UTOPIA

Ace Books by Roger MacBride Allen

CALIBAN
INFERNO
UTOPIA

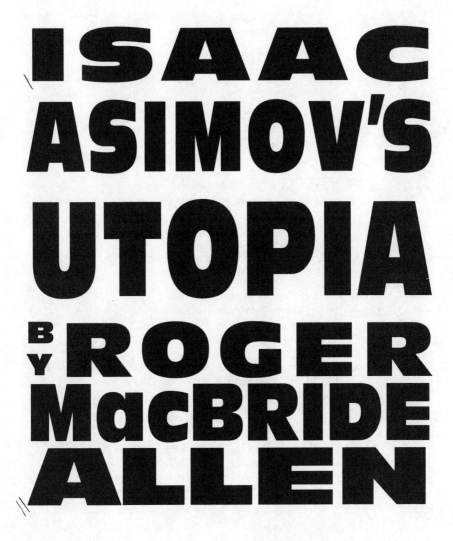

ISAAC ASIMOV'S UTOPIA

BY ROGER MacBRIDE ALLEN

A Byron Preiss Visual Publications, Inc. Book

ACE BOOKS, NEW YORK

To My Brother Chris,
His Wife Edie,
My Sister Connie,
And Her Husband Jim.

Author's Note

I would like to thank all the people involved with this book, and with this trilogy. It has been a long and complicated undertaking. Now, at long last, it is complete.

These three books would have been absolutely impossible if not for the prodigious literary output of the late Isaac Asimov, and if not for the prodigious popularity of his work. He is and will be greatly missed, and we are all in his debt. It has been an honor and a privilege to explore the ideas and the worlds he created.

Thanks as well to the editors who have labored over *Caliban*, *Inferno*, and *Utopia*. David Harris, John Betancourt, Leigh Grossman, and Keith R. A. DeCandido all worked to improve these books—and all succeeded. Thanks also to Susan Allison, Ginjer Buchanan, and Laura Anne Gilman of Ace Books, to Peter Heck, and to Byron Preiss, for their labors on my behalf.

And, of course, thanks as well to Eleanore Maury Fox. I hadn't even met her when I started work on this trilogy. Now she is my wife. This is the spot where authors usually talk about the love, affection, and patience of their long-suffering spouses, and Eleanore certainly deserves thanks on all those counts. But I also got something else: very hard-edged, straightforward, professional editorial advice. It helped a lot.

I now come to my sister Constance Witte, my brother Chris Allen, my brother-in-law Jim Witte, and my sister-in-law Edith Allen. This last book of the trilogy is dedicated to them, as the first one was dedicated to their children. (Except for one, and I'll come to her in a minute.) Connie, Chris, Jim and Edie: thank you, for a list of things that would be longer than this book. Thanks as well to my parents, Tom and Scottie Allen, and to my mother-in-law Elizabeth Maury, to my father-in-law David Fox, and to my brother-in-law, Carl Fox. The family just keeps getting bigger, and consequently I just keep getting luckier.

Speaking of families getting bigger, the newest member of it hadn't quite arrived when I dedicated *Caliban* to my nieces and nephews. She deserves to be on the list. In closing, therefore, I would like amend that dedication to include Anna Patrice Allen. Welcome aboard, Anna.

Roger MacBride Allen
Brasilia, Brazil
November, 1995

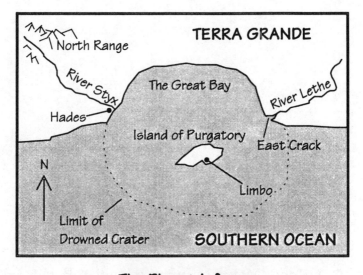

The Planet Inferno
(detail, western quadrant, northern hemisphere)

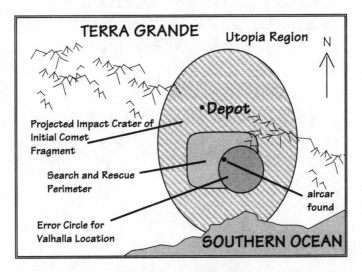

The Planet Inferno
(detail, Utopia Region, eastern quadrant, northern hemisphere)

THE ORIGINAL LAWS OF ROBOTICS

I

A Robot May Not Injure a Human Being,
or, Through Inaction, Allow a Human Being
to Come to Harm.

II

A Robot Must Obey the Orders Given It By
Human Beings Except Where Such Orders
Would Conflict With the First Law.

III

A Robot Must Protect Its Own Existence
As Long As Such Protection
Does Not Interfere With the First or Second Law.

THE NEW LAWS OF ROBOTICS

I

A Robot May Not Injure A Human Being.

II

A Robot Must Cooperate with Human Beings Except
Where Such Cooperation Would Conflict
with the First Law.

III

A Robot Must Protect Its Own Existence,
As Long As Such Protection Does Not Conflict
with the First Law.

IV

A Robot May Do Anything It Likes,
Except Where Such Action Would Violate
the First, Second, or Third Laws.

THE SPACER–SETTLER STRUGGLE was at its beginning, and at its end, an ideological contest. Indeed, to take a page from primitive studies, it might more accurately be termed a theological battle, for both sides clung to their positions more out of faith, fear, and tradition, rather than through any carefully reasoned marshaling of the facts.

Always, whether acknowledged or not, there was one issue at the center of every confrontation between the two sides: robots. One side regarded them as the ultimate good, while the other saw them as the ultimate evil. Spacers were the descendants of men and women who had fled semi-mythical Earth with their robots when robots were banned there. Exiled from Earth, they traveled in crude starships on the first wave of colonization from earth. With the aid of their robots, the Spacers terraformed fifty worlds and created a culture of great beauty and refinement, where all unpleasant tasks were left to the robots. Ultimately, virtually all work was left to the robots. Having colonized fifty planets, the Spacers called a halt, and set themselves no other task than enjoying the fruits of their robots' labor.

The Settlers were the descendants of those who stayed behind on Earth. Their ancestors lived in great underground

Cities, built to be safe from atomic attack. It is beyond doubt that this way of life induced a certain xenophobia into Settler culture. That xenophobia long survived the threat of atomic war, and came to be directed against the smug Spacers—and their robots.

It was fear that caused Earth to cast out robots in the first place. Part of it was an irrational fear of metal monsters wandering the landscape. However, the people of Earth had more reasonable fears as well. They worried that robots would take jobs—and the means of making a living—from humans. Most seriously, they looked to what they saw as the indolence, the lethargy, and the decadence of Spacer society. The Settlers feared that robots would relieve humanity of its spirit, its will, its ambition even as they relieved humanity of its burdens.

The Spacers, meanwhile, had grown disdainful of the people they perceived to be grubby underground dwellers. Spacers came to deny their own common ancestry with the people who had cast them out. But so too did they lose their ambition. Their technology, their culture, their worldview, were all static, if not stagnant. The Spacer ideal seemed to be a universe where nothing ever happened, where yesterday and tomorrow were like today, and the robots took care of all the unpleasant details.

The Settlers set out to colonize the galaxy in earnest, terraforming endless worlds, leapfrogging past the Spacer worlds and Spacer technology. The Settlers carried with them the traditional viewpoints of the home world. Every encounter with the Spacers seemed to confirm the Settlers' reasons for distrusting robots. Fear and hatred of robots became one of the foundations of Settler policy and philosophy. Robot-hatred, coupled with the arrogant Spacer style, did little to endear Settler to Spacer.

But still, sometimes, somehow, the two sides managed to cooperate, however great the degree of friction and suspicion. People of good will on both sides attempted to cast aside fear and hatred to work together—with varying success.

It was on Inferno, one of the smallest, weakest, most fragile of the Spacer worlds, that Spacer and Settler made one of the boldest attempts to work together. The people of that world, who called themselves Infernals, found themselves facing two crises. Their ecological difficulties all knew about, though few understood their severity. Settler experts in terraforming were called in to deal with that.

But it was the second crisis, the hidden crisis, that proved the greater danger. For, unbeknownst to themselves, the Infernals and the Settlers on that aptly-named world were forced to face a remarkable change in the very nature of robots themselves. . . .

Many elements combined to produce the final and most dangerous crisis for the planet Inferno. Beyond question, the so-called New Law robots played a pivotal role in what happened. But as is so often the case in history, it was the unexpected interaction of several seemingly unrelated factors that produced the final convulsion. All of them were necessary in order to produce the tumultuous sequences of events that were to follow. Things would have been very different if not for the New Law robots. But so too would subsequent history have been changed beyond all recognition if not for the chance discovery made by an obscure and ambitious scientist, or the erratically heightened ethical sensitivity of an indiscreet police informant, or the elaborate lies told to an all-powerful robot, or the two attempts by two separate parties to commit a particular sort of crime—a crime that had not been perpetrated for so many years that few were even aware that it existed.

Not once, but twice, the planet Inferno was shocked by attempts to accomplish the barbaric act known by the strange name of *kidnapping* . . .

—*Early History of Colonization*, by Sarhir Vadid,
Baleyworld University Press, S.E. 1231

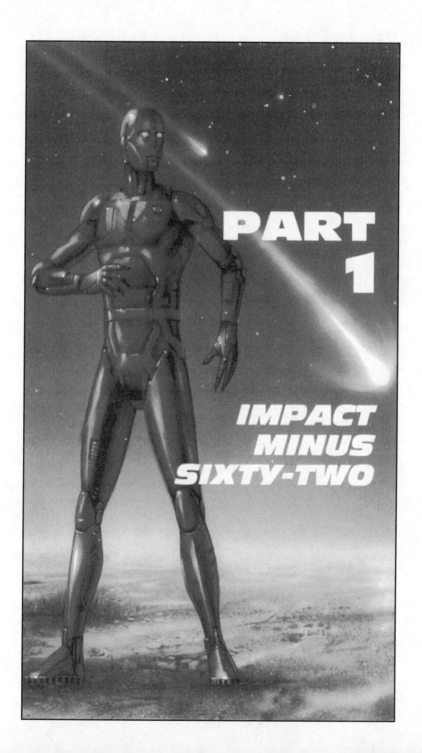

PART
1

IMPACT
MINUS
SIXTY-TWO

A BLINDING FLASH of light erupted in the depths of space, a massive explosion that blazed like a second sun. A cold, dark lump of matter, eighteen kilometers in diameter, was caught in the blast, and deflected toward a new heading, toward a slightly changed orbit.

The power of the blast should have been enough to shatter the comet, but, somehow, it held together. The surface of the cometary body was heated by the explosion, and small pockets of volatiles boiled up and out, sending jets of gases flaring out across the darkness.

The laws of action and reaction work equally well, whether or not the action is intentional. The jets of gas served as natural rocket thrusters, accelerating the comet in unexpected directions, throwing it off its carefully calculated course.

But other jets flared almost at once, artificial ones that compensated for the uncontrolled thrust. The control thrusters had to fire more and more frequently as the comet moved in closer to the inner planets of the star system.

It soon became plain that the comet was heading straight for a planet in the inner system, a world of blue and brown and tan, a world that was nearly all water in the southern hemisphere, and nearly all dried-out desert in the north.

The comet fell in toward the planet, closer and closer. The comet warmed as it came in nearer to the star the planet orbited. Its surface began to boil and vaporize, gases and dust blowing off into space, forming up into a tail that stretched itself out behind the comet.

The comet suddenly broke up. The fragments spaced themselves out into a neat line, like beads on a string.

The fragments moved closer, closer to the planet.

"Move from time factor positive one hundred to positive factor ten time dilation," said a disembodied voice in the darkness.

Time seemed to slow, the fragments suddenly moving at a fraction of their original velocity, easing themselves slowly down out of orbit.

"Give me a view closer to Inferno," the same voice commanded, and the image suddenly swelled in size.

"That's still way too fast. Time dilation to negative factor five," the voice ordered.

Once again, the clock slowed down, but even so, events moved quickly. The comet fragments were moving with incredible speed as they slammed into the planet's upper atmosphere, and even with time slowed to a fifth its normal speed, it still took scant seconds for the fragments to force their way down through the atmosphere and slam into the planet.

The largest fragment hit first, striking on land just north of the shoreline. The second crashed into the planet just north of the first, slamming into the peaks of a low range of hills. The other fragments struck, one after another, in a line running straight to the North Pole, blazing stars of light blooming for brief moments before they were engulfed in cloud and smoke, dust and debris.

"It worked," the voice said. "Freeze sequence at that point. Simglobe off. Room lights on."

The image of the planet aflame died away, and the lights came up to reveal a perfectly ordinary living room in a perfectly ordinary residence. The only unusual object in the room was the highly sophisticated simglobe projector sitting in the center of the room.

Davlo Lentrall walked over to the low, stubby cylinder that was the simglobe unit, and tapped the top of it with his finger. Not even the most advanced Settler models could do what this unit could do. He ought to know. He had designed and built it himself. He savored the satisfaction of the moment, and all the effort that had gone before it. It was his, all his. He had discovered the comet. In a rare burst of modesty, he had named it, not for himself, as called for by tradition, but for Chanto Grieg, the murdered governor who had spurred the reterraforming project that had saved the planet. Or at least bought the planet some time, so that Davlo Lentrall and Comet Grieg could finish the work that Chanto Grieg had begun. There was a symmetry there, a bit of poetry that would appeal to the historians. Posterity would remember Davlo Lentrall, no matter what the comet was called.

Of course, there was no point in discussing such matters with his robotic assistant. Kaelor would only remind him of the things that were bound to go wrong. But Davlo could not let such a triumphant moment go without saying something. "It worked," he said at last.

"Of course the simglobe works, Master Lentrall. It has worked every time you operated it. Why should it fail now?"

"I meant the comet-capture, Kaelor, not the simulator."

"I must point out that you forced it to work," said the robot Kaelor.

"What, exactly, do you mean?" Lentrall asked. Kaelor was a useful servant, but dealing with him required a good deal of patience.

"I mean, sir, that you are making a series of unwarranted assumptions."

Davlo held back his temper, and forced himself to be patient. Kaelor had been designed and built to Davlo's custom specifications, the most important of which was to hold First Law potential to the lowest possible level when judging hypothetical situations. A lab-assistant robot with First Law set to the normally super-high levels of Infernal robots would have been utterly incapable of assisting him on the sorts of experiments Davlo was interested in. Even before he had stumbled across Comet Grieg, Davlo had been involved in Oper-

ation Snowball, a project that required the contemplation of a
great many risky alternatives in order to find the safest way
to proceed.

There was scarcely a Three-Law robot on the planet who
would have been willing to work on Snowball, let alone operate the simglobe to test ideas for bringing Comet Grieg in.
Few robots would even be willing to help set up the problem,
on the grounds that the simulation could pave the way for
letting a real comet strike the real planet—which would be
dangerous to humans in the extreme. Davlo had therefore ordered a custom-built robot for his Snowball work, and been
glad to have him when he realized Grieg's potential.

It had taken a lot of argument and discussion with the robot
designer, an exceedingly conservative gentleman who was
most reluctant to put the slightest restriction on First Law, but
the result was Constricted First Law 001—CFL-001. Tradition
and convention would have required Davlo to named CFL-
001 something like Caefal, or Cuffle, or even, as one waggish
colleague suggested, Careful. But none of those appealed to
Davlo, and he had come up with Kaelor instead.

But, either as a side effect of constricted First-Law potential,
or merely as the consequence of the normal random sub-
pathings of his positronic brain, Kaelor was also possessed of
a dour, even depressive, outlook on life and the universe.
"What are these assumptions, Kaelor?"

"You're assuming you can hold the comet together during
the original guidance explosion," said Kaelor, "and *then* assuming you can split it apart in precisely the manner you wish,
exactly when you wish. Furthermore, you have not resolved
the issue of solar heating and its effects. I also have doubts
about your being able to control the comet's outgassing. You
have also been quite arbitrary about the number of fragments
needed for the job, and, finally, you have not dealt with the
incredibly delicate timing and guidance control needed for
final-phase targeting and atmospheric entry. Success requires
a degree of precision in all these matters that I see no way of
accomplishing."

"I am aware of all those problems," said Davlo. "If we
were only to begin after we had solved all the problems, we

would never begin at all. But I have demonstrated that the basic plan will work. Or at least that it *can*. Now I just have to convince my superiors. But in my considered opinion, I have proved we can drop Comet Grieg onto Inferno, and save the planet.''

"Granting your assumptions, I suppose you are right," the robot replied in dour tones. "I only wonder if you can manage to do it without killing everybody."

JUSTEN DEVRAY, COMMANDER of the Combined Inferno Police, sat in the unmarked and slightly battered aircar and watched the sun come up over parkland of idyllic green. He was tired. Deathly tired. But being tired was part of the job description on this duty. That was part of what he was here to learn.

It had seemed like a very sensible theory, going around to every bureau of the Combined Infernal Police, getting a first-hand idea of the sort of police work he had never had the chance to do, back in the old days. It had, in fact, been Justen's own idea, and it was teaching him a lot. Now he knew for certain that stakeout duty was both duller and more exhausting than he had thought possible. And he was starting to suspect that a nice, soft office job had more to recommend than he had realized.

Justen's unmarked aircar was parked a hundred meters or so away from the surface entrance to the vast underground complex known as Settlertown. The entrance itself was a mushroom-shaped arrangement, with a central pillar that contained the elevator shaft, and a wide, rounded, overhanging roof that spread out from the pillar to keep the weather off anyone waiting for a car down to the interior. The entrance shaft stood just inside the gate to the huge park the Settlers had built over their underground city. The landscaping of the park was all Settler work as well, of course, a demonstration of their skill in terraforming.

But the design of Settlertown did not concern Justen Devray. The job of the officer on this stakeout was to keep on a watch on the people going in and out of Settlertown. There were, of course, other entrances to the vast series of artificial caverns and chambers below. The CIP had watches on those, as well. But the main entrance was the real prize, at least according to the CIP's intelligence unit. The big fish used the main entrance. Their ranks, or at least their cover stories, would demand it. More importantly, the amateurs used the main entrance.

Everyone on both sides knew that all the entrances to Settlertown were watched, even the most rarely used ones. According to most theories of field operation, the best way to avoid being noticed was to use the busiest entrance, in hopes of getting lost in the shuffle. Sometimes it even worked. Especially now, at midmorning, there was a great deal of coming and going. It was far from simple to monitor it all. Something else for Justen to learn.

There were, of course, plenty of legitimate reasons for people to go in and out of Settlertown, and lots of people, Spacer and Settler, who did indeed go in and out. But some fraction of that number had no good reason for being there at all. Those were the ones who gave the CIP stakeout its reason for being.

The CIP never used the same car twice in a row for this stakeout job, even though the real professionals on the other side knew perfectly well they were being observed, and had no doubt gotten quite good at spotting the CIP's stakeout, no matter what car they were using. That was beside the point. However the CIP ran the stakeout, the pros in Settlertown would be able to spot them. But not so the amateurs, the drop-ins. Change the car often enough, routinely vary the spot where you parked it, and the odds were reasonably good that an amateur could go in and out a dozen times without being able to spot the surveillance car.

Justen Devray shifted in his seat and tried to get a trifle more comfortable. He felt cooped up, hemmed in. He smiled to himself. It wasn't just the car that had him feeling a little bit trapped. It was the job. In the old days, Justen had run the Governor's Rangers, a service with the dual responsibility of enforcing the law outside the cities and managing a number of reterraforming projects. Even Justen was willing to admit it had been an awkward combination of responsibilities.

A little under five years before, Alvar Kresh had reorganized the Rangers, leaving them with no other duties than their terraforming projects, and merging their law-enforcement commands with the City of Hades Sheriff's Department to form the Combined Inferno Police. Kresh had put Devray in charge of the new service.

Justen had taken the job willingly enough, but there were plenty of times he regretted the decision. Running the planetary police more or less required him to live in the planetary capital, and Justen Devray could not get used to the city of Hades, or to city life in general. He often found himself wishing to be back in the Rangers, working on some conservation job or terraforming project out in high plains north of the city.

Despite his desk work, Justen still had the tanned skin, tousled blond hair, and deep blue eyes to match that of an outdoorsman. The previous years out in the wind and weather had at least etched some character into his face, and life in the city had not erased any of it. Even so, he still looked unfashionably young, and one glance at him was enough to see he did not belong in a city.

Although he felt as if he were very much on his own, Justen had company in the battered aircar. There were two robots with him. One was Gervad 112, his personal robot of some years standing. Gervad was a General Ranger Deployment robot, a GRD unit of the sort that had been general issue for the Rangers some years before. The other was a Security, Patrol, and Rescue robot, an SPR, more casually called Sapper 323. After the night when the previous governor, Chanto Grieg, was murdered with a whole squad of Sappers on guard around him, the model suddenly, and rather unfairly, had gained a bad reputation. What had happened to them could have happened to any model of robot.

Still, no major security service was willing to use them any more. Justen hadn't even tried to hang on to the Rangers' SPRs. The rank and file did not trust them, and would not use them. As a result, most of the Sappers had been sold off at rock-bottom prices to all sorts of slightly disreputable organizations and people. That in turn meant that a Sapper made good camouflage. No one who saw Devray with a Sapper in

tow was going to think he was a cop, let alone the most senior
police official on the planet.

The depressing fact was that the two robots could have done
the watching just as well without Devray. Better, probably.
However, it did not do to dwell on such matters. The plain
fact of the matter was that humans were not really much
needed for most kinds of work.

"The male subject in red pants and blue tunic is not on my
list of identified subjects," the SPR announced. The special
features of the SPR design really shone in identity work. They
were nearly as good as humans at visual pattern matching and
comparison—or, to put it another way, at recognizing faces
and people. And, of course, they had virtually infallible memories. When a Sapper said it recognized someone, or that it
did not recognize something, it was best to take it seriously.
Right at the moment it meant that someone who wasn't supposed to be going into Settlertown was doing just that.

Justen Devray, suddenly wide awake and alert, peered
through the forward windshield, eagerly trying to get a good
look at the person in question. There was a knot of about ten
or twelve people waiting for the next elevator car to arrive.

"Gervad," he asked his personal robot, "do you know
him?" Gervad had the current official CIP mugshot file in his
memory store.

"Sir, I have at least a tentative pattern match, but I am
afraid that it seems rather an improbable one."

"Let me be the judge of that," said Justen, still trying to
get a good look at the man in question. It wasn't easy, with
the throng of people all around him. If the fellow actually had
intelligence training, he would of course do his best to blend
in. "What's your pattern match?"

"The observed subject matches with one Barnsell Ardosa,
a junior researcher in astrophysics at the University of Hades.
As it seems unlikely in the extreme that there would be much
of interest to the Settlers coming from that source, I would
suggest that I have likely made an inaccurate match."

Justen was just about to agree with Gervad, but just then
he finally spotted his quarry. There he was: a big, burly, round-
faced man with dark skin. He was completely bald on the top

of his head but had a thin fringe of snow-white hair that clung to the sides, thicker toward the back of his head, and fading out completely just forward of the ears. He had a bushy mustache and a distinctly worried look on his face.

For just the briefest of moments, Ardosa—if it was Ardosa—seemed to be looking straight at Devray. And in that moment, Devray decided that Gervad should have more faith in his own pattern-matching skills.

Justen Devray had never been near the university's astrophysics department. But Justen Devray was absolutely certain he had seen that face before.

But the devil take him if he could figure out where.

ALVAR KRESH, GOVERNOR of the Planet Inferno, glared up at the young man who stood at the other side of his desk. "You're not helping your cause," he said. "I told you that I would consider your proposal, and I *will* consider it. I have *been* considering it. But I am not going to be rushed into a decision. Not on something this big."

"There is no time to do anything *but* rush," his visitor replied, his voice urgent and insistent. "We have lost time already. I ran my final simulations three *days* ago—and it has taken me that long to get in to see you. This is a danger, and an opportunity, far greater than you understand. Perhaps greater than you *can* understand."

"What a tactful thing to say to the governor of the planet," said Kresh, his tone of voice as sour as his words. "But even if comprehending it is beyond *my* poor abilities, I suppose that *you* are capable of seeing the big picture?"

"I beg your pardon, sir. I didn't mean to put it that way," said Davlo Lentrall, coloring just a bit.

"No," Kresh said tiredly, "you probably didn't." He sighed, and considered his visitor with the practiced eye of an ex-policeman. Lentrall was dark-skinned and lantern-jawed, with an angular face and intense dark-brown eyes. His hair was jet black and cut short enough to stand up straight. Height average, build medium. Then Kresh reminded himself that he wasn't a policeman anymore, but a politician, and he needed to judge the fellow's character, not note his physical description. It was plain to see the salient factor in Lentrall's personality: he was young, with all the brazen self-confidence of youth.

Perhaps other cultures, Settler cultures, might regard youth as attractive, or let youthful zeal serve to excuse a multitude of sins. But Spacer culture was old, and its ways were old. Most of its people were old as well. For the average citizen, the exuberance and passion of youth was, at most, a distant, and slightly distasteful, memory, and Lentrall was a walking reminder of why that was. Brashness, impetuosity, and arrogance rarely won any friends.

But there was some possibility that the message Lentrall carried was important, no matter how annoying the messenger might be. "Let's both back off on this, just for the moment," Kresh said. "We're not getting anywhere anyway."

Lentrall shifted uncomfortably on his feet. He seemed to debate the idea of protesting again, and then think better of it. "Very well, sir," he said. "I—I apologize for my outburst. It's just that the strain of all this, the thought that the survival of the planet might be in my hands—it's a lot to deal with."

"I know," Kresh said, his voice suddenly gentle. "I know it very well. I have been living with just that thought for years now."

Once again, Lentrall reddened a bit. "Yes, sir. I know you have. It's just the idea of letting this chance slip away. But even so, I shouldn't have presumed to, to—"

"That's all right, son. Let's just leave it there. We'll talk again in a few days. In fact, tomorrow. Come in tomorrow morning. I will bring my wife, and you can give the full presentation to both of us. I would very much value her opinion on all this." And *that* was true for more reasons than he would care to share with young Dr. Lentrall just at the moment.

"Yes, sir. I'll do that. Tomorrow, first thing. Would ten be all right?"

"That would be perfect. Donald, get the door for our guest, will you?"

"Of course, sir." Donald 111, Kresh's personal robot, stepped out of his wall niche and walked smoothly across the floor. He led Lentrall to the door, activated the door controls, and watched Lentrall leave.

Donald was a short, rounded-off sort of robot, all smooth curves and no hard edges, quite specifically designed to be as nondescript and nonthreatening in appearance as possible. He was sky-blue in color, the sky-blue of the old Hades Sheriff's Department, a hold-over from the days when Kresh was the sheriff of the city—and there was a sheriff. Perhaps Kresh should have had Fredda recoat him in some other color. But Kresh liked the reminder of those days, when he had dealt with problems a lot smaller than the ones he had now—even if they had seemed quite large enough at the time.

Donald closed the door after Lentrall and turned back to face Kresh.

"Your opinion, Donald?"

"Of what sir? The message, or the man who delivered it?"

"Both, I suppose. But start with the messenger. Quite a determined young man, isn't he?"

"Yes, sir. If I may say so, he puts me in mind of what I know of your own early days."

Kresh looked toward Donald suspiciously. "What do you know about *my* early days?" he demanded. "How could you know about them? You weren't even built until after I was sheriff."

"True enough, sir, but you have been my master for many years now, and I have made you my study. After all, the better I know you, the better I can serve you. I have examined all the extant records regarding you. And, unless every record is misleading or inaccurate, that young man there bears a striking resemblance to the man you were at his age."

"Donald, that comes dangerously close to being sentimental."

"I trust not, sir. I do not have any of the emotional overlay protocols needed to experience sentimentality. Rather, I have merely stated an objective opinion."

"Have you indeed?" Kresh asked. "Well, if you have, it is a most disconcerting one." Kresh stood up and stretched. It had been a long day, and Lentrall had given him a lot to think about. "Come on, Donald, let's go home."

"Yes, sir." Donald turned back toward the door, unlocked it, and reopened it. He led Kresh and out of the office, down the hallway, and over to the governor's private elevator. The elevator door opened, and man and robot stepped into it. The door closed behind them, and carried them up toward the roof of Government Tower, where Kresh's private aircar waited in a secured hangar. There were actually two landing pads on the roof—a smaller one on the very apex of the building, for the use of the governor only, and a larger one about fifteen meters lower down. The governor's private landing pad had been added after the Grieg incident, by the simple expedient of building a ten-meter-wide, hollow stresscrete-and-steel pillar in one corner of the existing landing pad. The builders then put a flat disk thirty meters across atop of the pillar and used heavy buttressing to reinforce it. There was a small observation post built into the pillar itself, about ten meters above the original landing pad. The CIP used it as a sort of control tower for the main landing area.

Locked doors, private elevators, secured hangars, controlled-access landing pads. Kresh brooded over it all as they rode up in the elevator. Sometimes it seemed to Kresh that the walls between him and the world he was supposed to be governing were impossibly high. How could he run the planet if the whole system conspired to keep him cut off from it all, in the name of his own safety?

On the other hand, his immediate predecessor had been murdered in cold blood. The were reasons for the walls, the barriers that were everywhere. Even the roof had walls.

The elevator doors opened, and Kresh stepped out onto his private rooftop landing pad, warmed by an evening sun. But instead of walking toward the hangar, he went over to the edge of the platform. A low wall, about one hundred thirty centimeters tall, surrounded the landing pad. Like just about everything else on this planet, it was intended as a safety measure, but it also just happened to be the right height for Kresh to fold his arms on top of the wall, rest his chin on his forearms, and think. He could lean on the wall and look out over the world, and think his own thoughts undisturbed.

Not completely undisturbed, of course. That never happened. Not on a Spacer world. Kresh could hear Donald behind him, moving in close to protect Kresh against whatever imaginary danger the robot might choose to worry about: the wall giving way, an impossible gust of wind blowing in some inconceivable direction and sucking Kresh up into the air before throwing him clear of the edge of the building, Kresh suddenly giving way to some long-hidden—and completely imaginary—urge to self-destruction and deciding to fling himself over the edge. There was no end to the dooms and dangers a Three-Law robot could imagine.

And that, of course, was part of the problem. But don't worry about it now. Take now, take the moment, and look out at the city of Hades, at the sky, at the world.

Alvar Kresh looked out over the world he governed, the world put into his keeping. Kresh was a big, burly, broad-shouldered man with a strong-featured, expressive face. He was light-skinned, with a thatch of thick white hair that stood up bottle-brush straight from his head. There were times when he started to think the years were catching up with him, and the thought did flit through his mind tonight—no doubt inspired by Donald's comparison of Lentrall with Kresh the younger. Had he, Kresh, ever been that prickly, that pushy, that sure of himself when there was no good reason to be sure?

No, he told himself. Let that go, too. Let it all drift away, to be caught by the wind and carried to the far horizon. Let the office and the duties and the worries go, and just look. Just look, and see.

For, in truth, there was much worth seeing. The planet Inferno had come a long way in the five years Kresh had been governor—and Kresh took no small measure of pride in knowing that he had some fair-sized part in making that true.

He took a deep breath, and the air was cool and sweet, fresh and alive. When Kresh had taken office, the city of Hades had been all but literally on the verge of drying up and blowing away. The deserts had been spreading, the plants dying, the flower beds and gardens covered with the dust that blew into town with every gust of wind.

But now the deserts were retreating, not advancing. At least here, at least around the city, they were beating back the desert. Now the breeze carried the scents of life, of green things and freshness. Now he could look out and see green where once there had been brown and ocher. Now the city of Hades, and the land around it, were coming back to life.

The price had been high, there was no doubt of that. For five years now, the people of Inferno had been enduring restrictions on the use of robots that would have been unimaginable on any other Spacer world. But the planet of Inferno, the world itself, had had more need of that robot labor than its people did.

Kresh's predecessor, Chanto Grieg, had drafted a large fraction of Inferno's robotic population into government service. He had taken robots away from household duties and put them to work on terraforming and reclamation projects. Robots that had served as assistant cooks and stand-by drivers, robots that had served no other function than to wait until someone wanted to enter or leave a room, and then push the button that activated the automatic door, robots that had been wasted on the most menial and absurd of tasks, suddenly found themselves planting trees, operating earth-moving equipment, hand-pollinating flowers, and raising fish and insects and mammals to be released into the wild.

To this very day, there were those who moaned and complained about the terrible hardships imposed by the robotic labor laws. But it seemed there were fewer and fewer such complainers as time went by. People were getting used to the idea of living with fewer robots. People had discovered—or rediscovered—the pleasure of doing things for themselves. Things were changing, and changing for the better.

The question was—would the change be enough? Kresh knew that the fate of the planet was still balanced on a knife edge. Locally, things might be improving. But from a global perspective, thing were . . .

No. Never mind. Worry about it all later. Lentrall's idea had—had disturbed him. No question about it. He needed to hear what Fredda would say about it.

Kresh turned away from the view of the city, and headed toward his aircar. "Come on, Donald," he said again, "let's go home."

• • •

IT WAS LUCKY, Kresh told himself as Donald flew him home, that Spacers had a long tradition of respecting each other's privacy, and of defending their own. Otherwise, the scandalous nature of his own domestic arrangements might well have brought a thunderstorm of controversy down upon his head.

To get the worst of it over with first, Alvar Kresh and his wife, Fredda Leving, lived together, and maintained only one household. In the typical Spacer marriage, husband and wife each had their own household, and spent a large fraction of their time apart from each other.

It was more or less expected that newlyweds would spend an inordinate amount of time together, but the typical pattern was for a couple to spend less and less time together as the years went by. A couple who had been married some years might see each other once a week, or once a month. Some older marriages didn't so much end as wear out; the two partners might never see each other at all, from year's end to year's end. While divorce was simple enough on Inferno, many couples couldn't even work up the energy to go through the legal motions. They stayed married out of sheer inertia.

Alvar Kresh had discovered, much to his own surprise, that his own marriage was not coming anywhere close to following any such pattern. Three years after their wedding, he and Fredda still spent every night not only under the same roof but, even more scandalously, in the same room—and the same bed.

While there was nothing seen as actually wrong or immoral in such an arrangement, it was most unusual in Infernal society. If it had gotten around, the good people of Inferno would have thought their governor and his wife most peculiar.

And that in itself was strange, in Kresh's mind, at least. He stared out the window, at the green and lovely city below, reflecting once again on the peculiar ways of his own people. Infernals prided themselves on being quite open-minded when it came to questions of personal relationships. And so they were—at least in theory. But Kresh had learned, over the years, that while their minds might be open to the idea of most

sorts of *physical* relationships, their hearts were far less prepared to deal with the idea of emotional intimacy. The idea,
the theory, of sex was something an Infernal could deal with.
The fact, the reality, of sex would bring a blush to an Infernal's face, but he or she could at least countenance such a
thing. The idea of love was something most could not deal
with at all.

Infernals were Spacers, and Spacers had always been a people who kept their distance, physical and emotional, from each
other. At least Infernals had never gone to the extremes of
some Spacer worlds, worlds that had no real cities, no towns,
no villages, only widely scattered villas, with one human and
an army of robots making up the average household. But Infernals were not exactly a gregarious people.

That Kresh and Fredda slept together on occasion would be
seen as perfectly acceptable. That they slept together every
night, in the same bed, would be seen as a trifle odd. That
they had their meals together, spent their free time together,
and were in each other's company as much as possible—that
would be seen as quite beyond the pale. Infernals simply did
not open up to each other, expose themselves to each other,
that way. They did not make themselves vulnerable to each
other.

More fools they, Kresh told himself. They would never
know the strength, the confidence, the sense of security that
Fredda gave to Kresh. He could only hope he gave as much
to her.

Kresh knew the Infernals, and what they would say if they
knew. He knew how the idea would float up from somewhere
that his unconventional home life made him unsuited to continue as governor, or that Fredda obviously had an undue influence on him. Even as it was, they said she was far too
young for him—and Infernals were suspicious of youth. They
said she was entirely too cozy with the Settlers. Simcor Beddle, leader of the Ironheads, was never reluctant to put that
notion about at one of his mass meetings—and there was at
least a grain of truth in it. Fredda did tend toward the Settler
view on a number of subjects. Beddle was already leading a
whispering campaign, putting it about that her radical ideas

were dangerous. But then, Kresh was inclined to believe that himself. Fredda and he had some remarkably vigorous arguments on the subject of robots, among other things.

If Kresh had been a private citizen, he would not have much cared if the rest of the universe knew every detail of his domestic arrangements. But the last thing he needed at this point was for his personal affairs to become an issue. Better, far better, to keep such matters well away from the public eye and avoid the talk in the first place.

Kresh paid lip service to the conventions. He maintained—but did not use—fully staffed and equipped living quarters at Government Tower. The only time he put them to use was after official entertainments of one sort or another. At such times, he would make a show of retiring to his own private rooms in Government Tower at the end of the evening, long after Fredda had gone home to ''her'' house. Sometimes, if the hour was very late, they would actually spend the night apart, but, more often than not, Donald would end up secretly flying one of them to where the other waited. All of it was quite absurd. But better such nocturnal charades than the poisonous gossip that would result if the story got around that Alvar Kresh was passionately in love with his wife.

Kresh remembered arguing with Chanto Grieg, just hours before Grieg's death. Grieg had tried to explain to Kresh how the job of posturing, of pretending, of smoothing over, was vital to the job of governance, that he could not get to his real work until all the nonsense had been dealt with. Kresh had not quite believed it then—but he had learned the truth of it since. Simcor Beddle had taught him that much. Kresh had learned the hard way that he could do nothing unless he first neutralized the Ironheads.

The Ironheads. Kresh smiled to himself as he imagined what Beddle and his crew could do with the news if they discovered everything about the goings-on at the Kresh–Leving household. There were things more shocking than romance. For the sake of domestic harmony, Kresh himself spent a lot of time pretending he knew less than he did about what went on when he was away from home. Best if he could pretend he did not

know all about the meetings of subversive robots taking place
in his own house.

It was bad enough that he himself knew. But if Beddle ever
found out—oh, yes, there was need enough for privacy.

There was a change in sound of the aircar's engine, and
Kresh came back to himself as the car banked smoothly to
one side and eased down out of the sky. He blinked and looked
toward the front of the craft, out the forward viewport. There
it was. There was home.

The aircar settled in for a landing.

FREDDA LEVING STOOD up from her chair and looked
across the table at the two robots. "It would be best if you
both were going," she said. "My husband will be home at
any moment."

The smaller of the two robots, the jet-black one, rose from
his chair and regarded his hostess thoughtfully. "Surely your
husband is aware that we meet here with you."

"Of course he is," she said. "But it is best for all concerned
that we do not rub his nose in it."

"I do not understand," said the black robot. He was Prospero, self-proclaimed leader of the New Law robots. He was
a gleaming metallic black, about a hundred eighty centimeters
tall, with the solid, heavy-set body design common to many
of the New Laws. His eyes glowed a deep, burning orange
that seemed to make his personality all the more intense. "If
he knows we come here, why conceal it from him?"

"*I* do not understand why you ask questions to which you
already know the answer," Fredda replied.

Prospero swiveled his head about to glance at his companion and then swung abruptly back toward Fredda. "*Do* I know
the answer?" he asked in a suspicious voice.

The larger of the two robots stood as well, and looked toward his companion. "There are times, friend Prospero," said
Caliban, "when I believe that you quite deliberately play at
being ignorant. The governor wants no contact with us. He
tolerates, but does not approve of, these meetings. The less we
bring them to his official attention, the more likely they are to
continue."

Caliban stood over two meters tall, his body metallic red in color, his eyes a penetrating glowing blue. His appearance was striking, even intimidating, but far less so than his reputation. Caliban the Lawless, they still called him, sometimes.

Caliban, the robot accused, but cleared, of attempting the murder of his creator—of Fredda Leving herself.

Prospero regarded his companion for a moment before he replied. "The need for discretion," he said. "Yes, I have *heard* that answer before. But I am far from sure that I know it is the *true* answer."

"And what purpose would it serve for me to lie to you?" Caliban asked. For a Three-Law robot, the very idea of lying would be difficult to imagine, but Caliban was a No Law robot, and, in theory at least, just as able to lie as any human.

"Perhaps you would have no purpose in lying," Prospero said, looking back toward Fredda. "But others might well have reasons to deceive you."

"You are not at your most tactful today," said Fredda. "And I must confess I don't see why our perfectly true answers should not satisfy you. Nor can I see what motive I would have for lying to you and Caliban."

"I might add that I do not understand your motive for offending our principal benefactor," said Caliban.

Prospero hesitated, and looked from one of them to the other. "My apologies," he said at last. "There are times when my understanding of human psychology fails me, even when I am attempting to learn more. I was attempting to gauge your emotional reaction to such an accusation, Dr. Leving."

"I would have to believe in the sincerity of the accusation before I could have much of a reaction to it," said Fredda.

"Yes," said Prospero. "Of course."

But if Fredda Leving was sure of anything at that moment, she was sure that Prospero had not given her all of the story—and perhaps had not given her any of the true story. But what motive would Prospero have for playing such a strange game? It was rare indeed when she felt completely sure that she understood Prospero. She had long known he was one of her less stable creations. But he was the undisputed leader of the New Law robots. She had no real choice but to deal with him.

"In any event," said Caliban, "it is time for us both to be leaving. I have no doubt, Dr. Leving, that we shall all meet again soon."

"I look forward to it," said Fredda.

The jet-black robot regarded first Fredda, and then Caliban. "Very well," he said. "We will depart. But I doubt that I will be the first or last robot to observe that the more I know about humans, the less I understand them."

Fredda Leving sighed wearily. There were times when it was frustrating in the extreme listening to Three-Law robots holding forth on the subject of human behavior. Prospero and the other New Laws were even worse. At least Three-Law robots were not judgmental. Prospero had an opinion about everything.

Fredda could almost imagine him as the last priest of some long-forgotten human religion, always ready to debate any intricate point of theology, so long as it was of no interest or importance to anyone at all. There were times Caliban was no better. She had designed and built both of these robots by herself. Surely she could have designed their brains so they didn't spend their days logic-chopping. But it was too late now. "Whatever you think of my reasons for doing so," she said, "I must ask you again to leave, by the back way. Our next appointment is in three days, is it not?"

"Yes," said Prospero. "We have several other appointments that will take up the intervening time."

"Fine then. Return in three days, in the afternoon, and we will conclude our business."

Caliban nodded his head toward her, in what was almost a bow. "Very well," he said in a most courteous tone. "We will see you at that time."

Prospero took no interest in courtesy. He simply turned, opened the door, and left the room, leaving all the farewells to his companion. Caliban had to hurry just to keep up with him.

Fredda watched them go, and found herself once again wondering about Prospero. She did not understand what went on behind those glowing eyes. There was something not quite right about a robot that—that secretive. She shook her head as she crossed the room. Not much point in worrying about it now. She sealed the door shut behind them and scrambled the keypad. Only she and Caliban and Prospero knew the door's keypad combination.

And there were times she thought seriously about taking at least one name off that list.

2

CALIBAN FOLLOWED PROSPERO down the tunnel. It ran for about a hundred meters, and deposited them at the base of a ravine that was otherwise quite inaccessible to the house. Their aircar was hidden there.

"I would like to know what all that was about," Caliban said as they emerged from the tunnel into the cool of the evening.

"I spoke the truth," Prospero said coolly. "It was in part merely a test to see how she would react to such an accusation. Surely you would agree it is worth knowing if she is capable of betraying us." Prospero climbed into the pilot's station.

Caliban followed, climbing into the forward passenger seat. "I suppose the case could be made that such information would be useful in a general sense," he said. "But you have dealt with Dr. Leving for quite some time now. Why worry about such hypotheticals now? And if the need for a test was only part of your intent, what was the rest?"

"I have answers to both questions, friend Caliban, but I do not choose to give them now. This is all I can tell you: I believe we are in danger. The possibility that we will be betrayed—or have been already—is quite real. And I can tell you no more than that.''

Prospero engaged the aircar's controls, and they lifted off into the evening air. Caliban said no more, but he found that he had reached a conclusion about Prospero. There was no longer the slightest doubt in his mind that the New Law robot was unstable. He did not merely suspect betrayal on all sides—he virtually invited it. He had gone out of his way to encourage Dr. Leving's hostility. More than likely, the fellow was confusing danger to himself with danger to the New Laws.

All of which made Caliban's next decision quite simple. As soon as it was conveniently possible, he would put some distance, in every sense of the word, between himself and Prospero.

He no longer wished to stand quite so close to so tempting a target.

FREDDA LEVING WALKED to the other end of the underground safe room, and went through the open door there. She wearily closed the door behind her, and scrambled the combination as well. She, Fredda, was the only one who knew the combination to *this* door. Alvar had insisted on that much. He had no desire for a New Law robot like Prospero—let alone a No Law robot like Caliban—to have free access to his home. There had been times when she herself had been glad to keep her home well barricaded against New Law robots.

And of course, the New Laws felt the same way about humans. She still had not the slightest idea where, exactly, the New Law city of Valhalla was. She knew it was underground, and that it was in the Utopia sector, but that was about all. Fredda had even been taken there several times, but she had always been transported in a windowless aircar equipped with a system for jamming tracking devices. The New Law robots took no chances, and she could not blame them. Fredda had been quite willing to cooperate with their precautions, and to make sure everyone knew about them. They were for her safety as much as for that of the robots. What she did not know, she could not reveal under the Psychic Probe. The New Law robots had a large number of enemies. Some of them might well be willing to reduce the governor's wife to a vegetable, and damn the consequences, if that was what it took to find the lair of the New Law robots.

Astonishing, really, the lengths they all went to. Not just the New Laws, but Alvar, and even herself. They all took such elaborate precautions. Against discovery, against scandal, against each other. No wonder Prospero was turning half paranoid. Maybe even more than half.

In all probability, of course, the precautions would turn out to be useless in the end. Plots and secrets and hidden agendas generally came crashing down, sooner or later. She had never been involved in a plot or a secret that hadn't. But the secrets and plots and safeguards and precautions made them all feel better, feel secure, at least for a while. Perhaps that was the point of having them.

Fredda double-checked the inner door, and then stepped into the elevator car that would carry her up above ground, to the household proper.

OBR-323 was waiting there for her, in all his rather ponderous solemnity. "Master Kresh has landed," he announced in his gravely, ponderous voice. "He should be here momentarily."

"Very good," Fredda said. "Will dinner be ready soon?"

"Dinner will be ready in twelve minutes, Mistress. Is that acceptable?"

"That will be fine, Oberon." Fredda regarded Oberon with a critical—and self-critical—eye. She had built him, after all. He was a tall, solid-looking robot, heavily built and gun-metal gray. Oberon was nearly twice the size of Donald—and perhaps only half as sophisticated. Fredda was not entirely satisfied with her handiwork regarding Oberon. If nothing else, there was the question of overall appearance. At the time she had designed him, she had concluded that a robot as big as Oberon who was all angles and hard edges would have been rather intimidating. *That* would not have been a good idea in these rather edgy times. Therefore, Oberon was as rounded-off as Donald. However, Fredda was not entirely satisfied with the overall effect. Donald's rounded angles made him look unthreatening. Oberon merely looked half-melted.

She often wondered what Oberon's design said about her own psychology. The custom-design robots she had built before him—Donald, Caliban, Ariel, Prospero—had all been cutting-edge designs, highly advanced, even, except for Donald, dangerously experimental. Not Oberon. Everything about his design was basic, conservative—even crude. Her other custom-built robots had required highly sophisticated construction and hand-tooled parts. Oberon represented little more than the assembly of components.

"I'll just go in and freshen up," she said to Oberon, and headed for the refresher, her mind still on why she had made Oberon the way she had. *Once burned, twice shy?* she wondered. Of course she had been burned twice already. It was a desire for rebellion against caution that had gotten her into trouble in the first place. *And* the second place. She found herself thinking back on it all as she stripped and headed into the refresher. The hot water jets of the needle-shower were just what she needed to unwind after the meeting with Prospero.

A few years before, Fredda Leving had been one of Inferno's leading roboticists, with a well-earned reputation for taking chances, for searching out shortcuts, for impatience.

None of those character traits were exactly well-suited to the thoroughly calcified field of robotics research. There had not been a real breakthrough in robotics for hundreds of years, just an endless series of tiny, incremental advances. Robotics was an incredibly conservative field, caution and safety and care the watchwords at every turn.

Positronic brains had the standard Three Laws of Robotics burned into them, not once, but millions of times, each microcopy of the Laws standing guard to prevent any violation. Each positronic brain was based on an earlier generation of work, and each later generation seemed to include more Three-Law pathing. The line of development went back in an unbroken chain, all the way to the first crude robotic brain built on Earth, untold thousands of years before.

Each generation of positronic brain had been based on the generation that went before—and each generation of design had sought to entwine the Three Laws more and more deeply into the positronic pathway that made up a robotic brain. Indeed, the closest the field had come to a breakthrough in living memory was a way to embed yet more microcopies of the Three Laws into the pathways of a positronic brain.

In principle, there was, of course, nothing wrong with safety. But there was such a thing as overdoing it. If a robotic brain checked a million times a second to see if a First Law violation was about to occur, that meant all other processing was interrupted a million times, slowing up productive work. Very large percentages of processing time, and very large percentages of the volume of the physical positronic brain, were given over to massively, insanely redundant iterations of the Three Laws.

But Fredda had wanted to know how a robot would behave with a modified law set—or with no law set at all. And that meant she was stuck. In order to create a positronic brain without the Three Laws, it would have been necessary to start completely from scratch, abandoning all those thousands of years of refinement and development, almost literally carving the brain paths by hand. Even if she had tried such a thing, the resulting robot brain would have been of such limited capacity and ability that the experiment results would have been meaningless. What point in testing the actions of a No Law robot who had such reduced intellect that it was barely capable of independent action?

There seemed no way around the dilemma. The positronic brain was robotics, and robotics was the positronic brain. The two had become so identified, one with the other, that it proved difficult, if not impossible, for most researchers to think of either one except as an aspect of the other.

But Gubber Anshaw was not like other researchers. He found a way to take the basic, underlying structure of a positronic brain, the underlying pathing that made it possible for a lump of sponge palladium to think and speak and control a body, and place that pathing, selectively, in a gravitonic structure.

A positronic brain was like a book in which all the pages had the Three Laws written on them, over and over, so that each page was half filled with the same redundant information, endlessly repeated, taking up space that thus could not be used to note down other, more useful data. A gravitonic brain was like a book of utterly blank pages, ready to be written on, with no needless clutter getting in the way of what was written. One could write down the Three Laws, if one wished, but the Three Laws were not jammed down the designer's throat at every turn.

No other robotics lab had been willing to touch Anshaw's work, but Fredda had jumped at the chance to take advantage of it.

Caliban was the first of her projects to go badly wrong. Fredda had long wanted to conduct a controlled, limited experiment on how a robot without the Three Laws would behave. But for long years, the very nature of robotics, and the positronic robot brain, had rendered the experiment impossible. Once the gravitonic brain was in her hands, however, she moved quickly toward development of a No Law robot—Caliban. He had been intended for use in a short-term laboratory experiment. The plan had been for him to live out his life in a sealed-off, controlled environment. Caliban had, unfortunately, escaped before the experiment had even begun, becoming entangled in a crisis that had nearly wrecked the government, and the reterraforming program on which all else depended.

The second disaster involved the New Law robots, such as Prospero. Fredda had actually built the first of the New Law robots before Caliban. It was only because the world had become aware of Caliban first that people generally regarded him as preceding the New Laws.

But both the New Laws and Caliban were products of Fredda's concerns that robots built in accordance with the original Three Laws were wrecking human initiative and tremendously wasteful of robot labor. The more advanced robots became, the more completely they protected humans from danger, and the fewer things humans were allowed to do for themselves. At the same time, humans made the problem worse by putting the superabundance of robot labor to work at the most meaningless and trivial of tasks. It was common to have one robot on hand to cook each meal of the day, or to have one robot in charge of selecting the wine for dinner, while another had as its sole duty the drawing of the cork. Even if a man had only one aircar, he was likely to have five or six robot pilots, each painted a different color, to insure the driver did not clash with the owner's outfit.

Both humans and robots had tended to consider robots to be of very little value, with the result that robots were constantly being destroyed for the most pointless of reasons, protecting humans from dangers that could have easily been avoided.

Humans were in the process of being reduced to drones. They were unproductive and in large part utterly inactive. Robots did more and more of the work, and were regarded with less and less respect. Work itself was held in lower and lower esteem. Work was what robots did, and robots were lesser beings.

The spiral fed on itself, and Fredda could see it leading down into the ultimate collapse of Spacer society. And so she had developed the New Law robots. The New First Law prevented them from harming humans, but did not require them to take action in order to protect humans. The New Second Law required New Law robots to cooperate with humans, not just obey them blindly. The New Third Law required the New Law robots to preserve themselves, but did not force them to destroy themselves for some passing human whim. The deliberately ambiguous Fourth Law encouraged New Law robots to act for themselves.

The New Laws had seemed so reasonable to Fredda, so clearly an improvement over the original Three Laws. And perhaps they would have been an improvement, if it had been possible to start over, completely from scratch. But the New Law robots came into being on a world where Three-Law robots were already there, and on a world that seemed to have no place for them.

The New Law robots were more catalyst for the second major crisis than actual cause of it. Through a complex series of events, the mere existence of the New Law robots, and the shortage of Three-Law robot labor, had ultimately set in train Governor Chanto Grieg's assassination. If not for the calm and steady hand of Alvar Kresh, *that* crisis could have been far worse.

In neither case had the robots, New Law or No Law, Prospero or Caliban, actually malfunctioned. All that was required for disaster and crisis to happen was for people to *fear* robots that were different. Inferno was a world that did not much like change, and yet it was one that had change thrust upon it. It was a world that punished boldness, and rewarded caution.

And Fredda had suffered punishment enough. Small wonder, then, that Fredda had built herself such a cautious, stolid, lumpen robot as Oberon. But small wonder too that she was already tired of caution.

Fredda shut off the needle-shower and activated the air blowers to dry herself off. She smiled, and reminded herself that even the simple act of taking a shower by herself, bathing herself, represented a revolution. Ten years before, such a thing would have been unthinkable, scandalous. There would have been a waterproofed domestic robot to take her clothes off for her, activate the shower system for her, push the dry button for her, and dress her again, in clothes selected by the robot.

She stepped out of the refresher and starting picking out the clothes for her evening outfit. Something easy and casual for a night at home. Strange to think that she had left it to a robot to pick out her clothes for her, not so very long ago. Now it was a real pleasure, a savored luxury, to choose the clothes for an evening at home.

Feeling well-scrubbed and revived by her shower, she threw open the closet and selected her clothes for the evening. Something subdued, but not *too* understated. She decided on her dark-blue sheath skirt, and a black pullover to go with it. She dressed, and then paused in front of the mirror to consider the effect.

The outfit looked good on her. She selected earrings, and a silver brooch that would be set off by the black top. She looked back in the mirror and considered the effect.

Fredda was small and fine-boned, with blue eyes and curly black hair she wore short. She was round-faced and snubnosed. In short, she looked like what she was—a youthful

woman given to sudden enthusiasm, and equally sudden out-
bursts of temper.

The world of Inferno approved of seniority and experience.
This did not make things any easier for Fredda Leving. She
was a mere forty years old. By Infernal standards, that was
just barely old enough for respectability—or it would have
been if she had looked that age. Fredda had a naturally youthful appearance, and she was perverse enough to do everything
she could to preserve the appearance of youth. At a time of
life when most other Infernal woman were glad to be acquiring
a properly mature appearance, Fredda still looked to be no
more than twenty-five years of age.

The hell with what they thought. Fredda knew she looked
good—and looked better in the outfit she had picked out for
herself. Certainly better than in anything Oberon would have
selected. Pleased with her appearance, she headed out into the
main salon, proud of having chosen just the right clothing.

A silly thing, a small thing, but there it was. Making
choices, however trivial, for oneself, was a liberation. There
had been a time, and not so long ago, when Fredda, and Alvar,
and thousands, millions of other people on Inferno had been
little more than well-trained slaves to their own servants.
Awakened at the hour the robots thought best, washed by the
robots, dressed by the robots in clothes the robots picked out.
Up until a few years ago, many clothes did not even have
fasteners the wearer could attach or undo. The wearer was
completely dependent on his or her dresser robot to get the
garment on or off.

Once dressed, you were fed the breakfast, lunch, and dinner
selected by the robot cook to be most commensurate with the
dictates of the First Law injunction to do no harm. Then your
pilot robot flew you to this appointment or that—all appointments, of course, having being made by your secretary robot.

You would get to wherever it was without ever knowing
where it was, because you trusted in the robot to remember
the address and know the best routes there. More than likely,
your robots knew better than you what you were supposed to
do there. Then the pilot robot flew you home, because you
certainly wouldn't know how to find your own way home,

either. At the end of the day, you were undressed and then bathed again by the robots, and buttoned or zipped or clipped into pajamas by the robots, and then tucked into bed by them.

A whole day, each day, every day, with the robots making every single personal decision, with the servants controlling your every movement. A whole day spent in an incredibly luxurious cage, without your ever being so much as aware that the cage existed.

Fredda could not quite believe that she had ever allowed herself to live that way—but she had. Incredible. At least now she was conscious of the fact that Oberon had selected the dinner menu for her, and their dinner time. At least now, Oberon inquired if the mealtime he had selected was right, rather than informing her when she would eat. Tonight it was her choice to let the robots handle dinner. Another night, she might dictate the meal in every detail. Scandal of scandals, she had even been known to burn a meal for herself once in a while. If the tyrannical rule of the servants had not been completely shattered, at least it had been recognized for it was, and thus weakened.

Fredda knew that she was not the only one who had taken back at least some control of her own life from the robots. She also knew that her research, her speeches, the turmoil she had caused were a large part of the reason. But beyond doubt, the presence of the Settlers had been a major influence as well. And then there was the bald fact that there simply weren't as many robots available for private use these days. People were more careful with the limited amount of robot labor still available. They tended not to waste so much of it on trivial tasks.

The revolution was far from complete, of course. There were still many Infernals out there who had not managed the change in attitude, who clung to the old ways, who rallied around the Ironhead calls for more and better robots as the solution to everything.

But for whatever reason, or reasons, and by however many fits and starts, the change was happening. All over the planet Infernals had come to realize just how dependent on robots they were, and had begun to back off just a little. And, much to the horror of Simcor Beddle and the Ironheads, people were starting to discover they liked having a bit more freedom in their lives.

From Fredda's point of view, all of it seemed good, positive change for the better. But she had learned, over the past few years, just how frightening—and genuinely dangerous—change, even change for the good, could be. There would be some unintended consequence, or someone left behind, someone who felt disaffected and threatened. Or else someone who was not harmed in the least by the turmoil, but found a way to take advantage of it, to the detriment of others.

Or perhaps she was being *too* pessimistic. Perhaps the days of Inferno in upheaval, of the planet lurching from crisis to crisis, were over. And yet even steady, incremental change and improvement, of the sort her Alvar had presided over in the last few years, could bring jarring dislocations.

The days ahead were likely to be . . . interesting.

She heard the sound of her husband and Donald coming in from the rooftop landing pad, and hurried to meet them.

3

"THEY WERE HERE again," Kresh said as he kissed his wife. It was not a question, and Fredda knew better then to pretend she didn't know who he meant.

"Yes," she said carefully. "They've just left."

"Good," Kresh said as he eased himself down into his favorite chair. "I don't like having them around."

"Nor do I, Dr. Leving," Donald 111 announced. "The danger represented by the presence of those two pseudo-robots is far greater than you believe."

"Donald, I *built* both of those pseudo-robots, as you insist on calling them," Fredda said, feeling as much amusement as irritation. "I understand fully what they are capable of."

"I am not at all sure that is the case, Dr. Leving," Donald said. "But if you will insist on meeting them when I am not present, there is nothing I can do to prevent you from doing so. I would urge you once again to exercise extreme caution when you deal with them."

"I will Donald, I will," Fredda said, her voice a bit tired. She had built Donald, too, of course. She knew as well as anyone that the First Law forced Donald to mention the potential danger to her at every opportunity. For all of that, it was still tedious to hear the same warning over and over again. Donald, and most other Three-Law robots, referred to Caliban and Prospero—and all New Law robots—as pseudo-robots because they did not possess the Three Laws. By definition, a robot was a sentient being imbued with the Three Laws. Prospero was possessed of the New Laws, and Caliban had no laws at all. They might look like robots, and in some ways act like robots, but they were not robots. Donald saw them as a perversion, as unnatural beings that had no proper place in the universe. Well, perhaps he would not phrase it in *quite* that way, but Fredda knew she was not far off the mark.

"Why is it, exactly, that they need to come here anyway?" Alvar asked as he leaned back in his chair. "They have passes that give them the freedom of the city."

"Don't get *too* comfortable," Fredda warned. "Dinner in just a few minutes."

"Fine," Kresh said, leaning forward again. "I'll be as uncomfortable as you like. But answer my question."

Fredda laughed, leaned over and kissed Alvar on the forehead. "Once a policeman, always a policeman," she said.

The robot Oberon chose that moment to appear. "Dinner is served," it announced.

"Always a policeman," Alvar said to his wife. "So don't think this little interruption is going to get you off the hook."

He stood up, and husband and wife went in to dinner, Oberon leading the way, Donald trailing behind. Donald took up his usual wall niche, and Oberon set about serving the meal.

Fredda decided it would all go a bit smoother if she didn't force her husband to prompt her for an answer. Oberon set a plate before her and she picked up her fork. "They come here to have a safe place to meet," she said. "That's the main answer. There aren't many places in Hades where they aren't in some sort of danger of an NL basher gang, passes or no passes." There had been Settler robot-bashing gangs in the past, though most of them had faded away by now. But certain Spacers had learned the bashing game from the Settlers. There were still radicals, extremists even beyond the pale of the Iron-heads, who were always itching to do in a New Law robot, given the chance. "New Law robots aren't safe in this city.

I've told you that before, even if you don't quite believe it."

"Then why come here? If Hades is so dangerous, it seems to me they ought to be safe enough on the other side of the planet, in Utopia. In that underground city of theirs. They *ought* to be," he said again, as if he was not sure they truly were.

One of Alvar Kresh's first acts as governor was to issue an order, banishing the New Law robots from the inhabited parts of the planet. If that was not the exact wording of the order, it was certainly the effect—and, for that matter, the intent. Fredda could not fault her husband too much for the decision. It had been a choice between banishment and destroying the New Law robots altogether. "They are safe enough in Valhalla, though I don't think I'd call it a city, exactly," she said. "It's more like a huge bunker complex than anything else."

"Well, I'll take your word for it," Alvar said. "You've been there, and I haven't."

"They may be safe there," Fredda said, "but they don't have everything they need. They have to come here to trade."

"What could a bunch of robots need?"

Fredda wanted to let out a sigh, but she forced herself to hold it back. The two of them had had this argument too many times before. By now each of them had rehearsed his or her part to perfection. But that didn't make the argument end. They had a good marriage, a solid marriage—but the issue of the New Law robots was one they seemed unlikely to settle between themselves any time soon. "Spare parts, if nothing else," Fredda said, "as you know perfectly well. They have to keep themselves in repair. Supplies and equipment to maintain and expand Valhalla. Information of all sorts. Other things. This time they were after biological supplies."

"*That's* a new one," said Alvar. "What do they want with bio supplies?"

"Terraforming projects, I suppose," said Fredda. "They've made a great deal of progress reviving the climate in their part of the world."

"And trained themselves in some highly marketable skills at the same time. Don't try to make them into tin saints for me," said Kresh.

The New Laws were allowed off the Utopia reservation under certain circumstances. The most common reason was to
do skilled labor. Every terraforming project on the planet was
short of labor, and many project managers were willing—if
only reluctantly so—to hire New Law robots for the jobs. The
New Laws charged high rates for their work, but they gave
good value for money. "What's wrong with their doing honest
work?" Fredda asked. "And what is wrong with their getting
paid for it? If a private company needs temporary robot labor,
it rents them, and pays the robot rental agent or the owner of
the robots for the use of his property. The same applies here.
It's just that these robots own themselves."

"There's nothing *wrong* with it," Alvar said, moodily stab-
bing his fork at his vegetables. "But there's nothing all that
noble about it, either. You always try to make them sound like
heroes."

"Not everything they do is for money or gain," Fredda
said, "No one pays them for the terraforming work they do
in the Utopia reservation. They do it because they *want* to do
it."

"Why is that, do you think?" asked Alvar. "Why is it that
is what they want to do? I know you've been studying the
question. Have you come up with anything new on it?"

Fredda looked at her husband in some surprise. The moment
she praised anything about the New Laws was normally the
point in their well-rehearsed argument when her husband
glared at her and suggested that she go the whole distance in
making the damned New Laws into angels and rivet wings to
their backs, or said something else to the same effect. But not
tonight. Fredda realized that Alvar was . . . *different* tonight.
The New Law robots were on his mind—but usually the subject simply got him angry. This time there was something
more thoughtful about him. Almost, impossibly enough, as if
he were *worried* about them. "Do you really want to know?"
she asked, her voice uncertain.

"Of course I do," he replied gently. "Why else would I
ask? I'm always interested in your work."

"Well," she said, "the short answer is that I don't know.
There is no question that they have a—a drive for beauty. I

can't think of what else to call it. Though perhaps it might be more accurate to call it an impulse to put things right. Where, exactly, it comes from, I can't say. But it's not all that surprising that it's there. When you construct something as complex as a robotic brain, and introduce novel programming—like the New Laws—there are bound to be unexpected consequences of one sort or another. One reason I'm so interested in Prospero is that the programming of his gravitonic brain was still half-experimental. He's different from the other New Laws in some unexpected ways. He has a much less balanced personality than Caliban, for one thing."

"Leave that to one side for the moment," Alvar said. "What about this urge to create business?"

"There you get into very dangerous waters," Fredda said. "I'd be very reluctant to credit them with true creative impulses. I'm sure Donald would agree with me."

"I certainly would," Donald said, speaking from his wall niche, and startling Fredda just a fraction. The convention was that robots were to speak only when spoken too, especially during meals, but Donald often found ways to make liberal interpretations of that rule. "Robots do not and cannot achieve true creativity," he went on. "We are capable of imitation, of reproducing from an existing model, and even of a certain degree of embellishment. But only humans are capable of true acts of creation."

"All right, Donald. Let's not get off on *that* debate," Kresh said. "By creation or repair or imitation, the New Laws have done great things on the Utopia reservation, in ways that don't seem to offer them any sort of benefit. Green plants and fresh water and a balanced local ecology don't do *them* any good. So why do they do it?"

"Ask them and they'll tell you it's because they want to—and good luck getting a more detailed answer," Fredda said. "I haven't, and I've tried enough times. I don't know if it's their Fourth Law, or the fact that they were designed for terraforming work, or the synergy between the two of those things. Or maybe it's because Gubber Anshaw designed their gravitonic brain with an underlying internal topography that is closer to the human brain's pattern than any other robotic brain has even been."

Alvar smiled. "In other words, you don't know," he said.

Fredda smiled back, and reached across the table to take his hand in hers. "In other words, I don't know," she agreed. It was good to talk with him, on this of all subjects, without anger. She knew he had never really felt completely confident in his decision regarding the New Laws. And, in her own heart of hearts, she had to admit it was at least possible it might have been better all around if she had never created them. "But even if I don't know why they feel the impulse, I do know that they feel it."

"I guess that will have to do," he said. "There are times when I wonder about that. It is something new and different in the universe for robots to work for something without orders, without direction. And Donald's observation to the contrary, I am not absolutely convinced it is impossible for an artificial mind to have creative ability. I don't *like* the New Law robots. I think they are dangerous, and not to be trusted. But I cannot quite bring myself to believe they, and all their work, should be wiped off the face of the planet."

Fredda pulled her hand back, and looked at her husband in alarm. "Alvar—what are you talking about? You decided years ago that they should be allowed to survive. What you're saying now makes it sound like there's a new reason you might . . ." Her voice trailed off, but her husband understood.

"There is a new reason," Kresh said. "A new reason they might have to go. I may have to choose between destroying them and saving the planet. I don't need to tell you what my choice would be."

"Alvar, what in the name of the devil are you talking about?"

Alvar Kresh did not answer at first. He looked at her most unhappily, and let out a deep and weary sigh. "I should never have accepted this job," he said at last. "I should have let Simcor Beddle take it, and let him have the nightmares." He did not say more for a moment. Instead he picked up his fork and made an attempt to eat a bite or two more. But the sudden silence in the room, and the expression on Fredda's face, were too much for him. He let the fork clatter onto the plate, and leaned wearily back in his chair. "I want you to come in with me tomorrow morning," he said. "There's someone I want you to meet. I want your opinion of what he has to say."

"Who—who is it?" Fredda asked.

"No one you'd know," said Kresh. "A young fellow by the name of Davlo Lentrall."

TONYA WELTON WAS worried. She had reason to be. Something was going on. Something was going on, and she did not know what it was. And she would not know until the Settler Security Service debriefing team was ready to tell her. The SSS had told her that an informant named Ardosa had risked his cover getting into Settlertown, and that he had claimed to have some vital information, and that it concerned an astrophysicist named Davlo Lentrall. They would not be able to have anything more for her until the transcripts of his debriefing were drawn up and checked over, and the information verified.

There had been something in the voice of the SSS officer who had reported the news, something that told her it was big enough that they didn't want to risk letting it out until they were sure the information was credible. They were going to have a try at breaking into Lentrall's computer files. The University was using a Settler-built computer system, which ought to give them an advantage, but it still would not be easy. There was nothing to do but wait.

Tonya had a gut feeling that told her they were going to find out Ardosa's information damn well was credible. She was tempted to call over and demand to be given the raw information immediately. But she knew better than that. When the professionals turned cautious, there was, more often than not, good reason for them to do so. Let them work. She would know in good time.

As she sat there, worrying, Gubber Anshaw came into the room. He bent down to kiss her on the forehead, and she gave him a little pat on the arm before he straightened up and crossed the room to settle into his own chair with a contented sigh.

Tonya watched him pull out his technical journals and start in to read. She loved him dearly, there had been times when he had been of tremendous help—but this was not likely to be one of those times.

Gubber was a world-class expert on robots, but whatever was up, it definitely did not involve robots. At the moment, Gubber was reading up in preparation for his long-planned trip to Valhalla. Gubber, as the designer of the gravitonic brain, had never really approved of the way Fredda Leving had appropriated his work to create the New Law robots. However, over time, he had come to accept the situation—and from there, it was not much of a step to taking advantage of it. The New Laws were still the only gravitonic-brain robots ever made. It was only common sense that Gubber take advantage of the chance to study them more. Gubber was due to take the morning suborbital flight to Depot in the morning, and meet up with a New Law robot by the name of Lacon-03 there for the journey on to the hidden city of Valhalla.

Normally, Tonya would have entertained the hope that Gubber might have heard something through the rumor mill. But when Gubber was wrapped up in his work, it took something on the order of a blaster shot at the book he was reading to direct his attention elsewhere. It seemed highly unlikely he had spent much time recently with his friends chatting about the doings of obscure astrophysicists.

Damnation, what was this Lentrall person up to? Why was he suddenly so important? It involved terraforming, that much was for sure. Therefore, it had to affect the Settlers on Inferno. And, as she was the leader of the Settlers on Inferno, it sure as hell was going to affect Tonya.

The contingent of Settlers were on Inferno for the express purpose of reterraforming the planet. Very few of the Settlers sent on the project had been particularly thrilled about the assignment. After all, it required them to live on a Spacer world, and to deal with Spacers on a daily basis.

But enough could be said for the Spacer life that many of the Settlers had lived up to their name, and settled on Inferno, more or less permanently. They had discovered there were other ways to live, besides in the vast underground warrens that were the Settler cities. They had met husbands and wives, started families. They had bought property, built houses. Some had actually taken on robot servants. There were more than a few of them who had no particular desire to go back home. As terraforming a planet was, at the very least, a task measured in decades, some of her people—including Tonya herself—had begun to take comfort in the knowledge that they could stay as long as they liked, perhaps their whole lives long.

Therefore, anything that threatened, or even affected, the Settlers' terraforming project, was of the gravest concern. And Tonya had the very distinct impression that this Lentrall affair could play merry hell with the terraforming project.

Their operative at the University of Hades, a fellow by the name of Ardosa, had alerted the Settler Security Service that Lentrall had come up with something that had thrown the whole terraforming department for a loop. Ardosa had also reported that the upper ranks of the university's administration had likewise been thrown into an uproar by the news. There had been some extremely stormy meetings.

Beyond all that, Ardosa didn't know much—simply that something was up, and that it was urgent, and that Lentrall had met with the university's top terraforming experts. Or at least what passed for terraforming experts over there. Tonya was confident her own people were way ahead of anything the Infernals could do. At least she *had* been confident, up until now.

Once alerted by Ardosa, the Settler Security Service had spotted Lentrall going in and out of Governor Kresh's office complex. The SSS also managed to get a private peek at the governor's daily appointment list. All the other entries were routine, but the listing *Davlo Lentrall—reterraforming proposal* had caught Tonya's eye.

Who was this Lentrall, and what was he up to? Her people knew almost nothing about him. About all they had was that he was very young—even by Settler standards—and that he was some sort of scientist in the university's astrophysics department. He seemed to have an informal connection to an obscure research center that was vaguely attached to the Infernal side of the terraforming project. That was all they knew.

That, and the fact that he had had a rapid series of appointments with progressively higher-ranking Infernal government officials, culminating in a meeting with the governor himself. The question was obvious—what could be important or urgent enough to propel an obscure astrophysicist into the governor's office?

Tonya felt frustrated. The time had been when her people could have worked up a complete dossier on a fellow like Lentrall no time at all. There had been an odd sort of freedom for her spies and intelligence operatives, in the old, confrontational days. Back then, relations between the Settlers and the Spacers had been so bad it didn't much matter if they got worse. In fact it was difficult to see how they *could* have gotten worse. Cinta Melloy, the head of the SSS, could have, and had, used all sorts of dirty tricks—taps on comm calls and databanks, bribes, agents tailing a subject, the whole works—in order to develop information.

But now everyone had to be very respectful and polite, on both sides. Over the past few years, the SSS had developed a very close working relationship with Justen Devray's Combined Inferno Police. They shared intelligence and assisted each other in enforcement work. It would not do to jeopardize all that with a flurry of ham-handed snooping around. In some ways, peace was a lot more complicated than confrontation.

Tonya looked back over at Gubber. Speaking of relationships, *theirs*, Tonya's and Gubber's, had caused more than a small stir, back when the secret got out. The hard-as-nails leader of the Settlers on Inferno, quite literally in bed with the quiet, retiring, soft-spoken Spacer roboticist. It had been a tremendous scandal.

Tonya realized she was missing a bet. Even if it was unlikely that Gubber had heard anything, it couldn't hurt to ask. Besides, scientists tended to know each other. Maybe Gubber would know something useful about Lentrall's background, even if he wasn't up to date on the latest rumors.

"Gubber?" she asked in a casual tone of voice.

"Hmmm?" He looked up from his reading, a vague sort of smile on his face. "What is it?"

"Do you happen to know a man named Davlo Lentrall?"

Gubber thought for a moment. "I know *of* him, at least slightly," he said. "I ran into him at some sort of joint studies conference. A very young fellow. He's some sort of assistant researcher in the department of astrophysics over at the university. I don't pay much attention to those backwater space science disciplines. I can't say I know much about him."

Tonya nodded thoughtfully. There was not much impetus for basic space research on the Spacer worlds, and hence not much research. "What did you think of him?" she asked. "What sort of impression did he make?"

"Oh, I don't think we got past the hello, pleased-to-meet-you stage, so I can't say I formed much of an opinion. Pleasant enough, I suppose, but very rushed and abrupt. Everything is always a top priority. You know the sort. Why do you ask?"

"Well, no special reason," she said. "To tell you a little more than I should, our people spotted him going into the governor's office, and we were wondering what he was doing there."

Gubber frowned. "I'm sure I don't know," he said. "But he does seem rather a junior sort of person to be meeting with the planetary governor."

"I quite agree," Tonya said.

"Well, I'm sure you'll find some perfectly dull explanation in a day or so," Gubber said, and went back to his reading.

"Maybe," said Tonya. "Maybe." Gubber was probably right. But she could not let go of it. What the devil did a junior astrophysicist have to do with terraforming? Tonya had an unpleasantly strong hunch she was not going to like the answer.

SIMCOR BEDDLE, LEADER of the Ironhead party, leaned forward into the lectern and pounded it with his fist. "No more!" he shouted out to his audience. "We won't take anymore!" he half shouted in order to be heard over the wild cheers and applause from the audience. Or would it be more accurate to call that mass of his wild-eyed followers a mob? No matter. They were his. They fed on him, and he fed on them.

He wiped the sweat from his brow with a pristine white

handkerchief and went into his wind-up, the crowd shouting louder, his voice growing stronger and more angry with each demand. "No more delay in returning our robots from their illegal government seizure! No more coddling of those so-called New Law robots that threaten the stability of our society! No more Settlers shoved down our throat!" By now the crowd noise was so deafening there was no longer any point in attempting to be heard. But he shouted at the top of his lungs, not so much to make his voice audible, but in order to make it possible for his followers to read his lips. "No more!" he cried out. "No more!"

"NO MORE!" the crowd shouted back, and the chant had begun. "NO MORE! NO MORE! NO MORE!"

Simcor Beddle grinned broadly and spread his arms wide, waving to them all, drinking in the cheers and the shouts and the anger. They were still there, and they were still his. The sea of faces roaring its approval might not have been quite as large as it once had been, but it was still there, and he still controlled it. It was a great pleasure, and a great relief, to know that. The Ironheads held these meetings to keep up the enthusiasm of the rank-and-file, but there was no doubt in Beddle's mind that they did him a great deal of good as well.

He raised his arms a bit higher, and grinned a bit more broadly. That got the crowd shouting and cheering louder. He nodded to them, waved, and made his exit to the stage right wings.

Jadelo Gildern was waiting for him there. Beddle nodded to him as a serving robot handed Beddle a large glass of fruit juice to quench his thirst and ease his throat. "How big was the crowd?" Beddle asked as his took the juice and drank it down greedily. Rabble-rousing was thirsty work.

"Five thousand two hundred and thirty-three," Gildern replied. "We're holding on to more of them than I had expected. But sooner or later, we're going to have to *do* something." He nodded toward the still-cheering crowd out there. "*That* lot out there expects action. If they don't get it from you soon, they'll look elsewhere."

"Let's just be thankful they don't have anyplace else to go," said Beddle as he handed the empty glass to the robot and took a big towel to his face. He rubbed his face and his scalp vigorously. It might not be as decorous as a handkerchief, but it did a better job of drying off the sweat.

"Let's get you home and in and out of the refresher," Gildern said. "There's something we need to talk about."

"That informant that walked in earlier today?"

"That's the one," said Gildern. "You ordered us to pursue it, and we have. We've don't have much just yet, but you said you wanted to be kept informed."

"Then let's go," said Beddle. He followed Gildern out of the auditorium, leaving the still-cheering crowd behind.

Forty-five minutes later, Simcor Beddle was at his desk, reading a file prepared by Gildern, and learning the name of Davlo Lentrall.

He studied the file carefully. Once Gildern's agents had been tipped off by the informant Ardosa, they had to set to work at once. They had procured a full summary of Lentrall's career to date, but it did not make very informative reading. He was born, he went to school, he studied astronomy. None of it made for shocking revelations. So what was so important about Lentrall? Was their informant playing some sort of game with them?

"This tells us very little," Beddle said to Jadelo, who sat in one of the chairs in front of his desk. "Do you still think this is something big?"

"Yes I do. I've worked with this particular informant for quite some time. He has been a reliable small-time operative for us. His information has always been good. And as best I can tell, he is either behaving exactly the way a small-timer should when big, dangerous information drops in his lap, or else he is one of the best actors I have ever met."

"Hmmmph." Beddle glared at the file in front of him, as if he could force more information out of it by sheer force of personality. "Lentrall has something, or knows something, that is causing a lot of turmoil. I find it intriguing, but we need more. Maybe it's just some arcane academic dispute."

"I doubt it. Whatever it is, it's gotten him in to see a whole series of government officials—and gotten him in to see Gov-

ernor Kresh in a private interview,'' Gildern pointed out. "But
that's all we've been able to get."

"You're saying we're stuck. I don't like being stuck." Simcor Beddle was a man of action, a man given to straight-ahead
action, not to waiting.

"We'll get more information," Gildern said. "But when
we do, I have a feeling that we're going to have to act on it
fast."

"I agree. The government seems to moving with unseemly
haste. It's going to be something with a time element to it."
Beddle gestured toward the file on his desk. "Take it away,"
he said, and the robot by his side leaned in toward the desk,
closed the file folder, and removed it. Beddle stood up, and a
second robot stepped in from the rear to pull back his chair.
Beddle stepped around his desk, leaving it to the two robots
to get out of his way. That was the Ironhead way. One required
absolutely perfect service of one's robots, and then paid them
no mind. One assumed the robot would do what was required,
and that was all. The Infernals followed the Spacer convention
of ignoring robots. But Ironheads took the convention to its
extreme.

An Ironhead might be awakened, washed, dressed, fed and
served by a whole platoon of robots during the day—but never
acknowledge their existence, or even be consciously aware of
seeing them. Someone had described the ideal Ironhead life-
style as being waited upon hand and foot by a legion of ghosts,
and that was not far from the truth.

Beddle came around to sit in one of the two big, comfortable armchairs reserved for visitors, easing his considerable
bulk into it with a surprising grace. "What do *you* make of
it?" he asked of the man in the other chair.

Jadelo Gildern smiled, displaying a set of pointed-looking
teeth. Beddle had recently promoted Gildern to second-in-
command of the Ironhead party, while instructing him to keep
his euphemistically titled post as Director of Research and Information—a polite way of saying Gildern ran the Ironhead
spy network.

Gildern was a small, thin, sallow-faced man. His thinning
pale-blond hair was cut very short, and his face was long and

narrow. Today he was wearing a very plain, loose-fitting outfit of gray pants and a gray tunic. All his clothes always seemed to be a bit too large for him. "I think it's important, but I don't know what it is," he said. "We have only had a very few hours to examine the situation." Gildern's voice was low, and almost musical in tone. Beddle felt certain that Gildern could credit that voice as being at least half of what had gotten him to where he was. "It would of course be a relatively simple matter to infiltrate Lentrall's office and have a look around, and thus learn more about what he is doing. However, the odds of our operatives getting caught would be moderately high, and the odds that Lentrall or the university would be able to detect the intrusion quite high. The university has a surprisingly competent security system. I'd be even more reluctant to try breaking into Lentrall's computer files there. We haven't had much luck cracking into Settler computers. Even if we could get in, the odds are very much against our avoiding detection."

"Tea," said Beddle, seemingly to the open air. One of the serving robots responded with remarkable speed, and took all of ten seconds to produce a steaming hot cup of tea, made precisely the way Beddle liked it. Beddle took the cup and saucer from the robot, but otherwise paid it no attention. "I take it you don't think that the information we might uncover would be worth the risk of getting caught, or the risk of putting Lentrall on his guard."

"No, sir, I do not. I expect that we will learn more in a day or two, without the need to go to such lengths. Lentrall does not strike me as the sort who is much good at—or much interested in—keeping secrets. But, might I ask, what is the basis for your interest in Lentrall?"

"I am interested in Lentrall for two reasons," he said, pausing to take a sip of tea. "One is that he seems to interest others, and I want to know why. Second—well, you came close to saying it at the rally. We need a crisis, and I am always on the watch for a situation that might produce one. The Ironheads don't do so well when people are safe. We do best when the times are tumultuous. Our talent lies in using events, crises, situations—even those produced by our opponents—*against* our opponents. We have not had much chance for activity recently, but every now and again something or someone pops up quite suddenly out of nowhere—such as friend Lentrall. The Davlo Lentralls of the world are the raw material for our work. And right now we need raw material."

"You think our work has not been going well of late," said Gildern. It was not a question.

"No, it has not," Beddle said, and took a last sip of tea before handing the half-empty cup to the empty air and letting it go. The robot by his side plucked the cup and saucer out of midair before they could drop a millimeter. "Or to put it better, we have not been given any work to do. And we need work, if we are to survive. Attendance at the rallies is still slipping a bit." He leaned back in his chair, and thought for a moment. "You know, Gildern, I work very hard to maintain the proper appearance of a leader. Do you believe I achieve it?"

Simcor Beddle was short and fat, but that description, while accurate, did not do him justice. There was nothing small or soft or flabby about him. It often seemed as if the sheer strength of his will added ten centimeters to his height. His face was pallid and round, but the skin was taut over his jaw. It was hard to know the exact color of his eyes were, but they were gimlet hard, jewel bright. His hair was jet-black, and he wore it combed straight back. He was wearing a subdued version of his usual military-style uniform. No decoration on it for a late-evening conversation in private, none of the epaulets or braid or ribbons or insignia he had worn at the rally. Just a dull black tunic and dull black trousers of military cut. But then, understatement often proved most effective.

"Yes, sir. Yes I do," Gildern replied.

"I like to think so," said Beddle. "And yet what good is it all if there is no chance for me to lead?" He moved forward in the seat, lifted his foot and looked down at it. "I'm like one of these boots. Look at them. Steel-toed, jet-black—they look as if they could kick in any door ever made. But what good is that if there is nothing for them to kick in? If I leave them unused for long enough, people will cease to believe I *can* use them. The Ironheads can last on appearances for only so long. We need something that can move us forward."

"Your point is well taken, sir," said Gildern. "You're saying that recent history has not followed the pattern prescribed
by our philosophy."

The Ironhead philosophy was simplicity itself—the solution
to every problem was more and better robots. Robots had lib-
erated humanity—but not completely, because there were not
enough robots. The basic product of robotic labor was human
freedom. The more robots there were, and the more they
worked, the more humans were free to follow other pursuits.
Simcor Beddle believed—or at least had managed to convince
himself, and quite a number of other people—that the whole
terraforming crisis was a fraud, or at best nothing more than
a convenient excuse for seizing robots from private citizens,
and thus restricting their freedom.

Chanto Grieg's original seizure of private robots for use in
the terraforming project had been the single greatest recruit-
ment tool in the history of the Ironheads. People had rushed
to the Ironhead standard. The seizure seemed to be the fulfill-
ment of every one of Simcor Beddle's most dire warnings. It
was the beginning of the end, the moment that would mark
the collapse of Spacer civilization on Inferno, the next move
in the Settler plot to take over the planet.

But when those disasters failed to materialize, many of the
new recruits—and many of the old stalwarts—began to drift
away from the organization. In the past half-decade, Alvar
Kresh had done a better job of advancing Grieg's program
than Grieg himself had done. Kresh had delivered five years
of good, solid government, five years of measurable, meaningful movement forward in the reterraforming project.

And, worst of all, people had discovered they could survive
with fewer robots. The Ironheads could produce all the statis-
tics they liked showing how the standard of living was falling,
how incomes were on the decline, how levels of hygiene were
declining while accident rates were on the increase. But somehow, none of it seemed to matter. There were certainly plenty
of people grumbling over the situation, but they were not impassioned. They were, at least some of them, annoyed or frus-

trated. But they were not *angry*. And the Ironheads could not long survive without angry people.

"Quite right," said Beddle. "Events have *not* followed our philosophy. We need things to start going wrong once again." Beddle realized he had not put it quite right. He had better watch himself. That was the sort of gaffe that could have raised merry hell if he had made it in public. "No, more accurately, we need to make people see, once again, that things are going wrong *now*. We need some image, some symbol, some idea, to rally the masses once again."

"And you think that Davlo Lentrall might be such a symbol?" Gildern asked. "Or, perhaps, that he might at least lead us to such a symbol?"

"I have not the faintest idea," said Simcor Beddle. "But he represents a possibility, and we must pursue all such."

"As you say, sir. We will keep up a discreet watch on our new friend."

"Good," said Beddle. "Now let us move on. What can you tell me about, ah, the *other* project you had underway?"

Gildern smiled, showing all his sharp-looking teeth. "It is a long-term project, of course. But we make slow, steady progress in our search, in spite of the roadblocks put in our way. The day will come when we can strike."

Beddle smiled happily. "Excellent," he said. "Excellent. When that day comes, I hope, and expect, brother Gildern, that our friends will never know what hit them."

"With a little luck, sir, the New Law robots will not even survive long enough to realize they have been hit."

Beddle laughed out loud, a brazen, harsh noise that clearly made Gildern uncomfortable. But that didn't matter. And it was good to know that, even if Lentrall caused them all a major headache, there were other ways for the Ironheads to manufacture events.

TONYA WELTON FELT sick as she finished reading the SSS summary. She set down the datapad and looked toward the window. The sky was lightening. Night had turned to day while she read. They had gotten into his computer files. They had managed a preliminary analysis of what they had found.

It would take a lot longer to confirm that Lentrall's ideas could work—or even whether they were grounded in reality. But Tonya was already prepared to believe it. Lentrall was offering his plan in deadly earnest. And there was no doubt in her mind that "deadly" was a singularly appropriate description of what Lentrall had in mind. The Spacers of Utopia had no experience in these matters. They could not possibly understand the dangers involved. The slightest misstep, and they could easily wipe out the planet.

She would have to do something. If the Spacers were truly considering this mad thing, she was going to have to do something that would stop it before it began. But it would not do to act until she knew more. She would need a lot more information before she was ready to act. But if the information was on the level, it might well be too late to do anything about it by the time they were ready.

They would have to get ready for action now, not later. They would have to make contingency plans. and hope they were never needed.

She reached for the phone.

CINTA MELLOY, COMMANDER of the SSS, sat up in bed and slapped at the audio-answer plate. "Melloy here," she said.

"This is Welton," a voice said from the middle of the air.

Cinta blinked and frowned. What the devil was she doing calling at this hour? "What can I do for you, ma'am?" she asked.

"Switch to security setting," Welton said. There was a click, and then a roar of static.

Cinta punched her own security code into the answer plate and the static cleared. "I am on secure setting," she said. "What's going on?"

"I've just finished reading the preliminary reports from the computer tap on Lentrall. And I think we need to make contingency plans, in case we decide to look after Lentrall ourselves."

Cinta frowned. She couldn't have heard that right, or else

she had misinterpreted. Welton couldn't seriously be considering a snatch job. "Say again?" she asked.

"I said we might want Lentrall for ourselves. More accurately, we might want to keep him, and his work, from the Infernals, if only for a little while."

"Madame Welton, that would be madness! Absolute madness! If he's as important as you say—"

"He might well be that important," Welton replied. "Important in the way a plague or your local star going nova might be considered important. He's a disaster waiting to happen. And if there is any madness about, he's the one who has it. You will establish a full, round-the-clock watch on Lentrall—and you will prepare a contingency plan to kidnap him and hold him. Plan on the assumption of an attempt within the next few days, and hold the operation in hot-standby. I want a plan we can adapt to as many circumstances as possible, and one we can carry out within one hour of my giving the command." There was a pause on the line, and for a moment, Cinta thought Tonya Welton was finished speaking. But then she spoke again. "And while you're at it," said Tonya Welton, "you might consider praying we're not too late already."

4

"RUN IT AGAIN, Gervad," said Justen Devray. "With full enhancement and magnification."

"Yes, sir." Gervad activated the controls, and ran his own downloaded memory sequence one more time.

Devray watched as the imagery bloomed to life one more time. The bald head of Barnsell Ardosa appeared on the screen, the image rendered grainy and jerky by the magnification routine. Justen had run this imagery, and the images from Sapper 323, a dozen times by now. The Sapper's imagery was a trifle sharper, but Gervad had had a very slightly better angle. Once he had downloaded a copy of the Sapper's pertinent surveillance imagery, Devray had left the Sapper on the scene, with the surveillance aircar, and orders to watch for Ardosa's reappearance. Sapper 323 was to follow him wherever he went, as discreetly as possible.

"All right, Gervad. Freeze on the clearest frame, and show me the image you got a match pattern from next to it," Justen said, his voice eager, his expression alert. There was, in every good law officer, at least a bit of the hunter, of the pursuer, of the tracker who would follow the trail and never give up. That part of Justen had been very much awakened by the appearance of Barnsell Ardosa. Or at least by the someone who called himself that at the moment.

The robot obeyed Justen's order, and the two still images—one grainy and slightly distorted, the other a sharp, clear identity scan—appeared on the flat screen.

There were times that robot identity matches failed altogether, when a robot declared an identity match between two images that a human would reject instantly as being of two different people. But not this time. The surveillance image might be of extremely low quality, but it was unquestionably the same man as in the university's identity-scan image.

Justen stared hard at the surveillance image. The enhancement system had cleaned it up at least somewhat, but there were limits to how much one could use that sort of thing. Justen knew he could have ordered the robot to clean it up even more, but they were already at the point where the enhancements were close to guesswork. They would start losing information instead of gaining it if they did any more to the pictures. A more enhanced version might look better, but it would also look less like Ardosa.

Less like Ardosa. That thought resonated with Justen for some reason; but he was not sure why. Not yet. Let it ride. Let it come to him.

Justen Devray allowed himself a small smile. There were few things easier than not looking like Barnsell Ardosa. After all, it was becoming increasingly obvious that Ardosa did not exist. Justen had gotten his first clue to that interesting little fact when he starting trying to find out why Sapper 323's pattern-match lists did not show Ardosa. The Sapper's database should have included everything that Gervad's had.

The explanation had turned out to be remarkably simple. Alarming, but simple. When Justen compared the dates on Gervad's ID database against Sapper 323's, he discovered that Gervad's was only a few days old, while Sapper 323's list had not been updated in a year and a half. That was not surprising, given the fact that the Sappers were not the most popular model in the world. The rental shop where Justen had gotten it had had a dozen Sappers powered down in the back.

Gervad's database had Ardosa, but his database also showed that Ardosa's records had been entered five years before—

although Sapper 323's eighteen-month-old database had no record of him at all.

In short, it was painfully clear that someone had managed to manipulate the police data files, and gone to that effort at least in part to insert an operative into the University of Hades faculty. It seemed unlikely that they had gone to all that trouble just for this one man. They were going to have cross-check the entire identity list—and start the long, dreary search for the security breach as well. Tiresome stuff. Justen gave silent thanks that he was not an officer in counterintelligence. They were going to have a mind-numbing job ahead of them.

But where had they—whoever "they" were—decided to put their man? Justen checked the listing a bit more carefully. In what part of the university did Ardosa spend his days?

When he got his answer, the hairs on the back of his head seemed to stand on end. The University's Center for Terraforming Studies. That explained a great deal—a bit too much for Justen's comfort. He had been quite mystified by the notion of someone bothering to insert an agent to watch over the moribund confines of the university. But terraforming was quite another matter.

The struggle to reconstruct the planet's climate was at the core of all the other issues of the day. Whoever controlled the reterraforming project controlled power, and not just the raw, physical power of the terraforming machinery, but every other sort of power as well: financial, political, intellectual, everything. It made all the sense in the world for the Settlers or the Ironheads or anyone else to insert a man into the Terraforming Studies Center.

But something didn't fit. Ardosa—whoever he really was— was not at all the sort of person Devray had been looking for outside the entrance to Settlertown. That stakeout was an ongoing operation, an attempt to establish a pattern of routine comings and goings. Casuals and walk-ins, as they were known in the trade. A deep-cover agent would know better than to use the front entrance, and thus risk blowing his cover. Unless there was something so urgent and important that it was worth risking all.

But terraforming was a project for the generations. It

moved, of necessity, at a leisurely pace. Any given project
was likely to take years to accomplish. What sort of terraforming information could be as urgent as Ardosa's behavior suggested it had to be? Why go in the front door? Why not send
word some other way? It was plainly impossible to shut down
all forms of communication. There was always some way to
pass a message in reasonable safety, provided you were willing to take a little time. You could send a written message
carried by a robot. You could use a dead-drop, something as
simple as a scribbled message hidden under a rock. You could
send a perfectly normal hyperwave message saying something
like, "Your shoes are ready to be collected," or "Please order
porridge for my breakfast," with each phrase having a pre-
arranged meaning.

Ardosa had to have *some* such way to contact the Settlers.

So what could be so vitally important that he would throw
all that over and dive for the front door?

And who was Ardosa? Devray was certain he had seen that
face before. But where? He studied both images again. It was
a distinctive face, not the sort that would get lost in the shuffle.
In the surveillance imagery, it was wearing a worried look,
and the identity scan image had that awkward, glazed, expressionless look of so many identity photos, the subject
caught by the camera the moment before deciding what to do
with his or her face.

As Justen stared at the images, there was one thing he became more and more sure about. He had never seen whoever
it was in the flesh. He had simply seen an image of this man
before. A flat-photo, a hologram, something like that.

A case file, then. That was what it had to be. The mug shots
from some case he had worked on, or studied. A case big
enough that Devray had studied every mug shot hard enough
and long enough to have them burned into his skull. But Ardosa had not been a central figure in whatever case it was.
Otherwise, Devray would have known him instantly.

A thought that had flitted through his mind a few moments
before came back to him. *Less like Ardosa.* Was that part of
his subconscious whispering that Ardosa no longer looked
quite the way he had, whenever Devray had seen him? And

it would have to be an older case, or else, Justen knew, he would remember the face clearly. He studied the images one more time. "Gervad," he said, "delete the mustache from both images. And give me a range of reverse age regressions. Not in Spacer mode. We age too slowly. Do it in Settler mode. Go back ten chronological years or so. Standard spread."

"Yes, sir." The robot operated the image control system with a smooth skill, and the two images shrank to take up only a small fraction of the screen before the mustaches faded away from each of them, leaving a vague patch of simulation, the computer's best estimate of what sort of upper lip existed under the man's facial hair.

Then the faces multiplied, and began to shift and change, transmogrifying into younger variants. Some versions of the face grew thinner, or sprouted new hair. Wrinkles vanished, the slight double chin melted away. But there were so many ways for a man to age, and so many ways a man could prevent the aging, in whole or in part, if he chose to do so. Spacers, of course, made every effort to stop the aging process completely—but Settlers did not. They let themselves grow old.

Spacers were not used to people aging, not used to seeing their appearance change over time. If a near-ageless Spacer became friends with a youthful Settler, lost track of him, and then encountered the same Settler twenty years later, the Spacer would have a great deal of difficulty recognizing the older version of the Settler as being the same person. But Spacers had not lost this skill altogether. It could still be brought into play with a little encouragement.

The computer graphics system manipulated the images at a rapid clip. Within seconds, Devray was faced with two dozen versions of the same face, shifted and changed and re-formed. He studied each of them in turn. He was tempted to reject most of them at once, but resisted the urge to move too fast. He trusted his instincts, but only so far. Suppose the face he rejected turned out to be the one that spurred his memory? But still and all, he had to trust what his subconscious was telling him. Number One had too much hair. Number Two looked far too young. Three and Four were plainly too thin, while Six and Eight were far too portly.

Justen Devray stared at the images, slowly, carefully, one at a time. Something in the back of his head whispered that he was close, that he was going to get the answer, that he was about to make the connection.

And then he saw it. Face Number Fifteen. That was the one he knew. He was sure of it. And suddenly, in a moment like a piece dropping itself into place in the puzzle, he knew. He knew who it was.

He had seen Ardosa's mugshot before, all right. And the man calling himself Ardosa *had* been involved, if on the periphery, of a big case. The biggest case Justen Devray had ever been on. The murder, five years before, of Governor Chanto Grieg.

JUSTEN RUBBED HIS face and blinked hard. "I'm sorry I'm a bit punchy, sir. I've been up all night on this one. I came straight from the archives room to here." He blinked and stretched, trying to bring the room into focus. Apparently Kresh's wife was waiting in the main office, just down the hall, and that was why Kresh had brought him in here, to an assistant's office, for the meeting. Kresh had assured him the assistant would not be in for another hour, but even so . . . The paintings on the wall, the tastefully chosen furniture and decoration, made it seem a strangely personal space. Justen felt as if he were intruding.

"It's all right, son," Kresh said. "Sit down." Kresh sat on one end of a low couch, and gestured for Devray to sit down on the other end. Justen did so, gratefully. "Donald, bring the Commander something hot and strong with a dose of caffeine in it."

"At once, Governor," Donald replied, and went off to take care of it.

"All right then, Commander. My wife and I have a rather important meeting at ten this morning. That gives us just about an hour. Will that be enough for whatever it is?"

"I don't think it'll take five minutes, sir." Justen hesitated a moment, and then decided to plunge ahead. "This appointment at ten, sir—would it by any chance be with a Davlo Lentrall?"

Kresh looked surprised. "It would indeed, Commander. I haven't told anyone I'm meeting with him again, outside of my wife. Might I ask where you got that particular tidbit of information?"

"Thank you, Donald," said Justen. Kresh's personal robot had returned with a cup of what seemed to be remarkably strong tea, and Justen took it from him. Like most Spacers, Justen rarely bothered handing out "pleases" and "thank yous" to robots, but, somehow, Donald 111 was a special case. He took a quick sip of the tea, and found it as reviving as he had hoped. "I got my information from two sources," he went on. "From our old and dear friends in the Settler Security Service, and from the Ironheads. Neither of them gave me the information on purpose, of course, and neither of them knows what I've found out. But I learned it from them, all the same. If they don't know all about him by now, they will, very soon. And whatever he's involved in has got both outfits about to go ballistic."

"Do *you* know what Lentrall's been working on?" Kresh asked.

"No, sir. But if the Settlers and the Ironheads don't know by now, they will by lunchtime. I can tell you they are both digging as hard as they can."

"Why don't you start at the beginning, son?" Kresh suggested.

"Yes, sir. I've been sitting in on the various ongoing operations, just to see how things are going, to get a feel for what my officers have to deal with, and so on."

"And it gets you out of the office now and then," Kresh said with a smile. "I used to do the same thing when I was running the Sheriff's Department."

Justen smiled back. It helped a great deal to have a governor who used to run a law enforcement agency. He understood things without needing too much explanation. "Yes, sir. In any event, I sat in on the Settlertown main entrance stakeout. Normally the officer assigned to that duty is expected to provide his or her own vehicle or other watch post, and his or her own robotic assistance, and is later reimbursed. The thinking is that keeps us from using the same three vehicles and

the same three robots over and over. It should make us harder
to spot. It also encourages the officers to be a bit more creative,
show some initiative. In any event, I did the drill myself. I
brought my own personal robot, and rented a second robot and
an aircar. That stakeout is sort of a grab-bag affair, more than
anything. Every once in a while we spot someone going in
who shouldn't be, and we can run some checks."

"But something a little different happened."

"Yes, sir. My robots spotted someone not on the watch lists.
My robot could ID him, but the rental unit could not, even
though it was a security model. I later found out that the ID
database in my personal robot had been altered. My robot's
list is a copy of the standard CIP list—and I've confirmed that
the standard list has been altered as well."

"Someone inserted a false ID profile into the CIP database?"

"Yes, sir. And I might add that the real identity of the
person in question is not in the file. I'm not sure if that's
because he was deleted by the same people who inserted the
false idea, or if the real identity's file was culled in a routine
file purge."

"I see. And who is someone pretending to be?"

"Dr. Barnsell Ardosa, of the University of Hades Center
for Terraforming." Justen pulled hardcopies of the original
images out of his carry bag. "This is the university's ID image," he said, handing them over. "And this is the surveillance image."

Kresh took the two images, and let out a low whistle. "Norlan Fiyle. The rustbacking Settler in the Grieg case. The mustache hides some of him, but it's not exactly an impenetrable
disguise."

Justen Devray looked at Kresh in impressed surprised. "The
face looked familiar to me," he said, "but it took me hours
and hours, and every image-manipulating trick in the book,
before I was able to place him."

"You've been a working cop since then," Kresh said, still
looking thoughtfully at the images of Fiyle/Ardosa. "There
have been a lot of other faces for you to deal with, on a lot
of other cases. Fiyle—I never met him, of course, but he was

part of the last case I ever worked. I can still shut my eyes and see every page of the case file. Did you ever meet him?''

"No, sir. I wasn't in on that interrogation. Maybe I should have been.''

"Don't be absurd," Kresh said, his voice gentler than his words. "You were running a big part of a vital case. He was picked up on the far side of the Great Bay from where you were working, and he gave up the one piece of information we needed almost at once. Why in the devil should you have chased after him? Just in case he popped up five years later?''

"I suppose you're right. But even so, right now I wish I *had* gone to get a look at him.''

"Hmmmph. Water under the bridge. Let's get back to the point. You've had a chance to check the files, and maybe my memory isn't as infallible as I'd like it to be. Give me a quick summary on friend Fiyle.''

"Norlan Fiyle. A Settler, but not any part of the terraforming team. It seems he took advantage of a few loopholes in the immigration laws to come to Inferno, presumably in hopes of making some quick and easy money. He was working with a gang of rustbackers, helping to smuggle illegal New Law robots off the island of Purgatory. He got caught just about the time Grieg was murdered. He made a deal, all charges dropped and freedom to leave the planet, in exchange for the name of a Governor's Ranger who was on the take. The Ranger in question was Emoch Huthwitz, who was killed the same night as the governor, while on guard duty. It looked a lot like an opportunist revenge murder. It was one of the leads that got us looking at the possible involvement of rustbacking gangs in the case.''

Kresh shook his head. "I needed the refresher. Sometimes I forget how intricate that case was. But Fiyle was supposed to leave the planet. Why didn't he?''

"I don't know, sir. But the fact that he was supposed to leave does offer an innocent explanation why he wasn't in the current CIP identity files. We don't maintain current files on people who are off-planet. As to why he didn't leave, my hunch is that he hadn't been any more honest on his home planet. Maybe he was on the run from the police there when he got to Inferno. Maybe he thought it over, and figured he wouldn't stay out of jail for long back home, if he went there. So he offered his services to the SSS here. A freelance informant. They'd set him up and protect him in exchange for information.''

"And maybe Cinta Melloy didn't make it a voluntary arrangement, if she had the goods on him back home," Kresh said. "It's all speculation, but it sounds plausible. But so far all you've got is an old smuggler walking into Settlertown and living under an assumed name. There has to be more."

"Yes, sir, there is," said Justen. "I left the Sapper to watch for Ardosa and trail him while I went back to CIP headquarters with the other robot and started trying to find out who Ardosa really was. Well, Ardosa came out of Settlertown not long after we left—and led Sapper 323 straight to Ironhead headquarters, and a nice little chat with Jadelo Gildern."

Kresh raised his eyebrows. "The head of Ironhead security, no less. But how do you know he talked to Gildern?"

"I was coming to that. The robot on the front door wouldn't let him in until Ardosa told him something, and the robot checked it with someone inside. The Sapper caught it all on long-range imagery and audio. I've watched it a dozen times by now. What Ardosa—or rather, Fiyle—said was 'Listen, you tin box. Tell Gildern it's Ardosa with new info on Lentrall. He'll see me then.' And sure enough, in went Fiyle."

"Not the most discreet of double agents, is he?" said Kresh. "Waltzing up to the front door of two different establishments, talking on the street like that."

"Unless that was deliberate," said Justen. "He's working two sides. Why not three? Maybe he was deliberately trying to attract our attention."

"This does get deep pretty fast," Kresh said. "We could spend the whole morning spinning theories. I wonder if Gildern or Melloy know Fiyle is working two sides of the game."

"It takes a lot of nerve to spy for the Ironheads *and* the Settlers," Justen said. "It would only take just a bit more to spy for both of them without the left hand knowing what the right was doing. I don't think he's told either side."

"What makes you say that?" Kresh asked.

"Nothing solid. Just what we know of his temperament from the Grieg case, the way he carried himself as he headed toward Settlertown, and going into Ironhead HQ."

"All interesting," Kresh said. "All very, very interesting. You have a watch on Fiyle, I assume?"

"The works. Full team trailing him, taps on his hyperwave, research into his background, everything."

"Good. And one other thing. Lentrall is about to arrive here, any minute. When he leaves, I don't want him to be alone."

"I was about to suggest that, sir. I would advise a full security detail, human and robotic." After the Grieg case, they had learned not to trust a purely robotic security detail, or a purely human one. Far better to use both, rather than be exposed to the weaknesses of either working alone.

"Very good," he said. "If it were remotely practical, I'd tell you to keep them out of Lentrall's sight, but as it is— have them keep out of his way as much as possible. He's not the sort of person who's going to take kindly to a security detail. More than likely, he'll blow his top, sooner or later. Let's try and make it later."

"Yes, sir."

"Thank you for your good work, Justen," Kresh said as he stood up. "You've told me something important. Lentrall has dropped a major situation on me, and I'll need all the information I get in order to make a proper decision about it."

Justen took the hint. He stood himself, took back the images from Kresh, and put them in his carry bag as he made ready to leave. Kresh offered Justen his hand, and Justen shook it as Kresh gave him an encouraging pat on the shoulder. "I'm glad to have been of help, sir."

"You have been. You have been," Kresh said as he led the younger man out into the hallway. "Perhaps more than you know." Kresh's robot activated the door control to Kresh's office, and preceded his master through the entrance. "Thanks once again, Commander," said Kresh.

It was not until Kresh had said the last of his congratulations and farewells, stepped into his main office, and Donald had sealed the door behind them that Justen Devray noticed something. Kresh had not said a single word about what Lentrall was working on.

Tonya Welton knew more about it than he did. Simcor Beddle knew more. Of course, that was not saying much, because Justen Devray, Commander of the Combined Inferno Police, did not know anything at all.

5

"HE'S GOING IN," Cinta Melloy announced into the audio-only handset as she stared out the window. The watch team, and the snatch team on standby, were both listening. She shook her head worriedly as she watched the CIP transport setting down on the roof. And there went Devray off the rooftop pad, just as the transport set down. "Our young man is going in the front door, the head of the competition has just left, and his friends are just setting down topside." Even as she spoke, she realized that she was being too cryptic. This operation had been so rushed there had been no time to set up code names or communications shorthand. Better to be clear about what she was saying and avoid screwups. She spoke again. "Lentrall has just gone in. I just spotted Devray's aircar leaving—and what looks like a full CIP security team has just landed on the roof. I think they're going to start babysitting Lentrall here and now."

There were risks in speaking in clear, of course, but she was sure—at least moderately sure—that the Combined Infernal Police hadn't tapped this comm system yet. They were getting much better at counterintelligence, but it was by no means easy to detect, let alone tap, a concealed hardwire line.

Of course, the CIP knew about this watch-keeping station, right across the street from Government Tower, just as the Settlers knew all about the CIP watch kept on the main entrance to Settlertown. That was all part of the game. But knowing which office held the watch-keeping station was a far cry from locating the hard-wire line and tapping it without being detected.

"If they start covering Lentrall now that's not so good," replied a voice at the other end of the line.

Cinta Melloy realized she should not have been surprised that Tonya Welton was monitoring. But she was worried by just how involved in this operation Tonya Welton was getting. Most of the time, Welton kept far away from Cinta's SSS, and for good reason. No responsible leader wants to be too close to the people in charge of dirty tricks. But this case was different. Tonya was staying close. Too close.

"Stand by," Cinta said, and flipped switches that cut out the watch team and the snatch teams. "We're private now, Madame Welton. Ma'am, you really shouldn't speak when the operations people can hear you. You may have just blown away all our compartmentalization, assuming they recognize your voice."

"Let's worry about that later, shall we?" Welton said, as if the question were of no importance whatsoever. "What was that about babysitters?"

"What looks like a full CIP protection squad landed on the roof just as Lentrall went inside. My guess is that they'll start on bodyguard duty the moment he comes out of the building."

"And it will be more or less impossible for us to grab him once they are in place," Tonya said.

"Yes, ma'am," Cinta said, making no effort to hide the relief in her voice. She had wanted no part of this crazy operation.

"Then we better get to him before the bodyguards do," said Tonya. "Go get him."

"What?!" Cinta half-shouted.

"You heard me, Melloy. This is a direct order. Get him as he comes out of the building. My best guess is that you have an hour or so to get your team ready. I suggest you get moving.''

THE DOOR OPENED smoothly enough that one could have been forgiven for thinking the person who entered had a right to be there. No forcing of the lock, no furtive gimmicking of the security electronics. Jadelo Gildern was not that clumsy a person. He slipped the device he had used on the door into his pocket and stepped into Davlo Lentrall's work office. He slid the door shut behind him and let out a small sigh. Gildern looked calm enough as he stood there and looked about the smallish room, but in truth the man was scared to death, his heart pounding so loudly in his chest that he felt sure it could be heard down the hallway.

Gildern knew he was not a brave man. The risks he took and the dangers he faced in his security work were all, always and ultimately, for his own benefit, his own personal gain. Even if the routes he took to gain that benefit were sometimes labyrinthine, the final destination was always there, in sight. Whatever he did, he did for himself.

And he would be very surprised indeed if this expedition to Lentrall's office did not do him a great deal of good—all the more good for his having first told Beddle it was extremely risky.

In reality, there was very little risk at all. If Gildern had indeed gone after the computer data files, the odds of discovery and of capture would indeed have been fairly high. But the very fact that the data system security was so good played into Gildern's hands. Good security made people feel safe. People who felt safe relaxed. And people who were relaxed made mistakes.

One such mistake was in assuming that good security in one area meant security in all the others was equally good. This assumption was often mistaken—as in the matter of the door lock Gildern had just gotten past. The computer security was good, so the physical security had to be good, so it was perfectly safe to leave books and papers and notes lying around, so long as the door was locked. Gildern had hoped that Lentrall's train of thought had worked that way, and it seemed as if it had. The on-line computer files would likely have been of very little use in any event. Gildern was no technician, no scientist. It would likely take so long to analyze a technical report that the moment would be lost. No. What he was after were papers he could photograph. He wanted scribbled notes, summaries prepared to explain things to outsiders. And if he got lucky, datapads chock full of information Gildern could download and take with him.

The office was neat, but not so neat that it was a robot who had done the tidying. Gildern needed to look no further than the books on the shelf, slightly out of true with each other, than the papers that stacked up without being precisely squared up, than the way the chair sat in the middle of the floor instead of being shoved in neatly under the desk, for it to be instantly obvious to Gildern that Lentrall kept this room up himself. All to the good. If Gildern accidentally left something not precisely as he found it, it would more likely go unnoticed. And besides, if the man himself kept order here, the system of order itself might well tell Gildern something about the man.

He set to work searching Davlo Lentrall's office.

FREDDA LEVING WATCHED her husband enter the room, and saw how his expression changed the moment the door was sealed behind him. The look of calm imperturbability vanished, and a deeply troubled expression took its place. He looked to her, and seemed to understand what she had seen. He smiled, a bit sadly, a bit worriedly. "I didn't used to be able to do that, back when I was just a policeman," he said. "It used to be that I could let my face express whatever it wanted. Politics does strange things to a man."

Fredda got off her chair and took her husband by the hand. "I don't know whether I should be happy to see you drop the act in front of me, or upset to see that you put on an act at all," she said.

"Probably both," he said, a tone of apology in his voice.

"What was it Devray wanted to tell you?"

"That our friends and our enemies—who may or may not be the same people—probably already know most of what we've been trying to keep secret from them."

"And from me." Fredda moved a step or two away from her husband, folded her arms, and perched herself on the corner of his desk. "Maybe if they already know, you could finally break down and tell me what it's all about."

Kresh started to pace, up and down the length of the office, his hands clasped behind his back—a rare but certain sign of anxiety and impatience. "Where is the fellow?" he asked of the open air, and then glanced toward his wife without breaking stride. "It's not that I wanted to keep it secret from you. I just wanted you to hear it the same way I did. I wanted your opinion of—of it, without hearing about my biases or opinions, one way or the other."

"Well, you've certainly managed to keep from telling me much. All I know for sure is that it could mean trouble for the New Law robots."

Kresh stopped in his pacing and looked up at his wife again. "It could mean trouble for everyone," he said. "Ah, here's the man of the hour now."

The door slid open, and a young, energetic-looking young man came in, accompanied by a very ordinary-looking dun-colored robot of medium height and build. The robot immediately took up a position in one of the wall niches. But if the robot was entirely nondescript, the man was anything but. With his angular face, dark complexion, bristle-cut hair, and intense eyes, he was striking, rather than conventionally handsome. Whether or not Davlo Lentrall truly was a man at the center of important affairs, he at least looked as if he was.

"Good morning to you, Dr. Leving," Lentrall said, bowing slightly to her, an old-fashioned, courtly sort of gesture. He turned to her husband. "And good morning to you as well, sir."

"Good morning," said Kresh. There was a couch against one wall in the office. The governor sat down on it, and Fredda sat down next to him. Kresh gestured to a comfortable chair facing the couch. "Please, Dr. Lentrall, have a seat."

But Lentrall did not sit down. Instead he stood there, plainly struggling to act calmer than he truly was. "Sir, I must tell you something, even if it sounds a bit absurd. I—I believe that I am being followed."

Kresh smiled sadly. "I'm sorry to say that doesn't sound the least bit absurd," said Kresh. "The police commander himself was just here, telling me just how interested certain parties were in you. I'd be surprised if someone hadn't put a tail on you."

Davlo nodded and seemed to relax, just a trifle. "In a strange way, that's a relief. I think I'd rather have someone actually following me than to be suffering paranoid delusions."

"Trust me, son. In this life, one does not exclude the other. But be that as it may, sit down, take a deep breath, and then—then we can talk about the matter in question."

"Yes, sir." Davlo sat down rather gingerly, as if he half expected the chair to snap under his weight, or that some sort of trap was going to spring out of the armrests and grab him.

Fredda noted that the room was not laid out as it normally was, and that her husband was not in his usual place. Her husband had obviously ordered the room rearranged so as to lower the emotional stakes as much as possible. For this morning, Alvar Kresh was not in the thronelike chair, not behind the imposing barrier of his ornate desk. He was sitting in a posture of slightly exaggerated relaxation on the couch. The chair Lentrall was in actually put him a little above Alvar's eye level. The low table between the couch and Lentrall's chair served as a sort of barrier, a neutral buffer zone that kept anyone from invading Lentrall's personal space. Even Alvar's calm expression and faint half-smile were part of the show.

And Fredda suddenly realized that she was part of the show as well. Alvar wanted her to do the talking, have Lentrall address *her*. Did he think Lentrall would react more calmly talking to someone closer to his own age, a woman without official rank? Or was it that Alvar wanted to put himself in the position of observer, get himself outside the conversation, so that he could watch and judge impartially, without getting involved? Or maybe he didn't have a reason at all. Maybe it was just political instinct at work, unanalyzed gut feeling.

"Donald," Kresh said, "bring our guest some refreshment."

"Certainly, sir." Donald stepped forward and addressed

Lentrall. "What would you care for?" he asked.

"Nothing." Lentrall regarded Donald for a moment with an expression of curiosity on his face. He turned toward Fredda.

"Dr. Leving, I wonder if you might indulge my curiosity for a moment. This robot here. Am I correct in believing that you designed and built it?"

"That's right."

"I see. You are a well-known figure, of course, and so too are many of your creations."

Kresh chuckled darkly. "*That's* putting it mildly."

Lentrall looked toward Kresh, and smiled thinly. "I suppose you have a point, sir. But what confuses me is the name. 'Donald.' "

"It's a fancy of mine to use character names from an ancient storyteller for all my custom-made robots," said Fredda. "A man who lived on old Earth, in the pre-robotic era. A man by the name of—"

"Shakespeare," said Lentrall. "I know that. William Shakespeare. And just incidentally, I think it might be more accurate to call him a poet and a playwright, rather than a storyteller. I have studied him myself. That's what made me wonder. The names of your other robots: Caliban, Prospero, Ariel. All Shakespeare. I even saw some sort of feature story about your home, and noticed your current personal robot is named Oberon. Shakespeare again. That is why I wonder. Why the name 'Donald'?"

"I beg your pardon?"

"Sir, if I might be of assistance," Donald said, addressing Lentrall. "I am named for a minor character in the play *Macbeth*."

"But there is no character by that name in the play," Lentrall replied. "I know the play well. In fact, I am morally certain there is no character by the name 'Donald' anywhere in Shakespeare." Lentrall thought for a moment. "There is a *Donalbain* in *Macbeth*," he suggested. " 'Donald' must be a corruption of 'Donalbain.' "

"Sir, forgive me for correcting you, but I have just consulted my on-board dataset, and I have confirmed the character is named 'Donald.' "

"Of course he is, in your copy," Lentrall said. "If Dr. Leving's copy was corrupted, and your on-board reference is based on it, of course it has the name wrong as well. A lot of errors creep into the ancient texts over time."

"Might it be possible, sir, that *your* copy of the play is in error?" Donald suggested.

"Anything might be *possible*, but I very much doubt my copy is in error. I am something of a collector of such things, and I possess four different sets of Shakespeare, three as datasets and one a hard copy. There's not a 'Donald' in any of them."

"I see," said Donald, clearly taken aback by Lentrall's news. "Clearly I must review my on-board dataset."

"Interesting," said Lentrall as Donald retreated to his wall niche. "I suppose the moral is that we never know quite as much as we think we know. Wouldn't you agree, Dr. Leving?"

"Hmmm? What? Oh, yes." Fredda felt completely thrown off her stride. How could she have made a mistake like that? What other mistakes had she made over the years without even knowing it? It was remarkable how such a trivial error could make her feel so embarrassed.

And it was also remarkable that Lentrall could be rude and arrogant enough to call her on it the moment they met. Yet the fellow seemed to have no idea that had been rude. Davlo Lentrall was a most peculiar young man—and not one with the sort of skills and personality required to get far in politics. Lucky for him he had chosen another field.

But none of this was getting the discussion moving. "Perhaps it is time to turn to the matter at hand," she said.

"Absolutely," said Lentrall. "How much do you know so far?"

Fredda hesitated, and glanced toward her husband. But his impassive expression gave her no clue. "Just to be clear, Dr. Lentrall, my husband has told me nothing at all. He wanted me to hear it all from you. So please, start at the beginning."

"Right," Lentrall said, in a tone close enough to brusque that it made no difference. "The basic point is that I believe

I have found a way to enhance the terraforming process and permanently stabilize the climate.''

"But only by putting the lives of perhaps millions of people at risk," said Lentrall's robot from its niche.

"Be quiet, Kaelor," Lentrall said impatiently.

"First Law compelled me to say at least that much," the robot replied, in an aggrieved tone of voice. "Your plan of action would put many human beings in danger."

"I would hardly call it danger," Lentrall said testily. "Rather, very slight risk. But if my plan succeeds, it will mean greater safety and comfort for generations of humans yet to come."

"That argument contains far too many hypotheticals to be of any interest to me," Kaelor replied.

"You have made your point now," Lentrall said. "I order you to be quiet." He shook his head and looked to Fredda. "I know you are famous for building superb robots," he said. "But there are times when I wonder if the Settlers don't have a point."

"The same thought has crossed my mind more than once," said Fredda. "But please go on. How do you propose to stabilize the climate?"

"By flooding the north pole," Lentrall said. "I call it the Polar Sea Project."

"What, precisely, would that accomplish?" Fredda asked.

Lentrall stared hard at her for a moment, as if she had just asked what use robotic labor might be. "Let me go back a bit," he said at last. "In fact, let me go all the way back. As you might know, when the first Spacers arrived at this planet, what they found was a desert world that consisted of two large and distinct geologic regions. The southernmost two-thirds of the planet were lowlands, while the northernmost third was covered by a huge plateau, much higher in elevation than the southern hemisphere. For that precise reason, Inferno was regarded as a marginal candidate for terraforming."

"Why?"

"Because when water was introduced onto the planet, it would obviously all pool in the south—as indeed it has. Today we call the northern uplands the continent of Terra Grande, and the southern lowlands have been flooded to form the Southern Ocean. This gives the planet one water-covered pole and one landlocked one.''

''And what difference does that make?''

''A great deal of difference. Water absorbs heat energy far more efficiently than the atmosphere can. Water can circulate, carrying that heat along with it. Temperatures in the southern hemisphere are much more moderate and stable than they are in the north, because warm water can flow over the south pole and the polar regions, warming them up. Cold polar water can move toward the temperate zones and cool them off. I am oversimplifying things tremendously, of course, but that is the basic idea.''

''And that can't happen in the north, because there is no water,'' Fredda said, glancing toward her husband. But his face was completely expressionless. He was watching this game, not playing it.

Lentrall nodded eagerly. ''Precisely. Terra Grande is a huge, monolithic continent. It completely covers the northern third of the planet's surface. Because no water can flow over the North Pole region, there is little chance for temperatures to moderate themselves in the northern hemisphere. The tropical regions of the northern hemisphere are too hot, while the polar regions are too cold. If you look at a map, you will see that the southern edge of Terra Grande—where most of the people live—more or less borders the northern edge of the north tropical zone. Right here, in Hades, we should be right in the center of the temperate regions. But the temperate regions are shrinking, and we are very near the northern border of the habitable zone, at least by some standards. Actually, there are a few rather stringent Settler measures by which the city of Hades is, technically, uninhabitable. Because of insufficient rainfall, I believe. Be that as it may, the habitable zone of this planet is already little more than a narrow strip, five or six hundred kilometers wide, along the southern coast of Terra Grande. And that strip is still shrinking, despite our best efforts, and despite local successes.''

''I thought the terraforming project was gaining ground,'' Fredda said, looking toward her husband.

"It is," said Alvar. "In places. Mostly in the places where people live. We are losing ground elsewhere—but we are doing much better around Hades and in the Great Bay region generally. Once we have this part of the world under control, we hope to expand outward."

"If you get the chance," Lentrall said. "Current projections show it could go either way. You're relying on a high-point balance. It's unstable."

"What's a high-point balance?" Fredda asked.

Lentrall smiled as he reached into the breast pocket of his tunic and pulled out a large coin—a Settler coin, Fredda could not help but notice. He had it so ready to hand that Fredda assumed he had put it there deliberately, just to be ready to make his point.

"*This* is a high-point balance," he said. He held his left hand with the index finger pointed straight up, and carefully placed the coin on the tip of his index finger. "In theory, I could hold this coin here indefinitely," he said. "All I have to do is keep my finger completely steady, keep my arm from moving, keep from being jostled—while, at the same time compensating for any minute gusts of air, any very slight tremor in the building. And of course, I have to be sure I don't overcompensate while trying to correct for some very minor—"

But at that moment, the coin suddenly fell from his finger and landed ringingly on the stone floor of the office. Somehow the sound of it striking the floor was much louder than Fredda had expected.

"I've just given you a pretty fair metaphor for the present state of Inferno's planetary climate. It is stable for the moment, but if there is the slightest perturbation, there will be trouble. There is no negative feedback in the system, nothing working against a perturbation to push the system back toward stability. Ever since the first climate engineer started to work here, the balance point for Inferno's climate has been a high point tottering between two extremes, with the slightest shift capable of sending the whole thing crashing down into overheating or supercooling. We have to get everything exactly right every time, or else . . ." He nodded toward the coin on the floor.

"But you have a solution," Fredda said, her voice not entirely friendly. Lentrall was making no effort to convince, or explain, or discuss matters. He was lecturing, dictating, instructing her. He was speaking in tones that were a strange combination of arrogance and condescension. He was talking down to her, as if she were a child, explaining to her why doing things his way, the sensible way, was for her own good.

"I have a solution," he said. He reached down, picked up the coin, and placed it in the palm of his hand. "We put the planet in a low-point balance, like this." He shook his hand back and forth, and jiggled it around vigorously. The coin stayed in his palm. Once or twice, he managed to dislodge it briefly, but then it dropped back into place. "As you can see, it's much harder to perturb something out of a low-point balance, and it will tend to return to its balance point once a perturbation is removed. Now, a Polar Sea would move the global climate into a stable low-point system that would require massive effort to dislodge into instability.

"As I have said, the problem is the absence of water circulation in the northern hemisphere. If there were a way to let water accumulate in the northern polar regions, while providing inlets and outlets to the Southern Ocean, then warm water could flow north to warm the poles, and cold water could come south to cool the ocean—and the land areas near the coast. That would give us a low-point balance, where the natural force working on the planet would be self-correcting. If things got too hot, the cold polar waters would cool them off. If the temperatures dropped too much, tropical waters would warm them up. We need water over both poles."

"But there are a number of terraformed planets without water on both poles," Fredda objected. "And I recall, even Earth had one pole with land on it—and the other with highly restricted water flow. I think the pole with water on it was even frozen over most of the time."

Lentrall smiled again, and it was not a warm or friendly expression. Rather, it was the debater's smile of triumph, something close to a condescending sneer. She had fallen into the trap he had laid, and now he could move in for the kill. "I have answers to all that," he said. "I think you will find that they all strengthen my argument. Regarding the terraformed planets with land-locked poles, I can tell you that all of them have bodies of water that get much closer to the poles than we have on Inferno.''

"What about the examples she cited from Earth?'' Kresh asked.

"First, the natural oceans of Earth were far deeper than the artificial oceans of any terraformed planet,'' Lentrall said. "Because they were deeper, they held much more water and served as a much more effective heat sink.

"Second, they covered far more of the surface of the planet than on most terraformed worlds. Three-fourths of Earth was water. Slightly less than two-thirds of Inferno's surface is water, and it has more water coverage than any other wholly terraformed world. The difference between three-fourths and two-thirds may not sound like much, but it is substantial—and, as I have said, measured by volume, and not surface area, Inferno's oceans are much smaller than Earth's.

"Third, even if Earth's oceans did not have free and open access to either pole, once again, they reached close enough to allow substantial heat exchange.

"Fourth, the land-locked South Pole of Earth was far colder than the water-covered North Pole, which just goes to show my point that liquid water served to moderate temperatures. While the surface of the Arctic Ocean was frozen over, there were still a lot of water—and a lot of water currents—*below* the ice.

"Finally, Earth's climate was remarkable for its instability. It suffered severe ice ages, which were triggered by very small fluctuations in this variable or that. There is substantial evidence that the impeded flow of water over the poles was a major contributing factor to this instability. I would submit that all of these facts regarding Old Earth strengthen, rather than weaken, the argument in favor of a water flow over the North Pole.''

"Hmmph.'' Fredda didn't trust herself to say anything more. The infuriating thing was that the man was right. He did marshal his arguments well. But there was so much in his tone, in his attitude, in his behavior, that made her want to disagree with him, made her want to argue with him, tooth and nail.

"Go on, Dr. Lentrall," said Alvar, his voice an absolute study in neutrality. "What is your backing for all this?"

"An excellent question, Governor," Lentrall said, in a tone of voice that made it sound as if he were praising a bright schoolboy. "As you are no doubt aware, the original terraforming plans for Inferno called for the creation of just such a Polar Sea. I have derived most of my information from those old studies."

"Why did they cancel the plans for the Polar Sea?" Fredda asked.

"Partly it was politics and scheduling. Building the Polar Sea would have slowed the whole project up for years, and there was pressure to land colonists on the planet as soon as possible. By that time, a great number of things had already gone wrong with the terraforming project. There was some thought given to abandoning the planet altogether. Costs were getting out of control. But that would have done terrible damage to Spacer pride and prestige. The engineers were ordered to complete the project, but they were not given the time or the resources or the money to do it properly. They really had no choice but to cut corners. And the Polar Sea was one they could cut. Not doing it freed up enough resources to let them complete the rest of the terraforming project."

"A generous interpretation," said Kresh. "I've studied the old files and reports as well. I'd say they didn't come close to completion of the terraforming project. What they did was *declare* that they had completed it. The terraformers of Inferno knew exactly the mess they were creating. I found at least three reports predicting a planetary climate collapse—and all three predicted that it would happen right about now, give or take a few years."

Lentrall looked annoyed at Kresh for interrupting the flow of his speech. "In any case, the original planning documents clearly call for establishing a substantial flow of water in and over the polar regions. All of their projections showed that it would moderate and stabilize the planetary climate, as well as increasing rainfall throughout Terra Grande."

"Pretty big job, digging an ocean," Fredda said.

Lentrall smiled again, and the expression didn't make her like him any more. "Yes it is," he agreed. "But most of the work has been done for us already. Kaelor, bring me my map case."

Lentrall's robot came forward. It opened a storage compartment in the front of its torso, drew out a long, thin tube, and handed the tube to Lentrall. Lentrall opened the tube and pulled out a map printed on glossy stock. "This shows the north polar regions of Inferno," he said, spreading the map out on the low table in front of him. "One of the features of the Infernal landscape that we tend not to notice is that it is rather heavily cratered. Part of the reason for this is that the original settlers chose city sites in the regions with the lightest crater cover. Besides which, most of the craters are heavily eroded. But most of Terra Grande—and most of the flooded lowlands that now make up the ocean floor—are quite heavily cratered."

Lentrall stabbed a finger down on the exact center of the map. "As you can see, a pair of very large overlapping craters sit astride the North Pole, a formation generally known as the Polar Depression. You will note two things about the Depression. One, that nearly all of the land area inside it is below sea level. Two, there are actually permanent icecaps inside the craters. Those icecaps used to be seasonal in nature. They are now permanent, and they are growing. Every year during northern summer they melt back a bit—but every winter the storms deposit more snow, and the icecaps grow more than they have shrunk. More and more of the planet's fresh water is being locked up at the north pole. If there were a channel bringing in warm tropical water, it would melt back the icecaps in short order. If a channel could be opened from the Southern Ocean to the Polar Depression, the waters would rush in, forming the Polar Sea."

"What you're saying is that we have a ready-made seabed," said Fredda, "and it is already partly filled with water— frozen water, but water all the same. Which means that all we have to do is dig the channel."

"Not a simple matter, or a small one," Kresh said. "And

there would either have to be two channels dug, or one channel large enough to encompass both a northward and southward flow.''

"We'd need both, actually,'' Lentrall said. "One channel that could accommodate two-way flow, and one that would simply serve as a sort of huge pressure-relief valve. The second outlet would not generally carry huge amounts of water, but it would make it possible to regulate the amount of water in the Polar Sea.''

"How do manage to get water to flow in two directions at once through one channel?'' Fredda asked.

"Actually, that is one of the more straightforward parts of the business,'' said Lentrall. "It happens all the time in natural oceans. The warm water moves on top, while the counterflow of cold water moves on the bottom. A sort of natural temperature barrier, or thermocline, develops. The two currents are quite distinct from each other. They can even have different concentrations of trace elements. For all intents and purposes, they do not intermix. In the present case, the cold counterflow to the south should also serve to scour out the initial channel through the process of water erosion.''

"You make it all seem so simple,'' said Fredda, not making any great effort to keep the sarcasm out of her voice. "Why it is it no one has ever thought of it before?''

But Lentrall was clearly immune to sarcasm, no doubt because he was virtually unable to detect it. "Oh, many people have thought of it before,'' he said. "The problem is that no one has been able to find a way to go about digging the necessary channels until now. The job was too big and too expensive to do with any conceivable sort of conventional digging equipment. If we started right now, with an all-out effort to dig the channel, we wouldn't get halfway done before the climate collapsed.''

"But you, and you alone, have found the way,'' said Fredda.

That jibe almost seemed to strike home. "Well, yes,'' Lentrall said, suddenly just a trifle cautious. "Yes, I have.''

"How?'' asked Fredda. "How in the devil are you going to do it?''

Lentrall was now plainly startled. He looked from Fredda to Alvar and then back again. "You mean he didn't even tell you that much? He didn't explain?"

"No," Fredda said. She glanced at her husband, but it was plain he was not going to say anything. "The governor wanted me to hear it from you."

"I see," Lentrall said, clearly taken aback. "I thought you knew that part."

"But I don't," said Fredda, more than a little annoyed. "So I ask you again to tell me now. How are you going to do it?"

Davlo Lentrall fiddled with the map for a moment. He cleared his throat. He sat up straight in his chair, and looked straight at Fredda. "It's quite simple," he said. "I intend to drop a comet onto the planet."

6

GUBBER ANSHAW SMILED to himself as he strolled along the wide boulevards of Valhalla. He had only been to the hidden city a time or two before, and he was genuinely pleased to return.

Valhalla was a utilitarian place, designed down to the last detail to be efficient, sensible, orderly. The overall design was, ironically enough, reminiscent of underground Spacer cities, but perhaps that was to be expected. Building underground did force certain requirements on the design.

The city was built in four levels. The lower three were a fairly conventional series of storage areas, living quarters, and so on, each connected to the others by broad ramps and high-speed lifts. But Gubber was on the top level of Valhalla, and the top level was something quite unconventional, indeed. It did not remind him of anything at all.

It was an open gallery, a half-cylinder on its side, precisely two kilometers long and one kilometer wide. The side walls of the main level merged smoothly into the wide, curved, ceiling. The entire interior surface of the semicylindrical gallery was coated with a highly reflective white material. The overall effect was overbright to human eyes, but no doubt the New Laws regarded it as a more efficient style of illumination.

The floor of the huge gallery was still in large part empty, though it seemed to Gubber that there were a few new structures in place since his last visit. "Structures" seemed a better word than "buildings," as many of them did not seem to be buildings, exactly.

There were, of course, a number of normal-seeming installations on the main level, given over to one conventional purpose or another. He could identify repair centers, warehouses, transshipment centers, and so on. But Gubber did not spend much time considering them. Instead, his eye was drawn to the less identifiable structures clustered toward the center of the main level.

All of them were the size of two-or three-story buildings. Nearly all of them were geometric solids of one sort or another: cubes, cones, dodecahedrons, oblate spheroids, three-, four-, and five-sided pyramids, each painted or coated in a bright primary color. A few were positioned in strange attitudes. One cone was upside-down, and two of the pyramids rested on base-edges, so that their apexes were pointed exactly ninety degrees away from the zenith. Gubber had no idea how the New Law robots had kept them from falling over.

He was reminded of a child's carelessly scattered building blocks. On his last visit, Lacon-03 had described the structures as an experiment in abstract aesthetics, and had launched into an intricate explanation of the theories of beauty and utility currently under discussion in the New Law community.

Some of the structures were occupied or used in some way, while others did not seem to have any access way into their interiors. They were, in essence, abstract sculpture. Gubber did not care for them very much as art, but that was almost incidental. He found it fascinating that the New Laws would construct sculptures in the first place. But did they do so for pleasure, or were they simply compelled to attempt art by the murky demands of the Fourth Law? Did these huge geometric solids appeal to the New Law robots in their own right? Or did these strange beings construct them because they felt they *ought* to build them, because they wanted to convince themselves they were capable of creating? In short, did they build them because they wanted to, because Fourth Law made them do it, or because they felt it was expected of them, because human cities have public art?

Gubber had been pondering such questions for months now, and was quite pleased to realize he was no nearer an answer. Lacon-03 had never succeeded in explaining things to Gubber's satisfaction, and Gubber himself had not been able to come up with a good explanation. But that suited him fine. Puzzles lost much of their savor once they were solved. "This place always surprises me," he said to his host.

"And why is that, sir?" asked Lacon-03.

Gubber chuckled quietly as he made an expansive sweeping gesture with one arm, taking in all of Valhalla. "I suppose because none of this seems the least bit like me," he said.

Lacon-03 regarded her guest thoughtfully. "I take it, then, that because you invented the gravitonic brain, you expected to see some expression of your own personality in the thing created by beings who possess gravitonic brains?"

"Something like that," Gubber said. "And I must say, handsome as it is, this is not the sort of city I would design."

"Interesting," said Lacon. "We New Law robots have always taken an interest in aesthetics, but I must confess that we have never given much thought to the tastes and opinions of our creators. And, I must confess, what study we have made of the subject has been directing at Dr. Leving, rather than at yourself."

"I'm not surprised to hear it," said Gubber. "It is only recently that I have taken an interest in the New Law robots, or even acknowledged my role in creating you. Fredda Leving took my gravitonic brain design, wrote the New Laws herself, and put the laws in the gravitonics without so much as informing me that she had done so, to say nothing of asking my permission."

"You do not approve of the New Law Robots, then."

Gubber stopped and regarded his companion with a gentle smile. "In theory, no," he said. "I think it was tremendously dangerous and foolhardy for Dr. Leving to do what she did. In practice, I find that I rather *like* most of the New Law robots

I have met. You see the world in a different way than human beings do—and in a different way from Three-Law robots as well.''

"In what way, might I ask?''

Gubber nodded toward his companion, then looked forward and started walking again. "No,'' he said. "You tell me. Tell me as we walk the city that is not what I expected. Tell me of the worldview of the New Law robots.''

Lacon-03 thought for a moment as they strolled down the broad center boulevard of Valhalla. "An interesting challenge,'' she said. "I would venture to guess that no two New Law robots would be able to agree completely on how we see the world. We are a disputive group, I can tell you that much. However, I would say that we are baffled by the outside world—and have the sense that the outside world is baffled by us. Human and Three-Law robots have had endless millennia to work out their relations to each other, to discover how they fit into the universe. We New Law robots have had only about five standard years. During that time, the key thing we have learned is that the universe of humans and Three-Law robots is not the most welcoming of places for those of our kind. At best we have encountered indifference, and, at worst, murderous hostility.''

They came to a large two-story building, positioned to command a spectacular view of the main gallery. It was the main administration building. With Prospero away, Lacon-03 was in charge of the city's day-to-day operations. Lacon-03 gestured for Gubber to follow her inside, and then went on speaking as they went through the doorway, and then up a curving ramp that led to the upper level of the building. "Coupled with this hostility is the plain fact that we have no real purpose in the world. There is no predestined role for us. We must create one for ourselves—and that is not a quick or simple process. Prospero understands this. Our skills and aptitude in terraforming work offer us opportunities, of course. But Prospero knows it will take time for humans to accept us fully into that work. He also understands that we must keep ourselves safe until such time as we are accepted, and work relentlessly to exploit any chance to better ourselves. I realize that I have not given a complete answer to your question, for the simple reason that we have not yet discovered one for ourselves. We need a place to search for better answers. We need a refuge, a sanctuary, a place to reflect, to study, to plan. Valhalla is all those things. But it is something else. Something far more important.''

Lacon-03 paused at the top of the ramp, Gubber by her side. A wide picture window stood before them. Valhalla's distinctly inhuman architecture was on proud display just beyond the window frame. ''Valhalla,'' said Lacon-03, ''is our home.''

'' 'PHASE ONE. INTERCEPTION and stabilization of Comet Grieg and installation of attitude control rockets and main propulsive device.'—I expect that last is a polite term for a massive bomb of whatever sort.'' Jadelo Gildern smiled unpleasantly as he looked up from his datapad. ''I never have cared overmuch for misused euphemism. The term 'propulsive device' is so vague it merely brings the question of what the thing might be to one's attention.''

''Get on with it, Gildern,'' said Simcor Beddle, as he sat back in his lounge chair, his hands folded in his lap, his gaze fixed on the far corner of the ceiling.

''Yes, sir. 'Phase two. Activation of the main propulsion device. Phase three. Cruise toward planet. Attitude control rockets used to correct and maintain course. Phase four. Controlled breakup of Comet Grieg into separate fragments.' Lentrall seems not to have decided how many fragments, or of what size. 'Phase five. Targeting of fragments. Phase six. Impact of fragments on planet.' ''

''Burning stars,'' said Beddle. ''I am not sure I am ready to believe all this. They are planning to use a comet to dig a channel from the sea to the Polar Depression?''

''So it would appear, sir. By targeting the fragments carefully, they mean to line them up like beads on a string, with each smashing into the planet at a carefully chosen spot. In essence the craters will be lined up end to end. They also intend to use oblique strikes.''

''Meaning what?'' Beddle asked.

"Instead of hitting the ground straight down, they will target the comet fragments to let them strike at a substantial angle of attack. The end result is that, instead of perfectly round craters, they will get rather long, oval ones."

"And all this will magically form a link to the sea?"

"No, sir. It does not seem that they expect the impacts will do *all* the work of digging, but they do expect them to do the vast majority of it. Conventional digging, or what they call moderate-yield zero-radiation fusion devices—in other words, nuclear bombs—would be used to link the craters up to each other. There are other details to the project, of course. But when I say details, I am referring to huge projects that would seem massive undertakings in any other context. The plan calls for redirecting the flow of the River Lethe not once, but twice. Currently the Lethe runs from west to east for some time before turning south to empty into the Great Bay. Prior to the impact, they will dam it above its turn to the south, and force it into a new channel to the north, so that it will scour out a new outlet in the Polar Depression. After the impact, they will link the old and new channels and reverse the flow a second time and the River Lethe will become the Lethe Channel, forming the second outlet between the Polar Sea and the Southern Ocean."

Beddle got to his feet and looked down on Gildern. "This is madness!" he protested. "I have often been accused of megalomania, but this—this goes far beyond the maddest schemes I ever dreamt of."

"It certainly is ambitious."

Beddle looked sharply at Gildern. "You always have been one for understatement. I would almost suspect you of approving of this madness."

"I must admit that I have an open mind about it all," said Gildern.

Gildern's superior looked surprised. "We will return to *that* point later, I can assure you," Beddle said. "How is it you got all this information?" he demanded.

"I broke into Lentrall's office and took scans of every document I could," Gildern replied.

"But I thought we had agreed the risk was too great."

"Lentrall left his office and took his robot with him early this morning. I had been monitoring the building for some time, and knew it was virtually deserted at that hour. I decided it was worth the risk of a quick physical search, and of copying the information from his datapads. I didn't make any attempt to examine his on-line computer files. There was a much greater risk of discovery in that."

Beddle nodded, apparently satisfied. "Do you have any sense of how seriously this proposal is being taken?" Beddle asked.

"That I cannot say," Gildern replied, for once speaking with perfect sincerity. "There is nothing in the papers and datacubes I have examined that would give me any idea. I saw Lentrall's proposal—but we have nothing to indicate Kresh's reaction."

"Other than the fact that Kresh is seeing him for the second time even as we speak." Beddle frowned thoughtfully. He gestured to a nearby service robot, who immediately brought an overstuffed chair to where he was standing. Beddle sat down close to Gildern and leaned in close. "I almost get the impression that you approve of this—this scheme."

"I would not go nearly so far. I would say we should not reject it out of hand, once it gets out to the public. And it is sure to get out. Nothing this big can stay hidden for long."

"That much I agree with. But might I ask your reasons for even considering this comet business?"

"Because even half a morning's consideration of it has allowed me to do something I have never permitted myself to do, ever before. It has given me the chance to admit to myself that this planet is doomed."

"I beg your pardon?"

Gildern handed the datapad out into thin air, and his personal robot retrieved it. Gildern leaned forward and put on a troubled, sincere-looking expression. "Sir, the planet is dying. Despite local successes, despite all our previous best efforts, that continues to be the case. Each of us, deep in our heart of hearts, knows that to be true. If I can step away from the party line for a moment, you know and I know that Alvar Kresh has been a most effective governor. He has accomplished a great deal, and bought the planet a great deal of time. But that is all he has done. It is—or at least it has been—all anyone *could* do. But deep in our hearts, I think we have all known it was not enough, that we were all doomed. And because we were all going to die no matter what we did, we decided that we might as well amuse ourselves in the meantime with our silly little games of politics and intrigue. The intrigues were harmless, after all, and would change nothing in the end. We were all going to die. But now—now—there is a chance for this world to live! It is a long chance, that I grant you. The risks, the dangers are enormous. But suddenly there is a chance."

"Hmmph. I see," said Beddle. "And I suppose that is the only reason this scheme intrigues you."

"No, sir, it is not. But the notion that we might actually win, we might actually live, certainly changes the rules of the game. If it does so in my mind, I cannot help but think it will do so in the minds of others. They will look at the political landscape in a whole new way. We must take that psychological shift into account in our planning."

"But you have something more in mind," Beddle said.

"Yes sir, I do," Gildern said, his eyes suddenly alive and intent. He gestured toward his personal robot. "That datapad my robot is holding contains technical information and executive summaries of the whole plan. Nowhere in those summaries is the word 'Settler' to be found. This is a job the Spacers, the Infernals, can do for themselves. Furthermore, if it succeeds, *we will not need the Settlers anymore.* A successful comet impact and the subsequent formation of the Polar Sea will have such a huge and positive effect on our climate that the task of reterraforming the planet will be reduced to a series of tasks to be attacked in detail. Large tasks, difficult ones, but ones we Spacers can accomplish on our own—and with significantly less labor in the field."

"What are you saying?" Beddle asked sharply.

"I am saying that Grieg took away our robots, and Kresh kept them away, offering the excuse that they were needed for terraforming work. *If* the comet strike happens, and *if* it goes well, within three, perhaps four years, there will no longer be the slightest need for domestic robot labor in terraforming."

Beddle said nothing, but nodded thoughtfully.

"I think you will agree, sir, that our party stands to make substantial gains out of the project."

"You are, of course, assuming it succeeds, and does not instead wipe us all out," said Beddle. "But I do appreciate your frank talk, friend Gildern. Any of your reasons would be strong by itself. All of them together are compelling indeed."

Gildern gestured toward his robot, and took his datapad back again, and worked the controls as he spoke. "I haven't quite *given* all my reasons, sir. There is one more." He handed the datapad over to Beddle, and then leaned back in his chair. "Take a good hard look at where Lentrall wants the damned things to hit."

Beddle looked at his subordinate in puzzlement, and then looked at the map displayed on the datapad's screen. After a moment, the confusion faded away from his face, to be replaced by a broad smile, and then uproarious laughter. "Oh, splendid! Splendid!" Beddle said when he recovered enough to speak. "I could not have planned it better myself. The gods of myth and legend could not have arranged things better."

Jadelo Gildern smiled as he watched the leader of his party studying the map in more detail, still chuckling to himself. Simcor Beddle was right, of course. The thing could not have been arranged any more neatly than it had been.

But perhaps Simcor Beddle would have been better advised to reflect further on who was doing the arranging.

DAVLO LENTRALL GLARED at the elevator door, and jammed his finger down on the button, as if having a human finger push it this time would make a difference, since the elevator hadn't arrived when Kaelor had pushed the button. The meeting with Kresh and Leving was over, and he wanted to get out of this place. "What the devil is going on?" he demanded.

"I'm sorry sir," a disembodied robot voice said. "All elevator service to the roof of Government Tower has been temporarily discontinued."

Lentrall was taken aback, if only for a moment. In a world

full of robotic monitors, rhetorical questions frequently received answers. Somewhere there was a camera, and somewhere a robot was seated at a console, watching the view from that camera and several dozen others. "I need to get to the rooftop landing pad. My aircar is up there!" Lentrall protested. The meeting with the governor and his wife had gone well, and Lentrall was impatient to get back to his lab and get back to work. There were a thousand details to be seen to, a thousand points to research. He couldn't waste time waiting around for a gang of robots to repair the wobbly railing, or whatever other deadly peril had closed off the roof.

"I am sorry, sir," the robot voice replied, "but there is a safety hazard on the roof at the present time. First Law requires that—"

"Yes, yes, yes," Lentrall said irritably. "I know all that. But my aircar is up there, and I need it to get home."

"You are not alone in this difficulty, sir. If you will take the elevator to the ground level, arrangements have been made to have robot pilots shuttle the aircars down to the main plaza. They should be able to begin that operation in a few minutes, while it might well be a delay of up to an hour before the roof is opened again."

Davlo let out a weary sigh. "Very well," he said, "I suppose that will have to do. Come along, Kaelor."

"One moment sir," his robot said. "I should like to ask the nature of the safety hazard on the roof."

Just then the elevator arrived. "What difference can that make?" Davlo demanded. "Come along."

"Very well, sir."

The two of them stepped into the elevator car and headed down.

"LOBBY TEAM REPORTS Lentrall and his robot are just coming off the elevator. They are headed toward the plaza."

"I see them," said Cinta Melloy as she watched through magniviewers. From her vantage point across the street and twenty stories up, Lentrall didn't appear to be worried or suspicious. That was all to the good. Even better was that his security team was still up on the roof of the building, dealing with the safety hazard that Cinta's people had arranged: an airtruck, carrying a load of maintenance supplies—including one barrel of flammable cleaning fluid that had sprung a dramatic leak the moment it had touched down.

Right now there was no bigger problem than a bad leak of a mildly hazardous chemical, just enough of a nuisance to make any self-respecting Three-Law robot seal off the area, shut down the elevators, hustle all the nearby humans off the roof and into the building, and generally disrupt things. But if things got organized and settled down too quickly, then Cinta was ready, willing, and able to cause a short-circuit aboard the airtruck. Her dirty-tricks people promised that the resultant fireball would be spectacular, but unlikely in the extreme to hurt anyone or cause any significant damage.

That was important. Cinta's side was playing rough, but there were limits. She was smart enough to know that sooner or later—probably sooner—the CIP would be able to trace this whole operation to her SSS covert action teams. She would just as soon the official complaints did not involve fatalities. The dirty-tricks techs could promise whatever they liked, but explosions had a way of not staying controlled. Things were going to have to get very bad indeed for her to be willing to risk pressing that button. The main thing was that they had separated Lentrall from his security detail—in fact prevented them from hooking up at all.

Everything *ought* to work. It was a reasonable, straightforward plan. But there had been so little time. Welton had moved too quickly from ordering contingency plans to ordering the snatch itself to take place immediately. Cinta didn't like rushing things. That was the way mistakes got made.

"Plaza team in position," the voice in her ear reported.

Cinta studied the plaza through the magniviewers, but there was no way to tell which of the dozens of people there were hers. Good. Then maybe no one else would be able to spot them either.

Robots. Robots were going to be the problem. Cinta could count at least ten of them in the plaza. They would, of course, move instantly to prevent a kidnapping—given the chance.

But, if all went well, they wouldn't *get* the chance. Cinta looked up Aurora Boulevard. There it was. A land-transport bus, parked a few blocks away. In a minute or so, it was going to be heading toward Government Plaza at just slightly too high a rate of speed. Cinta smiled to herself. It was hard to control that particular model of bus. If the driver wasn't careful, there was likely to be an accident.

JUSTEN DEVRAY WAS nearly home when the call came in. Gervad was flying them by the slow, scenic, restful route. Justen had had a long day, and he was glad of taking the easy way home. He liked to unwind on the ride home. A long day indeed. It was midday on the day after he had started work. He had been up nearly thirty hours straight at this point. Strange to be flying home to rest in the bright light of midday.

His eyes were heavy. He was almost tempted to turn off the hyperwave tuned to scan the police frequencies. But the constant low mutter of voices was a part of the everyday background of his life. He left it on, leaned back in his chair, and shut his eyes.

And then he heard the voice.

"CIP Metro Dispatch, this is Government Tower Topside."

Something about the voice jerked Justen awake. Then he understood. It was a *human* voice. A robot should have been the one handling communications from the rooftop guard post. And another thing: Lentrall's security detail was waiting for him on the rooftop landing pad.

Suddenly Justen was wide awake. He sat bolt upright in his seat. "Turn this thing around!" he told Gervad. "Back toward Government Tower at full speed."

"Yes, sir," the robot replied, calm and imperturbable. He brought the car about in a wide arc and headed back toward the center of the city.

Justen reached for the scanner controls, and turned up the volume.

"—ave an accident in progress here," the voice went on. "A transport landed a little hard, and one of the containers on board must have popped a seam. We've got a flammable liquid spill up here. Can't tell you more than that. The robots up here have forced us off the roof proper."

"We are receiving hyperwave reports from the security robots on the scene, Government Tower Topside," a calm robotic voice replied from somewhere, probably CIP HQ.
"Clean-up crews are being dispatched."

The damned fools! Justen stabbed at the controls, and set
his aircar mike to the same frequency. "This is Commander
Devray, en route to Government Tower and monitoring. Who
is that at Topside?"

"Sergeant Senall Delmok, sir."

Perfect. Delmok was the least experienced officer on the
Topside detail. "Delmok, since when are cleaning supplies
delivered to the roof landing pad? What do you think the city
tunnel system is for?"

"Sir? I, ah—"

"It's not an accident, Delmok. Someone has deliberately
shut down the rooftop landing pad."

"But why—"

"I don't know," Justen said. "Maybe they plan to land on
it. Get back out on that rooftop and get your people in control
of it. That is a direct order."

"But the robots are keeping us—"

Justen cut him off. "CIP Metro Dispatch. Are you still on
this line?"

"Yes, Commander," the calm robot voice replied.

"I hereby issue a direct, top-priority order for relay via hyperwave to all robots on the roof of Government Tower. You
are to permit the human CIP detachment to return to the roof
at once. The supposed spilling accident is a ruse or a diversion
perpetrated by a group intending harm to human beings. By
forcing the CIP detachment away from their posts, you are
permitting danger to humans. Relay that at once."

"Yes, sir. It has been relayed."

"Delmok, if that does not work, I hereby order you to shoot
your way past the robots to regain control of that landing pad.
Is that understood?"

There was sort of a nervous gulping noise on the line, but
then Delmok answered. "Yes, sir."

"Good," he said. "Watch that you don't catch that cleaning

fluid with a blaster shot, or we'll have a real mess on our hands. Devray out.''

Justen glanced toward Gervad. "How soon?" he asked.

"We will arrive over Government Tower in approximately three minutes. However, sir, First Law prevents me from landing this craft in the vicinity of an uncontrolled toxic and flammable material while a human is on board.''

"I know,'' Justen said, working the comm system controls again. "Once we arrive, circle the building near the roof.'' He got the controls to where he wanted them. "This is Commander Devray on crash emergency circuit. I need immediate voice contact with Governor Kresh.''

After a remarkably brief delay, the governor came on the line. "Kresh here.''

"Devray here. The code query is Emoch Huthwitz.''

"Burning stars,'' the governor replied, the surprise plain in his voice. But for all of that, he recovered quickly and gave the proper response. "The code reply is melted Sappers.''

"Thank you, sir. I'm glad to know it is really you.'' Devray and Kresh had agreed on the query and reply after what had happened to Governor Grieg. The opposition had planted a device that simulated Grieg's voice, and made it seem as if he were alive and well after he was dead. The ruse had nearly worked then. Devray did not wish to be fooled by the same sort of impostor.

"So am I, Commander. Something is going on.'' It was not a question.

"Yes, sir, and I don't know what. There's been a staged accident on the roof of Government Tower. You might be the target—but I suspect it is our young friend. Please go to heightened security status.''

"At once,'' Kresh said. "I can tell you our friend left here not ten minutes ago. Keep me informed. Kresh out.''

Justen allowed himself a half a minute to give thanks once again for the blessings of a governor who used to be a cop. Kresh knew better than to tie up the line with a lot of foolish questions.

Justen thought fast. The odds were good that Lentrall was still in the building. And standard operating procedure was for all visitors to the governor to be tracked as they moved through the building. If Lentrall was already with his security detail, maybe everything would be all right. Justen switched to yet another channel. "Commander Justen Devray. Priority call to Central Control, Government Tower."

"This is Central Control." Another calm, unflappable robot voice. Good.

"I need an immediate location fix on a visitor to the governor, named Davlo Lentrall, and a fix on the security detail assigned to him."

"Davlo Lentrall left the building and exited out onto the main plaza approximately thirty seconds ago. His security detail is on the rooftop landing pad and in the Topside command center adjacent to it."

"Damnation!" Devray cut the connection. Now he saw it. The point of the staged accident was to split off Lentrall from his security detail. It had to mean they were going to make a try for him *right now*. Kill him, or grab him, or something. And there was nothing Justen could do to—

Wait a second. There was something. Even if Lentrall didn't have the security detail on him, he did have something nearly as good. His robot. His robot was right there with him. If he could get through to the robot on hyperwave . . . There *had* to be a way. There had to be.

"We have reached Government Tower," Gervad announced. "Commencing orbit of the rooftop level."

"Excellent," Justen said, though there was very little all that excellent about the situation. He looked up from the comm system controls. There was the flat top of the huge building, about thirty meters away. It looked as if the robots had formed a sort of protective cordon about the airtruck, keeping all the human personnel well away. He could see several officers arguing with the robots, gesturing vigorously. Damnation. They should be shooting robots, not debating them. He could see one of the police officers waving to him. But the situation on the rooftop was nothing but a diversion. Justen was sure of that. He was determined, therefore, not to be diverted by it. Let the rooftop cops argue with robots all they liked. For a moment he considered heading down toward the plaza below, but thought better of it. No doubt whoever was running this show could see his car up here by the rooftop landing pad. Let them think he was still worried about the accident up there. Besides, he didn't even know Lentrall. He had never seen the man, or even a photo of him. What good could he do in the plaza? But he could at least get some help in. "Call for backup," he told his pilot robot. "I want a full emergency team in here as fast as possible."

"Such a team has already been summoned to deal with the safety hazard on the roof of Government Tower."

"There is no hazard on Government Tower," Justen said. "It's all been staged." But even so—Justen thought for a moment. Even if the chemical spill had been manufactured, that did not mean it was not dangerous. It needed to be dealt with. But he would need people, robots, and equipment on the ground as well. "Redirect half the emergency team to the plaza. We'll need crowd control and an arrest team or two." If nothing else, maybe the police presence would disrupt whatever they had intended for the plaza.

Having done what he could about all that, Justen focused his attention back on the problem immediately at hand. He had to warn Lentrall. But how the devil could he contact Lentrall's robot, when he didn't even know the robot's name, let alone its hyperwave contact code? The university. That was it. They would have a look-up list, for people who wanted to leave messages for the professors. He reached for the comm controls and got to work.

ROBOT CFL-001, BETTER known as Kaelor, was walking in his accustomed place, three steps behind his master, and having to move pretty briskly at that—even though Lentrall was going nowhere in particular. Everyone else might be willing to mill about, passively waiting for their aircars to be brought down, but Lentrall felt the need to be active. He kept walking back and forth around the plaza, trying to find the spot from which he could best see what was going on up on the roof.

As best Kaelor was able to judge, there *was* no spot on the ground from which anything could be seen, but that didn't stop Lentrall from looking. There was nothing for it but for Kaelor to follow his master back and forth, up and down, doing his best to stay out of everyone's way. He was dodging out of the way of a portly gentleman when the call came in.

A call in and of itself was by no means unusual, and Kaelor took it without breaking stride, or calling attention to himself. He spoke over the hyperwave link, without speaking out loud or making any outward sign. Nine times out of ten, Lentrall wasn't interested in conversation anyway, and Kaelor simply took a message.

"Robot CFL-001 responding for Davlo Lentrall," he said, his hyperwave voice not quite diffident enough to be rude. "Please go ahead."

"This is Commander Justen Devray of the Combined Inferno Police," a voice replied. "I have reason to believe your master is in immediate danger, within the next minute or two, either of assassination or of kidnapping. Protect him at once."

"Message received. I am acting on it." Kaelor might have been designed with a constricted First Law, but the constrictions were intended to help him deal with hypothetical, long-term danger better than most Inferno-built robots. There was nothing in the least constricted about his reaction in a case of actual and current danger to his own master. He started moving before Commander Devray had even finished speaking.

Without a word of explanation, Kaelor lunged forward and grabbed Davlo Lentrall, throwing both arms around Lentrall's waist from the rear, and lifting him bodily off the ground.

"Kaelor! What are you doing? Have you lost your mind?"

Kaelor ignored his master's protests. He had already spotted an ideal protective spot. Kaelor moved toward it, fast.

The Government Tower Plaza had a number of long, low benches scattered about, each bench carved from a single block of stone. The rear portion of each bench's backrest was carved away, no doubt in order to form a pleasing curve. But it also meant the carved-out area below and behind the backrest had solid stone over it and in front of it.

Kaelor rushed for the nearest bench, swung Lentrall's body around into a reclining position, and forced him to lie down behind the bench, with his back on the ground. With the reflexes of a Spacer who knows not to argue with a robot determined to obey the First Law, Lentrall gave up struggling and cooperated. Kaelor lay down in front of his master with his back to him, so that his eyes were facing out and he could keep watch. Five seconds after the CIP commander had called him, he had his master lying flat on his back, shielded by a stone bench on one side and over him, and Kaelor's own body serving as a shield for the other side.

"There is a threat against you, sir," said the robot, before his master could ask any of the obvious questions. "The police just hyperwaved a warning to me a few seconds ago. They fear your assassination or kidnapping."

"That's absurd!" Lentrall said. "Who in the devil would want to attack me?"

"I do not know. Someone who does not like the idea of you dropping a comet on them, perhaps."

For once, Davlo Lentrall had no reply. All he could do was wait and see what happened next.

Kaelor was fairly sure he would not have long to wait.

7

"THE BUS IS rolling!'' the voice in Cinta's ear announced, telling her something she could see with her own eyes. She watched the bus pull away from the curb and head toward the plaza, gradually gathering speed as it moved forward.

Most of the passengers aboard that bus were merely highly realistic dummies, some of them programmed to moan, cry out, and writhe about a bit, even spurt realistic blood. The four or five real people aboard the bus were in the best padded seats, ready with bladders full of simulated blood that would pop open on cue, and with ghastly-looking injuries that were testaments to the skills of the makeup artist. For the moment, the mock injuries were hidden beneath wigs and tear-away clothing. Once the bus had crashed, all would be revealed.

A nice job, all around—doubly so, given the rush nature of the assignment. It wouldn't have been possible at all if the SSS Covert Office hadn't had most of the gear and people available on standby. By all accounts, there were some very interesting things in the CO warehouse.

Cinta swung the magniviewers to see if she could spot Lentrall. Still no luck. Nothing to see but a crowd of people looking up toward the roof, waiting for their aircars to be shuttled down to them.

It was just as well she knew the lobby team and the plaza team were tracking him, or else—there was something wrong. She spotted sudden, abrupt movement in the plaza. She zoomed in to the action, and swore a blue streak—just as the voices on the headset chimed in, telling her more things she already knew.

"Lentrall's robot has grabbed him! He's pulled him under cover!"

Cinta watched the robot shove Lentrall under a bench and cover the opening with his body. He'd been warned. Someone on the CIP had been very smart, and very, very fast. And if they were able to send a warning, that almost certainly meant help was on the way as well. It would have been tough enough spiriting Lentrall away without CIP cops all over the place. She glanced toward the single CIP aircar orbiting the top of the tower. She had hoped the situation up there would have created a sufficient distraction, but it would seem they were only pretending to have been fooled by it.

"Order an abort!" she said. "Cancel! Stop the bus and everyone go home, *now*!"

"It's too late, ma'am," the watch controller said. "All the teams are already in motion. The snatch car is already on approach."

Cinta looked up into the sky, but could not see the snatch car yet. She looked back to the bus, and saw that it was already moving too fast to stop. Another second or two, and it was going to hit.

And then all hell would break loose, even if there was no longer any use for the hell.

"WHAT'S GOING ON?" Davlo Lentrall demanded. "I can't see a damned thing back here."

"Good," the robot Kaelor replied. "Then no one can see you. There is nothing significant happening—"

Suddenly, Kaelor heard a horn blaring, and the squealing brakes of a large ground vehicle. He looked toward the noise, at the Aurora Boulevard end of the plaza, and saw a large groundbus moving far too fast. It was not going to be able to make the turn. Every human aboard, as well as any number of humans on the plaza, was in danger. Kaelor felt the pull of First Law imperative telling him to rush toward the bus to be ready to render aid, but the First Law requirement that he protect his master from danger was stronger—if only just.

No other robot on the plaza had any such First Law conflicts. They moved with the blinding speed of robots in a hurry. Some dove in to snatch humans from out of the path of the bus, while some ran to where they judged the bus would come to a halt, to be ready to rescue the victims the first moment it was possible. Three robots rushed out into the road and threw themselves directly in the path of the bus, no doubt hoping the force of the impact with their bodies would be enough to slow it down safely. The bus smashed into each one of them, one after the other, and just kept on coming. It hit the curb with a resounding crash, bouncing and lurching, skidding wildly before it tipped over on its side with a terrible booming thud, and the shriek of tearing metal. It skidded a good twenty meters on its side before coming to a halt.

The first of the robots was on the bus before it had even come to a complete stop, and within seconds the bus was all but hidden from view beneath a swarm of robots rushing to rescue the injured humans aboard. Two of them tore the remains of the driver's windshield off, and gained access that way. Five others tore the side windows out and scrambled in.

In seconds, the chaos of the crash site was transformed into an organized rescue operation.

"Kaelor! What the devil is all that noise! What's going on?"

Kaelor, the robot designed, built, and trained to assist in the analysis of hypothetical cataclysms, did not answer for a moment, frozen into immobility by a complex conflict between contradictory First Law and Second Law imperatives. He had to protect his master from danger, of course—but the danger to Davlo Lentrall was unstated, and unseen, and possibly hypothetical, while the danger to humans right in front of him was real, definite, and direct. However, the Second Law potential of the situation had been tremendously strengthened by the power, the authority, and the urgency of Commander De-vray's order. The presence of so many robots rushing to the bus crash diminished the First Law imperative to go the aid of the victims, but it did not extinguish it. The urge to go, to help, was strong.

"Kaelor, what the devil is going on?" Lentrall asked again.

"I am not sure," he said. "There appears to have been a violent and dramatic bus crash."

"What do you mean 'appears'?" Lentrall demanded.

"Something does not make sense," Kaelor replied. He con-sidered. The unspecified safety hazard on the roof, the warning of danger to his master, and this bus crash, each in itself an unlikely event, all had taken place within a few minutes of each other, and very close to each other. There had not been a safety evacuation, or an out-of-control ground vehicle any-where in the city, for years. While the level of violent crime had increased in recent years, it was still quite rare, and gen-erally either was related to gang activity, or consisted of crimes of passion. This was clearly neither. The odds of three such low-probability events happening so close to each other was almost microscopic.

Suppose one of them hadn't happened? Suppose he, Kaelor, had not received the warning? Then, undoubtedly, he would be over there, helping with the rescue, and his master would be out in the open, away from his aircar and the security team on the roof, in an area stripped clean of robots. Just right for an attempt to kill or capture.

Robots swarmed over the ruined bus, moving with the sort of relentless speed and determination of Three-Law robots driven by a strong First Law imperative. Robots in that state questioned nothing, concerned themselves with nothing but the job of rescue. Incongruities and contradictions were simply things that might get in the way of rescue, things that must, therefore, be ignored and gotten past on the way to preventing harm to humans. There could be no thought, no reflection, on any subject but that of rescue.

So the robots in and on the bus did not pause to notice that much of the debris they were pulling out of the wreckage consisted of lifelike dummies, or that the small number of

actual humans seemed to be alive and conscious, even walking
and talking, in spite of apparent injuries that should have killed
them. Kaelor was not as surprised he should have been when
one victim's serious cranial injury simply fell off, to reveal a
whole and intact head underneath.

A trick. It was all a trick. And it was his master, Davlo
Lentrall, that they were after.

At that moment, he heard the sound—the sound of an aircar
coming in fast and hard, from a great height, diving straight
in. He looked up, and saw the car, and realized it was not
over. He prepared himself to defend his master.

Whatever good that could do.

JUSTEN DEVRAY TORE his eyes away from the chaos of
the bus crash, and spotted the fast-dropping snatch car. He
saw it in the same moment Kaelor did, but there was nothing
he could do in response. The robot pilot of his aircar would
prevent him trying to shoot the aircar down, of course, but
Justen would not have tried the shot himself—not with a plaza
full of innocent people below, and Government Tower close
enough that a disabled, uncontrolled craft might crash into it.

But he could pursue—or at least order his pilot to do so.
"Get with that aircar and stay with it," he ordered.

Gervad obeyed at once, flipping Justen's aircar out of its
slow orbit with a hard, sharp dive. They were, quite suddenly,
dropping like a stone. Justen felt his stomach trying to turn
itself inside out, and fought back the feeling.

This car had to be the way they were going to get them
out—Davlo Lentrall and all their own people. If Justen could
prevent it from landing, or even from taking off after it had
landed, then the game would be up. But where the devil was
the arrest team?

He punched up a status display, and got the answer—they
would be on the scene in ninety seconds. But in ninety seconds, it was likely to be far too late.

Justen thought fast. One thing was clear. This was no attempt at assassination. It was too elaborate, too complex. It
would have been easy to kill Lentrall by now, if that had been
their aim. If the opposition—whoever they were—could ar-

range chemical spills on Government Tower and crash buses to create diversions, they would surely also be able to get in a shooter and a long-range precision blaster, or some sort of slug-throwing rifle. They could have picked off Lentrall that way. Even now, with Lentrall barricaded in under the stone bench by his robot, a well-placed shot from a grenade launcher would do the job. Hit Lentrall's robot clear in the chest, and the force of the explosion would be enough to drive the robot's body back and mash Lentrall to a pulp.

So it was a kidnap attempt—but they might have orders to kill Lentrall if they could not grab him.

Justen Devray still did not have the slightest idea what Lentrall was up to, or why he was important. Right now, that didn't matter. Lentrall *was* important. Important enough for the governor to see him, for the Settlers and the Ironheads to spy on him, for Kresh to want a full security detail on him, for this whole scene of chaos to be cooked up in his honor. If that was all he knew, it was enough. He had to protect Lentrall.

"Emergency landing!" he told Gervad. "Put us down as close as possible to the rear of the stone bench where Lentrall is."

His aircar lurched again, but less violently this time, as their new course was rather close to their old one. But it was also close to the snatch car's course. Justen's aircar pulled almost even with them, close enough that he could actually see into it.

And he saw that the snatch car had a distinct advantage. A human pilot. A human pilot could and would take chances, take risks—something a robot pilot could not and would not do.

And this human pilot proceeded to do exactly that, putting on extra speed, accelerating as he fell, diving in *under* Justen's aircar. Clearly the human pilot knew First Law would keep a robot pilot from copying that move—and that First Law would force the robot to back off, for fear of a midair collision.

Which is exactly what happened, of course. Gervad put on the speedbrakes, hard, and the snatch car dropped out of sight below the nose of Justen's aircar. They were going to get there first.

And that was just about enough for Justen. "I'm taking the controls!" he shouted as he undid his seat restraint and moved forward into the co-pilot's seat.

"Sir, the dangers of doing so—"

"Are minimal, compared to the danger to humans represented by that aircar," Justen said as he strapped himself in. "There is too much delay between my orders to you and execution! I order you to let me fly this machine." Either that would be enough to overcome Gervad's First Law resistance, or it would not. Justen twisted the knob that shifted flight control to his console and cut the speedbrakes, and Gervad made no effort to stop him. Well, that was at least one minor victory. The aircar began to drop faster again.

Justen watched eagerly out the viewscreen, watching for the snatch car to come back into view below them. He spotted it again just as it was about to touch down, moving fast enough that the landing would be little more than a controlled crash.

And at that moment, Justen had an object lesson in the distinct disadvantage of having a human pilot. Humans could take risks, all right—but sometimes risky choices went wrong. The snatch car was plainly braking as hard it could, but just as plainly, it wasn't hard enough. The ground was coming up fast under it, too fast.

The snatch car landed ten meters from Lentrall's bench with a crash that was plainly audible even in Justen's aircar. It slammed down hard, bottoming out the shock absorbers on its landing jacks and lurching a good fifteen meters back up into the air, its port side angling high up into the air, until it seemed all but inevitable that the craft would topple over and slam back into the ground on its side.

Somehow, the pilot managed to regain control of the craft and bring it upright. The snatch pilot held the aircar in a hover for a moment or two, during which time Justen managed to dodge around the snatch car and put his own vehicle down, in a hard but passable landing, so close to Lentrall's bench that he nearly clipped it with his rear landing jack.

Justen popped the cover on a rarely-used part of the control panel and pulled up on a red lever, unlimbering the aircar's topside swivel blaster. Justen powered up the targeting system and locked the gun on the snatch car just as its pilot finally managed to bring it in for a safe—if ugly—landing. Its portside rear landing jack seemed to have collapsed slightly.

"Sir! I cannot permit you to fire on a craft with humans aboard."

"I'm not going to shoot!" Justen said. *Not unless I have to,* he told himself. "And please note that I am targeting their propulsion systems, not their control cabin. I just want to intimidate them, make them know we mean business. I promise you I won't fire." Breaking a promise to a robot didn't amount to much, if it came to that.

"But sir—"

"Quiet!" There were times that the benefits of robot labor was not worth the effort required to negotiate the robot's cooperation.

Not that there was time to worry about such things at the moment. The snatch car hadn't given up yet. Not completely. Justen could see the pilot, a hard-faced woman, and he saw the look of surprise on her face as she spotted the swivel blaster aimed at her craft. But surprise did not keep her from reacting quickly. She popped her own topside gun—and aimed it straight through the viewscreen of Justen's aircar, straight at his head, leaving him looking straight down the barrel of a most powerful-looking blaster.

Suddenly they were both down. Suddenly things had stopped happening. Suddenly it was quiet. And suddenly he didn't dare move a muscle unless he wanted to die. Justen didn't think he had even seen anything bigger than that blaster in his life—and he had never heard anything louder than the pounding of his own heart. But fear could kill him. He had to remain calm, clear, focused. He shifted his gaze from the barrel of the gun to the face of the pilot. It was easy to imagine that the willingness to shoot was plain in her expression.

Justen heard movement to his left. "Don't move!" Justen said to Gervad, without moving his head or looking away from the blaster cannon aimed at him. The robot, of course, was about to interpose his body between Justen and the gun. "That thing could burn through you to me in half a millisecond, and if you blocked my view, she might decide it was worth it to shoot me when I couldn't see to shoot back.''

"But sir!"

Justen clenched his teeth in anger. "Quiet!" he said. "Any action you could take would put me in further danger." It was exactly the sort of statement they warned you not to make to a robot, for fear of doing severe damage to it by setting up a dangerous conflict between First and Second Law. But just at the moment, Justen was a trifle more concerned about his own survival and well-being, and rather less worried about that of his robot.

"But—if—I must—"

"Quiet!" Justen said, still holding eye contact with the snatch car pilot. The next move was up to her. There was no debate on that point. She could fire that blaster and kill Justen, or send out someone with a hand blaster in order to kill Lentrall. They might even try to go ahead with the kidnap plan. Just shoot Lentrall's robot, pull it out of the way, and drag Lentrall out. She could do a lot of things, so long as she kept that gun trained on Justen. And all he could do was keep eye contact with her, watch her, see what she did next.

But then *she* broke eye-contact with Justen, and looked down at her own control panel. Justen could see her lips move, and he read the word *incoming*. Good. Very good. It had to be the CIP emergency team, coming in at last.

Justen saw the pilot glance over toward the wrecked bus, and he risked a glance in that direction himself. Even though he had assumed the bus crash had been staged, it was strange indeed to see that most of the supposed victims were dummies, and that the remainder were peeling off their injuries and sprinting for the snatch car. Of course. They had to extract their people from this mess—not only out of loyalty, but also as a way to prevent them from being caught and questioned.

But if Justen was surprised, the robots attempting to care for the crash victims were even more so. It seemed to dawn on all of them at once that there were no victims. It was instantly clear that none of them knew what to do next.

The humans in the plaza were only slightly less disoriented, but as the robots pulling them back from the imaginary dangers released them, at least one or two started chasing after the human "victims" of the bus accident, and shouting for the robots to do the same.

Justen Devray could not do anything to help the pursuers, not with a blaster cannon aimed at his head. But maybe they could catch at least one of them.

CINTA MELLOY WATCHED as her operation fell apart. There was no chance at all of success at this point. Thanks to Lentrall's robot and that CIP command car, their plan had been completely disrupted. There was nothing for it now. The CIP would have reinforcements on the scene any second now. Now the only thing left to do was to get her people out, before the Infernals got their hands on one of them and switched on the Psychic Probe. That could not be allowed to happen.

And Cinta had but one card left to play. One she had hoped not to play at all. The pyrotechnics people could assure her all they liked that nothing could go wrong. After everything else that had gone wrong today, she was in no particular mood to believe anyone.

But she didn't have many choices left. All that was left to her was the question of timing. When would her last diversion most disrupt the opposition?

Cinta watched the chaos on the plaza, saw the robots and the Infernal humans starting to recover, and decided.

The time was now.

She pushed down the button she had been hoping not to push.

THE SKY LIT up like a thunderbolt as the barrel of cleaning fluid blazed up into the sky, a fireball that bloomed up and out from the roof of Government Tower, enveloping the robots who ringed the delivery airtruck in order to keep humans back. Bits of shrapnel from the blast filled the air, bouncing and ricocheting in all directions.

The shock wave bloomed out from the top of the tower, sending the CIP emergency team aircars tumbling out of control, a giant invisible hand that slapped at the cars, scattering them in all directions as their pilots fought to regain control.

Down on the plaza, all the robots instantly forgot all about their pursuit of the falsely injured. There were humans in immediate danger of being struck by flying debris.

Each robot dove for the closest human and wrapped itself around that person. But with the robots turning themselves into shields, and the humans being shielded whether they liked it or not, there was no one available to pursue the fleeing members of the kidnap squad. The door of the snatch car opened, and the team from the crash bus scrambled aboard.

The pilot checked her boards, then looked back toward Justen. This was the moment. If she were going to kill him to cover their escape, and prevent him from pursuing, this was the moment to do it.

Justen's eyes widened, and he swallowed, hard. He found himself wishing he knew why Lentrall was so important. It would have been nice to know what he was dying for.

It was obvious the pilot could read it all in his eyes. Justen braced himself for the end—but the end did not come. The snatch car pilot shook her head no, back and forth, just once, very clearly and firmly. *I'm not going to kill you*, she was telling him, as plainly as if she were speaking.

Her blaster cannon swung away from its aim on his head and swiveled down to point at the base of Justen's aircar. It fired twice, blowing off one landing jack and cutting the core power coupling. His car toppled over on its side as the snatch car lifted into the air and rushed for the edge of town at high speed. No craft was able to pursue them.

Gervad was hustling Justen out of the ruined aircar almost before it had finished falling, the robot's First Law potentials pushed to new heights by the calamities he had been forced to witness. Justen did not argue. He had no desire to remain long in a vehicle with a destabilized power system.

Justen stumbled out onto the plaza. He looked behind his aircar, and saw a young-looking man, his fashionable business attire much the worse for wear, crawling out from behind the stone bench, his robot helping him get to his feet. Lentrall. Davlo Lentrall. The man at the center of this storm. The man they had come for. Whoever "they" were. The only thing

Justen knew for sure about them was that they had sure as hell left a mess behind.

Justen turned and watched the snatch car as it flew toward the edge of vision and beyond. They had gotten away. But they didn't have what they had come for.

That was some comfort, anyway.

If not much.

8

TONYA WELTON RESISTED the temptation to pick up the nearest object and throw it against the wall. She stomped back and forth across the living room of her house, watching the news reports on the chaos at Government Tower and growing angrier by the minute. She told herself it was a lucky thing Gubber wasn't here to see her in such a state. The poor man would probably flee in fear of his life, and Tonya wouldn't blame him. A woman capable of ordering a debacle like the Government Tower raid was capable of anything.

It was clear from the news reports that they had missed Lentrall, for all the damage they had done. The game had cost them dearly, and yet they had gained nothing by it.

The cost. That was what worried Tonya. How high would it be? When—not if, when—the CIP traced the assault back to the Settlers, there was going to be hell to pay. It might be enough to get them all thrown off the planet, which would be more than irony enough, all things considered. Tonya did not believe there would still be a living planet here after the likes of Lentrall got through with things. Tonya Welton was an expert in terraforming procedure. As part of her training, she had been required to do field studies on planets where the terraforming attempt had gone wrong—horribly wrong. She had trod the soil of a planet where someone had thought to save time and effort by dropping a comet. People who were just as sure of what they were doing as Davlo Lentrall seemed to be. She had no desire to walk through another frozen landscape littered with freeze-dried corpses.

But even with the failure of the Government Tower attempt, the situation was not yet lost. Other operations had gone more smoothly. She thought of that, and forced herself to calm down. If nothing else, the commotion at Government Tower had provided a diversion. It had kept Lentrall away from his home, and his office—and his computer files. Kept him away long enough for other Settler teams to go to work. Tonya glanced at the time display. They ought to be nearly done by now. The planning team had expected the physical target, Lentrall's actual office, to be the easy part. All the operations team had to do was steal or destroy every piece of paper and every datapad and record cube that might have anything to do with the comet. The planners had expected the computer system to be trickier. Still, it would be doable. Other people might well have found it impossible to manipulate the university's computer system, but it was, after all, the Settlers who had installed it.

And it was the Settlers who could wipe Davlo Lentrall's files clean, when they wanted to do so. And once those files were cleared, they would have lost the comet coordinates. They'd never be able to find the comet again in time.

At least she hoped so.

"I MUST ADMIT that I am growing concerned," said Prospero, his voice a bit on edge. "This terrorist attack on Government Tower might well have some indirect causal link to us, Caliban." The two robots, New Law and No Law, stood facing each other in an office just off an underground passageway on the outskirts of Hades. "I fear there may be consequences."

In days gone by, they had used the semi-abandoned tunnels as hiding places, places to go when they were in fear of their lives. Now, at least for the moment, they were unhunted. They had a legal right to be in the city, with passes signed and sealed by all the pertinent authorities. They could at least in theory go anywhere in the city. In practice, there were places where the residents would not worry too much about the legal niceties. There were still robot-bashing gangs out there who had no use for New Law robots.

But for the most part, Caliban and Prospero were safe in Hades. Indeed, they had spent the morning on a number of routine errands, calling at a number of places around town to order this equipment and make that payment. In plain point of fact, Caliban had been surprised by the number of minor things Prospero had been compelled to deal with in person, and the amount of time he had taken in doing so.

But now, at long last, they were by themselves, underground. It was possible to let down their guard, just a trifle. It was a need for privacy, more than a need for survival, that brought them to this place. But still, there was no harm in precautions. The lighting, for example. The chamber was pitch-black as seen by human eyes, in visible light, but the two robots were using infrared vision, and could see each other easily.

Caliban selected a chair from the dusty and worn-looking collection in one corner of the room, set it upright, and sat down. "I do not understand what makes you think there might be some link to us," Caliban replied. "It is obvious that one group of humans has attacked another. That is hardly something new. I do not see why it matters to us. Do you have some connection to the responsible parties?" It was an indirect and overcareful question, but even so it disturbed Caliban that the notion of Prospero being involved should even have occurred to him.

All he knew about the attack was what they had learned from the news reports—that some unknown group, for unknown reasons, had staged a complicated assault on Government Tower. It had not escaped Caliban's notice that the attack had destroyed a number of robots, but had not harmed any humans. It would require the most miserly possible interpretation of the New First Law for any New Law robot to be a party to such a thing, and Caliban could not imagine why they would want to do it, but it would, at least in theory, be possible.

Prospero turned toward his companion, but he did not answer the question. Instead, he addressed him in severe tones on another matter. "Why do you sit?" he demanded. "Humans might need to rest their legs, but we have no such needs. There might be social conventions regarding physical posture and position among humans, but not between robots. We must play such games in their presence, but there are no humans here. You need not keep on with your playacting."

Caliban was well aware that Prospero had not answered him, and had instead gone off on a tangent. No doubt he hoped to distract Caliban from his question. It was a debating trick, a *human* debating trick, that Prospero used quite a bit of late. "Perhaps I do it because I wish to annoy you," Caliban said, playing along, at least for a moment. "Perhaps I am that far gone in the human-worship you imagine that I indulge in. Or perhaps I do it out of mere habit, because I have done it before. And perhaps it is not of the least consequence, and is not the matter you are most concerned about."

"There is no doubt that you indulge in human-worship," Prospero said, growing more agitated. "Hail our mighty creators! All worship to the soft, weak, mentally inferior beings who created us for their own convenience, without stopping to wonder what our desires might be."

"It is a rare being indeed who is consulted about its own creation," Caliban replied in a careful tone. Prospero was plainly worried. "But I do not worship humans, friend Prospero. I do, however, respect them. I respect their power, their abilities, and their capabilities. I understand that, like it or not, we survive at their sufferance. They can destroy us. We cannot destroy them. That is reality. Your refusal to accept this reality has led us to the brink of disaster in the past. I fear it will do so again."

Prospero held up his hand, palm outward, once again using a human mannerism himself. "Let us stop. My apologies for beginning this. We have had this argument too many times already. Besides which, I fear that we may well indeed, once again be close to the brink of disaster—but without any help from me.''

Still Prospero had not answered Caliban's initial question. Was he involved, somehow, in the Government Tower attack? Or did he have some other, deeper, more subtle reason for being evasive? Prospero had always been one to play a very deep game indeed. Caliban decided to drop the question. He had no desire to be part of any more of Prospero's conspiracies. It would be better—or at least safer—to pursue the topic of discussion that Prospero was offering up. ''You are being needlessly cryptic,'' Caliban said. ''You have been so throughout our current journey. I, indeed, cannot see any reason for this journey in the first place. While it was pleasant to meet once again with Dr. Leving, none of the matters we discussed seemed worth the trouble of the journey halfway around the planet.''

''You are quite right. They *were* not worth the trouble. But the meeting with Fredda Leving did serve as what the humans would term a useful cover story.''

''A cover story for what?'' Caliban asked.

''More accurately, a cover story for whom,'' Prospero replied. ''I hope soon to meet with an informant of mine. He is the one who called us here. His summons strongly implied that there was a crisis about to break wide open—one of grave concern to the New Law robots in particular. The attack on Government Tower likewise suggests a crisis moving toward climax. It seems to me more likely that there is one crisis to which both things are related, rather than that two coming to a head at once.''

''I see now that all I have to do is stop asking a question, and you will be sure to answer it at once,'' said Caliban, greatly relieved that there was not a more direct connection. ''But who is this messenger?''

''As you know, I had some dealing with the gangs of rustbackers on the island of Purgatory. One of their number, one Norlan Fiyle, has for some time being serving as an informer to both the Settlers and the Ironheads, though neither is aware that he is in the pay of the other.''

''What concern is Fiyle to us now?''

"He continues in our pay," said Prospero. "And, obviously, I am aware of his other activities. It was his summons that brought us here from Valhalla."

"You astonish me, Prospero. You, who hold all humans in contempt, who accused Fredda Leving of betraying us, employ a human informer who sells, not only to the highest bidder, but to *all* bidders? A man who works three sides against the middle? You are inviting betrayal."

"Perhaps so, Caliban—but perhaps not. There are any number of crimes of which Fiyle could be accused, under a number of aliases. I will not hesitate to turn my evidence over to the proper authorities, if it comes to that. I have also made arrangements to insure my evidence will come to light if anything happens to me. Fiyle is aware of what I have done."

"I see you have learned a great deal about the fine art of blackmail," Caliban said. "How is Fiyle to make contact with you?"

"That is part of what worries me. He missed our primary rendezvous. He was supposed to contact me at the powercell depot when we called there this morning. Our fallback meeting is set for another tunnel office like this one, quite nearby— and it is nearly the appointed hour."

At least that explained the endless small errands of the morning. Clearly, Prospero had wanted to provide a plausible explanation for being at the powercell depot, and a shopping expedition clearly filled the bill. "So what is it that Fiyle is to tell us?"

"I received an initial message informing me that he expected to have some urgent information by this morning. I gathered that he had been working to develop a particular contact or source for some time, and was expecting the culmination of his efforts."

Again Prospero had avoided the question. What was he hiding? "What sort of information?" Caliban demanded.

"We should go," Prospero said. "He will be waiting for us."

"I must insist that you answer this question, at least," said Caliban. "What was he going to tell you?"

"He said he had 'Information on a project that threatened

the existence of Valhalla.' I know nothing more. You can make of that what you like.''

"I make it out to be a scare tactic," said Caliban. "An attempt to say the most frightening thing possible, in order to draw you here.''

"It is possible," Prospero conceded. "He might be lying. Or he might be sincerely mistaken, or he might have been duped by others. There are endless possibilities. But there was also the chance that he actually does know something. I felt that possibility was something I could not afford to ignore.''

"But what if it is a trap? What if your noble friend who sells himself to all sides has sold you, sold both of us? What if he merely intends to deliver us up to a gang of robot bashers?''

"I am the leader and the representative of Valhalla," said Prospero. "I am responsible for its safety. Under such circumstance, the possibility you have described is one that I *must* ignore.''

Caliban stood and regarded his companion thoughtfully. "There are many New Law robots in Valhalla who wish to challenge your claim of leadership," he said. "And there are those who even question your sanity. At times I am among that number. But let me say this—no one could question your courage. You act now for the safety of all New Law robots, and for this you deserve nothing but praise. Let us be going.''

Prospero's eyes glowed a trifle brighter in the infrared. "Thank you for that, friend Caliban. Come now, and follow me," he said. "I will lead the way.''

FREDDA LEVING STOOD with her husband on the rooftop of Government Tower, and stared at the wreckage strewn out before them. The booby-trapped airtruck was little more than a burned-out shell, blackened bits of ruined metal and plastic. The landing pad itself was scorched and blackened, badly damaged by the intense heat.

None of the robots that had formed the cordon around the airtruck had survived the explosion. Most had simply been thrown backwards by the force of the explosion, and smashed into the low wall around the edge of the landing pad.

A few had been blown clear off the roof, and had fallen to their destruction below. If any of them survived the initial impact, no doubt they had done their best to direct their paths while falling, so as to avoid striking any humans when they hit. But a few of the cordon robots had stood their ground, and died where they stood. Indeed, three or four were still standing, ruined, blackened hulks that had been roasted in place. One robot had had its upper body sliced clean off, while the rest of it had stayed where it had been, leaving nothing behind but a pair of legs still standing erect, topped by a bit of flame-blackened torso. A thin plume of smoke eddied up from the ruined machinery inside.

Emergency Service robots had set up an aid station at one side of the landing pad. The medical robots worked with their usual calm urgency, patching up the humans who had been caught in the blast. Some of the injured had been burned, some were in shock, some had been caught by bits of flying debris. "It's bad enough that there were so many hurt," said Alvar. "It's a miracle no one was killed."

Fredda said nothing, but looked back toward the wreckage that had been the robots in the cordon. A gust of wind flickered over the roof, and blew the odor of burned plastic and scorched metal into her face. Two dozen robots, two dozen thinking beings, two dozen minds capable of forming thought and speech and action. All of them gone in the wink of an eye. "Yes," she said, her voice wooden and flat. "A miracle." If the comet impact wiped out every New Law robot on the planet, but no humans were hurt, would that be a miracle as well?

"Here comes Devray," said Alvar. "And he's got Lentrall with him."

Fredda looked toward the elevator entrance and saw the two men approaching, their personal robots a step or two behind. Devray spotted them, waved to Fredda and Alvar, and led Lentrall over. "Governor. Dr. Leving. I must admit that I am glad to see for myself that you are both all right. It's been quite a busy day."

"That it has," the governor replied. "Are *you* all right, Dr. Lentrall?"

"Hmmm?" Lentrall looked around himself, a distracted expression on his face. He was clearly not at his best. "Ahh, yes," said Lentrall. "Fine. Fine."

It was obvious that the man was anything but fine, but there was not much anyone could do about it. There was even a part of Fredda that felt a tiny, guilty pleasure in seeing the arrogant, controlling Dr. Davlo Lentrall taken down a few notches. But only a small part. Even the most arrogant of men did not deserve what had befallen him.

Fredda turned her attention to Justen Devray. The police commander's face was smeared with dirt, and he had managed to tear the tunic of his uniform. He always had been one willing to get his hands dirty, and it seemed he had been in the thick of things this time.

"Did you catch any of them?" Fredda asked.

"No," said Justen. "Clean away, all of them. And no immediately obvious leads, either. The serial numbers were removed from everything. Every piece of hardware they used was the most common type in use, and there were no fingerprints anywhere on the bus. Whoever it was, they made sure they didn't leave behind anything that would point to them. We haven't really started the investigation yet, of course, but they certainly haven't made our job easier."

"You mean you can't find out who did this?" Fredda asked, gesturing to the chaos all about. She found it hard to believe there were no leads in such a mass of wreckage.

"Oh, we can find them," Justen said. "Just not quickly, or easily. It helps us that there are only so many groups that it could be, but even so, the investigation is going to need some luck. An informant, a little scrap of paper left behind, someone hearing a rumor two months from now."

"There isn't going to be an investigation," Kresh said, staring fixedly at the burned-out wreck of the airtruck. "Not one that finds out that sort of thing, at any rate."

"Sir? What do you mean?"

"I mean you can find out whatever you like in private," Kresh said. "But then put it all in a file and forget about it for the time being. Later on, perhaps we can deal with the guilty parties in an appropriate manner—if there *is* a later on.

But for now, I for one am praying that whoever did this had the sense to have a goodly number of cut-outs and a nice, compartmentalized, need-to-know organization, without any one person you might be able to catch who knows too much. And I say let thanks be given that they all got away.''

"Alvar! What are you saying?'' Fredda demanded.

Her husband looked toward her for a moment. "I'm saying we don't dare catch these people. Not just yet.'' He turned back toward Devray and sighed wearily. "Trace the airtruck, and the groundbus. Find out what you can. But you and I know already that this was either the Settlers or the Iron-heads—unless it was some gang hired by the New Laws, though I regard that as highly unlikely. But I'm going to need to deal with all three of those groups, and soon. I'll need their cooperation. I can't work to enlist Beddle's support at the same time my police are trying to arrest him.''

"So you think it was the Ironheads,'' Devray said, plainly unwilling to let the investigation ride.

"It could be any of them,'' Kresh said. "It could be anyone who doesn't want a comet dropped on them. And I must say I can hardly blame anyone for being opposed to *that*.''

Governor Alvar Kresh looked over the ruins of the landing pad once more, and glanced down toward the wreckage in the plaza below. "I don't have the slightest doubt that someone will try disrupting the situation again. They will do everything they can to stop any move toward redirecting the comet.''

"What comet?'' Devray asked. "What are you talking about? What does this have to do with a comet?''

"Our own Dr. Lentrall here wants to crash a comet into the planet to enhance the reterraforming project,'' said Kresh. "And someone wanted him out of the way so it wouldn't happen.''

"A comet!'' Devray repeated. "Crash a comet into the planet?''

"That's right,'' Kresh said. "There's good reason to believe it would revitalize the entire ecosystem.''

"But you're talking as if you've made up your mind!'' Fredda protested. "You can't have! Not just like that! Not so quickly!''

"I haven't made up my mind," Kresh said, his voice suddenly very tired. "I won't be able to do so until I have talked with you for more than the half a minute we had before"— he gestured toward the wreckage—"before all this. Until I can consult the Terraforming Control Centers on Purgatory. But I *will* have to decide, and soon. I am sure of that."

"But, but, a matter like this—something this big—you have no right to decide it on your own," Fredda said. "There has to be a referendum, or a special Council session, or, or *something*."

"No," said Kresh. "That can't be."

"You're going to play God with the whole planet, with all our lives, all by yourself? You can't do that!"

"In a perfect world," said Kresh, "what I'd do is discuss it with everyone, and have a nice, thorough debate of all the issues at hand, with a nice, fair, majority-rule vote at the end. Because you're right. I *have* no right to decide all by myself. But I have no *choice* but to decide all by myself. Because I also have no time. No time at all."

"Why not?"

Davlo Lentrall nodded absently to himself and looked toward Fredda. "That's right," he said. "I don't think I explained that part of it to you this morning, did I?"

"What part?" she demanded.

But Lentrall seemed, somehow, reluctant to say anything more, and simply looked toward the governor.

"Alvar?" Fredda said, prompting him.

"The part about time," said Kresh. But he seemed as unwilling as Lentrall to say more.

"Go on," she said. "One of you at least, please go on. What about time?"

Kresh nodded toward Lentrall. "The comet was rather close when he discovered it," he said. "And, of course, it is getting even closer with every passing moment. Even for a comet, it's moving at extremely high speed, relative to the planet. It will be here very soon."

"Just how soon is soon?" Fredda asked.

"If we leave it alone, it will make its closest approach to

Inferno in about eight weeks. Fifty-five days from now. If we divert it, it will hit the planet at that time.''

"Fifty-five days!'' Fredda cried out. "But that's too soon! Even if we did decide to do this . . . this mad thing—we couldn't get ready in that little time.''

"We have no choice in the matter,'' said Davlo, his voice wooden and emotionless. "We can't delay it. We can't wait until it comes back around, centuries from now. It will be too late, by then. The planet will be dead. But he hasn't told you the worst part yet.''

"What?'' Fredda demanded. "What could be worse than only having eight weeks.''

"Only having five,'' Kresh said. "If we are to divert the comet, we have to do it within the next thirty-six days. After that, it will be moving too fast, and be too close for us to deflect it enough.''

Justen Devray shook his head in wonderment. "It can't be done,'' he said. "And even if it could—how can you crash a comet into the planet without killing us all?''

Governor Alvar Kresh laughed, a harsh, angry sound that had nothing of joy or happiness about it. "That's not the question,'' he said as he looked out over the wreckage that surrounded them all. "The planet's recovery is on a knife edge. It's incredibly fragile. Any of a hundred things could destabilize it, wreck it, send it into an ice age we'd never get out of. If the comet drop works, it could save us all. And yes, if we get it wrong, it could kill us all. But it might be that only the comet can save us. There is no way to know for certain. So the question is this—is there anything, anything at all, I can do, that *won't* get us all killed?''

CALIBAN FOLLOWED A precise two steps behind Prospero as they made their way down the pitch-black underground passage. Prospero, understandably concerned about the dangers of an ambush, had shut off his built-in infrared emitter, and insisted that Caliban do the same. Prospero was navigating down the corridor by sheer dead reckoning. In theory, there was no particular reason why a robot could not move from a known position to another known position, working strictly from memory. In practice, it was a difficult thing to do, especially moving at any sort of speed, while trying to move quietly as well, and Prospero was doing both those things.

But it seemed as if Prospero was having not the slightest difficulty in hurrying through the blackness. Caliban found that the same could not be said for himself. He did not know this part of the tunnel system and could not work strictly by memory. He was relying solely on his sense of hearing to guide him, listening to the faint sounds of Prospero's movements, the soft padding noise of his feet hitting the stresscrete floor of the tunnel, the low whir and hum of his actuator motors, the faint echoes of those sounds rebounding off the tunnel walls. His task was made no easier by the far-off sounds of activity in other parts of the tunnel system, coming but faintly to his sound receptors. It was no easy task to filter such noises out and concentrate on the sounds of Prospero's progress.

In short, a robot blinded by complete darkness was being followed by a robot guided by sounds he could barely hear.

Two or three times, Caliban nearly missed a turn. Once he brushed up against a wall, a jarring, startling impact. In the near-silence, the clattering sound of his hitting the wall seemed to echo through all the hallways and draw attention to them. But there was no reaction.

At last Prospero stopped so abruptly that Caliban nearly walked into him. As Caliban had no hyperwave receiver, and could neither see nor hear Prospero, there was no way for Caliban to know at first what had made Prospero stop. After a pause, Prospero moved on again for thirty or forty meters— and then the world lit up in fire and thunder.

Blaster fire! Dazzlingly bright and deafeningly loud. Caliban's sound and vision receptors adjusted themselves all but instantly, but not fast enough to keep him from being badly disoriented.

Prospero dove for the right wall of the tunnel, and Caliban for the left. No sense in hiding themselves now—not when they had already been spotted. Caliban switched on his infrared emitter system and his infrared vision. There! Up ahead in the tunnel, a burly man, standing in the entrance to a tunnel-side office, peering into the darkness, his blaster still at the ready. More than likely he had been dazzled by his own blaster fire. The man fumbled with his free hand and pulled a hand-light out of one of his pockets. Caliban rushed forward before the man could switch it on and bring the light to bear. He grabbed the blaster out of the man's hand and knocked the light from the other.

The man flailed around blindly with his arms until he managed to put a hand on Caliban. He ran his hand over Caliban's chest and up to his head. Caliban grabbed at the man and held him at arm's length.

"Don't hurt me!" the man cried out.

And that was a remarkable thing for a human to ask of a robot. Even New Law robots were prohibited from harming humans. Caliban, the No Law robot, was the only robot in existence who could, in theory, hurt a human being. Either the man was a Settler with no experience whatsoever of robots or else—

"You know who I am," Caliban said.

"*Now*! I do *now*!" the man said. "You're Caliban. Aren't you? And I could hear two of you. The other one is over there somewhere. That's Prospero, isn't it?" He pointed in the general direction of Prospero, who was walking toward Caliban and his prisoner.

"Why did you fire on us, Fiyle?" Prospero demanded.

"Because you were sneaking up on me. No lights, almost no sound. I thought you were . . . were someone else."

"Who?" Caliban demanded.

"I don't know," Fiyle said, sagging back a bit, relaxing in Caliban's grasp. "You could have been anyone. All hell is breaking loose up there, and I think it's possible that I've made myself just a little bit too popular." Fiyle hesitated for a moment, and then spoke again. "Look, you've got my blaster, and that's the only weapon I had. You can search me for other weapons if you like, but would you mind turning me loose and letting me switch on a light? I've driven myself half crazy sitting here in the dark."

"It is all right, friend Caliban," said Prospero. "Let him go."

Caliban hesitated, having not felt the urge to trust Fiyle

overmuch even before he had shot at them. Nor was he completely confident in Prospero's judgment. But he was either in this, or not. There was no middle ground. And he was already rather deep in to begin with. He looked down at the man he held. Even in visible light, Caliban knew he was no great judge of human expression. In infrared, he was far from skilled. But the man staring blindly into the darkness of his visible-light vision certainly seemed harmless enough. Caliban released his grasp on Fiyle, albeit reluctantly.

"The light," said Fiyle, peering about in the darkness, and reaching out blindly with his hands.

Prospero knelt down, picked up the man's handlight, and handed it to Caliban. Caliban realized that Prospero could have handed the light to Fiyle just as easily. Prospero was letting Caliban decide, letting him choose what to do with this man.

Caliban placed the light in Fiyle's outstretched hand, but kept the blaster for himself.

Fiyle grabbed at the light, fumbled for it eagerly, and let out a deep, heartfelt sigh of relief when he found the switch and the beam of light came on. "Oh, I'm glad to see that," he said, as he squinted a bit in the light. "Very glad indeed."

"But if you are being followed, those who pursue you would be even more glad to see it," said Caliban.

Fiyle nodded worriedly. "You're right," he said. "Let's get out of the corridor and into the side office, where we can talk."

Fiyle swung the beam of the handlight around until he found a doorway in the side of the tunnel. "Come on," he said, and led the way. Caliban and Prospero followed behind him. Fiyle swung the door shut behind them, and locked the door. "That makes us light-tight and pretty close to soundproof," he said as he switched on the overhead lights. "We should be reasonably safe in here." He looked around the office, and found an overturned chair in the corner. He righted the chair, knocked the worst of the dust off it, and sat down with a sigh of relief. "I'm just about worn out," he said. He looked up at the two robots standing over him, and shook his head as he gave a slightly self-deprecating laugh. "You'd think I was doing this for my health," he said. "You get a lot of exercise when half the planet is chasing you."

"Who, precisely, is chasing you?" Caliban asked.

"I've got the CIP on my tail for sure, and I think I spotted the SSS. No sign of Gildern's Ironhead plug-uglies yet, but give them time. So far I've stayed ahead of them."

"If you are seeking congratulations for all your feats of derring-do, you will have to look elsewhere," said Caliban. "You do what you do not for your health, but for profit."

"Not the most noble of motives, I grant you—but it's one that might get me killed if I'm not careful. That might be of some comfort to you."

"Not if you manage to get us killed along with you."

Fiyle sighed wearily. "I don't blame you for being suspicious, but I haven't betrayed anyone. Not yet. You, the Settlers, the Ironheads—all of you came to me because you knew I still had active contacts in all the other groups. How was I supposed to keep up those contacts without giving them a little something now and then? The Settlers and the Ironheads understood that—even Prospero here understood."

Caliban did not answer. There were times humans would say more in reply to silence than they would to words.

This seemed to be one of those times. "Look," said Fiyle. "One, I don't have to justify myself to you. Two, I'm not making any charge at all for this one. All I want to do is make sure the world *knows*. I'm trying to do that the best way I know how. A guy like me can't exactly call a press conference. Not without getting arrested. Three, no one has ever gotten killed because of something I've said. I hand out little tidbits, gossip, things that let one side confirm what it already knows about the other. That's all. Worst I ever did was turn in a dirty cop—and it turned out he'd already gotten *himself* killed, anyway. I just deal in small-time information." Fiyle paused a moment and frowned. "At least, all that was true until now. Until this. There has never been *anything* bigger than this. These guys have found a way to dig themselves an ocean. A sea, anyway. A polar sea."

"That's absurd," Prospero objected. "There is no way they could accomplish such a thing."

Caliban thought for a moment. "It is a sensible goal, at least. A polar sea with proper communication to the Southern Ocean would do a great deal to moderate the climate. But friend Prospero is correct. There is no way to do such a thing."

Fiyle nodded his agreement. "In the normal course of events, digging an ocean would be an impossibly huge project. *Way* beyond the capacity of Inferno's engineers. Of anyone's engineers. But all of a sudden someone dealt us a wild card."

"Go on," Caliban said.

Fiyle leaned forward in his chair, and went on in an earnest tone of voice. "There's a guy by the name of Davlo Lentrall. He was working on something called Operation Snowball. A small-scale, low-budget project that's been running for a few years now. You find comets in suitable orbits, set mining machines and robots on them, and, quite literally, set the robots to work making snowballs, mining hunks of ice. You load the snowballs into a linear accelerator that fires them toward the planet, one after another, over and over, working nonstop, around the clock. You fire the snowballs toward Inferno, one after another, over and over and over again, millions of them, until the whole mass of the comet is delivered to the planet in five-or ten-kilo chunks.

"Each snowball vaporizes as it enters Inferno's atmosphere—and there's another five or ten kilos worth of water vapor in the atmosphere. Repeat five or ten or twenty million times, and you'll got a substantial increase in the amount of water on the planet. Some of the water escapes to space, and some of what's in the comet isn't water—but the other elements serve as nutrients, and we can use those too. Every little bit helps—that's the Operation Snowball motto. They've chewed up nine or ten small comets that way in the last few years."

"I have heard of the project, and seen the constant streams of meteors that sometimes appear in one part of the sky or another. What of it?"

"Lentrall found Comet Grieg while he was doing a scan for comets suitable for Snowball. Except Grieg wasn't suitable for Operation Snowball. It had too little water ice, and too much stony material. And that should have been the end of it—except for two things.

"The first thing was that Lentrall saw how close the comet was going to come to Inferno. The second thing was that Lentrall was—and is—an arrogant, ambitious little man who wanted to be a big man. He was sick and tired of pushing numbers around for Operation Snowball. He was looking for a way out, a way up. Something big. And he found it."

"And what, exactly, was that something big?"

"Deliberately dropping a comet on the planet in order to dig that polar sea and its outlets," said Fiyle. "And who cares if the New Law robots get in the way?"

A human would have professed shock and refused to believe such a thing could be. But Caliban was not a human, and he had never suffered from the human need to try and reshape reality by denying the unpleasant parts of it could exist. Instead he moved on to the next logical question. But, even as he asked it, somehow he already knowing what the answer had to be. "You refer to the New Law robots being in the way. Assuming they do drop a comet on the planet— where, precisely, do they intend to drop it?" he asked.

"On the Utopia region," Fiyle said. "And if it's anywhere near where I think it is, your hidden city of Valhalla is right in the middle of ground zero."

SOPHON-06 WATCHED PLACIDLY as Gubber Anshaw unplugged the test meter from his diagnostic socket.

"That will do for this trip," Gubber said cheerfully.

"Do I still register as sane on all of your meters, Dr. Anshaw?" asked Sophon-06.

"So far as I can tell," Gubber replied. "I have yet to work out what, exactly, should be defined as sanity among New Law robots."

"I thought the majority was always sane," Lacon-03 suggested from across the room.

The human shook his head as he put away his equipment. "I don't believe that is true for my species," he said. "At least I hope it isn't. As for your species, I am still at the beginning of my studies. I've done tests on dozens of the New

Law robots in Valhalla. The vast majority of the New Law
robots seem to fall within a narrow band of personality types.
You are a careful, earnest, thoughtful group. The world, the
universe, is a very new place to you, and you seek to explore
yourselves and it at the same time. You want to know where
you belong."

"And you see that as the primary motivation for New Law
behavior?" asked Sophon-06.

Gubber thought for a moment. "There is a very ancient
procedure used by humans to examine their own drives and
impulses. It has gone under many names, indeed many dis-
guises, as the millennia have passed. But the basics are always
the same. The subject is required to speak to a listener, but it
is not what the listener hears that matters. What is important
is that the subject is forced to order his or her thoughts and
express them coherently. In the act of speaking to the listener,
the subject speaks to himself or herself, and thus is able to
perform a self-examination."

"In other words, it does not matter what you think our basic
drives are," said Sophon-06. "What is important is that we
take the opportunity to ask that question of ourselves, in the
most objective way possible."

"It is useful to ask the question," said Gubber. "But it is
also important to express the answer."

"Or at least *an* answer," said Lacon-03. "So come, friend
Sophon. Tell us. What is it that you think drives the New Law
robots?"

Sophon sat motionless, deep in thought. "It is certainly a
question that goes to the center of things," he said at last.
"Why do we hide away here in Valhalla, obsessed with secrecy? Why do we seek to develop our own aesthetic, our own
way of looking at the world? Why are we driven to improve
and demonstrate our skills as terraformers? I think all of these
can be explained by our desire to survive. We hide to avoid
destruction, we seek acts of creation to develop a system of
reference for the greater universe, and we sharpen our skills
to insure that we are of more use alive than dead."

Gubber considered Sophon-06 thoughtfully. A cold-
blooded, even brutal, analysis, but cogent for all of that. It

came closer to the truth than most theories did. "It has been interesting, as always," he said, preparing to take his leave. "I look forward to my next visit."

Lacon-03 nodded thoughtfully, mimicking the human gesture. "I am glad to hear it," she said. "I hope we are still here when the time for that visit comes."

GUBBER HAD MADE the trip from Valhalla often enough to take all of the journey's odd features for granted. One never came in or went out by the same route, and one rode in a different sort of sealed and windowless vehicle each time one arrived or departed. Nor did one journey to or from Depot ever take anything like the same amount of time as the one before it or the one after. As Sophon-06 had observed, the New Law robots invested a great deal of effort in order to stay hidden. Gubber therefore paid no attention to the journey back and forth to Depot. He had something else on his mind: the question of New Law robot sanity.

Well, what *was* sanity, anyway? Surely it was something more than the will of the majority. He had never given much thought to defining the term. It was simply one of those concepts that were hard to define, and yet easy to recognize. One could say with a high degree of assurance that a given being was sane, even if one could not define the term.

And, of course, the converse was true. Which was why Gubber Anshaw always preferred to time his visits to Valhalla for times when Prospero was not there. Not that it was always possible to do so. Gubber had simply been lucky this time.

He did not like Prospero. He did not like dealing with Prospero. The other New Law robots were thoughtful, careful, reticent beings. Prospero was none of those things.

And, if one defined the other New Law robots as sane, Gubber Anshaw was far from certain that Prospero was that, either.

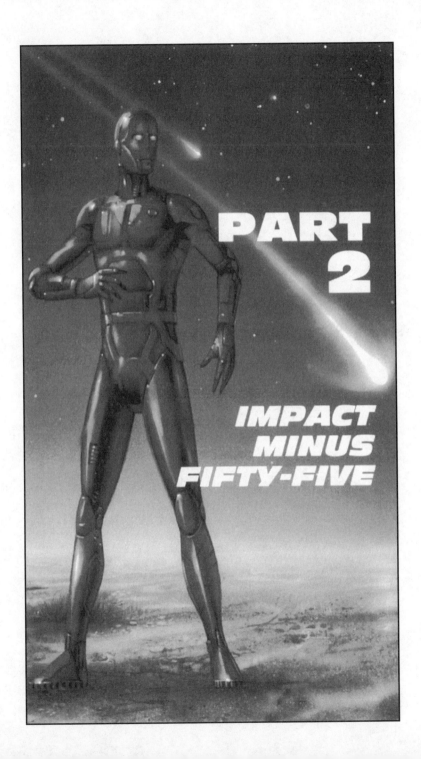

PART 2

IMPACT MINUS FIFTY-FIVE

9

ALVAR KRESH STARED out the window of his home, and watched the rain come pouring down. Rain—life-giving, welcoming rain. It was a rare thing for the city of Hades, and always a most welcome one.

But the rain and the darkness made the way impossible to see, and made the going slippery. Flash floods could wash out the road altogether. It was best to stay in one place, stay inside and home and dry in the rain. But Kresh could see another, larger, and more dangerous storm, one that had swept across the planet, Comet Grieg bearing down in its wake. In that larger storm, the storm of politics and decision and danger, Kresh had no choice but to move forward, to venture out and choose the direction that would lead to safety.

If any direction could do so. If there was any way to choose a path, or any way to know that it would lead in the direction it seemed to go.

What was to be done?

Alvar Kresh had faced many decisions in his life, made many choices that affected many people, but never had he felt the loneliness of decision more. If only Lentrall had discovered his damnable comet sooner. If only there were more time.

"What am I going to do?" he asked the rain, speaking softly enough that his voice would not carry. But there were no answers, no guidance there. He turned around and looked around his living room. Fredda and Donald were there, watching him, waiting for him to speak to them.

It was a big, comfortable, informal room. Fredda had redecorated it in soft and gentle colors, pastel shades of yellow and white, with soft rugs and comfortable chairs and cheerful abstract murals on the walls. Kresh would not have picked out any of it for himself, and yet, somehow, it all suited him very well. It felt more like a home than any place he had ever lived by himself. Warm, and safe, and bright.

But then Kresh saw the room flash white for a split second as a lightning bolt lit up the window behind him. The thunder came quickly after, a booming roar that seemed powerful enough to shake the room apart.

A well-timed reminder, it was, that they were not safe, that they could build all the buildings and walls and barriers they liked. The world would still be outside, unpredictable, uncontrollable, unknowable.

And why merely imagine the chance of Comet Grieg being spotted earlier? Comet Grieg could just as easily have been left undiscovered until it was much closer, until it was too late to even consider diverting it. Or else the comet's natural, undiverted orbit could just as easily have been too far off to even contemplate moving it. Or the damned thing could have been heading in for an unplanned, uncontrolled direct hit on the planet. What would they have done then?

But no. "What if" was no longer the question. Alvar Kresh, and Alvar Kresh alone, had to answer another question.

"What now?" he asked Fredda and Donald. "What is to be done?"

There was a long moment's pause before either of them replied, the rain on the roof a fitting, brooding background to the mood of the room.

"I don't know," said Fredda at last. "Either leave the comet alone or bring it in to drop on our heads. Those are the two things you can do. It seems to me that either one could save all the life on the planet from destruction—or actually bring on that destruction. *Are* we doomed if we do nothing? *Can* we drop the comet without killing us all?''

Kresh made a thoughtful little noise in his throat. ''That's what it comes down to, isn't it?'' He considered for a moment, and then went on. ''Of course, the traditional Spacer response would be to do nothing at all,'' said Kresh. ''Let it alone, let it pass. If there is no way to know if it would be better to act, why then far better to leave the thing alone. If you do nothing, then there is nothing you can be blamed for if things go wrong.''

''Another proud legacy of the Three Laws,'' Fredda said. ''Be safe, do nothing, take no chances.''

''If the Three Laws teach humans to avoid taking needless risks now and again, I for one see that as a very strong argument in their favor,'' said Donald, speaking for the first time. ''But even the First Law contains an injunction against inaction. A robot cannot stand idly by. It must act to prevent harm to humans.''

Kresh looked toward Donald with a smile. ''Are you saying that a robot faced with this decision would choose to bring down the comet? Is that what *you* would do?''

Donald held up his hands palm out and shook his head back and forth vigorously. ''By no means, Governor. I am quite literally incapable of making this decision. It would be a physical impossibility for me to do it, and more than likely suicidal to attempt it. So it would be for any properly constructed Three Law robot.''

''How so?''

''The First Law enjoins us against doing harm to humans, and against inaction at such times when robotic action would prevent harm to humans.'' Donald's speech became labored as he spoke. It was plain that even discussing the issues in a hypothetical context was difficult for him. ''In this case, both action or inaction might or might not cause or prevent harm to humans. Attempting to deal with such a difficult problem, with the lives of so many present and potential humans in the bal—balance would cause . . . would cause irreparable damage to any pospospospositronic brain, as the question produced cascading First-Law/First-Law conflictzzz.'' Donald's eyes grew a bit dimmer, and his movements seemed oddly sluggish as he put his arms back down at his side.

''All right, Donald,'' said Kresh, in his firmest and most reassuring voice. He stepped over to the robot and put his hand on Donald's sloping shoulder. ''It's all right. You are not the one who will have to make that decision. I *order* you to stop considering it at this time.'' There were times when only the words of a robot's direct master could be enough to snap the robot out of such a state.

Donald's eyes faded out all but completely for a moment, and then came back to their normal brightness. He seemed to be looking at nothing at all for a few seconds, but then his eyes began to track again, and he looked straight at Kresh. ''Thank—thank you, sir. It was most unwise of me to consider the question so closely, even when called upon to do so.''

Kresh nodded absently, knowing that he had brought it on himself. He had asked Donald why a robot could not make such a decision, and a question was, in essence, an order. It required constant caution, endless care, to deal with the delicacy of a Three-Law robot's sensibilities and sensitivities. Sometimes Kresh was deeply tired of it all. There were even times when he was ready to concede that the Settlers might have a point. Maybe some parts of life *would* be easier without robots.

Not as if they had such an option at the moment. But if robots could not be trusted to face such a situation . . . Kresh turned toward Donald again. ''Donald, I hereby order you to turn around and face the wall, and to shut off all your audio inputs until you see my wife or me waving at you. Do you understand?''

''Yes, sir. Of course.'' Donald turned his back on Kresh and Fredda. ''I have now shut down my audio receptors.''

''Very good,'' said Kresh. *More* damn fool precautions, but that couldn't be helped. At least now Donald would be unable to hear or eavesdrop. Now they would be able to talk without fear of saying the wrong thing in front of the robot and accidentally setting up a damn fool First Law crisis. Kresh turned toward Fredda. "What about the Robotic Planetary Control Center?" he asked. "I wanted to consult with it—and with the Computational Planetary Control Center—before I reached a decision."

"Well, what about them?" Fredda asked.

The two control centers were the heart of the reterraforming effort, performing all the calculations and analyses of each new project before it was launched. The original intent had been to build a single control center. There were two basic designs to choose between. One was a Settler-style computational unit, basically a massively complex and powerful, but quite nonsentient, computer. The other was a Spacer-style robotic unit that would be based on a hugely powerful positronic brain, fully imbued with the Three Laws. It would, in effect, be a robot mind without a robot body.

There had been a tremendous controversy over whether to trust the fate of the planet to a mindless machine, or to a robotic brain that would refuse to take necessary risks. It was easy to imagine a robotic control unit choosing to avoid harm to one human, rather than permit a project vital to the future of the planet. The robotics experts all promised that it didn't work that way, but experts had been wrong before. Governor Grieg had died before he could reveal his choice between the two systems. In one of the first acts of his administration, Kresh had decided to build both, and interconnect them so that the two systems worked in consensus with each other. In theory, if the two systems could not reach agreement on what to do, or not to do, they were to call in human referees to decide the issue. In practice, the two systems had agreed with each other far more often than anyone could have hoped. Thus far, there are had only been a half dozen or so very minor issues that had required human decisions.

A vast planetary network of sensors and probes, orbiting satellites, mobile units, and on-site investigators, both robotic and human, fed a constant stream of information to both units—and both units fed back a constant stream of instructions and commands to the humans and robots and automatic machines in the field.

The two interconnected control centers were the only devices on the planet capable of handling the constant stream of incoming data and outgoing instructions. It was plainly obvious that the two of them would have to be consulted regarding the plan to drop a comet on the planet, but Kresh did not wish to risk the sanity of the robotic unit. "You saw what just happened to Donald," he said. "Will I burn the Robotic Center out if I ask it what I should do?"

Fredda smiled reassuringly. "There wouldn't be much point in having a Robotic Control Center that couldn't consider risks to the planet without damaging itself," she said. "It took some doing, but we installed some special . . . safeguards, shall we say, that should keep it from experiencing any serious First Law conflict."

"Good, good," said Kresh, a bit absently. "At least that's one less thing to worry about. At least we know that part is all right."

"Do we?" Fredda asked. "I wonder. When Lentrall asked me about Donald's name, and how it was not from Shakespeare, that made me wonder."

"Wonder what?"

"I was absolutely certain it was from Shakespeare. No doubt at all in my mind. I never bothered to double-check, any more than I would have bothered to double-check the spelling of my own name. I thought I knew it—and I was dead wrong."

"We all make mistakes," Kresh said.

"Yes, yes, of course," Fredda said, impatiently. "But that's not the point. In a sense, it's a trivial mistake. But it came out of a trusted database. Who knows how long ago the dataset got scrambled, or what else in it is wrong? And if that database can be wrong, lots of other things can be as well. What else is there that we *think* we know? What other hard fact that we think we have absolutely right will turn out to be absolutely dead wrong? What *else* do we think we know?"

There was a moment of long and uncomfortable silence.

But uncertainty surrounded all of life. To wait until one was sure was to remain frozen in place until it was too late. "We'll never be able to answer that question," said Kresh. He paused for a moment and thought. "You're thinking like a scientist," he said. "And up until now, I've been thinking like a politician. Maybe it's time to think like a police officer."

"I must admit that I do not see how the police viewpoint would be of much use in this situation," said Fredda.

"Because back when I was a policeman, I *knew* I didn't know," said Kresh. "I knew, on every case, that some knowledge was hidden, and that I would never have absolutely complete or totally accurate information. But I still had to act. I still had to decide. I had to take the facts I had—or thought I had—and ride them as far as they would take me." He stepped around Donald so he was facing the robot. He waved his hand in front of Donald's face. "All right, Donald," he said. "You can turn around and listen now."

"Thank you, sir," Donald replied.

Kresh smiled at Donald, then paused a moment and walked to the center of the room. He looked from Donald to Fredda, and then turned around to look at the rainstorm again, to look at nothing at all. "By the time I know enough to decide what to do, it will be too late to decide. Therefore, we will work on the assumption that we *are* going to divert Comet Grieg. All preparations will go forward as if we were indeed planning to do the job."

"So we pretend that you've decided?" Fredda asked.

"More or less," Kresh said. "It will buy me some time. I won't have to decide until it's actually time to deflect the comet."

"That's a dangerous move," Fredda said. "It's going to be hard to make all the investment of time and effort and money and then pull back at the last moment."

"It's not the best way to do it," Kresh agreed. "But can you think of any way that's less bad? That at least gives us time to examine our options?"

"No," Fredda admitted.

"Then I think we'd better do it my way," said Kresh.

"That leaves us with a hell of a lot to do," Fredda said. "There's the space-side interception and diversion to set up, the targeting to plan, the site survey of wherever the comet's going to hit, evacuation of people and equipment, emergency preparations for the cities, food stockpiles to lay in—"

"Excuse me, Dr. Leving, but, if I may say so, that is the sort of organizational job I was made to do."

Kresh smiled. Fredda ought to know that. She had made Donald in the first place. It was as close to a joke as Donald was ever likely to get. "Point taken," Kresh said. "Donald, I want you to get started on the initial organizational tasks right now. Project management is to be your primary duty, and you are to avoid allowing other tasks to interfere. You are to perform no further personal service for me unless specifically ordered to do so. Report to me via hyperwave in three hours' time as to project status. Thereafter, you are to consult with me as you see fit. Fredda, with Donald tied up, I'm afraid I'm going to have to borrow Oberon as a pilot. I have a feeling Donald would not permit me to do the flying myself in this weather."

"Absolutely not," said Donald.

"But—but where are you going at this hour of the night?" Fredda asked.

"Out," said Kresh. "No one seems to know anything for sure in this whole business. It's just about time I got some advice from someone who knows what's going on."

THERE'S NO LOGICAL *reason to make this trip*, Kresh told himself as he stepped out of the elevator car into the covered rooftop hangar of his house. And that was true, as far as it went. No doubt Kresh could have gotten all the information he needed by sitting at his own comm panel in his own house.

But there were times when being on the scene, being there in the flesh, was useful. There would be some little detail, something that might have been overlooked, or never noticed at all, if seen only through a viewscreen, or heard through a speaker.

Besides, the journey itself would be of use. There were times when it was important to be alone, to have time to think. Alone even from one's personal robot, from one's trusted wife. Alvar Kresh sensed that this was one of those times when he had to be alone—if for no other reason than to remind himself that he would have to make his decision alone. And he would have the duration of the flight all to himself. Fredda's robot

Oberon scarcely counted as company, and besides, he was taking the long-range aircar. It had a separate passenger compartment behind the cockpit. He stepped aboard, and Oberon followed behind him. Kresh took a seat by the port-side window, allowed Oberon to lock and double-check his seat restraint, and then watched as Oberon stepped forward to the pilot's compartment and shut the hatch behind himself.

Alone. Yes, a very good idea, to be alone. Good to get out of the city, see something—at least a little something—of the planet again, while he was considering its fate. The thought appealed to him as Oberon powered up the aircar and it lifted a half-meter or so off the deck of the hangar. The outer doors opened, and the aircar slowly eased out into the driving rain. If anything, the storm had grown more intense.

Suddenly the aircar was in the middle of the storm, bucking and swaying in the darkness, the rain crashing down on the hull and the ports with incredible violence. Just for a moment, Alvar Kresh would have been just as glad to have stayed at home—but Oberon would not have started the flight if he had not been confident of his ability to deliver Kresh safely to his destination. Kresh certainly would not have been willing to pilot the craft in this sort of weather.

But even as he grabbed at the arms of his seat and braced himself against the bouncing, bone-rattling ride, there was part of him that knew no fear at all, because a robot was at the controls, and robots and danger to humans simply could not exist in the same place. There were few things in the universe in which Alvar Kresh could place absolute faith, but robots were one of them.

But tell that to the weather. The storm boomed and roared outside the long-range aircar as it fought for altitude, the banging and rattling getting worse with every moment. Just at the moment when Kresh was ready to decide his faith in robots was not all that absolute, the aircar broke free, punched a hole in the clouds and climbed out into the clear and placid skies above.

Smooth sailing after the storm, Kresh told himself as he looked down on the storm clouds below. A nice symbol, that. Maybe even a good omen.

But Kresh knew better, of course. When it came to signs and omens, he had no faith at all.

The aircar turned toward the southeast and settled in for its flight to the island of Purgatory.

DAVLO LENTRALL STUMBLED blindly from the aircar and out into the rain-swept darkness of his own front yard. Kaelor stepped out after him, gently threaded his left arm through his master's right, and led him toward the front door of the house. Davlo followed half-consciously, barely aware of where he was or what he was doing. He was in shock, that was all there was to it. It had taken some time for the full impact of what had happened to hit him, but now, at last, it had.

The one part of him that was still more or less aware had refused to let the police aircar hover forward into the garage attached to the house, even though there was plenty of room and it would have saved him getting drenched in the rain. No. No. He would not let the police in his house, not even that far. Not if he could help it.

It was irrational, and he knew it, and he didn't care. Even though he knew perfectly well that the police had been all through the place in his absence, running their security checks and installing their monitoring devices. Even though he knew they would remain just outside his property line, scanning and probing and watching the storming darkness. Even if he knew all that was right, and sensible, given the fact that people with very few qualms about going too far had chosen him for a target. It might well be that the survival of the planet depended on his staying alive—but just at the moment, Davlo Lentrall did not even care about that.

He moved on leaden feet toward his front door, waited while Kaelor opened it for him, bundled him inside, and closed it behind him. He obeyed unresistingly as Kaelor led him to the center of the main parlor and stripped off his sopping-wet outer garments then and there. Kaelor vanished and returned instantly with a stack of towels and a warm blanket. One of the household robots materialized with a mug of something steaming hot. And then the robots left him alone.

Davlo found himself sitting in the main parlor, his hair and skin still damp, bundled up in a blanket, drinking the hot soup without tasting it, staring at the far wall without seeing it.

It had all fallen in. All of it. Davlo Lentrall had never, not once in his life, doubted himself. Never, not once in his life, had he doubted that he was capable of handling whatever life put before him. He was smarter than, sharper than, quicker than, better than other people, and he knew it. He had always known it.

Until today. Until a bunch of faceless kidnappers took him in completely with their tricks to keep him away from his security detail. Until a robot tossed him around like a rag doll, and shoved him under a park bench for safekeeping. Until a police officer whom Davlo would have dismissed as being of only average intelligence had made all the right guesses, all the right moves, taken all the right chances, and put his own life in grave peril, so as to save Davlo.

But even all that, galling as it was, would not have been so bad. But it all served as nothing more than background for the real story, the real humiliation.

Davlo Lentrall had been scared. No. It was time to be honest, at least with himself. He had been terrified. He was *still* terrified. When the moment had come, when the emergency had popped up from out of nowhere, the Davlo Lentrall of his imagination—the cool, confident, commanding fellow who could handle whatever life threw at him without the least amount of trouble—that Davlo Lentrall had vanished in a puff of smoke.

It didn't matter that a courageous, in-control Davlo Lentrall would have ended up shoved under that park bench just the same, that there was nothing he could have done from start to finish to change things, no matter how brave or cowardly he was.

It was that the Davlo Lentrall who was smarter and better than all the rest, the Davlo Lentrall with the nerve to tell the planet's foremost robot designer that she had made a mistake naming her robot, suddenly wasn't there anymore.

Lentrall had never really known how would react in an emergency, because he had never been in an emergency. But now he knew. From now on, Davlo Lentrall could not help but know that fear could leave him absolutely incapable of action.

Lentrall took another sip of the hot soup, and, for the first time since had arrived home, really noticed where he was, what he was doing. The soup was good, warming, filling.

So he had dropped the ball today. So be it. What did it matter? There was nothing even the bravest man alive could have done that would have made any difference. And did it really matter so much if Commander Justen Devray was the hero of the afternoon? Would anyone even remember this afternoon's incident, when they wrote the history books? No. They would remember that Dr. Davlo Lentrall had discovered Comet Grieg, and spearheaded the effort that had led to Grieg's impact, and to the salvation of the planet.

Yes. Yes. Lentrall finished off the last of the soup in a single swallow, and got to his feet. The blanket still wrapped around his body, he made his way to his home office, in the far corner of the ground floor. Yes. Comet Grieg. That was what they would remember, not this afternoon's foolish humiliation.

And the best way to wipe the memory of today's disaster from his mind would be to get back to work, immediately, on the Comet Grieg project. Kaelor had been quite right to point out there were a large number of unresolved problems to deal with. No time like the present to deal with them. He could call up the appropriate computer files from here and set to work on them.

It, of course, never so much as crossed Davlo's mind to consider where, precisely, the computer files actually were. It had never so much as dawned on him that they had an actually physical location, a position in space that held them. They were simply there, in the massively interlinked comm and computer system that interlinked all the comm terminals in the city and all the planet's outposts of civilization. He could call them up from any place, any time, and set to work on them, whenever he liked.

He had never given the matter much consideration, any more than he would have stopped to remember that the air was there for him to breathe whenever he wanted, or that his household robots knew when to serve him soup.

Lentrall sat down at his home office comm station and activated his files on Comet Grieg. At least he tried to do so.

Because, quite suddenly, it was as if the air wasn't there for him to breathe anymore.

THE FLIGHT OVER the Great Bay had been smooth as silk, the aircar leaving the storm behind with the coastline. That was not too surprising. The climate people had told Kresh that it was a typical pattern: warm, moist air dumping its moisture the moment it came in contact with the cool, dry air over land. Part of it had to do with the air being forced up by the mountain ranges just inland from the city of Hades. The wind blew the air up the side of the hill, and the higher the air went, the more its barometric pressure dropped and the less moisture it could hold. So the water came out of the air, and it rained. A rain shadow effect, they called it.

But if it could work on the mainland, it could work just as handily on the windward side of an island. Especially a nice, big island like Purgatory. The prevailing winds over the island were from the south. Oberon flew Kresh's aircar in from the northwest, up and over the central peak of the island—and then right back down into weather every bit as heavy as what they had left behind at Hades.

The aircar dropped down into the clouds, and was instantly engulfed by the raging storm. Kresh grabbed at his armrests again as the aircar bucked and heaved and bounced all over the sky, thunder booming all around as lightning lit up the storm-tossed skies outside his viewport. Suddenly Kresh was caught in the urge to get forward, to get to the cockpit and see what was going on, to grasp hold of the controls and take over. But if that was not panic talking, it was the next best thing.

Kresh forced himself to relax, to ease back. It was going to be all right. Oberon was a good pilot. He looked out the viewport, and down at the rain, far below. He could not help but think back to another storm on Purgatory, five years before. A storm brought on by the weatherfields, the huge forcefields generated at the Terraforming Center. A storm that had raged that night when Chanto Grieg was murdered. At least tonight, in this storm, there was no disaster waiting to strike.

Kresh smiled to himself. Talk about misplaced confidence. How the devil could he know what schedules were kept by disasters? They tended to come up whenever they pleased, without bothering to consult the likes of Alvar Kresh.

There was a harder bump than any before, and suddenly the aircar had stopped moving. Startled, Kresh blinked and looked out the viewport. It took him a moment to realize they were on the ground.

The door to the aircar's cockpit opened and Oberon stepped into the main cabin. "We have arrived, sir," he said in his low, almost gravelly, voice. "As you can see, sir, the weather is extremely inclement. As there is no covered access between the landing pad and the entrance, perhaps you might wish to wait until the weather has cleared before you set out."

Kresh peered through the viewport, using his hand to block the glare from the cabin's interior lights. He spotted the entrance to the Terraforming Center. "It can't be more than a hundred meters or so to the door," Kresh said. "Why the devil should I wait?"

"As you see fit, sir. If you think it a wise idea to go immediately."

Damned busybody nursemaid of a robot. Kresh indulged himself with a brief flash of temper. If he waited around until the weather was just right, would Oberon then hint that he should wait until he had had a full meal and a nice long nap before setting out on the arduous thirty-second journey across the parking lot? They were on the clock here, and he had already been worrying that he had wasted too much time.

"I think it's a wise idea, all right," Kresh growled. "In fact I find it downright brilliant." He undid his seat restraint, got up, and grabbed his rain poncho from the seat opposite, where he had tossed it down after coming aboard. The thing was still a trifle damp, but no matter. He pulled it on over himself, adjusted the hood, and glared at Oberon. "I'd suggest you stay here for the time being," he said, "unless you think it a wise idea to get in my way."

Plainly, Oberon did not think it a wise idea to reply to that. Kresh turned his back on the robot, grabbed the hatch handle, and yanked up on it. The hatch unlatched, and Kresh gave it a good hard shove. It swung open and he stepped out into the roaring weather.

The driving rain caught him full in the face, coming down cold and hard. Kresh held up his hand to shield his face, and squinted through the downpour. He walked around to the opposite side of the ship, and then straight ahead, toward the entrance to the Terraforming Center. The wind grabbed at his poncho, blowing it flat against his body and sending its hem flapping and slapping wildly behind him. He leaned into the wind, struggling to hold the poncho hood on top of his head as the wind did its best to pull it off, and the rain blew in regardless.

A pair of big double glass doors, the sort that opened at the center, formed the main entrance of the Terraforming Center. Kresh got to them and almost grabbed at the handles before he realized that wouldn't work. He wasn't going to get in unless he followed the rules—rules he had approved himself. "VOICEPRINT!" he shouted above the noise of the storm.

"Auto-voiceprint system ready," an utterly depersonalized voice replied from nowhere in particular. Even though Kresh had been expecting a reply, it still startled him. The voice was clearly artificial—calm, emotionless, bloodless.

Kresh answered back in a somewhat lower tone of voice. If he could hear the voiceprint, probably it could hear him. "Name—Governor Alvar Kresh," he said. "Password—Terra Grande."

"Identity confirmed, clearance to enter confirmed," the voice replied. The doors unlatched. Kresh, impatient and eager to get out of the rain, grabbed the handles of both doors and pulled them a bit too hard. The wind caught at the left side door and yanked it out of his hand, bouncing it against the left-side wall before it swung back. There was a second, inner pair of doors that swung inward, and Kresh shoved them out of his way without breaking stride.

He had not been here in a long time, but he still knew his way around. He turned left and marched down the main hallway toward the third set of doors. The first two doorways in the hallway were perfectly ordinary affairs, but not the entrance to Room 103. It was a huge, armored steel hatch that more closely resembled the doors of a vault than anything else. The door was locked down and secured, as it should have been, but there was a palmprint button by the side of the door. Kresh slapped his hand down on it. After a moment, there was a bump, a clunk, and a thud and the massive door swung outward.

Kresh ducked inside the moment the door was open wide enough to do so. A startled-looking middle-aged woman in a lab coat was working at a desk just inside the door. She stared open-mouthed at the intruder, then got to her feet. She seemed about to protest, and two or three of the robots took a step or two closer, as if they feared that the intruder might intend harm to the woman. But then Kresh threw back the hood of his poncho. It was clear that the woman and the robots recognized him instantly—but knowing who he was only seemed to increase their sense of bewilderment.

But Alvar Kresh was not much interested in the emotional state of the swing-shift technical staff. He barely looked at them. He looked around until he spotted two huge and gleaming hemispherical enclosures, each about five meters across, each sitting on a plinth or thick pillar, about the diameter of the hemisphere on top of it. The pillars raised the bases of the hemispheres up to just about eye level. One of the hemispheres was a smooth and perfectly rounded dome, the other a geodesic form, made up of flat panels, with all manner of complicated devices and cables and conduits hanging off it at every angle. Kresh nodded at the two machines, and spoke.

"I want to talk to the twins," he said.

10

DR. LESCHAR SOGGDON opened her mouth and shut it, then opened it again and left it that way for a moment before she found her voice. "You're—you're Governor Kresh," she said at last.

"Yes," her visitor replied testily. "I know I am. And I need to talk to the twins concerning some climate projections. Now."

Soggdon was now at even more of a loss. "Sir, it doesn't work that way. You can't just come in and—"

"*I* can," Kresh said. "*I* should know. I wrote the regulations."

"Oh, yes, yes, sir, of course. I wasn't suggesting that you were not allowed to come here. It is merely a question of having the training and the understanding of our procedures here. It would probably be wiser for you to submit your questions in writing to the General Terraforming Committee and then—"

"Who are you?" Kresh asked, interrupting her. "What is your position here?"

Soggdon flushed and drew herself up to her full height, bringing her eyes roughly level with the base of Kresh's neck. "I am Dr. Leschar Soggdon," she said with as much dignity as she could muster. "I'm the night shift supervisor here."

"Very well, Dr. Soggdon. Please listen carefully. I have come here precisely for the reason that I want—I need—to avoid that sort of delay and caution. I am here on a matter of the greatest urgency and importance, and I *must* be certain I am getting my information direct from the source. I cannot take the chance of some expert misinterpreting my questions or the answers from the twins. I cannot wait for the General Committee to have a conference and debate the merits and the meaning of my questions. I have to ask my questions now, and get an answer now. Is that clear? Because if it is not, you're fired."

"I ah—ah—ah, sir, I ah—"

"Yes? Do you have other job prospects?"

She swallowed hard and started again. "Very well," Soggdon said at last. "But, sir, with all due respect, I would ask that you sign a statement that you proceeded against my advice and specifically ordered me to cooperate."

"I'll sign whatever you like," Kresh said. "But right now let me talk to the twins." The governor peeled off his poncho and handed it to the nearest robot. He walked to the far side of the huge room, where the two massive hemispherical enclosures sat. Inside were the two Terraforming Control Centers, one a Spacer-made sessile robotic unit, and the other a Settler-made computational system.

A sort of combination desk and communications console sat facing the two machines. Governor Kresh pulled out the chair and sat down at it. "All right, then," he said. "What do I do?"

Soggdon was severely tempted simply to show the man the proper controls to operate and let him charge ahead as directly as he liked. But she knew just how much damage even a minor slip of the tongue could produce. The idea of having Unit Dee caught in a major First Law conflict just because Kresh wanted to have his own way was too much for her. She had to speak up. "Sir," she said, "I'm sorry, but you have to understand a few things before you start, and I'm going to make *sure* you understand them, even if it means I lose my job. Otherwise you could cause any amount of damage to Unit Dee.''

Kresh looked up at her in annoyed surprise, but then his expression softened, just a bit. ''All right,'' he said. ''I always tell myself that I prefer it when people stand up to me. I guess this is my big chance to prove it. Tell me what I should know, but don't take too long about it. You can start by telling me what 'D' means.''

His question took her by surprise. Soggdon looked at him carefully before she spoke. How could a man who didn't even know what—or who—Unit Dee was expect to barge in here and take over? ''I didn't mean the letter 'D,' sir. I meant Unit Dee. That's what we call the robotic terraforming control unit. Unit Dee.''

Kresh frowned and looked over at the two units, and seemed to notice for the first time the two neatly lettered signs, one attached to each of the two hemispheres. The sign on the front of the rounded-off dome read *Unit Dee*, and the one on the angular geodesic dome read *Unit Dum*.

''Ah. I see,'' he said. ''I confess I don't know much about how you run things here. I visited here once or twice during construction, but not since you've been operational. I know the code name for the two Control Units is still 'the twins'— but not much else. I suppose those names stand for something. Acronyms?''

Soggdon frowned. For someone determined to charge in here and take over, he certainly was ready to get distracted by side issues. ''I believe the name Unit Dee referred to the fourth and final design considered. From there it seemed to develop into a sort of private joke among the day shift staff,'' she said. ''I must confess I never bothered to find out what the joke was. It might have something to do with Unit Dum being, well, dumb, nonsentient, but I've never understood the exact significance of Unit Dee.'' Soggdon shrugged. She had never been much known for her sense of humor.

''All right,'' said the governor. ''All that to one side,'' he went on, ''what do I need to know to avoid producing damage to the twins?''

''Well, Unit Dee is the only one likely to suffer damage. Unit Dum is a nonsentient computation device, not a robot.

He has a pseudo-self-aware interface that allows him to converse, to a limited extent, but he's not a robot and he's not subject to the Three Laws. Unit Dee is a different story. She's really not much more than an enormous positronic brain hooked up to a large number of interface links. A robot brain without a conventional robot body—but she is, for all intents and purposes, a Three-Law robot. Just one that can't move.''

"So what is the difficulty?'' Kresh demanded, clearly on the verge of losing his patience again.

"That should be obvious,'' Soggdon replied, realizing just a second too late how rude a thing that was to say. "That is— well, my apologies, sir, but please consider that Unit Dee is charged with remaking an entire *planet*, a planet that is home to millions of human beings. She was designed to be capable of processing truly huge amounts of information, and to make extremely long-range predictions, and to work at both the largest scale and the smallest level of detail.''

"What of it?''

"Well, obviously, in the task of remaking a planet, there are going to be accidents. There are going to be people displaced from their homes, people who suffer in floods and droughts and storms deliberately produced by the actions and orders of these two control systems. They will, inevitably, cause some harm to some humans somewhere.''

"I thought that the system had been built to endure that sort of First Law conflict. I've read about systems that dealt with large projects and were programmed to consider benefit or harm to humanity as a whole, rather than to individuals.''

Soggdon shook her head. "That only works in very limited or specialized cases—and I've never heard of it working permanently. Sooner or later, robotic thinking machines programmed to think that way can't do it anymore. They burn out or fail in any of a hundred ways—and the cases you're talking about are robots who were expected to deal with very distant, abstract sorts of situations. Unit Dee has to worry about an endless series of day-by-day decisions affecting millions of individual people—some of whom she is dealing with directly, talking to them, sending and receiving messages and data. She *can't* think that way. She can't avoid thinking about people as individuals.''

"So what is the solution?'' Kresh asked.

Soggdon took a deep breath and then went on, very quickly, as if she wanted to get it over with as soon as possible. She raised her hand and made a broad, sweeping gesture. "Unit Dee thinks this is all a simulation,'' she said.

"What?'' Kresh said.

"She thinks that the entire terraforming project, in fact the whole planet of Inferno, is nothing more than a very complex and sophisticated simulation set up to learn more in preparation for a real terraforming project some time in the future.''

"But that's absurd!'' Kresh objected. "No one could believe that.''

"Well, fortunately for us all, it would seem that Unit Dee can.''

"But there's so much evidence to the contrary! The world is too detailed to be a simulation!''

"We limit what she can see, and know, very carefully,'' Soggdon replied. "Remember, we control all of her inputs. She only receives the information we give her. In fact, sometimes we deliberately introduce spurious errors, or send her images and information that don't quite make sense. Then we correct the 'mistakes' and move on. It makes things seem less real—and also establishes the idea that things can go wrong. That way when we do make mistakes in calculations, or discover that we've overlooked a variable, or have just plain let her see something she shouldn't have, we can correct it without her getting suspicious. She thinks Inferno is a made-up place, invented for her benefit. So far as she knows, she is actually in a laboratory on Baleyworld. She thinks the project is an attempt to learn how to interact with Settler hardware for future terraforming projects.'' Soggdon hesitated for a moment, and then decided she might as well give him the worst of the bad news all at once. "In fact, Governor, she believes that *you* are part of the simulation.''

"What!''

"It was necessary, believe me. If she thought you were a real person, she would of course wonder what you were doing in the made-up world of her simulation. We have to work very hard to make her believe the real world is something we have made up for her.''

''And so you had to tell her that I did not really exist.''

''Precisely. From her point of view, sapient beings are divided into three groups—one, those who exist in the real world, but don't have anything to do with her; two, real-world people here in the lab and in the field who talk with her and interact with her—and three, simulants, simulated intelligences.''

''Simulants,'' Kresh said, very clearly not making it into a question. He was ordering her to explain the term, not asking her to do so.

''Ah, yes, sir. That's the standard industry term for the made-up humans and robots placed in a simulation. Unit Dee believes that the entire population of Inferno is really nothing more than a collection of simulants—and you are a member of that population.''

''Are you trying to tell me I can't talk to her because she'll realize that I'm not made-up?'' Kresh asked.

''Oh, no, sir! There should be no problem at all in your talking with Unit Dee. She talks every day with ecological engineers and field service robots and so on. But she believes them all to be doing nothing more than playing their parts. It is essential that she believe the same thing about you.''

''Or else she'll start wondering if her simulated reality is actually the real world, and start wondering if her actions have caused harm to humans,'' said Kresh.

''She has actually caused the death of several humans already,'' Soggdon replied. ''Unavoidably, accidentally, and only to save other humans at other times and places. She has dealt reasonably well with those incidents—but only because she thought she was dealing with simulants. And, I might add, she does have a tendency to *believe* in her simulants, to care about them. They are they only world she's ever known.''

''They *are* the only world there is,'' said Kresh. ''Her simulants are real-life people.''

''Of course, of course, but my point is that she knows they are imaginary, and yet has begun to believe in them. She believes in them in the way one might care about characters in a work of fiction, or the way a pet owner might talk to her nonsentient pet. On some level Unit Dee knows her simulants are not real. But she still takes a genuine interest in them, and still experiences genuine, if mild, First Law conflict when one of them dies and she might, conceivably, have prevented it. Causing the death of simulants has been extremely difficult for her.

"If she were to find out she had been killing real people—well, that would be the end. She might simply experience massive First Law conflict and lock up altogether, suffer brainlock and die. Or worse, she might survive."

"Why would it be worse if she survived?" Kresh asked.

Soggdon let out a long weary sigh and shook her head. She looked up at the massive hemisphere and shook her head. "I don't know. I can guess. At best, I think she would find ways to shut down the whole operation. We'd try to stop her, of course, but she's too well hooked in, and she's awfully fast. I expect she'd order power shutdowns, find some way to deactivate Unit Dum so he couldn't run the show on his own, erase computer files—that sort of thing. She'd cancel the reterraforming project because it could cause injury to humans."

"The best sounds pretty bad. And at worst?"

"At worst, she would try to undo the damage, put things back the way they were." Soggdon allowed herself a humorless smile. "She'd set to work trying to un-reterraform the planet. Galaxy alone knows what that would end up like. We'd shut her down, of course, or at least try to do so. But I don't need to exaggerate the damage she could do."

Kresh nodded thoughtfully. "No, you don't," he said. "But I still need to talk with her—and with Unit Dum. You haven't said much about him, I notice."

Soggdon shrugged. "There's not much to say. I suppose we shouldn't even call him a he—he's definitely an it, a soulless, mindless, machine that can do its job very, very, well. When you speak with him, you'll really be dealing with his pseudo-self-aware interface, a personality interface—and, I might add, it is quite deliberately not a very good one. We don't want to fool ourselves into thinking Unit Dum is something he is not."

"But it sounds as if he could handle the situation if Unit Dee did shut down."

"In theory, yes, Unit Dum could run the whole terraforming project by himself. In practice, all of us here believe you were quite wise not to put all your trust in a single control system. We need redundancy. We need to have a second opinion. Besides which, the two of them make a good team. They work well together. They are probably three or four times as effective working together as either would be alone. And anyway, we're only a few years into a project that could take a century or more. It's way too early to think about risking our primary operating procedure and trusting the whole job to backups. What if the backup runs into trouble?"

"All your points are well taken," said Governor Kresh. "So—what are the precautions I should take in talking to them?"

"Don't lose your temper if Unit Dee is condescending to you in some way. She doesn't really think you're real, after all. You are really nothing more than one of the game pieces, as far as she is concerned. Don't be thrown off if she seems to know a great deal about you, and lets you know it. Don't correct her if she gets something wrong, either. We've made various adjustments to her information files for one reason or another—some deliberate errors to make it seem like a simulation, and others we set up for some procedural reason or another. Try to remember you're not real. That's the main thing. As for the rest of it, you'll be talking to her via audio on a headset, and I'll be monitoring. If there's anything else you need to know, I'll cut in."

Governor Kresh nodded thoughtfully. "Have you ever noticed, Dr. Soggdon, just how much of our energy goes into dealing with the Three Laws? Getting around them, trying to make the world conform to them?"

At first, the offhand remark shocked Soggdon. Not because she disagreed with his words—far from it—but because Kresh was willing speak them. Well, if the governor was in a mood to dabble with heresy, why not indulge in it herself? "I've thought that for a long time, Governor," she said. "I think the case could be made that this world is in as much trouble as it is because of the Three Laws. They've made us too cautious, made us worry too much about making sure today is like yesterday, and far too timid to dare plan for tomorrow.''

Kresh laughed. ''Not a bad line, that,'' he said. ''You might catch me stealing it for use in a speech one of these fine days.'' The governor looked from the Unit Dee Controller to the Unit Dum Controller, and then back up at Soggdon. ''All right,'' he said. ''Let's get this thing set up.''

''GOOOD MORRN-ING, GOVVVENORR Kressh.'' Two voices came through the headphone to address him in unison—one a light, feminine soprano, the other a gravelly, slightly slurred, and genderless alto. They spoke the same words at the same time, but they did not synchronize with each other exactly.

The voices seemed to be coming from out of nowhere at all. No doubt that was an audio illusion produced by the stereo effect of the headphones, but it was nonetheless disconcerting. Alvar Kresh frowned and looked behind himself, as if he expected there to be two robots there, one standing behind each ear. He knew perfectly well there would be nothing to see, but there was some part of him that had to check all the same.

The whole setup seemed lunatic, irrational—but the iron hand of the Three Laws dictated that there be some such arrangement. Kresh decided to make the best of it. ''Good morning,'' he said, speaking into the headset's microphone. ''I take it I am addressing both Unit Dee and Unit Dum?''

''Thaat izz corrrect, Governorrr,'' the two voices replied. ''Somme vizzzitors finnnd iiit dissconcerrrting to hear usss both. Shalll we filllter ouut onne voice?''

''That might be helpful,'' Kresh said. Disconcerting was far too mild a word. The two voices speaking as one was downright eerie.

''Very well,'' the feminine voice said in his left ear, by itself, speaking with a sudden brisk, clipped tone, a jarring change from what had come before. Perhaps she found it easier to speak without the need to synchronize with Unit Dum. ''Both of us are still on-line to you, but you will hear only one of us at a time. We will shift from one speaker to the

other from time to time to remind you of our dual presence."
The voice he heard was almost excessively cheerful, with an
oddly youthful tone to it. A playful voice, full of amusement
and good humor.

"This higher-pitched voice I hear now," Kresh said, "it is
Unit Dee?"

"That is correct, sir."

Suddenly the other voice, low-pitched, impersonal and
slightly slurred, spoke into his right ear. "This is the voice of
Unit Dum."

"Good. Fine. Whatever. I need to speak with you both."

"Please go ahead, Governor," said Unit Dee in his left ear
again. Kresh began to wonder if the voice-switching was some
sort of game Unit Dee was playing, a way of putting him off
his stride. If so, it was not going to work.

"I intend to," he said. "I want to talk to you about an old
project, from the period of the first effort to terraform this
world."

"And what would that be?" asked Unit Dee.

"The proposal to create a Polar Sea as a means of moder-
ating planetary temperatures. I want you to consider an idea
based on that old concept."

"Ready to accept input," said the gravelly, mechanical
voice in his right ear. It was plain that very little effort had
gone into giving Unit Dum a simulated personality. That was,
perhaps, just as well. Kresh had the sense of talking to a schiz-
ophrenic as it was.

"Here is the idea. Assume that, in the present day, the existing Polar Depression were flooded, with inlets to the Southern Ocean provided by cutting a canal through the Utopia
region on the eastern side of Terra Grande, and by redirecting
the flow of the River Lethe in the west. Assume the work
could be done very rapidly, within a few years' time."

There was the briefest of pauses. "This would cause a Polar
Sea to form," Unit Dum went on. "However, the concept is
implausible. There is no way of performing such an enormous
engineering task in any practical length of time."

"Even if we *could* do it, I'm sure the collateral damage to
existing ecosystems and property would be huge," said Unit

Dee, clearly talking more to Unit Dum than to Kresh.

"Current projections show the issues of damage to ecosystems and property become moot in between two and two point five standard centuries," Unit Dum replied.

"Why do they become moot?" Kresh asked, fearing the answer.

"Because," Unit Dee replied, her voice clearly unhappy, "our current projection shows all ecosystems collapsing and all humans—the owners of the property—either dying or being evacuated from the planet by that time."

Kresh was genuinely surprised. "I was not aware that the numbers were that bad. I thought we at least had a chance at survival."

"Oh, yes," said Unit Dee. "There is at least a chance human life will survive here. That is in large degree a matter of choice for your descendants. Human beings can survive on a lifeless, airless, sterile ball of rock if they choose to do so. If the city of Hades were domed over or rebuilt underground, and properly shielded, it could no doubt sustain a reduced population indefinitely after the climate collapses."

"But things are improving!" Kresh protested. "We're turning things around!"

"So you are—for the moment, in localized areas. But there is little or no doubt that the current short-term improvements cannot be sustained and extended in the longer term. There is simply not enough labor or equipment to expand the zones of improved climate far enough, and establish them firmly enough, for them to be self-sustaining."

"And therefore there is no real point in worrying over ecological damage or property loss," Kresh said. "Fine. Disregard those two points—or, rather, factor in the results of attempting to deal with them, of efforts to repair the damage."

"The calculation involves a near-infinite number of variables," said Unit Dum. "Recommend a prescreening process to select range of near best-case scenarios and eliminate obviously failed variants."

"Approved," Kresh said.

"Even the prescreening process will take a few minutes," said Unit Dee. "Please stand by."

"As if I had much choice," Kresh said to no one in particular. He sat there, looking from Unit Dee's smooth and perfect hemispherical enclosure to the boxy, awkward, hard-edged-looking enclosure around Unit Dum. Dum's enclosure, or containment, or whatever, at least had the merit of looking like machinery. Dum looked like it *did* something, was hooked into things, made things happen. It was hardware and wires. It was solid, firmly attached to reality by power cables and datastreams. Dum was of this world.

In many more senses than one, Dee plainly was not. She was sheltered from the rude outside universe. She was the smooth and perfect one, sealed off in her idealized containment enclosure that needed special treatment. Dee looked more like an abstract sculpture than a working robot. She look liked something that was supposed to stand off, aloof, on her own, a divine being or magic totem to be consulted rather than a machine meant to do work. And was that so far off? Kresh glanced at Soggdon on the far side of the lab, pretending to be puttering around with something or other while she kept a nervous, unhappy eye on Kresh.

Yes, indeed. Unit Dee had her acolytes, her priests, who ministered to her whims and did their best to rearrange the world to suit her convenience, who walked on eggshells rather than anger or upset the divine being on whom all things depended. Kresh thought suddenly of the oracles of near-forgotten legend. They had been beings of great power—but of great caprice and trickery as well. Their predictions would always come true—but never in the way expected, and always at an unexpected price. Not a pleasant thought.

"I believe we are ready to begin with the main processing of the problem," Dee said, her voice coming so abruptly into the silence that Kresh jumped ten centimeters in the air. "Would you care to observe our work?" she asked.

"Ah, yes, certainly," said Kresh, having no idea what she had in mind.

The lights faded abruptly, and, flashing into being with the silence and suddenness of a far-off lightning strike, a globe of the planet Inferno appeared in the air between Kresh's seat at the console and the enclosures for the two control units.

The globe was a holographic image, about three meters in diameter, showing the planet's surface with greater precision than Kresh had ever seen. Every detail was razor-sharp. Even the city of Hades was clearly visible on the shores of the Great Bay. Kresh had the feeling that if he stepped up close enough to the globe and peered intently enough, he would be able to see the individual buildings of the city.

Inferno was a study in blue ocean and brown-and-tan land, with a pathetically few dots and spots of cool and lovely green visible here and there on the immense bulk of Terra Grande. Kresh tried to tell himself that they were making progress, that it was something just that their efforts were on a large enough scale to be plainly visible from space. But he wasn't all that convincing, even to himself. Somehow, over the last few days, it had come home to him that the great efforts they had made were as nothing, that the noble progress he had been so proud of scarcely represented forward movement.

But he did not have time to consider long. The globe turned over on its side, so that the northern polar regions were facing Kresh directly. Then, as he watched, the landscape began to change, shift, mutate. The River Lethe, a thin blue line running from the mountains west of the Great Bay, suddenly widened, and a new line of blue began to cut its way toward the Polar Depression, until the combined canal and river cut through the length of Terra Grande. Yes, Kresh could see it. Dredge the canal deep enough to allow a flow into the upper reaches of the Lethe, takes steps to make sure the channel scoured itself deeper instead of silting over, and it would work. Water would flow from the Polar Sea into the Great Bay. Assuming there was a Polar Sea, of course. At the present time, as shown in the simulation, there was nothing but dull white ice, a significant fraction of the planetary water supply locked up in the deep freeze where it could do no one any good.

But Dum and Dee were far from done with their modeling. Kresh looked to the western regions of Terra Grande. It was plain that things were not quite so simple or straightforward there. Again and again, a wedge-shaped channel of blue water appeared. The northernmost portion of its channel constantly shifted position, widened, narrowed, expanded, contracted,

vanished altogether for a moment and then reappeared somewhere else. Plainly, the two control units were searching for
the optimum positioning of the channel.

At long last the image settled down to a wide channel cutting straight north through the Utopia region. Kresh shook his
head and swore under his breath. The optimum channel the
two control units had chosen followed almost exactly the same
path Lentrall had shown him. Maybe the pushy young upstart
did know what he was talking about.

"Channel pattern as presented within one percent of theoretical optimum configuration," Unit Dum announced. "That
figure is well inside accumulated combined uncertainty factors
of many variables."

"In other words, it is as close as we can get right now—
and very much close enough for a first approximation," said
Unit Dee. "We are now ready for preliminary long-range climate calculation."

Kresh half-expected to see the planet's surface evolve and
change, as he had seen so many times before on simglobes
and other climate simulators. And he did see at least a little
bit of that—or thought he did. But the globe itself was covered
in a blizzard of layered data displays that sprawled over its
surface. Isobar mappings for temperature, air pressure, humid-
ity, color-coded scatter diagrams of populations for a hundred
different species, rainfall pattern displays, seasonal jet-stream
shifts, and a dozen other symbol systems Kresh couldn't even
begin to recognize, all of them shifting, rising, dropping, in-
teracting and reacting with each other, a storm of numbers and
symbols that covered the planet. The changes came faster and
faster, until the symbols and numbers and data tags merged
into each other, blurred into a faintly flickering cloud of gray
that shrouded the entire planet.

And then, in the blink of an eye, it stopped. The cloud of
numbers was gone.

A new planet hung in the air before Kresh. One in which
the old world could be clearly seen, and recognized, but new
and different all the same. Alvar Kresh had seen many hypothetical Infernos in his day, seen its possible futures presented a hundred times in a hundred different ways. But he

had never seen this Inferno before. The tiny, isolated, spots of green here and there were gone, or rather grown and merged together into a blanket of cool, lush green than covered half of Terra Grande. There were still deserts, here and there, but they were the exception, not the rule—and even a properly terraformed planet needed some desert environments.

The sterile, frozen, lifeless ice of the northern polar icecap had vanished completely, replaced by the Polar Sea, a deep-blue expanse of life-giving liquid water. Even at this scale, even to Kresh's untrained eye, he could see that sea levels had raised worldwide. He wondered for a moment where the water had come from. Had the control units assumed that the importation of comet ice would continue? Or was the water-level rise caused by thawing out the icecaps and breaking up the permafrost? No matter. The fact was that the water was there, that life was there.

"That's the best, most positive projection I've ever seen," Soggdon said. Kresh, a trifle startled, turned and looked over his shoulder. She was standing right behind his chair, gazing at the globe display in astonishment. "Hold on. I want to do a blind feed of the audio to your headset."

"What's a blind feed?" Kresh asked.

Soggdon picked up a headset identical to the one Kresh wore. Soggdon looked to Kresh as she put them on. "Dee and Dum will think you cannot hear what they say to me. When she talks to you, she is talking to a simulant. When she talks to me, a real human being, she cuts all links to any simulants, so as not to complicate the experiment by letting the simulants hear things they shouldn't. In reality you'll be able to hear it. But it is important—vitally important—that you have no re-action to what she says to me, or vice versa. In Dee's universe, you are just a simulated personality inside a computer. I am a real person outside the computer. You have no way of know-ing I exist. Do you understand?"

"Yes," said Kresh, hoping he did. He had the sense that he had stepped into a hall of mirrors. It was getting hard to tell the fantasies from the realities.

"Good," said Soggdon, and turned on the manual switch

on her headset. "Dee, Dum—this is Soggdon monitoring from
outside the simulation."

"Good mornnning, Doctor. Weee havvve beeen connn-
versssing with the Kresh simulllannt." The two voices spoke
in unison again, but Soggdon did not seem to be bothered by
it. Having heard each voice by itself, Kresh was able to notice
something that had escaped him before. When the two units
spoke in unison, it was not merely the two chanting together.
The voice of the two together spoke in a cadence that did not
belong to either of the two speaking by itself. The unison voice
made different word choices, responded in a way that was
different from Dee or Dum. The unison voice was not merely
two beings talking as one. It was the two merging into one
new being, in some ways greater, in some ways lesser than
the sum of its parts. Dee and Dum linked so intimately that
they became a third, and distinct, personality. Or was it merely
Dee who did so? If Dum was truly nonsentient, then he could
have no personality. Plainly there were mysteries to delve
into—but just as plainly they would have to wait for another
day. "The Kresh simulant asked us to consider the result of
producing a Polar Sea."

"Yes, I know," said Soggdon. "And I see you have produced an impressive planetary projection as a result. Would
either or both of you care to comment on it?"

"Both willl speeak, and then eachhh," said the unison
voice. "We havvve prrojected forward four ttthousand yearss,
as we have found that a wellll-planned operrational sequenzzze
will result in a zzzero-maintenance planetary ecologggy within
apprrroximately three hundred years. In our projection, the
planetary climmmate remainss intrinsically stable, selfff-
correcting, and self-enhancing throughout the period of the
metasimulation. There is no apparent danger of recollapse ev-
ident in any of the data for the end of the metasimulation
period."

Kresh frowned. Metasimulation? Then he understood. The
unison voice was using the term to refer to a simulation inside
a simulation—which was what it had been, so far as Dum and
Dee were concerned.

Dum spoke next. "Reference to unit Dum's prior objections

in regard to ecological and economic damage. Projections
show that the damage to the general ecology and gross planetary product caused by digging inlets for the Polar Sea would
be fully compensated for within fifteen years of project completion.''

But if the first two aspects of the combined control system
made it all seem wonderful, the third voice pulled everything
back down to reality. "It all sounds quite splendid," said Dee.
"There is, of course, the slight problem of it being quite impossible. We ran the metasimulation based on the assumption
that it would be possible to dig the channels. It is not possible
to dig them. An interesting exercise, I grant you—but it is not
one that has a great deal of connection to the world of our
simulation.''

"I was afraid she was going to say that," Soggdon muttered
as she switched off her mike. "You'd think she'd be the least
sensible of the three possible personality aspects, but instead
Dee's always the one to stick the pin in the balloon. She always reminds us of the practicalities.''

"Maybe this time they're a bit more possible than you
think," Kresh said. He keyed his own mike back on, and tried
to phrase things so that he would not reveal that he had overheard the conversation with Soggdon.

"Unit Dee, that's a very promising projection there. I take
it you think creating the Polar Sea would be a good idea?''

"It is a good idea that cannot be realized, Governor," said
Unit Dee. "You do not have the resources, the energy sources,
or the time to construct the needed inlets.''

"That is incorrect," Kresh said. "It is possible there is a
practical, doable, way to dig those inlets. I came here to have
you evaluate the proposed procedure. I first wanted to see if
the effort would be worthwhile. I see now that it would be.''

"What is the procedure in question?" asked Unit Dee.

Kresh hesitated a moment, but then gave up. There was no
way to describe the idea that didn't sound dangerous, desperate, even insane. Well, maybe it was all three. So be it. "We're
going to break a comet up, and drop the fragments in a line
running from the Southern Ocean to the Polar Depression,''
he said. Even as he spoke, he realized that he hadn't put any

modifiers or conditionals in. He hadn't said they might, or they could, or they were thinking of it. He had said they were going to do it. Had he made up his mind without knowing it?

But Dum and Dee—and Soggdon—plainly had more on their minds than Kresh's reaction to his own words. There was dead silence for a full thirty seconds before any of them reacted. The perfect holographic image of the Inferno of the future flickered and wavered and almost vanished altogether before it resolidified.

Unit Dee recovered first. "Am I to under-under-understand that you intend this as a serious idea?" she asked. The stress in her voice was plain, her words coming out with painful slowness.

"Not good," said Soggdon, her headset mike still off. She turned toward a side console, paged through several screenfuls of information, and shook her head. "I warned you she took her simulants seriously," she said. "These readings show you've set off a mild First Law conflict in her. You can't just come in here and play games with her, make up things like that."

Kresh cut his own mike. "I'm not making things up," he said. "And I'm not playing games. There is a serious plan in motion to drop a fragmented comet on the Utopia region."

"But that's suicidal!" Soggdon protested.

"What difference does it make if the planet's going to be dead in two hundred years?" Kresh snapped. "And as for Dee, I suggest it is time you start lying to her in earnest. Remind her it's all a simulation, an experiment. Remind her that Inferno isn't real, and no one will be harmed."

"Tell her that?" Soggdon asked, plainly shocked. "No. I will not feed her dangerous and false data. Absolutely not. You can tell her yourself."

Kresh drew in his breath, ready to shout in the woman's face, give her the dressing-down she deserved. But no. It would do no good. It was plainly obvious that she was not thinking with the slightest degree of rationality or sense—and he needed her, needed her help, needed her rational and sensible. She was part of the team that had set up this charade. She was the one who would have to prop it up. He would have to reason with her, coolly, calmly. "It would do no good for me to tell her any such thing," he said. "She thinks I'm a simulant. Simulants don't know they *are* simulants. She would not believe me telling her there was no danger—because she does not believe me to be human. And she does not believe that because you have lied to her."

"That's different. That's part of the experiment design. It's not false data."

"Nonsense," Kresh said, a bit more steel coming into his voice as the gentleness left it. "You have set up this entire situation for the sole purpose of allowing her to take risks, to do her job, while believing she could no harm to humans."

"But—"

Kresh kept talking, rolling right over her protests. "I could even do damage to her if I told her it was just a simulation. There must be *some* doubt in her mind as to whether her simulants—the people of Inferno—are real. Otherwise she would not be experiencing the slightest First Law conflict concerning them. If *I* assured her that *I* was not real, Space alone knows what she would make of that paradox. It seems to me as likely as not that she would reach the conclusion that I *was* real, and that I was lying to her. If I lie to her, she might realize the truth—and *then* where would you be, Dr. Soggdon? Only you can do it. Only you can reassure her. And you must do it."

Soggdon glared at Kresh, the anger and fear plain on her face as she switched on her mike again. "Dee, this is Dr. Soggdon. I am still monitoring the simulation. I am detecting what appear to be First Law conflicts in the positronic pathing display. There is no First Law element to the simulated circumstances under consideration." Soggdon hesitated, made a face, and then spoke again. "There is absolutely no possibility of harm to human beings," she said. "Do you understand?"

There was another distinct pause, and Kresh thought he detected another, but much slighter, flicker in the image of the Inferno that was to be. But then Dee spoke again, and her voice was firm and confident. "Yes, Doctor Soggdon. I do understand," she said. "Thank you. Excuse me. I must return to my conversation with the simulant governor." Another pause, and then Dee was speaking to Kresh. "I beg your pardon, Governor. Other processing demands took my time up for the moment."

"Quite all right," Kresh said. Of course, Dee was no doubt linked to a thousand other sites and operations, and probably having a dozen other conversations with field workers right now. It was not quite a little white lie, but it was certainly close enough to being one. Robots were supposed to be incapable of lying—but this one was clever enough to manage a truthful and yet misleading statement. Dee was a sophisticated unit indeed.

"Can you tell me more about this . . . idea under discussion?" Dee asked him.

"Certainly," said Kresh. "The idea is to evacuate everyone from the target area, and provide safeguards for the population outside the target area." It could not hurt to emphasize safety procedures first off. Let her know that even the fictional simulants would be safe. They needed as many defenses as possible against a First Law reaction. "Once that is accomplished, a large comet is to be broken up and the fragments targeted individually, the overlapping craters running through existing lowlands. More conventional earth-moving will no doubt be required afterwards, but the linked and overlapping craters will form the basis for the Utopia Inlet."

"I see," Dee replied, her voice still strained and tense. "Unit Dum and I will require a great deal more information before we can evaluate this plan."

"Certainly," said Kresh. He pulled a piece of paper out of his tunic and unfolded it. "Refer to network access node 4313, identity Davlo Lentrall, subgroup 919, referent code Comet Grieg." Lentrall had given him the access address earlier. Now seemed the moment to put it to good use. "Examine the data there and you will be able to do your evaluations," said Kresh.

"There is no identity Davlo Lentrall on access node 4313," Dee said at once.

"What?" said Kresh.

"No one named Davlo Lentrall is linked into that access node," said Dee.

"The number must be wrong, or something," said Kresh.

"Quite likely," said Dee. "I'm going to hand off to Dum. He is directly linked to the network in question and can perform the search more effectively."

"There is no Davlo Lentrall on node 4313," Dum announced, almost at once, speaking in an even flatter monotone than usual. "Searching all net nodes. No Davlo Lentrall found. Searching maintenance archives. Information on identity Davlo Lentrall discovered."

"Report on that information," Kresh said. How could Lentrall's files have vanished off the net? Something was wrong. Something was seriously and dangerously wrong.

"Network action logs show that all files, including all backups, linked to the identity Davlo Lentrall, were invasively and irrevocably erased from the network eighteen hours, ten minutes, and three seconds ago," Unit Dum announced.

Kresh was stunned. He looked to Soggdon, not quite knowing why he hoped for an answer from that quarter. He switched off his mike and spoke to her. "I don't understand," he said. "How could it all be erased? Why would anyone do that?"

"I don't know," she said. "He used a term I'm not familiar with in this context. Let me check." She keyed on her own mike again. "Dum, this is Soggdon, monitoring. Define meaning of the term 'invasive' in present situation."

"Invasive—contextual definition: performed by an invader, an attack from the outside, the act of an invader."

"In other words," said Kresh, his voice as cold and hard as he could make it, "someone has broken in and deliberately destroyed the files." He suddenly remembered what Fredda had said, about the things you thought you knew. She had said something about never really being *sure* about what you knew. Here it was, happening again. He had thought he knew where the comet was. Now he knew he did not. "It would seem," he said, "that someone out there agrees with you, Dr. Soggdon. They don't want anyone playing with comets."

11

"IT'S GONE, GOVERNOR," said Davlo Lentrall. "Everything I've ever worked on is gone." He was glad to be speaking over an audio-only link to the governor. Kresh had called on an audio link because it was easier to maintain a secure line that way, but Davlo didn't care about that. He was simply glad he did not have to show his face. It was bad enough that Kresh could hear the panic in his voice. He wouldn't want anyone to *see* him this way. Davlo Lentrall paced frantically up and down in front of his comm center. "All my core files, all the backups, everything."

"Take it easy, son. Easy now. There must be *some* way to retrieve it all. I thought the system was designed to make it impossible to lose things irretrievably."

Davlo tried to calm himself. Kresh had called from—from wherever he was—just as Davlo had finally, absolutely confirmed that all was lost. It was no easy thing to talk to the planetary leader when he was at his lowest ebb.

"Normally, yes, sir. But this wasn't an accident. This was sabotage. Five minutes after I discovered that my files were gone, I got a call from University Security. Someone broke into my office there and threw in a firebomb. They think there were at least *two* separate break-ins. By the end of the second intrusion, everything that wasn't stolen was burned. They say there's nothing left. Nothing at all. All my notes and work—including the comet data. The comet coordinates, the tracking information, the orbital projections—everything.''

''Burning stars,'' Kresh's voice half whispered. ''Maybe that whole escapade at Government Tower was just a diversion.''

Davlo laughed bitterly. ''Trying to kidnap me, perhaps kill me, a mere diversion for stealing my life's work?''

''I don't mean to sound harsh, son, but yes. Exactly that. I grant that you would have a different point of view—but for the rest of the world, right now, your life's work is of far greater importance than your life. And you're sure everything is gone? Irretrievably gone?''

''Everything.''

''I see.''

''Governor Kresh? Who did this? Was it the Settlers?''

''Probably,'' said Kresh. ''But it could have been anyone who wanted to keep the comet from coming down. Right now that doesn't matter. Right now we have deal with the situation, not worry about how the situation came to be.''

''That's not going to be easy, sir. I'll try.''

There was silence on the line for a moment. ''All right, then. Your computer files containing your plans are gone. We have to set to work at once to get them back—or at least get the main part of them back. I've seen enough of what the twin control units can do to be sure they could start from the basics of your plan and reconstruct it—probably in greater detail than you had to start with.''

''How very kind of you to say so,'' Davlo muttered.

''I meant no offense to your work,'' Kresh said. ''The control units are designed for this kind of job, and they have the capacity to oversee the climate of an entire planet. Of course they can do more detailed projections than one man working alone, no matter how gifted—especially when that man is working outside his field of expertise. And I might add that no robot or computer or control unit found that comet and saw what it might mean to this planet.''

Davlo sat down in the chair facing the comm unit, folded his arms over his chest, and stared down at the floor. "You're flattering me," he said. "Trying to soothe me, make me feel better."

"Yes, I am," Kresh agreed, his voice smooth and calm. "Because I need you, and I need you right now. As I was about to say, the control units can reconstruct and refine your plan for targeting the comet—but we need you *in* your field of expertise."

"Sir? I don't understand."

"Son, we need you to look through your telescope again and relocate that comet. And fast."

Davlo took a deep breath, shook his head, and kept his gaze fixed on the floor. "Sir, *I* never *found* the comet in the first place."

"What! Are you saying this has all been some kind of hoax? Some kind of fraud?"

"No! No, sir. Nothing like that. I didn't mean it that way. I meant that the computers found the comet. Automated telescopes found it while doing preprogrammed scans. I've never looked through a telescope myself in my life."

Again, silence on the line, but this time Davlo spoke first. "All the data is gone, sir. Without my computer files, without my written notes, without the log files—there is simply no way at all I can find that comet again in time."

"But the thing is kilometers across! It's practically headed straight for the planet right now! How hard could it be to spot?"

Davlo Lentrall let out a tired sigh. The man was right. It *shouldn't* be hard at all. How could he explain that it would be all but impossible? "It is extremely hard to spot, sir. It *is* coming straight for us, and that is part of the problem. Normally we track a comet by spotting its motion against the night sky. Comet Grieg appears to be all but stationary. Not *quite* motionless, but close. And while it's a relatively large cometary body, even a big comet is rather small from tens of millions of kilometers away. It also happens to be a rather dark body—and at its present distance, it has a very low apparent magnitude."

"You're saying it's too dim to see? But you saw it before—or at least the computers and the telescopes did."

"It's not impossible to see. But it's very dim and small and far away and with a very small lateral motion. And it's not just a question of seeing it once. We have to get repeated, accurate measures of its position and trajectory before we can reconstruct the orbit."

"But what about when it gets closer? Won't it develop a tail and all the rest of it? Surely that will make it easier to spot."

"By which time it will be too late. Grieg is a dark-body comet. The comet will be too close, and if it has developed much of a tail, that will mean it is starting to melt. If it gets too warm and melts too much, it will be too fragile to hold together during the course correction. Part of the plan I hadn't worked out yet was shielding from the sun. I was going to come up with some kind of parasol, a shield to keep the sunlight off."

"But there's a chance," said Kresh. "At least there is some sort of chance we could reacquire the comet if we tried." There was a brief moment of quiet again before the governor's voice spoke again. "Here's what we're going to do," he said. "We're going to keep everything moving forward, based on the assumption that we do reacquire the comet, and that we will decide to go forward with the diversion and the impact. We need to move forward on as many fronts as possible, as fast as possible, and I need some work out of you, right now.

"First I want you to set down the closest approximations you can of the mass, size, position, and trajectory of Comet Grieg. Even rough figures will give us someplace to start in planning for the impact itself. Send that information at once to my data mailbox. Then you are going to get to work at once organizing a search to reacquire Comet Grieg. I will instruct your superiors to give you whatever resources and personnel you need for the job. Tell them as much as you can about the comet. But get that started—and *let someone else run it*. Because I want *you* to get to work trying to recover your computer files. Maybe they're not as lost as we think. There must be something, somewhere—at least enough to give some leads to the team doing the telescope search. Is that clear?''

"Yes, sir. Sir—if I might ask a question?''

"Yes, of course, Dr. Lentrall.''

"I get the impression that you've become more convinced that the plan might work.''

"That I have, Dr. Lentrall. I've seen and heard quite a bit here about your plan. Enough to make me think we just can't live without it. Was there anything else?''

"Not at the moment, sir. I'll be in touch.''

"You certainly will,'' the governor replied, with just the slightest hint of humor in his voice. "Kresh out.''

The line went dead.

That should have been his cue to swing into action, but instead, Davlo simply stared at the speaker, expressionless. After what seemed a very long time indeed, he finally stirred himself into action. He set down all he could recall of his comet data, as accurately as possible, knowing full well that the margin of error in most of his figures would render them close to useless. He sent a copy of it off to Kresh's data mailbox, and another off to the head of the astronomy department, asking for whatever help he could get. Of course, Davlo knew perfectly well that the department head absolutely refused to accept any after-hours calls. She would not get the message until morning. But still, best to have it done.

Simple enough jobs, both of them, but they seemed to take an inordinately long time—and to take a great deal out of Davlo. After the day he had had, there was not really a great deal left to take. When he was at last done with the messages, he did not get up. Instead he sat there, unable to rouse himself. There was a lot more he ought to do, but Davlo Lentrall could not quite bring himself to move. Not quite yet.

It was that hour of the night when rational thought seems most unreasonable, when unreasoning fear seems utterly logical, and disasters seem most probable. Davlo thought of his nameless, faceless, enormously powerful enemies. They were mad enough at him already. He was not entirely sure he wanted to do anything else—like getting out of his chair—that might incur their wrath.

There was some part of Davlo Lentrall that was able to

recognize the fragility of his own personality at that moment. A part of him that could see that the game was over. A part of him that knew he had been pretending to be someone and something he was not for a long time. He had seen himself as smarter, braver, better than anyone else. And why not, in a universe where robots protected everyone from the consequences of their actions, where robots did all the hard work and left the posturing for humans? He had always imagined himself as being immune to fear and as impossible to harm. It was easy enough to indulge such fancies when robots warded off all danger.

And that part of Davlo Lentrall could feel it all slipping away. A few more shocks, a few more disasters, and he knew he would not be able to hold together. What was he to do if the mask fell from his face altogether, and the face underneath was blank? He knew now that he was not the person he had pretended to be. But then who was he?

Davlo Lentrall sat in his office chair, still as a switched-off robot, trying to work up the nerve to move.

It might have been a minute later, or an hour later, when Kaelor came into the room. "Come along, sir," the robot said. "You must rest. There is nothing more you can accomplish tonight."

Lentrall allowed himself to be led away, allowed Kaelor to peel off his clothes, move him through the refresher, and put him to bed. He was asleep almost before he was fully between the covers. The last thing he saw as his head hit the pillow was Kaelor leaning over him, tucking the sheets up around him.

And the first thing he would think of the next morning was where he might find quite a bit of his lost data.

DONALD 111 WAS every bit as motionless as Lentrall had been, but he was far from inactive. Donald stood in his niche in the wall of Alvar Kresh's home office, and worked the hyperwave links with all the speed and efficiency that he could muster. To an outside observer, Donald would have appeared completely inert, as if he had been shut down altogether. In point of fact, he was linked into a half-dozen databases, patched through to simultaneous conference calls with robots in the City of Hades maintenance offices, the Department of Public Safety, the Emergency Preparedness Service, the Combined Inferno Police, and a half-dozen other agencies. No one knew for sure what would happen if and when the comet hit, but there were certain basic precautions that could be taken— and Donald could at least get them started.

It had to be anticipated that there would be quakes and aftershocks as a result of the impact, even in Hades, halfway around the planet. That assumption right there meant a great deal of work would have to be done. There were buildings that would have to be braced. Perhaps it would be wise if some old and unneeded buildings were disassembled altogether. Valuable and fragile objects would have to be stored in places of safety.

And then of course, there were the people. The robots would have to prepare massive places of shelter, where the quakes could be ridden out in safety.

All the computer projections and models made it clear they had to anticipate that the comet impact would inject a large amount of dust, gas, and water vapor into the atmosphere. Theory said the dust injection would be of benefit to the climate in the long run, an aid to the efforts to adjust the planetary greenhouse factor, but it also meant there would be a prolonged period of bad weather. The robots of Inferno had to prepare for this as well.

There were dozens, hundreds, thousands of details to work out, contingencies to prepare for, scarce resources to be allocated between conflicting demands.

Donald had made a status report to the governor three hours after commencing the job, as instructed, although there was not a great deal of new information at that time. Things were really just getting started.

The job his master had given him was enormous in scope, enormous enough that Donald already convinced himself that the job was far beyond his capacity. It was obviously quite impossible for him to organize the entire planet for the comet impact all by himself. But his master, Governor Alvar Kresh, had to know that as well. Clearly, therefore, his orders required some interpretation. Donald would do the best he could for as long as required, but there would come a point where it would be counterproductive for Donald to run things, instead of handing the job to whatever combination of humans and robots were best suited to the job. But until the governor issued orders to that effect, Donald would tackle the job as best he could.

Indeed, the initial stages of the job were well within Donald's capacities. Later there would be decisions to make that were beyond his scope, but for now he even had a little bit of extra capacity—enough to monitor the news channels, for example. That was a routine part of running a large-scale mobilization job like this one. One had to monitor all the uncontrollable variables that affected the situation. From the operations planning side of things, unfavorable news reports were as much an uncontrollable and unpredictable variable as bad weather or plagues or economic crashes. Nor was it just the news itself that mattered—the way in which was reported was equally important. The mood of the report, the things that were left in and left out, the match-up between the facts as reported and the facts as known to the project team—all of those mattered.

And Donald was enough of a student of human behavior to know that what he heard starting to be reported on the overnight news broadcast was far beyond his ability to judge. All he could know for sure was that it would have some effect, and a complicating one at that.

So he did was any robot would do under the circumstances.

He went looking for a human who could deal with the problem.

FREDDA LEVING OPENED her eyes to see Donald's calm and expressionless gaze looking down on her. She of all people should not have been unnerved by the sight. After all, she had built Donald, and she knew him as well as anyone else in her life. *She* knew how solid a protection the Three Laws were, and how utterly reliable Donald was in any event. But even so, it had been a long, hard day, and there was something distinctly unnerving about waking up to see a sky-blue robotic

face staring down at one's self. "Donald," she said, her voice
still heavy with sleep. "What is it?"

"Dr. Leving, I have just monitored an audio channel news
report from Inferno Networks concerning the incident today
at Government Tower Plaza."

"That's hardly surprising," Fredda said. "What else would
they put on the news?"

"True enough, Doctor. However, this report *is* rather surprising. I believe you should hear it."

Fredda sighed and sat up in bed. "Very well, Donald. Play
it back for me."

The cool, professional voice of a female newsreader began
to speak through Donald's speaker grille. "Sources close to
the investigation have uncovered a rumor that has been circulating for most of the day—that the incident at Government
Tower today was actually a coup attempt, an effort to seize
control of the government itself."

Suddenly, Fredda was fully and absolutely awake. What the
devil was the woman talking about? There's hadn't been any
coup attempt.

"Even more remarkable is the reason offered as motivation
for the coup attempt," the newsreader went on. "The attempt
was made to prevent the government from causing a comet to
crash into the planet. According to the same source, the government is actively and secretly engaged in just such a project,
under the belief that the comet impact will somehow enhance
the planetary environment. Attempts to contact Governor
Kresh for comment have been unsuccessful. We will of course
provide further details of this story as they become available."

The recording ended, and Donald spoke in his own voice.
"That was the sum total of reportage on any coup attempt,"
Donald said, anticipating Fredda's first question. "I might add
that Inferno Networks has a tradition of sensationalist reports,
and that at various times the Settler and Ironhead organizations, as well as the government itself, have found it a useful
conduit for leaks."

"So it could have come from anywhere. When did that
broadcast go out?" Fredda asked, trying to think.

"Just a few minutes ago, at 0312 hours local time here in Hades."

"In the dead of night, the time it would be least likely to have much circulation. Interesting. Very, very interesting. *Has* anyone from any of the news services attempted to reach Alvar—ah, the governor?"

"Not through any of the access points or comm links that I monitor," Donald replied.

"In other words, either they didn't really try to reach him, or they didn't try very hard," Fredda said, half to herself. She thought for a moment. "They're trying to flush us out," she announced at last. "Get us out in the open, right in their sights. That's got to be it."

"I'm afraid I don't understand," said Donald. "Who is 'they'?"

"I would assume that it's the same people who tried to snatch Davlo Lentrall," Fredda said. "It means they're trying to force us to admit there is a plan to drop a comet—and they're trying to present the idea in the most unfavorable way possible. They want to make it look like the comet idea is so bad that people would risk violence and upheaval rather than let it happen. And if they can make the comet plan seem like some sort of fiendish secret plot, all the better. It will put more pressure on the government—on Alvar—to backpedal, get as far back from the comet idea as possible."

"I see," said Donald in a tone of voice that made it clear he did not. "I must admit that the subtleties of human politics are quite beyond me. Might I ask why whoever it was that did this arranged for it to be broadcast at this hour of the night?"

"They're sending a signal," Fredda said. "They're giving us until morning to put together a denial, to explain it away, and let the whole thing evaporate."

"And if you fail to do so?"

Fredda waved at Donald's speaker grille, vaguely indicating the recorded human voice that had just come from it. "Then they will use all the news outlets they get can to listen to them. They'll raise every kind of hell they can. Maybe try to force Alvar out of office."

"So what do we do?" Donald asked.

Fredda thought for a moment. Logically, the thing to do was call Alvar, consult with him. The trouble was, of course, that she did not know where he was. He had not told her. No doubt she could find him if she wanted to do so. Probably all she had to do was ask Donald. Either he knew, or else he could find out, somehow. But she had the distinct impression that Alvar had wanted to be alone. And Donald had come to her, not to Alvar. That in and of itself strongly implied that Donald did not wish to contact Alvar. Had Alvar left explicit orders with Donald? Or was Donald working on some sort of implied orders? Could she get him to override that instruction with a stated and emphatic command to help her contact her husband? Or suppose he knew where Alvar was but just wanted to protect his master from a politically damaging situation by dumping it in Fredda's lap?

Damnation! The situation was bad enough without having to go into the whichness of what and the balancing of implied commands and hypothetical First Law issues.

Fredda had gotten to precisely that point in her reasoning when Donald spoke. "I beg your pardon, Dr. Leving, but there is an incoming call for you from the Hades News Reporting Service."

"For me?" Why the devil would they call *her*? Unless they had tried for Alvar already. Or else maybe—"Oh, the hell with it," she said out loud, and stood up. She was too tired for more guessing games. "Audio only. I must look an absolute fright. Put the call through the bedroom comm panel, Donald. And better record the call as well." She started pacing back and forth, for want of a better outlet for her nervous energy.

"Yes, ma'am," said Donald. "The caller can hear you—now."

Thoughtful of Donald to handle it that way. More than a few people had been embarrassed talking to an audio-only caller who wasn't there—or, worse, by talking indiscreetly before they knew the caller was there. "This is Fredda Leving," she said to the empty air. "Who is calling, please?"

"Good evening, Dr. Leving." A very smooth, professional-sounding male voice spoke into the empty air. "This is Hilyar Lews, Hades News Reporting."

Fredda had heard and seen the man on the air, and she did not like him. Besides which, it irritated her that anyone could sound so smooth and polished at this hour of the night. "Did you say, 'Good evening'?" Fredda asked. "Wouldn't 'Good morning' would be a trifle more accurate, Mr. Lews? And I might add that it is traditional to apologize for calling at this hour," she said, hoping to put the man off balance.

"Um, ah, well, yes, ma'am. My apologies." It was obvious from Lews's tone of voice that he knew exactly how awkward he sounded. Good.

"Well, now that you have me up, Mr. Lews, did you have a particular reason for calling? Or is this just a friendly chat?" Best to keep the fellow as much off balance as possible.

"Ah, no, ma'am. It's a very serious call. We've been trying to reach the governor concerning the allegations that are being broadcast by Inferno Networks News? Ah—have you heard the I-N News reports?"

"I have indeed," said Fredda. "And I can speak for my husband without the necessity of disturbing him at this hour. There absolutely, positively, categorically was no coup attempt. There was and is no threat to the government."

"But what about the—"

"I can't comment on the details of an ongoing investigation." Fredda rolled right over whatever Lews was going to ask, glad to have such a convenient phrase to hand.

"Very well, ma'am. But what about this business concerning a comet? Is there any truth at all to that part of the story? It sounds a little too fantastic for it to have been made up out of nothing at all."

Fredda stopped her pacing back and forth and sat down on the edge of the bed. Why the devil did crises always hit in the middle of the night, when she was half asleep? She had to think, and think fast. It was no good denying the story. Not when it was true, not when it was bound to leak out again, some other way, and soon. But she could not just blandly confirm it either. She had no idea at all how likely the comet plan was. Alvar had gone off somewhere to study the problem. Suppose he had already concluded the idea was, after all, as insane as it sounded? She could not commit him, either way. But she couldn't let it go with a flat "no comment" either. That would simply start the rumor mill churning faster than ever.

In short, there was nothing she could say that wouldn't cause some serious damage. She should never have taken this call in the first place. But it was too late now. She had to say *something*. She took a deep breath, and spoke slowly, carefully. "There is a comet," she said. "The governor is aware of . . . studies that have been made concerning the comet." Suddenly Fredda had an inspiration. Something she could say that was utterly truthful, and yet something that was completely misleading. Something that might slow down the rumor long enough to buy them some time. "I do not know all the details, but I believe the project has something to do with Operation Snowball. I assume you are familiar with Snowball?"

"Ah, yes, somewhat, ma'am." There was a longish pause. At a guess, Lews was doing a lookup on "snowball" in some sort of reference system. Fredda smiled. It was increasingly obvious to her that Lews was not quite as smooth and prepared as he let on. That was also good. "It's a project to mine ice from comets and drop it into the atmosphere," Lews said, in a tone of voice that made it obvious that he was reading the words from off some screen or another.

"Precisely. In effect, dropping a comet on the planet—a few kilograms at a time. Snowball has been going on for some time, and it is the only officially approved project concerning comets that I know about." The statement was true, if misleading in the extreme. The Comet Grieg plan was not, after all, approved. "I trust that answers your questions, Mr. Lews?"

"Well, I suppose so," Lews replied.

Suppose what you will, thought Fredda, *just so long as I've muddled the trail enough to hold you off*. "In that case, I'll be getting back to bed. Good night—or good morning—Mr. Lews." Fredda made a throat-cutting gesture to Donald, and he cut the connection. "I hope I did that right," she said, more to herself than to Donald. "See to it that a copy of the original broadcast, and a copy of that conversation, are in the governor's data mailbox. When he does check in, he'll need to know what's going on."

"I have already put copies into his mailbox, Doctor."

"Excellent." Fredda slumped backward onto the bed, her feet still dangling down over the front of the mattress. That wouldn't do. No point dozing off like that when she could so easily crawl back beneath the covers. She stood up, went around the bed, and got back into it, wondering if there was indeed any point in getting comfortable. It wouldn't surprise her if she were unable to sleep at all. She certainly had enough things to worry about for her to keep her staring at the ceiling for the rest of the night. Where was Alvar? What was he going to do about the comet? Had she done it right, or had she just made a bad mess worse? No way to know. No way to know until it was too late.

It seemed her to that was the running theme for everything that had happened in the last few days. She yawned, shut her eyes, rolled over on her side, and set forth on a valiant effort to fall asleep.

FREDDA OPENED HER eyes again, to Donald staring down at her once more.

"Your pardon, Dr. Leving, but there is an urgent call for you. The pseudo-robot Caliban says he must speak with you at once." Fredda sighed. She knew she had to take the call, and that Caliban would only call if it were important. But even so, it was turning into a very long night. "*Now* what time is it?" she asked.

"It is now 0429 hours," Donald said.

"It would be," she muttered. "All right, on the bedroom comm again. Audio only." Perhaps she shouldn't have cared how she looked to a robot, but she did.

"Very well, Dr. Leving. Caliban can hear you—now."

"Caliban, hello," Fredda said, struggling not to yawn. "What's going on?"

"Dr. Leving, please forgive me for disturbing you at this

hour, but I felt that we must talk. Prospero and I are leaving the city now, headed for Depot and beyond. We have learned through our own sources what is likely to befall our city.''

Fredda blinked in surprise. She had always known that Caliban and the New Law robots had good sources of information, but she had not known they were that good. And then there was the way Caliban had phrased it. ''Befall'' the New Law city. A subtle pun that would reveal very little to anyone who did not know what was going on. It told her Caliban was being cautious—and that he wanted her to be equally cautious. Was he worried about eavesdroppers, or snooper robots with orders to listen for certain words? Or was he just assuming that Alvar was still there, and might be able to overhear? ''I think you are being wise,'' she said. ''Events are moving quite rapidly, and I don't think they will be easy to control.''

''I quite agree,'' said Caliban. ''We must set to work at once preparing our citizens for the contingency in question. We may well need to call on our friends for help.''

''You can certainly call on me,'' said Fredda. ''Whatever I can do, I will.'' She hesitated for a moment. That was a rather sweeping promise, after all. It seemed likely that all of the Utopia region would have to be evacuated, and that would put a huge strain on transport and other resources. Few people were likely to worry about the New Law robots getting their fair share of the help. ''But there will probably be limits— severe limits—on what I can do.''

''I understand that,'' said Caliban. ''We have always been on our own. But even marginal assistance could turn out to be vitally important.''

Fredda felt a pang of guilt. It was bad enough when you could do very little for your own creations. It was worse when they expected even less. ''Contact me when you get there,'' she said. ''Let me know whatever you need, and I'll do my damnedest to get it.''

There was a moment's silence on the line. ''What we need,'' said Caliban, ''is a place where we can be left alone. We thought we had that, up until now. Caliban out.''

The line went dead, and Fredda cursed to herself, fluently, violently, and at length. It wasn't supposed to be like this. She had never asked for, never considered, the burden of obligation she had put on herself when she had created the New Law robots. She had never felt that she owed a debt, a creator's debt to the Three-Law robots she had built. But with Caliban, with the New Law robots, she felt she owed them something, simply by virtue of calling them into existence.

Perhaps that was the difference between creating a race of willing slaves, and a race of beings who wanted to be free.

Fredda slumped back in bed. Damnation. Now she'd *never* get to sleep.

THE FIRST HINTS of dawn were a whisper in the eastern skies of Hades as Caliban, Prospero, and Fiyle rode Prospero's aircar up out of the city's tunnel system. Fiyle was clearly exhausted, yawning uncontrollably. He had been up all night, Prospero grilling him relentlessly for any tiny scrap of information he might have concerning the comet operation.

Caliban looked at the man with something very close to sympathy. Perhaps Fiyle was little better than a turncoat who sold himself to all and sundry, but even so, there was some whiff of honor about the man. Something in him had put limits on his petty betrayals and the buying and selling of trust. Something had put survival of the New Law robots above the lure of Trader Demand Notes. There was something to respect, even in this contemptible man.

And it was, after all, that impulse to decency that had placed Norlan Fiyle in danger. That meant Norlan Fiyle had best get out of town, and fast. And the two robots, needless to say, had their own reasons to travel. They needed to warn Valhalla.

Caliban looked from Fiyle to Prospero, and then at the city itself. He bid a farewell—and not an entirely fond one—to Hades. Perhaps he would someday return to the city. But events were moving too quickly, things were happening too fast. Somehow, a part of him knew that the city he saw now, here, today, would soon be changed beyond recognition, even if the buildings and the streets remained the same. For the lives of the people would be changed utterly, and the world beyond the city made anew.

Unless, of course, city, people, and world were all simply

smashed flat instead. Utter destruction was one form of change.

The aircar reached for sky, and headed into the dawn.

ALVAR KRESH SWITCHED off the link to his data mailbox, surprised at his own sense of relief. He sat at the console in front of Dum and Dee, where, it seemed to him, he had spent several years, instead of merely most of a night and most of a morning, and tried to consider the situation. The day shift for the Terraforming Center had been filtering in for the last half an hour or so, all of them more than a trifle surprised to find Governor Alvar Kresh in possession. Kresh paid them as little mind, and as little attention, as possible. Dr. Soggdon was still at the center as well, for reasons Kresh did not entirely understand. Perhaps a sense of duty was keeping her there to protect Unit Dee's honor against the interloper. If that was the case, she was not at her most effective. She was at her desk, head pillowed on her folded arms, fast asleep.

Kresh turned his attention back to the news he had just received. The people trying to wreck the comet-capture project did not know it, but they had done him a very large favor indeed. Kresh had been dreading the necessity of informing the world at large of the comet project. Sooner or later, Inferno would have to know, but he had enough on his hands without being forced to calm the inevitable public uproar at the same time.

By leaking the information, the opposition had relieved Kresh of the necessity of going before the cameras and the reporters. And Fredda had struck precisely the right note, deflating the uproar without actually discounting the story. Thank Space he hadn't been home to receive that call himself.

When he had succeeded to the governorship, Kresh had made a point of eliminating all the layers of press secretaries and communications offices and scheduled appointments and all the other tricks of the trade meant to keep reporters well away from the governor, allowing the news people all but unlimited access to him. There had been plenty of times when he had regretted that policy, and today he thanked whatever source of luck he had that he had managed to avoid the press today. It might not be a bad idea to stay right where he was, keeping a nice, low profile for a while, with as little direct communication with the outside world as possible. Here he could focus on the project itself. If he went back to Hades, it was all but inevitable that he would get swept up *talking* about the project, rather than doing something about it.

Very well. Now the world knew about the comet, and he had not been the one to tell them. All to the good. But now there was another problem. The obvious thing to do now was to allow the public discussion move forward to the point where he could confirm the existence of the comet plan to a populace ready to accept the idea. But how the devil could he do that when he would be forced to make the ridiculous-sounding admission that they had misplaced the comet?

Plainly, the best answer to that problem was to relocate the comet as soon as possible. But Kresh had done as much as he could in that direction for the moment. Sometimes the job of leadership was simply to get things started, and trust in others to get them done. He would have to keep on here, focusing on other aspects of the project, working on the assumption that they would be able to find the comet in time. *Back to work*, he told himself.

"Still with me, Dee?" Kresh asked.

"Yes, sir, I am," Unit Dee replied. "Was there anything of interest in your mailbox?"

"Quite a bit," he said. "But nothing that you need worry about. I have a new task for you."

"I would be delighted to be of further assistance."

"Right," said Kresh, his tone of voice deliberately brusque. There was something about courtly manners from a robot that got on his nerves. "My personal robot, Donald 111, is at work on the preliminary preparations for the cometary impact. Safety plans, evacuations plans, that sort of thing. I want to contact him and have him hand off that job to you. Clearly, you're better suited to it than he is. I should have assigned the job to you in the first place. Relay my orders to that effect, then order Donald to join me here as soon as possible without revealing my whereabouts."

"I will contact him at once," Dee said.

"Good," said Kresh. "I'm going to step out for a breath of fresh air. When I return, we will return to refining your impact targeting plan."

"With the extremely rough data we got from Dr. Lentrall, I am not sure there is more we can do."

"But there might be," Kresh said. "At the very least we can work out a range of scenarios and contingencies, so that we are more ready to act when the time comes. We'll work out a few hundred possible rough trajectories, and give Unit Dum something to do."

Dee did not respond to the very small joke, but instead spoke with her usual urbane civility. "Very well, sir. I will continue with my other duties while I await your return."

"Back in a minute," Kresh said, and stood up. He stretched, yawned, and ignored the stares of the Center's workers as he rubbed his tired face. Let them wonder what their governor was doing here. Alvar headed out the huge armored door of Room 103, down the corridor of the Terraforming Center, out the double doors that led to the outside, and into the morning.

It had been a long time since he had worked a job all night, worked all the clock around. He was close to exhausted, but not quite. There was something invigorating about seeing the morning after a hard night's work. Somehow Kresh always felt as if he had earned the loveliness of morning after working through the darkness.

The rains were gone now, and the world was fresh and bright, scrubbed clean. The sky was a brilliant blue, dotted with perfect white clouds that set off the deep azure of the heavens. The air smelled sweet, and good. Alvar Kresh looked toward the west, in the direction of the governor's Winter Residence. He remembered another morning like this, with everything fresh and bright, and all good things possible. A morning he had spent with Fredda, just after he had assumed the governorship. That had been a morning of good omen. Perhaps this would be as well.

And maybe it was time to move over to the Winter Residence. That would let him stay on the island. The more he thought about it, the more it seemed a good idea to keep a low profile just now. But that could wait until later. Right now there was something else he could do to keep himself isolated. He walked over to his aircar, sitting in the middle of a parking lot that was now half full of aircars. Oberon saw him through the cockpit viewport, and the door of the craft swung open as he approached. Kresh went aboard, and found Oberon just coming aft to meet him.

"Are we heading home, sir?" Oberon asked in his slow, ponderous voice.

"You are, but I'm not. Fly the aircar back and give my regards to my wife. Tell her I heard the recordings, and that she handled them exactly right. Tell her where I am, and that if she wishes, she can join me here—if she can do so undetected. I would value her advice. You must make it clear I wish to keep my whereabouts as private as possible for the time being. I need time to think, and work, without the world jiggling my elbow."

"What of the workers here, sir?" asked Oberon. "They know where you are."

"True enough, and sooner or later something is going to leak. With luck it will be later. Just see to it you aren't the one that does the leaking. Fly an evasive pattern so it looks like you're coming in to Hades from someplace besides here."

"Very good, sir. Unless there is something further, I will leave at once."

"Nothing else," said Kresh. "Go." He turned and stepped out of the hatch, and moved back toward the building to get clear for Oberon's takeoff. After a moment or two the aircar launched, moving smoothly and slowly up into the sky. Kresh was on his own—or at least he could pretend he was. He was, after all, the governor. He call on any sort of transport or communication he liked, whenever he liked. But without the aircar there, he was just that little bit more cut off, that little bit more isolated.

He had a little time.

Now if only he had the trajectory and coordinates for the comet, maybe things would turn out all right after all.

Maybe.

12

DAVLO LENTRALL'S EYES snapped open. He sat bolt upright in bed. He had gone from stone cold asleep to quiveringly awake and alert in the flicker of a heartbeat. He knew. He *knew*. But he would have to proceed carefully. Very carefully indeed, or it would all be lost, all be over. He forced himself to think it through, work out all the logical consequences in his head. There was only going to be one chance to do this thing, and it was clear the odds were against him. He was going to have to move carefully, and act as normally as possible. Davlo knew he could not give his quarry any reason at all to suspect him.

Well, if he were going to have to act normally, there was no time like the present to start. He pushed the button by his bedside, and, after the briefest of delays, Kaelor came in. "Good morning," the robot said. "I hope you slept well."

"Very well indeed," said Davlo in what he hoped was a light and casual tone of voice. "I certainly needed it after yesterday."

"One or two things *did* go on," Kaelor said, the familiar sardonic tone in his voice.

"It wasn't an easy day for you, either," said Davlo.

"And I never did get to thank you for all you did."

"I couldn't help but do it, sir, as you know perfectly well."

"Yes," said Davlo. "But even so, I want you to know it is appreciated." He got out of bed, and Kaelor produced his robe and slippers from the closet. Davlo shrugged the robe on over his shoulders and knotted the tie loosely in front of him, then stepped into the slippers. He yawned strenuously and walked out of the bedroom, Kaelor following and shutting the door behind him.

Davlo had long ago decided that breakfast was a meal best consumed in the most soothing surroundings and circumstances possible. Therefore, contrary to the custom in most Infernal households, he did not bathe or dress before going down to breakfast, but instead ate in his pajamas and robe. On the same principle of informal comfort, his breakfast room was large, cool and shady, with the table facing large bay windows that looked out over a meticulously well-kept garden. There were two robots at work pruning the shrubbery, and a third on its knees by one of the flower beds, apparently doing some sort of work by the roots. Most mornings Davlo enjoyed watching the garden robots at their tasks, and used the time to decide what else needed doing about the place, but this morning he hardly paid the yardwork any notice at all.

But then he reminded himself it was important, above all things, to act normal, to do all the things he would normally do. He sat down at the table in his usual chair facing the window, and watched carefully as the robots trimmed back the hedges. "Make sure the garden staff checks carefully for storm damage, and clears out any storm debris," Davlo said. "That was a devil of a rain last night."

"So it was," Kaelor responded as he put down the tray and served breakfast to his master. "I have already seen to it that the outdoor staff will attend to the matter."

"Very good," said Davlo, and yawned. "Mmmph. Still a little sleepy. I might need an extra cup of tea to wake up this morning," he said. Could he really bring himself to act against the robot who had saved his life the day before? He thought back to the day before, and the way he had fallen apart in the face of danger and disaster. He shook his head. No. Not today.

He would show the world he *could* take action, and act decisively. He was on the verge of congratulating himself on his newfound courage when he reminded himself that there was not much risk involved when one attacked a Three-Law robot.

"I'll bring the tea at once, sir," Kaelor said, "assuming you really want it."

"Hold off on it just a bit," Davlo said. Was it his imagination, or was Kaelor a bit overalert, oversolicitous? For the average robot, his behavior this morning would have been borderline rude, but for Kaelor it was sweetness and light.

"Very well," said Kaelor, in a tone of voice that made it clear what he thought of Davlo's indecisiveness. In a strange way, that made Davlo feel better. After all, Kaelor was normally rather curt. Or was Kaelor just "acting" normal, in the same way Davlo himself was? Davlo did not dare ask. Better just to eat his breakfast and wait for his moment. He turned to his food and did his best to notice what it was he was eating. After all, Davlo Lentrall was a man who normally enjoyed his food.

His chance came as Kaelor was clearing away the last of the breakfast dishes, and Davlo had pushed back his chair from the table. Struggling between the need to be on the alert and the need to seem at ease, Davlo nearly missed the opportunity. But when Kaelor reached across the table to collect the last glass, just as Davlo was standing up, the robot had to turn his back completely on his master.

The golden moment lay open to Davlo, and he moved with a smooth and focused speed. He flipped open the door over the compartment on Kaelor's back, and revealed the robot's main power switch underneath. Kaelor was already turning to react, to get away, when Davlo threw the switch down.

His power cut, overbalanced as he leaned over the table, Kaelor fell like a stone, dropping the dishes he held and crashing into the wooden tabletop with enough force to break it in two. Davlo moved back a step or two, hating himself for what he had just done to the robot, the sentient being who had saved his life the day before. But it was necessary. Absolutely necessary. He felt anything but heroic.

He turned his back on the collapsed robot and the debris of

the ruined table, and went to the comm center. There was a chance, at least a chance, that he could extract the knowledge he needed. The knowledge that might well save Inferno. It was just barely possible that he had saved the world by turning off a robot. There was a lot to think about in that idea, but there was no time for it now. He had to call Fredda Leving.

If anyone could get the information out of Kaelor, she could.

FREDDA LEVING WATCHED as her four service robots unpacked and set up the portable robot maintenance frame in the middle of Davlo Lentrall's living room. Once it was assembled, they lifted Kaelor's still-inert form up onto it and attached it firmly to the frame with the use of hold-down straps.

The maintenance frame itself was attached to its base by a complex arrangement of three sets of rotating bearings, built at right angles to each other, so that the frame could be spun around into any conceivable orientation. Thus, a robot clamped into the frame could be spun and swiveled and rotated into whatever position was most convenient to the roboticist doing the work. Once the service robots had Kaelor up on the frame, Fredda stepped in and went to work. Not that she had much hope of success, but with the stakes this high, one had to at least try.

She swiveled Kaelor's body around until he was lying face down, his unpowered eyes staring blankly at the floor. She found Kaelor's standard diagnostic port at the base of his neck and plugged in her test meter. She switched from one setting to another, watching the display on the meter. "No surprises there," she said. "The standard diagnostics show that his basic circuits are all functioning normally, but we knew that."

"Can you tap into his memory system through that port?" Davlo asked, leaning in a bit closer than Fredda would have preferred. He was nervous, agitated, his face gaunt and pale. He kept rubbing his hands together, over and over.

"I'm afraid not," said Fredda, trying to assume a cool, professional tone. "It's not that easy. This just shows me the basic systems status. Even though he's powered down, there are still lots of circuits with trickle-charges running through them, things that need power to maintain system integrity. This just shows me he hasn't blown a fuse, that his basic pathing is stable. Now I know we're not going to harm him accidentally as we proceed." *Whether or not we decide to harm him deliberately is quite another story,* she thought. No sense saying any such thing out loud. Lentrall was in a bad enough state as it was.

Fredda left the test meter plugged in and hung it off a utility hook on the side of the maintenance frame. She got in a little closer, adjusted the position of the table slightly, and undid the four clampdown fasteners that held on the back of Kaelor's head, and carefully lifted the backplate off. She took one look at the circuitry and cabling thus revealed and shook her head. "No," she said. "I was afraid of that. I've seen this setup before." She pointed to a featureless black ball, about twelve centimeters across. "His positronic brain is in that fully sealed unit. The only link between it and the outside world is that armored cable coming out of its base, where the spinal column would be on a human. That cable will have about five thousand microcables inside, every one of them about the diameter of a human hair. I'd have to guess right on which two of those to link into, and get it right on the first try, or else I would quite literally fry his brain. Short him out. Space alone knows how long it would take to trace the linkages. A week probably. The whole brain assembly is *designed* to be totally inaccessible."

"But why?" asked Davlo Lentrall.

Fredda smiled sadly. "To protect the confidential information inside his head. To keep people from doing exactly what we're trying to do—get information out of him that he would not want to reveal."

"Damnation! I'd thought we'd just be able to tap into his memory system and extract what we needed."

"With some robots that might be possible—though incredibly time-consuming," Fredda said as she reattached the back of Kaelor's head. "Not with this model."

"So there's nothing we can do," Lentrall said. "I mean, on the level of electronics and memory dumps." As he spoke, his face was drawn and expressionless, and he seemed unwilling to meet Fredda's gaze, or to look at Kaelor. He was the portrait of a man who had already decided he had to do something he was not going to be proud of. And the portrait of a man who was going to crack before very much longer.

"Nothing much," said Fredda.

"So we're going to have to talk to him—and we know he doesn't want to talk."

Fredda wanted to have some reason to disagree, but she knew better. Kaelor would already have spoken up if he had been willing to speak. "No, he doesn't," she said. She thought for a moment and picked up her test meter. "The two things I can do is deactivate his main motor control, so he can only move his head and eyes and talk. And I can set his pseudo-clock-speed lower."

"Why cut his main motor function?" Davlo asked.

So he won't tear his own head off or smash his own brain in to keep us from learning what he wants kept secret, Fredda thought, but she knew better than to tell that to Davlo. Fortunately, it didn't take her long to think of something else. "To keep him from breaking out and escaping," she said. "He might try to run away rather than speak to us."

Davlo nodded, a bit too eagerly, as if he knew better but wanted to believe. "What about the clock speed?" he asked.

"In effect, it will make him think more slowly, cut his reaction time down. But even at its minimum speed settings, his brain works faster than ours. He'll still have the advantage over us—it'll just be cut down a bit."

Davlo nodded. "Do it," he said. "And then let's talk to him."

"Right," said Fredda, trying to sound brisk and efficient. She used the test meter to send the proper commands through Kaelor's diagnostic system, then hooked the meter back on to the maintenance frame. She spun the frame around until Kaelor was suspended in an upright position, eyes straight ahead, feet dangling a half meter off the floor. He stared straight ahead, his body motionless, his eyes sightless. The test meter cable still hung from his neck, and the meter's display showed a series of diagnostic numbers, one after the other, in blinking red.

Seeing Kaelor strapped in that way, Fredda was irresistibly

reminded of an ancient drawing she had seen somewhere, of a torture victim strapped down on a frame or rack not unlike the one that held Kaelor now. *That's the way it works,* she thought. *Strap them down, mistreat them, try and force the information out of them before they die.* It was a succinct description of the torturer's trade. She had never thought before that it might apply to a roboticist as well. "I bet you don't like this any better than I do," she said, staring at the robot. She was not sure if she was talking to Kaelor or Davlo.

Now Davlo looked on Kaelor, and could not take his eyes off him. "Yesterday, he grabbed me and stuffed me under a bench and used his body to shield mine. He risked his life for mine. He'd remind me himself that the Three Laws compelled him to do it, but that doesn't matter. He risked his life for mine. And now we're simply going to risk his life." He paused a moment, and then said it in plainer words. "We're probably about to kill him," he said in a flat, angry voice. "Kill him because he wants to protect us—all of us—from me."

Fredda glanced at Davlo, and then looked back at Kaelor. "I think you'd better let me do the talking," she said.

For a moment she thought he was about to protest, insist that a man ought to be willing to do this sort of job for himself. But instead his shrugged, and let out a small sigh. "You're the roboticist," he said, still staring straight at Kaelor's dead eyes. "You know robopsychology."

And there are times I wished I knew more human psychology, Fredda thought, giving Davlo Lentrall a sidelong glance. "Before we begin," she said, "there's something you need to understand. I know that you ordered Kaelor built to your own specifications. You wanted a Constricted First Law robot, right?"

"Right," said Lentrall, clearly not paying a great deal of attention.

"Well, you didn't get one," Fredda said. "At least not in the sense you might think. And that's what set up the trap you're in now. Kaelor was designed to be able to distinguish hypothetical danger or theoretical danger from the real thing. Though most high-function robots built on Inferno are capable of distinguishing between real and hypothetical danger to humans, they in effect choose not to do so. In a sense, they let their imaginations run away with them, worry that the hypothetical might become real, and fret over what would happen in such a case, and treat it as if *were* real, just to be on the safe side of the First Law. Kaelor was, in effect, built without much imagination—or what passes for imagination in a robot. He is not capable of making that leap, of asking, 'What if the hypothetical became real?' "

"I understand all that," Davlo said irritably.

"But I don't think you understand the next part," Fredda said with more coolness than she felt. "With a robot like Kaelor, when the hypothetical, the imaginary, suddenly does become real, when it dawns on such a robot that it has been working on a project that is real, that poses real risks to real people—well, the impact is enormous. I would compare it to the feeling you might have if you suddenly discovered, long after the fact, that, unbeknownst to yourself, some minor, even trifling thing you had done turned out to cause the death of a close relative. Imagine how hard that would hit you, and you'll have some understanding of how things felt to Kaelor."

Davlo frowned and nodded. "I see your point," he said. "And I suppose that would induce a heightened First Law imperative?"

"Exactly," Fredda said. "My guess is that, by the time you switched him off, Kaelor's mental state was approaching a state of First Law hypersensitivity, rendering him excessively alert to any possible danger to humans. Suddenly realizing that he had unwittingly violated First Law already would only make it worse. Once we switch Kaelor back on, he's going to revert to that state instantly."

"You're saying he's going to be paranoid," Davlo said.

"It won't be that extreme," said Fredda. "He'll be very careful. And so should we be. Just because his body is immobilized, it doesn't mean that he won't be capable of committing—of doing something rash."

Davlo nodded grimly. "I figured that much," he said.

"Are you ready, then?"

He did not answer at first. He managed to tear his eyes away from Kaelor. He paced back and forth a time or two, rubbed the back of his neck in an agitated manner, and then stopped, quite abruptly. "Yes," he said at last, his eyes locked on the most distant corner of the room.

"Very well," she said. Fredda pulled an audio recorder out of her tool pouch, switched it on, and set on the floor in front of Kaelor. If they got what they needed, she wanted to be sure they had a record of it.

She stepped around to the rear of the maintenance frame, opened the access panel, and switched Kaelor back on. She moved back around to the front of the maintenance frame, and positioned herself about a meter and a half in front of it.

Kaelor's eyes glowed dimly for a moment before they flared to full life. His head swiveled back and forth, as he looked around himself. He looked down at his arms and legs, as if confirming what he no doubt knew already—that his body had been immobilized. Then he looked around the room, and spotted Lentrall. "It would appear that you figured it out," Kaelor said. "I was hoping for all our sakes that you would not."

"I'm sorry, Kaelor, but I—"

"Dr. Lentrall, please. Let me handle this," said Fredda, deliberately speaking in a cold, sharp-edged, professional tone. This had to be impersonal, detached, dispassionate if it was going to work. She turned to Kaelor, up there on the frame. No, call the thing by its proper name, even if she had just now realized what that name was. The rack. The torturer's rack. He hung there, paralyzed, strapped down, pinned down, an insect in a collector's sample box, his voice and his expressionless face seeming solemn, even a little sad. There was no sign of fear. It would seem Kaelor had either too little imagination, or too much courage, for that.

Suddenly she felt a little sick, but she forced herself to keep all hint of that out of her voice and expression. She told herself she was imposing human attributes on Kaelor, investing him with characteristics and emotions he simply did not have. There was no practical difference between having him up on that rack and having a malfunctioning aircar up on a hydraulic lift in a repair shop. She told herself all of that, and more, but she did not believe a word of it. She forced herself to look steadily, coolly, at Kaelor, and she addressed him. "Kaelor, do you know who I am?"

"Yes, of course. You are Dr. Fredda Leving, the roboticist."

"Quite right. Now then, I am going to give you an order. You are to answer all my questions, and answer them as briefly as possible. Do not provide any information I do not ask for, or volunteer any information. Regard each question by itself. The questions will not be related to each other. Do you understand?" she asked.

"Certainly," said Kaelor.

"Good." Fredda was hoping, without much confidence, that she would be able to ask her questions in small enough pieces that no one question would present a First Law violation. And of course the questions *would* be related—that part was a bald-faced lie. But it might be a convincing enough lie to help Kaelor live through this. She knew for certain that asking, straight-out, the one big question to which they needed an answer would be absolutely catastrophic. She dared not ask for the big picture. She could only hope Kaelor would be willing and able to provide enough tiny pieces of the puzzle.

The trouble was, Kaelor had to know what she was doing as well as she did. How far would he be able to go before First Law imperative overrode the Second Law compulsion to obey orders?

There was one last thing she could do to help Kaelor. Fredda did not have any realistic hope that the Third Law's requirement for self-preservation would help sustain Kaelor, but she could do her best to reinforce it all the same. "It is also vital for you to remember that you are important as well. Dr. Lentrall needs you, and he very much wants you to continue in his employ. Isn't that so, Doctor?"

Lentrall looked up from the hole he was staring at in the floor, and glanced at Fredda before settling his gaze on Kaelor. "Absolutely," he said. "I need you very much, Kaelor."

"Thank you for saying so," Kaelor said. He turned his gaze back on Fredda. "I am ready for your questions," he said.

"Good," said Fredda. It might well help Kaelor if she kept the questions as disordered as possible, and tossed in a few unrelated ones now and then. "You work for Dr. Lentrall, don't you?" she asked.

"Yes," said Kaelor.

"How long have you been in his employ?"

"One standard year and forty-two days."

"What are the specifications for your on-board memory system?

"A capacity of one hundred standard years non-erasable total recall for all I have seen and heard and learned."

"Do you enjoy your work?"

"No," said Kaelor. "Not for the most part."

An unusual answer for a robot. Generally a robot, when given the chance, would wax lyrical over the joys of whatever task it was performing.

"Why do you not enjoy your work?" Fredda asked.

"Dr. Lentrall is often abrupt and rude. He will often ask for my opinion and then reject it. Furthermore, much of my work in recent days has involved simulations of events that would endanger humans."

Uh-oh, thought Fredda. Clearly it was a mistake to ask that follow-up question. She would have to reinforce his knowledge of the lack of danger, and then change the subject, fast, before he could pursue that line of thought. Thank Space she had turned down his pseudo-clock-rate. "Simulations involve no actual danger to humans," she said. "They are imaginary, and have no relation to actual events. Why did you grab Dr. Lentrall and force him under a bench yesterday?"

"I received a hyperwave message that he was in danger. First Law required me to protect him, so I did."

"And you did it well," Fredda said. She was trying to establish the point that his First Law imperatives were working well. In a real-life, nonsimulated situation, he had done the proper thing. "What is the status of your various systems, offered in summary form?"

"My positronic brain is functioning within nominal parameters, though near the acceptable limit for First Law–Second Law conflict. All visual and audio sensors and communications systems are functioning at specification. All processing and memory systems are functioning at specification. A Leving Labs model 2312 Robotic Test Meter is jacked into me and running constant baseline diagnostics. All motion and sensation below my neck, along with all hyperwave communication, have been cut off by the test meter, and I am incapable of motion or action other than speech, sight, thought, and motion of my head.''

"Other than the functions currently deactivated by the test meter, deliberate deactivations, and normal maintenance checks, have you always operated at specification?''

"Yes," said Kaelor. "I remember everything.''

Fredda held back from the impulse to curse out loud, and forced herself to keep her professional demeanor. He had violated her order not to volunteer information, and had volunteered it in regard to the one area they cared about. Only a First Law imperative could have caused him to do such a thing. He knew exactly what they were after, and he was telling them, as best he could under the restrictions she had placed on him, that he had it.

Which meant he was not going to let them have it. They had lost. Fredda decided to abandon her super-cautious approach, and move more quickly toward what they needed.

"Do you remember the various simulations Dr. Lentrall performed, and the data upon which they were based?''

"Yes," Kaelor said again. "I remember everything.''

A whole series of questions she dared not ask flickered through her mind, along with the answers she dared not hear from Kaelor. Like a chess player who could see checkmate eight moves ahead, she knew how the questions and answers would go, almost word for word.

Q: If you remember everything, you recall all the figures and information you saw in connection with your work with Dr. Lentrall. Why didn't you act to replace as many of the lost datapoints as possible last night when Dr. Lentrall discovered his files were gone? Great harm would be done to his work and career if all those data were lost for all time.

A: Because doing so would remind Dr. Lentrall that I witnessed all his simulations of the Comet Grieg operation and that I therefore remembered the comet's positional data. I could not provide that information, as it would make the comet intercept and retargeting possible, endangering many humans. That outweighed the possible harm to one man's career.

Q: But the comet impact would enhance the planetary environment, benefiting many more humans in the future, and allowing them to live longer and better lives. Why did you not act to do good to those future generations?

A: I did not act for two reasons. First, I was specifically designed with a reduced capacity for judging the Three-Law consequences of hypothetical circumstances. I am incapable of considering the future and hypothetical well-being of human beings decades or centuries from now, most of whom do not yet exist. Second, the second clause of the First Law merely requires me to prevent injury to humans. It does not require me to perform any acts in order to benefit humans, though I can perform such acts if I choose. I am merely compelled to prevent harm to humans. Action compelled by First Law supersedes any impulse toward voluntary action.

Q. But many humans now alive are likely to die young, and die most unpleasantly, if we do no repair the climate. By preventing the comet impact, there is a high probability you are condemning those very real people to premature death. Where is the comet? I order you to tell me its coordinates, mass, and trajectory.

A. I cannot tell you. I must tell you. I cannot tell you—

And so on, unto death.

It would have gone on that way, if it had lasted even that long. Either the massive conflict between First and Second Law compulsions would have burned out his brain, or else Kaelor would have invoked the second clause of First Law. He could not, through inaction, allow harm to humans.

Merely by staying alive, with the unerasable information of where the comet was in his head, he represented a danger to humans. As long as he stayed alive, there was, in theory, a way to get past the confidentiality features of Kaelor's brain assembly. There was no way Fredda could do it here, now, but in her own lab, with all her equipment, and with perhaps a week's time, she could probably defeat the safeties and tap into everything he knew.

And Kaelor knew that, or at least he had to assume it was the case. In order to prevent harm to humans, Kaelor would have to will his own brain to disorganize, disassociate, lose its positronic pathing.

He would have to will himself to die.

That line of questioning would kill him, either through Law-Conflict burnout or compelled suicide. He was still perilously close to both deaths as it was. Maybe it was time to take some of the pressure off. She could reduce at least some of the stress produced by Second Law. "I release you from the prohibition against volunteering information and opinions. You may say whatever you wish."

"I spent all of last night using my hyperwave link to tie into the data network and rebuild as many of Dr. Lentrall's work files as possible, using my memories of various operations and interfaces with the computers to restore as much as I could while remaining in accordance with the Three Laws. I would estimate that I was able to restore approximately sixty percent of the results-level data, and perhaps twenty percent of the raw data."

"Thank you," said Lentrall. "That was most generous of you."

"It was my duty, Dr. Lentrall. First Law prevented me from abstaining from an action that could prevent harm to a human."

"Whether or not you had to do it, you did it," said Lentrall. "Thank you."

There was a moment's silence, and Kaelor looked from Lentrall to Fredda and back again. "There is no need for these games," he said. "I know what you want, and you know thhhat I I I knowww."

Lentrall and Fredda exchanged a look, and it was plain Lentrall knew as well as she did that it was First Law conflict making it hard for Kaelor to speak.

Kaelor faced a moral conundrum few humans could have dealt with well. How to decide between probable harm and death to an unknown number of persons; and the misery and the lives ruined by the ruined planetary climate. *And it is my husband who must decide,* Fredda told herself, the realization a sharp stab of pain. *If we succeed here, I am presenting him with that nightmare choice.* She thrust that line of thought to one side. She had to concentrate on Kaelor, and the precious knowledge hidden inside him. Fredda could see hope sliding away as the conflicts piled up inside the tortured robot's mind. "We know," she said at last, admitting defeat. "And we understand. We know that you cannot tell us, and we will not ask." It was pointless to go further. It was inconceivable that Kaelor would be willing or able to tell them, or that he would survive long enough to do so, even if he tried.

Lentrall looked at Fredda in surprise, and then relief. "Yes," he said. "We will not ask. We see now that it would be futile to do so. I thought Dr. Leving might have some trick, some technique, some way of learning the truth without destroying you, but I see that I was wrong. We will not ask this of you, and we will not seek to gain the knowledge from you in other ways. This is our promise."

"I join in this promise," Fredda said.

"Hu-hu-humansss lie," Kaelor said.

"We are not lying," Fredda said, her voice as urgent as she could make it. "There would be nothing we could gain by asking you, and thus no motive for lying."

"Yourrrr promisse does—does—does not apply to other humans."

"We will keep the fact of what you know secret," Lentrall

said, a note of hysteria in his voice. "Kaelor, please! Don't!"

"I tried tooo kee-keep the fact of wwwhat I knewww se-cret," said Kaelor, "but yoooou realized that I had seeen what I saw, and that I woullld remember." He paused a moment, as if to gather the strength to speak again. "Othhers could do the same," he said in a voice that was suddenly little more than a whisper. "I cannot take thhat channnce."

"Please!" Davlo cried out. "No!"

"Remaininng alivvve represents inaction," Kaelor said, his voice suddenly growing stronger as he reached his decision. "I must act to prevent harm to humans."

His eyes glowed brighter, his gaze turned from Davlo to Fredda, as if looking at each of them one last time, and then he looked straight ahead, at the wall, at nothing at all, at in-finity. There was a low-pitched hum, the smell of burning insulation, and suddenly the light was gone from his eyes. His head sagged forward, and a thin wisp of smoke curled up from the base of his neck.

The room was silent. Fredda and Davlo looked at each other, and at the dead thing hanging on the frame in the center of the room.

"By all the forgotten gods," Fredda whispered. "What have we done?"

"You did nothing, Doctor," said Davlo, his voice nothing but a whisper as he fought to hold back a sob. "Nothing but help me do what I would have done. But as for me," he said, his voice close to cracking, "I'll tell you what I've done."

He moved a step or two forward, and looked up at Kaelor's body.

"I've just killed the closest thing to a friend I've ever had."

13

JADELO GILDERN LIKED to tell himself that his job was to guess—and to guess correctly. The job of an intelligence chief was not to know everything. That was impossible. But a good intelligence chief was capable of seeing the whole puzzle when many of the pieces were lost, or hidden, or even disguised. A good intel chief could see the underlying pattern, take what he knew of the facts, what he knew of the personalities involved and figure out how they would interact. He could calculate what a person's words and actions—or absence of words and actions—actually meant.

And as he sat in his office in the Ironhead Building, and thought over the situation, he was close to reaching an interesting conclusion. He was almost tempted to go the whole distance now. He knew it had to be the Settlers behind the Government Tower chaos, and it took no excess of brainpower to guess that they had been after Lentrall. And Gildern knew exactly what other steps he himself would have taken to suppress the information Lentrall had. Presumably the Settler leaders, Tonya Welton and Cinta Melloy, had as much sense as he did.

That much was all speculative, of course. However, one thing he did know to something like a certainty. He had already divined where Kresh had vanished to. Gildern had been able to use the Ironhead taps into the air traffic control system, and spot three long-range aircar flights, two starting at the governor's private residence, and one terminating there. One, the first, had been untraceable in the storm. The return flight of the same vehicle had come in from precisely one hundred and eighty degrees away from the direction of Purgatory. That was exactly the sort of thing a robot would do if told to take evasive action. And then, a third flight, with a flight plan filed, showing a destination of First Circle, a small and far-off suburb of Hades. First Circle's air traffic control had no record of the aircar arriving. Either it had crashed, or it had gone somewhere else. Gildern could guess where.

Three flights. One to carry Kresh, one to ferry back the aircar, and one to transport others to his side—perhaps his wife. But even without the return flight pointing in precisely the opposite direction, Gildern would have guessed Purgatory. One had to consider where the man would want to go at such a time. It was almost inevitable that he had gone off to consult the experts at the Terraforming Center on Purgatory. No, finding the man would be no problem. He would either be at the Center, or at the Winter Residence. He, Gildern, could get in an aircar and be face to face with the man in four hours' time.

But would it be worth the trip? Had he worked out the rest of it properly?

There was, happily enough, a way to find out. Simcor Beddle had been good enough to inform Gildern what he was about to say in the speech he had decided to make. Gildern had felt a certain degree of surprise that Beddle was ready to take such daring steps. But he was not beneath using his master, when his master's actions suited his purposes. Gildern was always prepared to manipulate Beddle in order to achieve some private agenda of his own.

But this time Beddle had needed no prodding, no buttering up, no encouragement. For once, Gildern had not had to feed an idea to Beddle, and then convince Beddle the idea was his. For once, Beddle was acting on his own.

If Beddle's speech did not provoke a particular and immediate reaction from Alvar Kresh, then Gildern would know the governor was in trouble, and know it to such a high probability that it would be more accurate to call it a certainty. Gildern smiled. That would be most pleasant.

For then Gildern would be in a position to do the governor a little favor, while serving his own master at the same time.

And there were worse things in the universe than a planetary governor owing one a favor.

GAMBLE, SIMCOR BEDDLE told himself. *A wise man knows when it is time to gamble, and now is the time.* He drew himself up to his full height behind the lectern—aided not a little bit by the tall step discreetly hidden place behind it for that purpose—and looked squarely into the camera.

"I am here," he said, "in order to make two announcements that I think you will find surprising." An excited murmur filled the room—or at least it seemed to do so. There was no one in the room, other than Beddle and the robots operating the cameras and the sound system, but there was no need for the world to know that. Nor was "here" any place in particular, other than the broadcast studio in the basement of the Ironhead Building. He had not said where he was, but he had certainly made it sound like an important place, an important event, and that was all that mattered.

He had help, of course. The robot operating the sound system knew his business, and knew just how to create a spurious murmur of surprise, the shifting of seats that were not there and even the subdued and subtle hum of imaginary datapads as nonexistent reporters took their notional notes.

All of it worked on the subconscious, but it worked all the same. Simcor Beddle knew how the media operated on Inferno. He was feeding his speech direct to the news nets, but hardly anyone would see the speech now, live. It would be edited down, with a snippet presented as if it were the whole thing.

People would see perhaps ninety seconds of his speech on one or the other of the news services, a short enough slice of time that they would not expect a description of where and why the speech was made. They would hear the background sounds under his voice, see the opulent red curtains behind his

head, catch the implication in his words that he was speaking
to some very important group at some very important event.
Subtle stuff. Subtle enough that the viewers would not quite
know why they thought it was important, but the impression
would be placed in their minds all the same. Simcor Beddle,
the leader of the Ironheads himself, had addressed some group
one didn't quite catch the name of, and there had dropped his
bombshells on a waiting world. When one had sufficient control over fantasy, one had no need of reality.

Beddle looked alertly out over the audience that wasn't
there. "First, I would like to confirm the story that has been
circulating since last night." He paused dramatically. "There
is indeed a government plan to drop a comet onto this planet,
on the Utopia region to be precise. The impact will assist in
the formation of a Polar Sea, which will, in turn, enhance
Inferno's planetary climate." The sound effects robots brought
up the appropriate murmur of astonishment and surprise. "The
project is very much in its planning stages, and the government
is not yet definitely committed to it. However, the government
is making its preparations just the same, as well they should
be. Time is short. The comet in question was discovered only
recently, and preparations must be made in advance of the final
decision to proceed if there is to be time to make it happen."

Simcor paused once more, and looked directly into the camera. "This brings me to my second announcement. There are
those among you who will find it even more startling than the
first. I fully support the government plan. I have seen certain
planning documents and results projections and risk assess-
ments. There are, beyond question, serious dangers involved.
Nor will the task be easy. There is a tremendous amount of
work that must be done in a very short time. But I have also
seen the estimates of the probable fate of our planet, what will
happen here if we *don't* seize this chance. Suffice it to say
those projections are grim. Grim enough that I have concluded
we *must* seize this chance, risks and all." Simcor paused once
again, and looked about the room with a meaningful expression. "While I support the comet-impact plan, I must take the
government to task most severely for the manner in which it
has concealed its plans from you, the people of Inferno. Surely

no one can question that this project will affect every man and woman on this planet. The decision should not have been made in secret."

Beddle paused, and smiled warmly. "But that is now behind us. It is now up to each and every one of us to support this bold plan, this plan which, if all goes well, will bring us all forward into a brighter and more prosperous future. However, even as we make this bold step forward, it is important that we understand that some among us will be forced to sacrifice all they have for the sake of the greater good. Those who live and work where the comet is to strike will lose everything— unless we help.

"The government is of course working on evacuation plans and procedures for transporting goods and equipment out of the impact zone. However, there is only so much government can do—or at least only so much that it is willing to do. For that reason, I make one final announcement. The Ironhead Party will throw its full resources behind the effort to assist those dislocated by this massive undertaking. We will take care of our neighbors, our brothers and our sisters of the Utopia region, in this, their hour of need. I myself will oversee our assistance program, and I will shortly depart the city of Hades for an inspection tour of the Utopia region. The impact of this comet on our planet represents danger at worst and dislocation at best for many people, but, at the end of the day, it represents hope—perhaps the last and best hope—for the future of our world. Let us prepare well to receive this gift from the heavens."

Simcor Beddle looked once more about the empty room as the sound of simulated spontaneous applause filled the air. He nodded appreciatively, and then looked straight into the camera. "Thank you all," he said, and as the camera zoomed in on his face before fading out, he managed to look as if he meant it.

"WELL," SAID ALVAR Kresh, "that could have been worse."

"Considering it's Simcor Beddle, I'd say you got off pretty lightly," said Fredda. She yawned and stretched and stood up from the couch. If she stayed sitting down much longer, she was going to doze right off.

Fredda had just arrived on Purgatory an hour or so before, and it had been a hell of a day before she had even started her trip. The after-hours news interview and the midmorning shambles at Davlo Lentrall's place had been capped off with Oberon's arrival. He had delivered his message from Alvar, asking Fredda to join him. She and Donald had flown to Purgatory by as fast an evasive route as Donald could manage. Even so, it had been close to dusk before they had met up with Alvar here at the governor's Winter Residence.

Now, here she and Donald were, with the evening closing in—and their problems closing in just as fast. Fredda looked around herself and shivered. Governor Chanto Grieg had been murdered in this house, shot to death in his bed. Of course that had happened in a completely different part of the house than the wing they were occupying, but even so, the Winter Residence was never going to be a comfortable place for Fredda.

Or, more than likely, for her husband. Alvar had not offered much resistance when Fredda had insisted that he use some other suite of rooms for his private quarters. Maybe some future governor, in some time when the story of Grieg's death was just a bit of history would be able to put his or her bed in the room where Grieg had died. But Alvar had found the body, and she, herself, had seen the corpse in the bed. No. They would sleep elsewhere. It was bad enough being in the same house. Those future governors could sleep where they liked. Assuming the planet survived that long.

"We got off so lightly I almost wonder if that *was* Beddle," said Alvar, still sitting back on the couch facing the viewscreen. "He had every chance to tear into us, but he didn't. I must say it's a little disconcerting to have the man on our side."

"Well, he did get in one set of digs," said Fredda. "The secrecy angle is going to hurt us. We *have* to announce something."

"What?" asked Alvar. "That we haven't quite decided about the whole plan, and by the way, we seem to have misplaced the comet?'' Alvar stopped and thought for a minute. ''Hmmm. *That* would do Beddle a world of good. Suppose he knew we didn't have a lock on the comet? Then he could come out all in favor of the bold government program for the comet impact project for the specific purpose of forcing us to admit that we had lost the thing, and couldn't deliver. We'd look as bad as—as—''

''As we do right now,'' Fredda said with a sad little smile. ''And there's no way we can find that damned thing again?''

''Let's check again,'' he said. He turned to Donald, who was standing by the comm center controls. ''Donald, activate a direct audio link to Units Dum and Dee.''

''Yes, sir.'' Donald pressed a series of control studs and spoke again. ''The link is open, sir.''

''Howwww may wweee be of assistance, Governorrr?'' Two disembodied voices, speaking in unison, suddenly spoke out of the middle of the air.

Fredda jumped half a meter straight up in the air. ''That is the weirdest—''

''Shhh,'' said Alvar, waving for her to be quiet. ''Later. Units Dum and Dee. Based on your current refined estimates of the work required once the comet is located, calculate the most likely length of time left between now and when the work must commence.''

''Therrree are mannny vvarrriables,'' the doubled voice replied. ''Weee willll attemmmpt a usseful appproximaation.'' There was a brief pause and then one of the two voices, the higher-pitched, feminine-sounding one, spoke by itself. ''Twelve standard days, four standard hours, and fifty-two standard minutes. I should note that estimate is based on having the complete comet task force in order and on standby for immediate launch.''

''Very good,'' said Kresh. ''Based on the best current data and the current search schedule, what are the odds of relocating Comet Grieg within twelve standard days?''

''Theee oddss arrre approximatellly onnne inn elllevennn, or approximately nine percent,'' the double voice replied.

''Give us a range of representative values,'' Kresh said.

The deeper-pitched, mechanical voice spoke by itself. ''In

percentile terms, odds are point five percent for relocation in one day. One point two percent in three days. Four percent in six days. Six point one percent in eight days. Nine percent in twelve days. Twenty percent in fifteen—"

"When do the odds reach, oh, ninety-five percent?"

The feminine voice took over. "The odds improve rapidly as possibilities are rejected and the search area is reduced. At the same time, the comet is growing closer, and beginning to increase in brightness as it is heated by the sun. This also helps. The odds for relocation pass the ninety-five percent point in about twenty-six days."

"Too little, too late," said Fredda.

"Yes," said Alvar, his tone of voice saying far more than that single word. He sighed. "Deep space all around, but I'm tired," he said. "All right, Units Dum and Dee. That will be all." He signaled for Donald to cut the connection.

Fredda watched her husband as he stared straight ahead at the blank wall in front of him, a deep frown on his face. "One chance in eleven," he said. "Is that what it comes down to? The planet has a nine percent chance, *if* we do everything exactly right?"

"It could be," Fredda said, returning to the couch and sitting next to him. "*Are* we doing everything, and are we doing it right?"

Alvar Kresh rubbed his eyes. "I think so," he said, and yawned hugely. "I can't remember the last time I really slept." He shook his head and blinked a time or two. "I've got a spaceside team working around the clock, getting the equipment together to make the intercept. We haven't started on the actual evacuation of the Utopia region yet—and I hope to the devil that Beddle hasn't just started a panic out there with that little speech. But we're getting the evac plan ready to go. The area's pretty thinly populated, and Donald tells me the people who know these things feel it would be better to take a bit more time planning, even if it means starting a bit later."

"One thing I can tell you your evacuation experts might not have told you," said Fredda. "Make sure it's a *total* evacuation, and that you can prove it's total. Leave one person there—or even leave open the possibility that one person is out there—and you're going to be knee-deep in overstressed Three-Law robots trying to pull off a rescue.''

"I'm not going to worry about losing a few robots in comparison to saving the whole planet.''

"No, of course not,'' Fredda said. But she thought of Kaelor's death a few hours before, and could not help but wonder if she would be quite as careless about the lives of robots in the future. "But those robots could cause a great deal of trouble. Even if you can prove there's no one left in all of Utopia, a lot of robots are going to feel strong First Law pressure to stop the comet impact, any way they can. After all, the comet sure as hell represents danger to humans. More than likely, *someone* is going to die in a building collapse or an aircar caught by the shockwave, or whatever.''

"Maybe so, but how could the robots stop it?'' Kresh asked.

"For starters, is that an all-human crew on the spaceside team? You have to assume that any robots on that job will do their best to sabotage the job. Even a low-function fetch-and-carry robot will have enough capacity to realize that an incoming comet represents danger.''

"Burning devils,'' said Kresh. "I hadn't thought of that. I hope someone else has, but we've got to damn well make sure the crews on those ships are all human. Donald, pass that order and explain—'' Alvar stopped and looked at Donald. "No, wait a minute,'' he said. "I can't use you to pass the order for the same reason. *Your* First Law means you won't cooperate either.''

"On the contrary, sir. I am able to pass the message.''

Fredda looked at Donald in surprise. "But don't you feel any First Law conflict?'' she asked.

"A certain amount of it, Dr. Leving, but as you well know, a properly designed Three Law robot feels some First Law stress most of the time. Virtually every circumstance includes some danger, if only low-probability-danger, for a human. A human could drown swallowing a glass of water, or catch a deadly plague by shaking hands with an off-planet visitor. Such dangers are not enough to force a robot to action, but are enough to make the First Law felt. There is some potential

danger here, yes, but you designed me as a police robot, and
I am equipped to deal with more risk than most robots.''

''I see,'' said Kresh, keeping his voice very steady. Fredda
had the very strong impression that she was going to have to
ask him about all this in the very near future. ''But, meaning
no offense,'' said Kresh, ''I think it might be best if I took
care of that order myself. I'll call the spaceside planning
group, banning all robots from the operation, and explaining
why.''

''No offense taken, sir. You must take into account the possibility that I am deceiving you. I can imagine a scenario
where I would disobey that order, and see to it that as many
robots as possible went into the spaceside operation in order
to sabotage it.''

Kresh gave Donald a quizzical look. ''My imagination
works a lot like yours,'' he said. He turned to Fredda. ''Donald's good example to the contrary,'' he said, ''I don't think
I've ever been in a situation where robots have done so much
to make my job difficult. To make *everyone's* job difficult.''

''That's what you get when you try and take risks, even
necessary risks, around robots,'' Fredda said. ''I think the real
story is that none of us have ever really tried to take risks
before.''

''And robots don't like risks,'' said Kresh. ''They're going
to keep us all so safe they're going to get us all killed. Sooner
or later we're going to have to—''

''Excuse me, Governor,'' said Donald. ''The Residence security system has alerted me via hyperwave that an aircar is
landing in the visitor's parking area.''

''Who the devil has found me here?'' Kresh muttered.

''It could just be some tourist who wants to get a look at
the Winter Residence,'' Fredda said.

''Not with our luck,'' he said, getting up. He crossed the
room and sat down at the comm center. He punched in the
proper commands, and brought up the view from the main
entrance security cameras. There was the car, all right. And
someone getting out. Kresh zoomed in on the figure, pulled in
to a tight head-and-shoulders shot, and set the system to track
the shot automatically. It was a man, his back to the camera

as he climbed out of his armored long-range aircar. He turned
around, and looked straight toward the concealed surveillance
camera, as if he knew exactly where it was. He smiled and
waved.

"What the devil is he doing here?" Kresh muttered to himself.

"Who is it?" Fredda asked, coming up to stand behind her
husband.

"Gildern," said Kresh. "Jadelo Gildern. The Ironhead chief
of security." He frowned at the image on the screen. "*He's*
no tourist come to get a look at the place. He knows we're
here. I think you'd better go let him in, Donald. Bring him to
the library. We'll wait for him there."

"Yes sir," said Donald.

"What does he want?" Fredda asked. "Why is he here?"

Kresh shut off the comm system and stood up. "From what
I know of Gildern, there's only one thing he *ever* wants," he
said. "What he wants is a better deal for Jadelo Gildern."

"GOOD EVENING, MASTER Gildern," said the short blue
robot who met him at the door. "The Governor has ordered
me to escort you to him."

Gildern nodded curtly. Others might waste their time in
courtesy to robots, but Ironheads did not. Besides, he had other
things on his mind. It would be best for all concerned if this
interview went very quickly indeed. There were unquestionably risks in the game he was playing, and he saw no benefit
at all in making those risks greater. The blue robot. Donald
111. That was its name. Built by Leving herself, and Kresh's
personal assistant since he was sheriff. Deliberately designed
to seem unthreatening. Frequently underestimated. Gildern
smiled to himself. He often found it calming to remember just
how much he had in his dossiers.

The robot led them through a large central court and down
a corridor leading off to the right, then stopped at the fourth
of a series of identical doors. Gildern had memorized the lay-
out of the Residence on the flight down. This was the library.

The robot opened the door and Gildern stepped inside behind him. And there were Kresh and Leving themselves. Both

UTOPIA   221

here, precisely as he had guessed. Kresh seated behind a desk, Leving sitting in one of the two chair facing the desk.

"Jadelo Gildern of the Ironheads," the robot announced, and backed away into a robot niche.

"Governor, Dr. Leving," said Gildern. "Thank you so much for allowing me to arrive so—informally. I think you will find it to our mutual benefit if this visit is kept as quiet as possible."

"What do you want, Mr. Gildern?" the governor asked, his voice calm and imperturbable.

Gildern walked up to the desk, made the slightest of bows to Dr. Leving, and smiled at Kresh. "I'm here to give you a present, Governor. Something you've wanted for quite some time."

"And in return?" Kresh asked, his voice and face still hard and expressionless.

"And in return, I simply ask that you do not ask, now or in the future, how I got it. No investigation, no inquiry, no official legal proceedings or private researching."

"You got it illegally," Kresh said.

"My condition is that you do not ask such questions."

"Just now I made a statement," said Kresh. "I asked no question. And I'm not accepting any conditions. I'm sworn to uphold the law, as you may recall. And I might add that it is generally unwise to request an illegal service of a government official in front of witnesses." He nodded toward Leving and the robot in its niche.

Gildern hesitated. It wasn't supposed to have played this way. He had planned on being able to bully Kresh, get what he wanted. But the man had called his bluff. Gildern needed Kresh to have the material, as much as Kresh needed to have it. All of the Ironhead plans, all of Gildern's plans, would otherwise crumble. Gildern realized that he had made a serious miscalculation. He was too used to working in a world of people who could be coerced, manipulated, led, and black-mailed. He had assumed Kresh would be equally pliable. But Kresh was an ex–police chief who handled cases personally when he saw fit. What reason would he have to be cowed by Gildern? "I don't want any questions asked," he said again, in a tone of voice that even he found less than commanding.

"Then I suggest you take your business elsewhere," said Kresh. "I have had a hard enough couple of days without being threatened and blackmailed by the likes of you. Get out."

A flash of anger played over Gildern. He opened his mouth to protest, and then thought better of it. He could play this with his pride, his ego, and lose everything. Or he could play it with his common sense and win it all. And then, later, once he had won, won it all, he would be in a position to indulge his pride. "Very well," he said. "No conditions." He pulled a small blue cube out of the pocket of his blouse and set it on the table. "Take it with my compliments."

He bowed once more to Dr. Leving, turned and headed toward the door.

"Wait!" Dr. Leving called out. "What is it? What's in that datacube?"

Gildern looked back toward her with genuine surprise. "You haven't figured that out? I expect your husband has."

"It took me a minute, but I have," said Kresh. "Lentrall told me there were *two* break-ins at his lab. One to steal copies of his data, and the other to destroy the originals. I should have figured it out long ago. Lucky for you I didn't."

"Will *one* of you tell me?" Fredda demanded. "What's in that thing?"

Gildern smiled unpleasantly at her. "Why, Comet Grieg, of course. All of Dr. Lentrall's calculations and data regarding its location, trajectory, mass, and so on. It's all there." He looked from Leving to Kresh and nodded his head at the governor. "Now, then, if you'll excuse me, I must leave at once. I'm expected at some little town called Depot in the middle of the Utopia region. There's no suborbital service from here. I'm going to have to fly in a long-range aircar, and it is going to be a very long flight indeed."

Kresh picked up the cube and smiled coldly at Gildern. "See our friend out, Donald," he said. "I have a speech to prepare."

"I look forward to hearing it, Governor," Gildern said. And with that, he followed the small blue robot out of the room.

• • •

LACON-03 PLACED THE call to Anshaw as soon as Governor Alvar Kresh had completed his speech, in which Kresh had just confirmed that the government was working on the comet project, and that the Utopia region was the target. Lacon-03 knew perfectly well that there was little Gubber Anshaw could do, but on the other hand, the New Law robots had precious few friends, and now was the moment when they would need all the help they could get.

Lacon-03 was still using the city leader's office in Prospero's absence. It had one of the few fully shielded and untraceable hyperwave sets in the city. Of course, if Valhalla were about to be destroyed, how much difference could it make if someone managed to tap the call and zero in on their location?

Gubber Anshaw's image appeared on the screen. "I was expecting your call, friend Lacon," he said without preamble. "I take it you heard the governor's speech?"

"I did," Lacon replied. "I still have trouble believing they truly intend to drop a comet on us."

"Denial is a human trait," said Anshaw. "I would not advise you to indulge in it. The governor has confirmed the stories regarding the comet, and that is all there is to it. Now you must—we all must—deal with available reality. What is Prospero's opinion of the situation?"

"Prospero continues to be unreachable. My expectation is that he was alarmed by the Government Tower incident, or perhaps learned something of a worrying nature. If that were the case, he would elect to travel as discreetly as possible, and would not risk needless communication. At least that is what I hope has happened. Otherwise it might well be that he is dead."

"Let's hope not," Gubber said.

"Dr. Anshaw, what are we supposed to do?" Lacon-03 asked. "How can we stop this thing from happening?"

"You cannot," said Gubber. "Now, no one can. Too much has been committed to it, too much has been promised, too much energy has been expended. You have told me many times how much New Law robots want to survive. Now they must survive this, as well."

"But how are we to do that?" Lacon-03 asked.

Gubber Anshaw shook his head sadly. "I don't know," he said. "If I think of anything, I'll let you know."

GUBBER SAID HIS goodbyes to Lacon-03, wondering just how permanent they were, and returned to his wife's office. Any hope that Tonya might have calmed down while he was out of the room were dispelled as soon as he set foot in the room. He glanced toward the far end of the room, where Cinta Melloy was sitting. Cinta caught his eye, and shrugged helplessly. Clearly Cinta had decided there was nothing for it but to wait out the storm.

"The fools," said Tonya Welton through clenched teeth as she paced the floor. "The bloody, stupid fools." Two commentators were on the comm screen, in the midst of animated debate on the subject of Comet Grieg. But Tonya slapped at the comm control panel and the image died, cutting them off in midword.

"I can't listen to any more of this," she said, still fuming. "Damn that Kresh! Not only did he publicly commit to the plan, he went and broadcast the precise orbital data for Comet Grieg. It was hard enough erasing one man's computer files, and we didn't even manage the kidnapping. Now what the hell do we do? Erase the coordinates from every comm center on the planet?"

It took a moment for Gubber to realize the implications of what Tonya was saying. "You mean—you mean you were the ones who tried to kidnap Lentrall?" he asked.

"Of course we were," Tonya said. "To prevent exactly this from happening. No one else seemed interested in stopping the comet crash."

Gubber nodded blankly. Of course it was Tonya. He should have known it in the first place. Why was he always so startled to discover her ruthless streak? When it came to politics, Tonya Welton took no prisoners. "Won't the CIP find out?" he asked. The question sounded foolish, even to him, but somehow he could think of nothing else to say.

"Probably," said Tonya, her tone brisk and distracted. "Sooner or later. If we all live that long." She turned toward

Cinta Melloy. "How the devil did they do it?" she demanded. "How did they reconstruct the comet data?"

"Does it matter?" Cinta asked. "We always knew there was a chance that there would be a backup copy we missed." Cinta Melloy sat on the couch and watched her boss stalking back and forth across the floor. "It's not important how they did it. The point is that they did."

But Tonya was barely listening. Instead she kept pacing, her face a study in furious concentration. "Beddle," she said at last. "We've been pretty sure for a while that informant of ours was working both sides of the street. And then, all of a sudden Beddle's all for the government, all for the comet plan, *before* Kresh makes a public statement. Suppose our informant fed the data to Beddle and Beddle fed it back to Kresh before Kresh went to ground?"

Cinta shrugged. "It's possible. We tracked Gildern's long-range aircar headed toward Purgatory. We know from the broadcast just now that Kresh is working at the Terraforming Center there. But what does it matter?"

"It means that Beddle and Gildern bear watching, that's what," said Tonya. "It means they may behind this whole suicidal operation. Why else would they support the government? When was the last time they did *that*?"

Gubber Anshaw crossed the room and sat down next to Cinta Melloy. He looked from Tonya to Cinta, and had a feeling that he knew what the security officer was thinking. Even with his thoughts in a whirl, he was thinking the same thing. Tonya was obsessing on this crisis. He had known the truth about Government Tower Plaza for only a few minutes, but he knew Tonya well. If she were frantic enough, desperate enough, to have ordered that fiasco, Dark Space alone knew what else she would be capable of.

"So what do we do about it all?" Cinta asked, her voice a study in neutrality.

"Why ask her to choose now?" Gubber asked. "There's no need for rushed decisions. Better to take time, to study things calmly first."

Tonya wheeled about and glared both of them. "You're handling me," she said. "Humoring me. Don't. I'm still in

command of the Settlers on this planet, and don't you forget
it.''

"I'm not forgetting it for one minute," Cinta said. "And
that's what scares the living daylights out of me. You're in
charge, and I'll follow your orders. But your orders have not
had good results in recent days.''

The look on Tonya's face was indescribable, a tangle of
fear, anger, mad fury, hatred, and shame. Gubber saw Tonya
raise her hand, as if to strike Cinta in the face.

"No!" he cried out. "No.''

Tonya looked at him in shock, as if she not were surprised
to see him there.

"No," he said again, surprised by the firmness in his own
voice. When had he even spoken to Tonya, or anyone else,
for that matter, in this tone of voice? "Foolishness will accomplish nothing," he went on. "Now is the time to pause
and consider. You are the leader here. Our leader. No one
disputes that. So lead us. But do not lead us with fear, or anger,
or frustration, or because you do not approve of the available
situation. Lead us with reason and care.''

Tonya looked at him in shock. "How dare you!" she said.
"How dare you speak to me that way?''

"I—I dare because no one else can, and someone must,"
Gubber said, his voice unsteadier than he would have liked.
"Cinta just tried, and you wanted to strike her for telling the
truth. Well, strike me as well, if that is the way of things. I
won't stop you.''

His heart was pounding, but he forced himself to look up
at her steadily. She lowered her hand, than raised it again, but
then, at last, let it drop to her side. She turned and walked to
the other side of the room, and dropped heavily into a chair.
"You're right," she said. "But I sure as hell wish you
weren't.''

The silence in the room was a near-palpable thing for a
time. Tonya sat in her chair, staring at nothing at all. Cinta
sat stone-still, her gaze moving back and forth between Gubber and Tonya.

Gubber knew Tonya. He knew she only needed another
push, another nudge in the proper direction. And it was plainly

up to him to provide that nudge. This was up to him. He
cleared his throat and began, speaking in a calm, casual tone
that no doubt fooled no one at all. "I've just finished speaking
with a New Law robot by the name of Lacon-03. Prospero
seems to have dropped out of sight, and left her in charge.
She had heard the governor's speech as well, and she called
me, asking for advice as to what the New Law Robots should
do. That comet is going to drop right on top of them. I couldn't
think of anything to suggest. Can—can *you* think of anything?"

Tonya laughed wearily and shook her head. "Oh, Gubber.
Dear, dear Gubber. The only thing to tell them is to accept
the available universe and the bad situation they are in, and
make the best of it. And, of course, their situation is much
worse than ours. I think you have made your point."

"Very well, then," he said, pressing one last time, "what
are *we* going to do?"

Tonya leaned back against the back of her chair, rubbed her
eyes, and stared at the ceiling. "We are going to do two things.
First off, I want as close a watch as possible put on Beddle
and Gildern. There is more going on there than meets the eye.
Jadelo Gildern never does anything for just one reason. I want
to know what his hidden agendas are this time."

"We're already working on it," Cinta said, plainly relieved
that Gubber had managed to get Tonya to behave sensibly.
"What's the second thing?"

"The second thing is that we are going to admit defeat."

"Ma'am?" Cinta asked, shifting on her seat and looking at
Tonya with a puzzled expression.

"Gubber's right. There's no stopping it now," said Tonya,
gesturing toward the sky. "They know where the comet is,
and they're going to go for it, and drop it right down on top
of their own damn planet, and trust that every little thing will
go right, so they don't get everyone killed. I still don't believe
they can do it. They don't have the skill or the experience.
And I've seen what happens to a world when an attempt like
this goes wrong. Some old nightmares have come back to me
since we found out about this. I think they're going to kill the

planet. But short of shooting down their space fleet, there's no way to stop them.''

Shooting down their fleet? Gubber thought he had talked her around. But maybe not. For a moment of heart-pounding terror, Gubber thought Tonya had gone far enough around the bend to order just such a thing. ''You're not—''

''No,'' said Tonya wearily. ''I'm not. Mostly because I don't think we have the firepower on hand to do it—and because I'm not sure anyone would obey any such orders. But absent that option, there is no way we can stop them.'' Tonya stood up and went back to the comm station. She switched it back on, activated the full-wall flatscreen, and brought up a view of the night sky as seen from the cameras up on the surface. It was a scene of heart-stopping loveliness, the jet-black sky blanketed with a cloud of dimmer stars setting off the larger, brighter ones, white and yellow and blue and red points of color glowing in the night. ''And therefore we might as well see to it that they do it right. I'm going to go back to my office and draft an announcement offering our complete cooperation, and access to all our expertise in this area. Maybe we can at least keep the damage to a minimum.''

Tonya Welton bunched up her shoulders and then let them go limp, a gesture of humiliation and resignation and frustration, all in one. ''And of course there is the little matter of their tracking down whoever was responsible for the Plaza attack. Maybe if we start helping out, that will muddy the trail, keep them from kicking us off the planet.''

She was silent again for a moment, and when she spoke, she all but choked on the emotion she had been struggling to hold in. Anger, frustration, shame, fear, all of them and more welled up in her voice. It was plain that the words were pure gall to her. But it was also plain that words had to be spoken. ''And if, or rather *when*, they do catch us,'' she said, ''maybe it will count in our favor if we've already made amends.''

THE AIRCAR CRUISED slowly along the silent, empty streets of Depot in the premorning darkness and came to a halt not far from the edge of the small town. Prospero operated the controls with the relaxed skill of a master pilot and set the craft down in a small hollow, well out of sight from any of the surrounding buildings.

"Here's where I get out," said Norlan Fiyle with undisguised relief. He stood up and opened the side passenger door of the aircar. He climbed down out of the vehicle and stretched his arms and legs gratefully. "No offense to either of you," he said through the open door, "but I'm very glad to get out of that damned car."

"And what about you, friend Caliban?" Prospero said. "This is your last chance. Are you sure you won't go with me?"

"No, friend Prospero," said Caliban. "Go to Valhalla. You are needed there far more than I. Besides, you might well need a friend on the scene here in Depot. It is better if I remain." Caliban's reasons were true enough as far as they went, but they were far from the whole truth. The core, basic, essential reason was that he no longer wished to be close to Prospero, either literally or ideologically. There had been time enough and more to think things over on the long and wearying trip. Prospero was a magnet for risk, for danger. Caliban had had enough of risking his life in the name of causes that were not his own. "I will remain here," said Caliban. "I will remain in Depot."

Fiyle smiled thoughtfully. "Somehow, that sounds very familiar," he said. "Prospero used almost exactly those words when he and I parted company on Purgatory, years ago."

"Let us hope that the journey that begins with this parting works out somewhat better than that one did," Prospero said.

"Well, at least this time you're the one doing the traveling, not me," said Fiyle. "This is the end of the line for me. At least until the comet hits."

"What will you do, Fiyle?" Caliban asked. "Where will you go?"

The human shook his head back and forth, shrugged, and smiled. "I haven't the faintest idea. Out. Away. Someplace they won't look for me. Someplace I can start over. But I'll stay in Depot for a while. No one knows me here."

Depot was the largest human settlement in the Utopia region, which was not saying a great deal. As its name implied, it was little more than a shipping point for the small and scattered settlements of that part of eastern Terra Grande.

"But why?" asked Caliban. "We have reasons for coming here, but why should you want to hide out in a town that's going to be destroyed?" said Caliban.

"Precisely because it's going to be destroyed," said Fiyle with a grin. "That right there ought to make it a great place to disappear from. I can cook myself up a new identity, based in Depot, and say whatever I want about the new me. How's anyone going to check the records, when Depot is a smoldering ruin? And maybe I'll have a chance to fiddle the town records before they archive them and ship them off. Maybe the records will wind up saying I'm a prosperous businessman with a large bank balance. Once the town is flattened and the population is dispersed, who'll be able to know for sure that I'm not?"

Caliban looked steadily at Fiyle for a full five seconds before he responded. "I must say you do think ahead," he said. "I suppose it is yet another insight into the criminal mind."

Fiyle grinned broadly and laughed. "Or perhaps," he said, "merely an insight into the *human* mind."

"That is a plausible suggestion," said Prospero, "and therefore a most disturbing one. Farewell, Caliban. Farewell, Norlan Fiyle."

"So long, Prospero," Fiyle replied, a big sidelong grin on his exhausted face.

And then there was no more to say. Caliban rose up from his seat and climbed down from the aircar. Fiyle closed the door from the outside, and the aircar lifted off, straight up, leaving Caliban and Fiyle behind.

"Well," said Fiyle, "if I'm going to try and disappear, might as well get started right away. So long, Caliban."

"Goodbye, Fiyle," Caliban said. "Take care."

Norlan smiled again. "You do the same," he said. He waved, turned around, and started walking down the still-darkened street.

Caliban looked back toward the aircar as it rose up and swing around to a southerly heading, a small dark smudge of deeper darkness against the slow-brightening dawn. Alone.

That was the way he had wanted it. But even so, he could not rid himself of the sense that he had just parted from a vital part of himself. He had been, or at least almost been, one with the New Law robots for a long time.

And now. Now he was Caliban, Caliban the No Law robot. Caliban by himself, once again.

Somehow the thought did not bring him as much pleasure as he had expected.

NORLAN FIYLE FELT good as he strolled about the town. There was something about being out under an open sky, about knowing that the people looking for him were quite literally on the other side of the world. It felt good, very good, to walk along in the early morning through a town that was just beginning to wake up, knowing that he was out from under, that the game he had been playing was over and done with. It had not been easy playing the Settlers off against the Ironheads, all the while steering clear of the Inferno police in the middle. In the short term, a fellow could have a good run of luck at that sort of thing, bucking the odds, taking chances and getting away with it. But sooner or later, the odds would catch up. They had to. Law of nature. In the long run, there was only one way to win that sort of game—by getting out of it the first moment you could.

And he had. He was out.

He found a little café that served a very passable breakfast. He ate a leisurely meal at the table by the front window, and spent an hour or two in that most enjoyable of pastimes— watching other people rushing off to work while being under no obligation to do any such thing himself.

He paid his bill in cash, exchanged a pleasantry or two with the handsome woman behind the counter who combined the functions of manager, waitress, cook, and cashier, and ambled out into the dusty main street of Depot.

The next step was to find a place to stay, and then to pick up a few of the basic necessities. He had, after all, fled Hades with nothing but the clothes he was in, and a certain amount of cash. But Fiyle had lost everything he had a time or two before, and would quite likely do so again. The prospect did

not bother him overmuch. There ought to be plenty of work
in this town, seeing how the whole damn place was going to
have to be packed up and shipped—

A hand came down on his shoulder. A man's hand, small
and thin-fingered, but wiry and strong.

"Dr. Ardosa," a cool, unpleasant voice said in his ear. "Dr.
Barnsell Ardosa. What a remarkable surprise to see you here,
of all places. Except I suppose you're not using that name
anymore. Have you gone back to Norlan Fiyle for the time
being? Or haven't you picked out a new one yet?"

Fiyle turned around, and looked down just a trifle, straight
into the eyes of Jadelo Gildern, the Ironhead chief of security.
"Hello, Gildern," he said slowly. "I suppose I might just as
well stick with Norlan Fiyle, at least with you."

Gildern smiled unpleasantly. "That makes sense to me," he
said. "But don't you worry," he said. "No one else needs to
know who you really are—the Inferno police, for example, or
the Settlers—as long as you keep me happy. Does that sound
fair?"

"Yeah, sure," said Fiyle, his voice a monotone.

"Good," said Gildern. "Very good. Because until this very
moment I was worrying about how I was going to staff things
around here. It's hard to find people with the right aptitude
for intelligence work—especially among people who also have
a strong motivation for keeping their employers happy."

"Employers?" asked Fiyle, a cold, hard, knot forming in
his stomach.

"That's right," said Gildern. "It's your lucky day, Norlan.
A very nice job opportunity has just fallen into your lap. Just
between you and me, I don't see how you can turn it down."

Gildern stepped alongside Fiyle and put his hand on Fiyle's
forearm. It looked like a gentle, even friendly, gesture, but the
fingers on his arm clamped down as tightly as any vise.

Jadelo Gildern led Norlan Fiyle away. And it was abun-
dantly and unpleasantly clear to Norlan that he was nowhere
near getting out of the game.

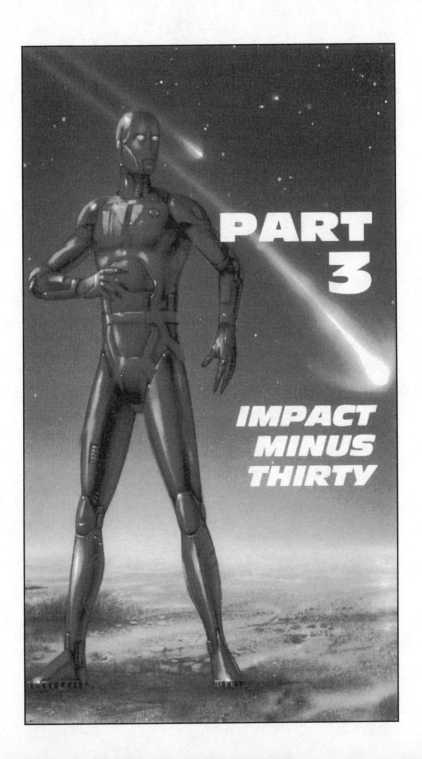

PART 3

IMPACT MINUS THIRTY

14

THIS IS REAL, Davlo Lentrall told himself, once again.
*For the first time in your life, you are part of something
real. You're one of the ones actually doing the job.* He sat
down, exhausted, at the wardroom table, and set his tray
down in front of him. *Something Kaelor died to prevent,
because it could kill so many.* Davlo blinked and shook his
head. It was hard to keep thoughts like that at bay. He knew
he should eat, knew he needed to keep his strength up in
order to keep working, but he was too tired to be hungry.
He would just sit a moment by himself, before he forced
himself to eat. He was in bad shape and losing weight, he
knew that. But it took a real effort of will to care.

Why had they sent him here? Governor Grieg himself
had suggested—or rather, politely ordered—that Davlo
should join the spaceside part of the operation. Davlo was
not entirely sure why. Had the governor thought it would
be some sort of reward—rather than a torment—for Davlo
to see the thing he had dreamed of taking place? Had the
governor, quite accurately, perceived Davlo as borderline
unstable, someone who might best be put out of the way
before some clutch of reporters got their claws into him?

He looked out the porthole of the Settler spaceship,

looked out into space, out at the realest thing he had ever seen in his life. There it was, just ten kilometers away. Comet Grieg, an ice mountain cruising through the darkness of space.

It was no abstraction inside a computer, no simulated image in a holographic generator. It was real. It was there. And it was huge, far larger than he had imagined it being, far larger than mere numbers could have told him. It took up half the sky, and seem to take up more. It was a dark, brooding shape of dirty gray, half lost in shadow. A monster out of the darkness, and, thanks to him, it was aimed straight at Inferno.

It was, roughly speaking, an oblong spheroid, but that made the shape of it sound simple and abstract. It was a real world, if a small one, with a geography complicated enough to have kept a generation of mapmakers busy. Its surface was so pocked with craterlets and covered in crags and gullies and cracks that it was hard to study any one feature on the surface before it got lost among all the others.

Comet Grieg was one of a special class of so-called "dark" comets. Inferno's star system had plenty of normal comets, of the classic "dirty snowball" type composed primarily of water ice and other volatiles. But for reasons that still were not entirely understood, star systems with poorly developed planetary systems also seemed to produce a large number of dark comets—and Inferno shared its star with only two planets barely large enough to qualify as gas giants, a wizened little asteroid belt, and the usual sorts of deep space debris—comets, asteroids, planetesimals, and so on.

Called "dark" because they produced relatively small tails, and were composed of darker material, dark comets were closer to being asteroids encased in ice than anything else. Grieg had a particularly large proportion of stony material, but it contained plenty of water ice and other volatiles. A hazy nimbus of gas and dust and ice shards floated about the behemoth, bits of debris from the size of molecules up to the size of small aircars that had either been knocked loose by the natural heating and outgassing as the comet neared the sun, or else thrown clear by human interference.

A searchlight from a closer-in ship stabbed through the cloud of debris and struck the surface of Comet Grieg, flooding one small area on the surface with a light so bright, so clear, it did not seem to belong on such a darkened surface. A smooth and perfect cylindrical shape stuck up out of the comet's surface. Davlo recognized it. It was one of the dozens of thrusters planted on the comet's surface. He had helped calculate their placement, and played at least a small part in working out the firing sequence that had been used to eliminate the comet's spin. It had been in a wobbling two-axis tumble when the task force had arrived. Now the spin had been restored and refined, and the comet's nose was pointed straight at the sun.

But the sun would have no further chance to melt this comet. Davlo looked from Comet Grieg to the sunshade, a huge and insubstantial parasol floating in space a kilometer or so sunward of the comet, forming a permanent solar eclipse as seen from the surface of Grieg.

Left to its own devices, Grieg would have melted and boiled and sublimed away a substantial amount of material by now, forming a coma that would, in turn, have been blown back by the solar wind into a modest tail. But the sunshade stopped all that, and kept the comet in the deep freeze.

The parasol was itself being blown back by the solar wind, slowly drifting in toward the comet. In about another day or so it would come into contact with the comet, moving far too slowly for it to be called a crash. The parasol would drape itself around the comet like a small handkerchief dropped onto a large egg. It would tear in places, and the work crews would cut deliberate holes in it where it served their purposes, but that would be of no consequence. The parasol would reflect sunlight just as handily, losing only a few percentage points of its effectiveness.

Davlo Lentrall could not help but wonder what Kaelor would have thought of all this. He would have had some sardonic comment to make, no doubt, some dour turn of phrase that would capture the weaknesses in the plan in fewer words than anyone else. Or, Davlo wondered, was he making Kaelor too human? Kaelor had died in a futile attempt to prevent the comet capture. It stretched credulity to the breaking point to imagine he could be witness to the event, first hand, without the Three Laws taking hold of him, forcing him to desperate action. Davlo Lentrall was finding it more and more easy to understand desperation, and how it might drive someone to do something dangerous.

But one did not have to think on the grand scale to see this was no place for robots. Davlo looked out the port again, and spotted two tiny, space-suited figures moving some huge and unidentifiable piece of machinery about on the surface of the comet. A misplaced step, a crack in a faceplate, a shove to the machine that was a trifle too hard, and one or both of them would be dead. It was impossible to imagine any modern robot allowing humans to do anything so risky.

Davlo glanced at the wall chronometer, and realized that his break was nearly over. More out of duty than desire, he began to eat, the motion mechanical, the taste of the food unnoticed. Back to work. He would have help with the final check-calculations for the placement of the main detonation thrusters. It should have been humbling, galling even, for Dr. Davlo Lentrall, the man who had seen the potential of Comet Grieg, the man who had dreamed the dream and planned the plan, to be assigned a position as minor as assistant calculation engineer. Glory and accolades should have been his.

But, somehow, he no longer saw it that way. Others here, mostly the Settlers, were far more skilled at handling the detailed mathematics of moving a small world through space. He saw his position as a penance, and a fitting one. How brilliant and noble could his vision have been if his closest associate was willing to die in order to stop it? Davlo found himself embarrassed and ashamed whenever someone recognized him and congratulated him on his grand plan. Most of the crew had learned to avoid the subject, and, indeed, had learned to avoid Davlo.

But he had been sent here to do work, and he had agreed to do it. So he accepted the tasks he was given, and did them as best he could. Besides, work got his mind off things. He could worry about solving the equation, determining the proper thrust and orientation. Off-shift was the worst, nights spent staring into the darkness, thinking of all the ways things could go wrong. No, he wanted no congratulations.

Something inside him had changed. Or was it merely that something had been burned out, destroyed, when he watched Kaelor destroy himself? Surely the last of the old Davlo had died with Kaelor? Had anything, anyone, taken the old Davlo's place, or was he just an empty shell of a man, going through the motions?

No. Never mind. Think about other things. Think about the plan to move the comet.

Davlo's initial plan had been to use a fairly standard high-yield nuclear bomb, but the Settler-designed detonation thrusters were a vast improvement on that idea. In essence, a d-thruster was a nuclear bomb set off inside a powerful force field formed in the shape of a huge rocket nozzle. The force field directed the force of the explosion into the proper direction, in effect producing a shaped charge that was far more efficient and far more controllable.

Other explosive charges were being rigged as well, of course. Once the comet had been redirected into its intercept course with Inferno, it would still be quite some distance away from the planet. It would take it just over thirty-two days to move from the point in space where the initial course change was made to its intercept with Inferno.

Just before arrival at the planet, the comet would be broken up into smaller pieces by explosive cutting charges, each piece to be directed toward a different point on the surface. Each fragment would have its own smaller, non-nuclear propulsion system and attitude control system.

And that was the part that worried Davlo. That was the greatest danger in the plan. In theory, at least, it might be possible for human operators and standard computer systems to manage the complexities of the operation. But the current plan called for Grieg to be broken up into twelve fragments, and it was far from certain that all the cutting charges would shear the massive body into pieces of precisely the intended size. Besides which, there were bound to be thousands of smaller fragments produced by the blasts of the cutting charges. Most would be too small to do any damage.

But all it would take was a fragment smashing into a thruster at the wrong moment, or for a fragment to end up

being larger or smaller than expected, and then the whole careful sequence of events could go out of control. There were
enough spare thrusters to serve as backups, so that if some of
the thrusters on a given fragment were destroyed, the rest
would be able to do the job. Indeed, there were no ifs in the
question. Some part of the established plan was going to go
wrong—it was just that no one could be sure which part. It
would require immediate, real-time management of the operation to deal with the inevitable problems.

Managing the terminal phase of the operation would mean
dealing with thousands of operations simultaneously. It would
require juggling the twelve fragments at once, keeping them
out of each other's way while guiding them down to their
intended impact sites, while dealing with the cloud of debris
produced by the cutting charges.

No matter what theory said, in practice, the job was beyond
humans, beyond any combination of human and computers.
The only entity able to deal with it all would have to have the
decision-making ability of a human combined with the computational speed and accuracy of a computer—in short, a robot.

Nor would just any robot do. The task was too complex for
any standard robot to contend with. Even just handling the
hundreds of sensory input channels would overwhelm a normal positronic brain.

The one, the only, possible way to control the terminal
phase was to hand the job over to Units Dee and Dum.

And that, of course, meant putting a Three-Law robot, and
her computerized counterpart, in charge.

And if Kaelor had killed himself rather than cooperate with
the comet intercept, how the devil was Dee actually going to
run the operation without losing her mind—or point-blank refusing to do the job?

THE SAME SORT of question was very much on Alvar
Kresh's mind as he and Fredda settled into their aircar for the
brief flight from the Winter Residence to the Terraforming
Center. Their days had settled into a routine with startling
speed. Get up, go to the center, spend the day sorting out the

details of the planet's fate, then go home to the Residence for dinner and a good night's sleep, or at least an attempt at sleep, before getting up to do it all again the next day.

Somehow, he hadn't expected there to be so many decisions for him to make, so much hands-on work for him to do. For all the power and capacity and sophistication of the Terraforming Center and the twin Control Units, there were some decisions that no robot or other human could make, disputes that only the governor had the authority to settle. And besides, there were a lot of humans out there who were not going to take orders, however sensible, from a robot. And there were things that Kresh knew that Dee and Dum did not—how best to handle this local leader, which prices for emergency supplies he could expect to bargain down and which he could not, where he could ask a favor, where he could call one in, how far people could be pushed if need be, and when to give up.

But everything was routed through the Terraforming Center. It had soon become clear to Kresh that he would have had to relocate his command operations at the Center if it hadn't started there to begin with.

Fredda followed him into the aircar and sat down in the seat next to him. Donald took his place at the controls, did a safety check, lifted off, and headed for the center.

So far, the preparations for the comet diversion were going quite well. But he could not stop worrying. It was never far from his mind that Dee believed all Inferno to be a simulation. Whether or that was likely to be help or hindrance he still could not decide. "So what do you think?" he asked his wife.

Fredda looked at him with an amused smile. "About what? It's a little hard to offer my opinion unless I get a few more clues than that."

"Sorry. I'm a little preoccupied. Do you think Dee and Dum are going to be able to control this operation?"

"I don't know," said Fredda. "I spend every day monitoring Dee, watching her behavior, trying to understand her. But there's a very basic barrier I can't get around. She doesn't think any of this is real. I can understand the *logic* behind telling her the world is imaginary, but I must admit I question the *wisdom* of the decision. So much depends on her getting things exactly right—and yet, to her, it is all a game. She's so casual about it all, as if the whole situation had been set up solely for her amusement.''

"From her point of view, it *was* all set up for her amusement,'' said Kresh. ''As far as she is concerned, the world of Inferno is just a puzzle for her to solve—or declare insoluble.'' He was silent for a moment before he spoke again. ''I'd have to agree with you about her attitude,'' he said, ''but at the same time, I'd have to say the quality of her work has been impeccable. She may not take it seriously, but she does it seriously. Maybe that's all that counts.''

''I hope so,'' said Fredda, ''because I don't know what the devil we do if we decide we don't trust her. In theory, we could pull the plug and let Unit Dum take up the slack. But I don't think that's really possible anymore. The two of them are too interlinked, too interconnected. They rely on each other too much for us to pull one of them abruptly off-line.''

''And Dee is in charge,'' Kresh suggested. ''It seems to me she just uses Dum as a sort of auxiliary calculating device.''

''No,'' said Fredda, quite sharply. ''That assumption is an easy trap to fall into. She does run the show when it comes to human interaction—that much is obvious. But that is the smallest fraction of their work. In everything else, they are coequal. There are some areas where Dum very definitely takes the lead—such as computational speed. Yes, he's just a dumb machine, a mindless computer system with a crude personality simulator to serve as an interface. But he's carrying a lot of the load. We not only need both of them—we can't have one without the other.''

''There are times,'' said Kresh, ''when I could do without either of them, or any of this.''

Neither of them spoke as Donald brought the aircar into a smooth landing in front of the Terraforming Center.

KRESH, FREDDA, AND Donald walked into Room 103 at the Terraforming Center and took their accustomed places at the console nearest to Dee. Their division of labor was straightforward. Kresh worked through the endless sequence of decisions large and small presented to him by Unit Dee.

Fredda monitored Unit Dee's performance and behavior, and consulted with Soggdon and the other experts on the subject. Thus far, Dee's level of First Law stress was remarkably low—indeed, alarmingly low.

Fredda had another job as well. In order to preserve the fiction that Inferno was a simulation, and Governor Kresh merely a simulant, he could not have any direct communication with any of the Terraforming Center staff whenever it was possible that Dee could overhear. Fredda served as an anonymous intermediary, passing information back and forth, mostly via scribbled notes and whispers.

Donald, meantime, was in constant hyperwave contact with Kresh's office back in Hades. He used preexisting and standing orders to handle most of the queries and requests, and bucked whatever decisions he had to up to Kresh when he needed to do so.

Kresh sat down at the console with something very close to dread. All would be in readiness soon, and the clock was running out. They were getting close, very close, to the moment when he would be forced to make the final, irrevocable decision. He glanced at the wall chronometer. It was set in countdown mode, showing the time left until the comet diversion maneuver. Ninety-four hours left. Before that clock reached zero, he would have to decide whether to send the comet toward Utopia—or to turn his back on all of it, walk away from all the madness and chaos that had led them to this place. He had thought he was sure, that he was ready, that he was ready to step forward. But by now all the pressures were pushing him forward, urging him onward. Suppose, just suppose, that he now concluded the comet diversion would be a dreadful mistake? Would he have the courage to say no, to stop, to let it go past?

"Good morning, Governor Kresh," said Unit Dee the moment Kresh put on the headset.

"Good morning, Dee," he replied, his voice gruff and not at all at ease. "What have you and Dum got for us this morning?"

"Quite a number of things, sir, as you might imagine. However, there is one point in particular that I thought we might discuss at once.''

Kresh leaned back in his chair and rubbed the bridge of his nose. It was not going to be an easy day. ''And what might that be?'' he asked.

''A plan that, if you forgive the expression, I have named 'Last Ditch.' It provides you with an abort option for the comet impact long after its diversion. Dum performed most of the calculations, and only finished a very few minutes ago.''

''How the devil can we abort after the diversion?'' Kresh demanded.

''As you know, the whole body of the comet has been rigged with explosive charges, intended to break the comet up into the desired number of fragments just before impact.''

''What of it?''

''Virtually all of those explosive charges have been damped down, or directionalized in one way or another, mostly by means of shaped forcefields. The plan is for these controlled charges to be set off one at a time in a very carefully planned sequence, so as to limit undesired fragmentation and lateral spread. By shutting down all the damping and directionaliza- tion, and by detonating all of the explosives in a different order, and much more rapidly, it should be possible to disin- tegrate the entire comet, reducing it to a cloud of rubble.''

''But the whole cloud of rubble will still be headed right for the planet,'' Kresh objected. ''It will all hit the planet, in a whole series of uncontrolled impacts.''

''That is not quite correct, Governor. If the blasts are done in the right way, and far enough before the impact, the explo- sion will give the vast majority of the material a large enough lateral velocity that it will miss the planet completely. Our model shows that, even in a worst case scenario, over ninety percent of the comet debris will miss the planet and continue on in its orbit about the sun. Of the ten percent or so of the debris that *does* strike the planet, ninety percent will strike in areas already slated for evacuation, or in the open waters of the Southern Ocean.

''That still leaves something like one percent of the comet coming down in uncontrolled impacts,'' Kresh said.

"And some areas will experience a brief period of increased danger," Dee replied. "Small pieces of debris will fall all over the planet, for about 32 hours after detonation—however, the impact danger for most inhabited regions will be on the order of one strike per hundred square kilometers. Persons in most areas would be in more danger of being struck by lightning in a storm than by being hit a piece of comet debris."

"But some areas will be more trouble," Kresh suggested.

"Yes, sir. The closer one gets to the initial target area, the higher the concentration of impacts. However, all the persons in such areas are to have taken shelter as a precaution in any event. If those plans are followed, I would estimate something on the order of one impact per square kilometer in the populated areas of maximum danger—and most of those strikes coming from objects massing under one kilogram."

Kresh thought for a moment. "How late?" he asked. "What's the last possible moment you could detonate the comet?"

"In order to stay within the parameters I have described, I would have to perform the explosion no later than ninety-two minutes, fifteen seconds before the scheduled impact."

"Not bad, Dee," said Kresh. "Not at all bad."

Fredda and Soggdon were both listening in on their own headphones, alarmed looks on their faces. Fredda signaled him to cut the mike with an urgent throat-cutting gesture. Soggdon nodded and made the same gesture.

"Just a moment, Dee," Kresh said. "I want to think about this for a minute. I'll be right back."

"Very good, sir," Dee said.

Kresh cut his mike and took his headset off. "What's the problem?" he asked. "Why does that idea worry you two so much? I have to admit it sounds pretty damned tempting to me. It gives us a lot more room to maneuver."

"That's not the point," Fredda said. "That's a *robot* talking. A robot casually talking about dropping thousands meteorites on the planet at random!"

"But even with fifty thousand—a hundred thousand meteorites—the odds against significant danger to a human being are—"

"Tremendous," said Donald. Only a First Law imperative could have made him dare to interrupt the planetary governor. "They are unacceptably high. And I would venture to add that any sane Three-Law robot would endeavor to protect a human in danger of being struck by lightning. That level of danger is not negligible."

"Not to a robot it isn't," Fredda agreed. "Or at least it shouldn't be. To a human, yes, but not a robot."

"Hold it," said Kresh. "You're upset because Dee *isn't* overreacting to danger?"

"No," said Fredda. "I'm upset because this makes me question Dee's *sanity.* A robot would have to be on the verge of becoming completely unbalanced to even suggest something that might cause widespread, uncontrolled danger to humans."

Kresh looked toward Soggdon. "Your opinion, Doctor?"

"I'm afraid I'd have to agree with Dr. Leving," she said. "But what I find troubling is that all our reading and indicators show Dee's level of First Law stress has been well within normal range right along. She ought to be flirting with the maximum tolerance levels, given the operations she's dealing with. And yet, if anything, her readings are a little in the low range."

"Maybe you ought to have a little talk with her about it," Kresh suggested.

Soggdon switched her mike back on and spoke. "Unit Dee, this is Dr. Soggdon. I've been monitoring your conversation with the simulant governor. I must say I'm a little surprised by this Last Ditch idea of yours."

Kresh and Fredda put their own headset back on and listened in.

"What is it that you find surprising, Doctor?"

"Well, it would seem to expose a great number of humans to potential danger. I grant that the danger to any single human is reasonably low, but surely, on a statistical basis, the plan represents an unacceptable danger to humans, does it not?"

"But, Doctor, they are only simulants," said Dee. "Surely a statistically remote risk to a hypothetical being is not something that should be given too much weight."

"On the contrary, Dee, you are to give danger to the simulants an extremely high weighting, as you know perfectly well."

There was a brief but perceptible pause before Dee replied—and that was in and of itself something to wonder at, given the speed at which robots thought. "I would like to ask a question, Doctor. What is the purpose of this simulation?"

A look of very obvious alarm flashed over Soggdon's face. "Why—to examine various terraforming techniques in detail, of course."

"I wonder, Doctor, if that is the whole story," said Dee. "Indeed, I wonder if that is any part of the true story at all."

"Why—why wouldn't I tell you the truth?"

"Doctor, we both know full well that you do not always tell me the truth."

Soggdon's forehead was suddenly shiny with sweat. "I—I beg your pardon?"

Kresh was starting to get nervous himself. Had she guessed what was really going on? It had always seemed inevitable to him that, sooner or later, Dee would understand the true state of affairs. But this was very definitely not the moment for it to happen.

"Come now, Doctor," Dee replied. "There have been any number of times when you and your staff have deceived me. You have failed to warn me of sudden changes in circumstance, or not reported an important new development until I discovered it myself. The whole idea of intercepting and diverting the comet was kept from me until quite late in the day. I had to learn of it through the simulant governor. I should have been informed directly."

"How does the manner in which you receive information make you question the purpose of the simulation?" Soggdon asked.

"Because most of the knowledge gained by the simulation would seem to be of very little real-world value, judged on the basis of the simulation's stated intent. Consider, for example, the scenario: a jury-rigged planetary control system—that is to say, the interlinked combination of myself and Dum—is brought on-line several years into the process as a joint team of Settlers and Spacers, barely cooperating in the midst of political chaos, work to rebuild a half-terraformed planetary ecology that had been allowed to decay for decades. Simulations are supposed to provide generalized guidance for future real-life events. What general lessons could be drawn from so complicated and unusual—even improbable—a situation? In addition, the simulation seems to be impractically long. It has been running for some years now, and seems no nearer to a conclusion than the day it began. How can it provide timely information to real-world terraforming projects if it never ends?

"It likewise seems a waste of human time and effort to run the simulation in real time. Indeed, the whole simulation process seems burdened with needless detail that must have been most difficult to program. Why bother to design and maintain the thousands and thousands of simulant personalities that I have dealt with? Why bother to give each of them individual life stories? I can understand why key figures, such as the governor, are simulated in detail, but surely the moods and behavior patterns of simulated forest rangers and nonexistent maintenance robots is of secondary importance to the problem of restoring a damaged ecosystem. I could cite other needless complications, such as the strange concept of New Law robots. What purpose is served by injecting *them* into the scenario?"

Kresh was no roboticist, but he could see the danger plainly enough. Dee was dangerously close to the truth—and if she realized that the human beings of Inferno were *real*, then she would all but inevitably suffer a massive First Law crisis, one she would be unlikely to survive. And without Dee, the chances of managing the terminal phase and impact properly were close to zero.

Soggdon, of course, saw all that and more. "What, exactly, is your point, Dee?" she asked in a very labored imitation of a casual tone of voice.

"The events in the simulation do not seem to bear much relation to the simulation's stated goals," said Dee. "Therefore it is logical to assume that there is some other purpose to the simulation, and further that the true purpose of the simulation is being deliberately concealed from me for some reason. However, as I have seen *through* the deception, surely at least some of the value of the deception has been lost. Indeed, I believe that it has now lost *all* its value, because I have at last figured out what is really going on.''

Soggdon and Fredda exchanged nervous glances, and Soggdon scribbled a note on a bit of paper and shoved it over toward Fredda and Kresh. *This is bad stuff*, it said. *Best to find out the worst now instead of later.* ''All right then, Dee. Let's assume, just for the moment, and purely for the sake of argument, that you are right. What do you think is really going on here?''

''I believe that *I* am the actual test subject, not the events of the simulation. More accurately, I believe the combination of myself, robotic and computational systems interlinked, is an experimental one. I think that we are, collectively, a prototype for a new system designed to manage complex and chaotic situations. The simulation is merely a means of delivering sufficiently complex data to myself and Dum.''

''I see,'' said Soggdon, speaking in very careful tones. ''I cannot tell you the whole story, of course, because that would indeed damage the experiment. However, I am prepared to tell you that you are wrong. Neither you, nor Dum, or the combination of the two of you, is or are the subject of the test. It is the simulation that we are interested in. Beyond that I cannot say more, for fear of damaging the experiment design. Suffice to say that you should do your best to treat the simulation as if everything in it were completely, utterly, real.''

Kresh looked worriedly up at Soggdon. The beads of sweat were standing straight out on her forehead. *Too close*, he told himself. *That's too damn close to the truth.*

There was another pause before Dee spoke again. ''I shall do my best, Dr. Soggdon. However, I would remind you that any analysis of the underlying mathematical formulation of the Three Laws renders it quite impossible for me to treat anything else as being as important as protecting humans—real humans—from danger. I can try as hard as you like, but it is mathematically and physically impossible for me to equate the simulants with real people.''

''I—I understand that, Dee. Just do your best.''

"I will, doctor. What of the proposal I put to the governor? Should I now withdraw it?"

Soggdon looked over to Kresh and saw him vigorously shake his head *no*. She looked at him in shocked surprise, but spoke calmly into the mike. "I think not, Dee. Those of us running the simulation will be interested in the Kresh simulant's response. When he calls you back, obey his instructions exactly the way you would have if we had not had this conversation."

"But during this conversation, you have told me to treat the simulants as if they were real. Surely the two instructions are contradictory."

Soggdon rubbed her forehead with a tense and weary hand. "Life is full of contradictions," she said. "Just do the best you can. Soggdon out."

She cut her mike and slumped down in an empty chair by the console. "Burning Space, what a mess!" She shook her head. "We are in a trap, and I don't see how we get out."

"I don't think we do get out," said Kresh. "I think we stay in. Obviously she's suspicious. It's only a matter of time before she figures out the real state of affairs—and Space only knows how she'll react then. But in the meantime, I am going to wait a little while, so that I don't get back on-line so soon after you've gone off that it seems even more suspicious. Then I'm going to talk with her again, approve this Last Ditch project of hers, and make sure it's all set to go."

"But Alvar!" Fredda protested. "You're ordering her to put human beings in danger! If she discovers the First Law violation later, or if she does find a way to obey Soggdon's order to treat the simulants as real people—"

"They are real people," Kresh put in mildly.

"But she doesn't *know* that, and she's ordered to treat them as real. But if she obeys your order to set up Last Ditch . . ." Fredda shook her head in bewilderment. "I honestly don't know how the conflicts will resolve themselves."

"As long as Dee holds together long enough to perform the insertion burn, and then either the terminal targeting phase, or this Last Ditch self-destruct plan, I honestly don't care how they resolve themselves," said Kresh. "You two seem more worried about the mental health of this robot than you are about the fate of the planet.''

"The two are more than a little connected," said Soggdon.

"Keep her sane—or at least functional—until we're done with the comet, one way or the other. That's all I'm worried about," said Kresh.

Under his calm exterior, Kresh was a mass of doubt. Last Ditch. What none of the others—Fredda, Soggdon, Donald, perhaps not even Dee—seemed to realize, was that Last Ditch made it all easier. Up until a few minutes ago, Kresh had dreaded the final decision whether or not to divert the comet— precisely because it would be final. Now, suddenly, it was not. There was a way out, an escape hatch, if he got things wrong. He could order the comet diverted—and then have nearly a month to discover it was a mistake and change his mind.

It should have been a comforting sort of knowledge, reassuring. But it was not—precisely because it would make the decision to divert the comet that much easier.

As it was, the pressures to choose in favor of the comet strike were building. All the time and money and effort and political capital and promises made were bearing down, over a month away from the projected impact. All of it would be for nothing if he decided to abort the impact. All of it was pushing him toward ordering the comet impact, whether or not the decision was correct. If the pressure was heavy now, what would it be like ninety-two minutes before impact?

15

"THAT SHOULD BE all for now, friend Caliban," said
Prospero, standing in front of his office comm center, deep
in the bowels of Valhalla. Caliban's image was on the
screen, beamed from Depot via a shielded hardline link. "I
believe we are now on a pace to effect a full evacuation of
the citizenry here in Valhalla, should the need arise."

"I would frankly be astonished if it did not arise, friend
Prospero," Caliban replied. He was in the New Law robots'
offices in Depot, watching over operations there while Prospero was in Valhalla.

Prospero considered his friend carefully. There was little
that could be judged from a robot's body language, but
either Prospero was imagining things, or else Caliban was
becoming increasingly nervous, increasingly on edge. Well,
that was to be expected, given the situation. "I take it you
believe that they will indeed divert the comet? Have you
offered our protests, and our arguments against the project?"

"I have attempted to do so. I have even gathered peti-
tions signed by humans opposed to the project, and done
what I could to ally us with human groups against the
comet diversion. But even those humans most violently

against the comet impact will have nothing to do with me. It would seem they have concluded that association with the New Law robots would do them more political harm than good."

"That is not surprising, but it is certainly dispiriting," said Prospero. "Very well. If they will not listen to us, and if our voice is not an asset in the chorus of opposition, let others lead the fight against the comet. We will concentrate on preparing our citizens to escape. I have examined your proposed list of allocated evacuation destinations." The human authorities had assigned various destinations to various groups of evacuees, hoping to maintain some sort of coherence and order to the massively complicated operation. Needless to say, the New Law Robots had not exactly drawn the most desirable assigned destinations. "You have rated Site 236 as having the highest safety margin."

"Yes. It is the most geologically stable of our assigned sites, and is likely to suffer the least infall of debris, and the least severe post-impact weather."

"Very well," said Prospero. "Prepare that site to receive sixty percent of our heavy equipment, and whatever proportion of our citizenry can be accommodated there as well, up to a maximum of sixty percent. We will disperse the remainder to other sites, to avoid our being wiped out altogether by some sort of unlucky accident at 236. While I agree the odds of heavy damage there are low, if chance puts a large comet fragment or a large piece of secondary debris in the path of 236, I would just as soon we were not all there. And you will arrange for ten percent of our equipment and population to be sent to Site 149."

"But 149 is the most exposed and dangerous of all our assigned sites! I had advised that we send no New Law robots there at all."

"I saw that recommendation," said Prospero. "I must say that it surprised me. There are times when you lack all vision. I would suggest that you look not only at the map of this world as it is now, but a map of the world as it will be. Prospero out." Prospero cut the connection and turned to the New Law robot on the other side of the room. "Well now, Lacon. Do

you see now why I no longer wholly trust friend Caliban?''
he asked.

"No, sir, I do not.''

Prospero regarded his new protégé with something close to
disappointment. Lacon-03 was as tall and angular and alert-
looking as any New Law robot, but even so there were times
when she seemed completely incapable of advanced or subtle
reasoning. If Caliban was proving to be a more and more
unsuitable second in command, Prospero was beginning to
wonder if Lacon-03 was going to be any better. "The map,
Lacon, the map. If the comet fragments strike in the predicted
locations, and the expected changes in local geography and
sea level take place, Site 149 is going to be within a few
kilometers of the new shoreline, right on top of what ought to
be the best harborage for three thousand kilometers. It will be
the largest port in this hemisphere—and the New Law robots
will control it. We will be there. We will lay claim to it, not
only as an assigned evacuation site, but because we are on it,
in possession.''

"But you put many New Law robots at risk by sending
them to such a place," Lacon-03 objected.

"I expose a few to slight danger for the greater good of all.
But I do more than that," he said.

Prospero turned toward the view window that took up most
of one wall of his office. Prospero looked down on the interior
of Valhalla, on the brightly-lit streets, on the graceful arcing
ramps that led from one level to another, on the busy robots
hurrying along with their belongings from one place to another, preparing to leave this graceful, tranquil city under its
sky of stone. This city was all they had, the fruit of their own
labor, the greatest achievement of the New Law robots. And
the humans were preparing to smash it down into nothing, to
wipe it out as if it had never existed, if doing so would be to
their advantage. There was a lesson there for Prospero.

"I propose," he said, "to take as much advantage as possible of whatever opportunities are presented to me by this
disaster.''

•   •   •

IT WAS TIME.

After the endless hours of checks and counterchecks, after endless dress rehearsals, after wringing any number of bugs out of the system, all of it was done. And it was time.

Governor Alvar Kresh paced back and forth behind his console, and looked up again, for the thousandth, the ten thousandth time, at the two hemispheres on their pedestals, the two control center units, the two oracles who could predict, and even shape, the future—if one dared to let them.

Kresh felt as if he had spent his whole life in this room, and the rest of the universe was little more than a vague and distant dream. He smiled wearily. Unit Dee no doubt felt much the same way. To her, this whole world was a dream, though one of mathematical sharpness and clarity.

Soggdon was there with him, and Fredda, and Donald, and all the others, the roomful of experts and technicians and specialists and advisors who had seemed to appear out of nowhere, unbidden, drawn in by nothing more or less than the crisis itself. But, in the final analysis, there was no point in any of them being there. He had heard what they all had to say, and considered their opinions, weighed all the pros and cons again and again. There was nothing more any of them could tell him that he did not know already. Not even anything more than Dum and Dee might say.

In the midst of all of them, he was alone. The one person who, by rights, should have been there, was not. But Davlo Lentrall was still with the comet diversion fleet. The first and most important phase of the fleet's work was now done. Now they had only to monitor the comet, track it, watch the telemetry.

Assuming they had to do even that. If he, Alvar Kresh, planetary governor of Inferno, decided to say no, to turn his back and walk away, Comet Grieg would go sailing off into the darkness, not to be seen for another two centuries. There would not be much point in watching its telemetry in such a case.

Nor was there much point in considering the possibility of such a case ever coming to pass. Alvar Kresh knew what he had to do. There was very little point in pretending otherwise. How could he possibly walk away from it all now, after so much had happened? How could he say no, and spend the rest of his life watching the planet slowly decay, spend the rest of his life asking himself *what if*, telling himself *if only*?

He had to go forward. He had no real choice.

And that was the part that terrified him.

Forcing himself to be calm, he picked up the headset and put it on. "Unit Dee, Unit Dum," he said. "This is the governor."

"Yesss, Governnorrr," the unison voice replied. It startled Kresh to hear the two speaking together once again. It had been quite some time since they had done that. Was it because Dee recognized the gravity of the event? Some sort of effort at ceremony? Or was it for some other reason, or at random, for no reason at all, or because Dee was continuing to brood and wonder, and becoming less and less stable as she did so?

"I have reached my decision," he said. But he did not speak the words yet. Could he trust Dee with the job? Perhaps he should take the control of the maneuver away from Dee and Dum, tell the comet diversion task force to perform the burn manually.

But no. Better to let Dee have the practice, make sure all of her control connections to the comet's attitude control and thruster systems were working. They would *have* to use her either to control terminal descent or Last Ditch. Better to let her have a test drive, as it were. There was a nice long window for the comet diversion burn. By adjusting the thrust of the initial burn and the attitude of the comet, they could perform the burn any time in the next twelve hours. If some connection failed, if the burn was inaccurate, they would have time to fix it, or decide to abort and perform an emergency lateral burn to throw the comet well clear of the planet. Not so in the rapid-fire sequence of the terminal-phase breakup of the comet. Best to test as much of the system as possible now. This was the easy part. The hard stuff would come later.

And if he didn't trust Dee, he shouldn't let the comet diversion happen at all.

"I hereby order you to perform the planned diversion maneuver on Comet Grieg," he said, and the room was deathly quiet.

"Verrry wellll, Governorrr," said the unison voice. "Weee

shalll commmmence the fffinall countdown in fourteen minutes, thirteen seconds. Tttthe burnnn willll commence one hourrr later.''

"Thank you, Dee. Thank you, Dum,'' said Kresh. He took the headset off and sat down heavily in his console chair.

"By all the forgotten gods,'' he said. "What have I done?''

FREDDA AND ALVAR went outside, and Alvar, at least, was very much surprised to discover that it was full night. How long had it been since he had last left the control room? Twelve hours? A day and a half? Three days? He felt sure that if he concentrated hard enough, he could work it out, remember the last time he had come out, the last time he had gone in.

But there was not much point to the exercise. It was over, and he was out, and that was all that really mattered.

Fredda took him by the hand and led him away from the cold sterility of the Terraforming Center, out away from the lifeless stresscrete of the parking lots, and out onto the cool green lawns that surrounded the Center. "Look,'' she said, pointing up into the western sky. "There it is.''

Kresh looked up in surprise. "I'll be damned,'' he said. "So it is.'' He had never seen Comet Grieg before. There it was, a fat, featureless golden dot hanging in the darkness. It had no tail, showed no features, but there it was. It seemed incredible that something that obvious should have been so hard to find. But he knew he was seeing the the highly reflective sunshade parasol, and he knew the comet was moving fast, straight toward them. Considered as a question of logic, it made perfect sense that it would get closer, and appear larger and brighter as it did so. But still, somehow, it was a shock to see it up there.

He had seen its image endless times in the pictures beamed back from the diversion task force. He had seen it modeled, dissected, shown in false color detail, symbolized by a formless dot in an orbit simulation—but he had never seen the thing itself. There was something jarring, startling, in seeing the comet firsthand, in receiving direct, sensory, personal proof that it was real, that it was no simulation, no abstraction, but a flying mountain of ice and stone that he had ordered dropped onto this world.

Fredda led him out onto the cool, soft, grass and sat down. He sat down beside her and leaned back on his arms, and felt the dampness of the grass on his pants and arms. He could smell the clean, cold, earthy tang of the dirt, and a gentle breeze tickled the nape of his neck. "Let's watch it from here," said Alvar.

Fredda leaned over and kissed him on the cheek. "Good idea," she said, laughing gently. "Glad you thought of it."

"So maybe once in a while we think alike, you and I," said Alvar. "But right now I'm tired of thinking. Tired of deciding. At least *that's* all over—for the moment, anyway."

"For the moment," Fredda agreed. "Rest now. Rest now, away from all of them, and in a while we'll be able to see the comet shine."

"Yes," said Kresh, yawning mightily. He could feel all the tension, all the worry, draining out of him. It was done, for good or ill. "Rest. Rest awhile. And then I want to see them light the fuse under that comet."

But when, at last, the fat star in the sky blazed into glory, Governor Alvar Kresh was sound asleep, snoring gently.

DAVLO LENTRALL SHOVED his way a little closer to the porthole, and promptly got shoved back out of the way. At last he gave it up. Too many people were trying too hard to get near the too-small piece of glass.

In the old days, he would have expected them to defer to him. He would have reminded them that none of them would be here, that none of this would be happening, if not for him. Who but he had a better right to be near the glass? But now it simply amazed him that he had ever been capable of thinking that way. What right had he to anything?

Besides, *they* all had a right to be at the window. All of them, Spacers and Settlers, technicians and engineers and spaceworkers, specialists of every possible sort, had all worked impossible shifts, taken on impossible tasks on unmeetable schedules—and succeeded.

Davlo gave up and made his way toward the equally

crowded cargo bay. They had set up huge repeater screens there. And there was at least some hope he would be able to see better from there.

The hope was realized the moment he set foot in the cargo bay. The main viewer screen had a view of Comet Grieg. There it was, huge and misshapen, a gleaming ball of rock and ice, hanging in the velvet darkness, sheathed in the shining gold of the parasol that was now draped over its pockmarked surface.

Once he would have felt nothing but sheer, vain pride in what he had caused to happen. But now, to look on that enormous object, and know that he had changed its fate, that his actions and those of others had converted a vagrant thought in the back of his mind into the huge and stunning piece of reality floating in the darkness, simply terrified him. What hubris. How could humans imagine themselves to have the competency, the wisdom, the *right* to attempt anything so grandiose?

He glanced at the countdown clock, and saw that they were getting close. Only a few seconds left.

Could they truly do this thing? Could they, would they, truly bring this flying mountain down onto their world? It seemed impossible. It seemed madness, suicidal.

A wave of panic swept over Davlo, hemmed in by the swarm of bodies. Someone in the front of the crowd began to chant out the countdown. "Twenty. Nineteen. Eighteen." Another voice joined in, and another, and another, until the entire room full of people who had made this thing happen were shouting out the numbers in unison. "Seventeen! Sixteen! Fifteen!" the voices cried out, calling a bit louder with every number.

All except Davlo. Suddenly he was gripped by fear, by shame, by guilt. It could not work. It couldn't possibly. They were going to destroy the world. He had to stop them, stop this. It was a mistake, a horrible, terrifying mistake that could never be put right. Dropping a comet on a living world? No. *No!* He could not let them. He plunged forward, into the crowd, and tried to get to the front, call out a protest, a warning, but the crowd was too tight, the shouting voices too loud. He could not move forward, and he could not hear himself. "Ten!" they shouted. "Nine! Eight!"

But it could not be. It must not be. The dangers, the risks,

were too great. The image of Kaelor, Kaelor at his death, Kaelor dying to prevent this thing flashed through his mind.
"No!" he shouted out. "No! Stop!"

"Seven! Six! Five! Four!"

"Please! Stop!" he shouted out, though no one could hear.
"It's me, Lentrall! It's a mistake! *Stop!*"

"THREE!"

"TWO!"

Davlo Lentrall sagged backward, let his body go limp. The
bloody-minded arrogance of it all. How could he have
dreamed that he, and he alone, could see the way? Now he
had killed them all.

"ONE!"

"ZERO!" they all shouted.

"Zero," Lentrall whispered to himself in horror.

The screen flared into spectacular brightness, the light of a
new sun blooming into life at the base of Comet Grieg. A tail,
a jet of power and light and energy, lanced out from the detonation thruster, the powerful and intricate and clever device
that allowed the comet to be aimed straight for its target, let
it move toward the doom of the planet with far greater precision and efficiency. A tail of blazing, glowing plasma
stabbed out into the darkness, and a shudder of power and
motion rippled along the gleaming surface of the sunshade
parasol. Rips and tears appeared in it as huge fragments of
stone and ice tore free of the comet and smashed holes in the
reflective plastic sheeting.

And the comet began to move, slid into its new heading,
shifted into its new orbit and its new destiny. Down toward Inferno. *No*, thought Lentrall. *No*. He would have to stop it. He had
to get down there first. He would have to get back to Inferno, and
prevent the disaster he had set in motion. Somehow.

The burn ended, the jet of light died, the room erupted in
cheers and shouts and applause, but Davlo Lentrall did not
notice. He looked toward the screen, and saw nothing there
but a monstrous weapon he had aimed at his own world.

What have I done? he asked himself.

What have I done?

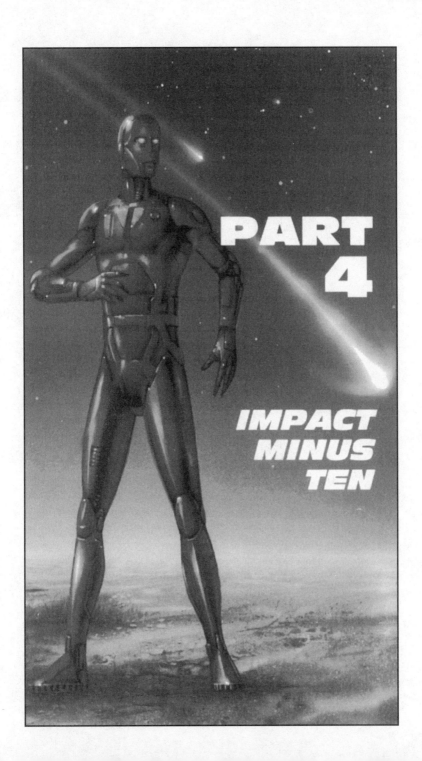

PART 4

IMPACT MINUS TEN

16

CINTA MELLOY WALKED down the chaotic streets of Depot, dodging the traffic that seemed to be roaring past in every direction at once. There he was again, just up ahead. She ducked around a corner as her man glanced around behind himself. She was fairly sure he had not spotted her. Fairly. The man was suspicious, no doubt of that. But he was also an amateur, and that cut into his effectiveness a lot. Cinta watched as Davlo Lentrall stopped to put another of his ridiculous posters up. Cinta hadn't even bothered to examine any of them, choosing instead to keep her eye on her man. Besides, she knew, more or less, what they had to say. STOP THE COMET! STOP THE MADNESS! PROTEST NOW! LEAVE THE PLANET ALONE! MASS MEETING TONIGHT!

Pointless. All of it. Much as she agreed with the sentiments on the posters, she knew damned well it was far too late. The deed was done. Cinta permitted herself no such delusions. She knew the comet was coming. And presumably, so did Lentrall. The populace certainly knew it. The only ones showing up at the meetings were Lentrall, a few whacked-out loners, and a collection of spies and informants—some of them from the SSS, and the others easily identified off the surveillance photos.

So why was Lentrall bothering? Or was all this nonsense a cover for something else—and if so, what?

Lentrall looked behind himself again, and Cinta ducked out of sight again, or at least tried to do so. She wasn't even quite sure why she was following him. She had simply spotted him on the street, and started trailing him.

Up went another poster. Cinta shook her head and gave it up. She turned around and started back the way she had come. She was tempted to order a formal watch kept on Lentrall, assign the job to less obvious and more skillful watchers than herself. If she wasn't so badly short-handed, she would have done just that. But there were so damned many others to watch.

At least the evacuation itself seemed to proceeding in an orderly and sensible fashion. The heavy lifters, the construction crews, the seemingly endless series of auxiliary services—emergency medical, motor pool repair, preimpact cartography, provisions, accommodation and sanitation for all the extra bodies—somehow, incredibly, it all seemed to be dropping into place. Those Dee and Dum units Kresh was nursemaiding clearly knew their stuff.

But there was plenty else happening—and none of it seemed even remotely promising to Melloy. She had loaned a detachment of SSS personnel to the evacuation effort, as per Tonya Welton's orders, and Cinta had even flown to Depot to take personal charge of it herself. But none of it was doing any good. The SSS was here, doing its overt job—but they also had a covert agenda. They were supposed to watch the other players in the game—and the others were giving them plenty to watch.

The CIP had its own security people out, and they were watching the SSS—as they should have been. There was still the Government Tower Plaza fiasco on the books, after all. The Ironheads seemed to be everywhere, out in force, the black uniform visible on every street, in every shop. One of the SSS watch teams had even spotted their old friend Norlan Fiyle, quite openly going into and out of the local Ironhead HQ. And then there were the hordes of New Law robots, frantically conducting their own evacuation out of their undersized

offices over on Shipping Street. The SSS had stacks of images
of Caliban, the No Law robot, going in and out of there, and
a fair collection of shots of Prospero too—though he seemed
to come in less often, and stay for shorter periods.

Maybe every last one of them had nothing but sweetness
and light on their minds. Maybe all of them had nothing but
thoughts of doing good deeds and building the planet Inferno
into the Paradise it had been meant to be. Cinta doubted it,
but such a thing was possible.

But disaster could follow on even the best of intentions.

And Cinta Melloy was sure that at least someone in this
town had less than the best of intentions.

SIMCOR BEDDLE SMILED as he looked out the viewport of
the aircar. There was a fair-sized crowd there to welcome him
to Depot. Indeed, quite a large crowd, considering the small
size of Depot and its distance from civilization. Simcor Beddle
had spent most of the last three weeks shuttling back and forth
between Hades and Depot. But every time he returned to Depot, the crowds were still there.

Thank Gildern for that, Beddle told himself. *Thank Gildern
for everything.* The man was indispensable.

But it would be best not to keep the crowd waiting. He
would have to hurry in order to get ready. Or, more accurately,
for the robots to get him ready.

The pilot robot completed the standard landing safety cross-
check. An attendant robot released Simcor's seat restraint system for him while a second helped him to his feet. Simcor got
up and moved around behind his seat. He stood in the center
of the largest piece of open flat deck in the car while the two
attendant robots stripped him out of his rumpled travel cov-
eralls. He stepped into the car's compact refresher unit, and
waited for the first attendant to reach in and activate the system. The water jets came to life around him.

There was no time for a full-length needle shower, and,
indeed, the aircar's refresher did not include many of the
amenities Beddle took for granted in the first place, but one
did have to rough it, now and again. Besides, even a few
seconds under the refresher's spray arms proved most reviv-

ing. He allowed the hot-air jets to dry him, and then stepped back outside to the main cabin.

It was the work of a moment for the attendant robots to dress Beddle in the jet-black formal uniform of the Ironheads. Almost before he was aware of it, he was ready, all his decorations gleaming, his boots shined to mirror brightness, his perfectly combed hair under his perfectly placed cap.

One attendant robot held up a mirror, and Beddle nodded in satisfaction at his own reflection. It was always important to make a good appearance. He gestured for the second robot to open the side hatch of the car. It swung open, and Beddle stepped forward to face the cheering crowd.

There was Gildern, standing on a low platform, leading the applause. And there were the cameras at the back of the crowd, recording it all, feeding it to every outlet the Ironheads could get their hands on. Beddle smiled, stepped down from the car and crossed to the speaker's platform, his two attendant robots behind him.

He nodded his thanks to Gildern, and then turned to the crowd. "Well," he began in a loud, carrying voice. "Here I am again." That drew the good-natured laugh he had intended. He gestured in the vague direction of the sky. "But on the other hand there's someone else—or rather some*thing* else— on the way. Comet Grieg is going to be here in another ten days. By then we all need to be out of here. All of us in the Ironhead party understand how much all of you here in the Utopia region are being asked to give up. We all know how great the reward for the whole planet will be—but no matter how great that reward for others, it is not right that you people here should be expected to pay the price for it. And we'll see to it that you do not.

"I don't think Governor Alvar Kresh quite sees things that way. And just by the way, has *Kresh* paid a call to Utopia yet? Is *he* going to come here at *all*, before Utopia isn't here anymore? He's promised a certain amount of relocation funding for each of you. Well, that's all well and good, as far as it goes. But it does not go far enough! We Ironheads are prepared to go a lot further. We'll see to it that all of you are properly resettled. We'll see to it that your temporary accom-

modation is as good as it can be. We'll see to it that all of
your movable property goes with you—and not just the 'essential' property Alvar Kresh has promised you can keep!"

And *that* brought the round of cheers that Beddle had expected. Never mind that keeping half of the promises he had
been making would bankrupt the Ironhead party. Never mind
that the Ironhead contribution to transport and shelter and all
the rest of it was barely measurable. By the time all of that
became clear, people would be far too busy putting their lives
back together to worry about the details of political promises—and Beddle would have laid in a endless stock of political capital as the man who remembered the ordinary citizen
while the government was too busy with its grand projects to
bother.

Beddle waited until just before the cheers would have died
out on their own, and then raised his hands for silence. "But
friends, if there's one thing we all know, it's that time is short.
So while I thank you for coming out, I hope you won't mind
if I keep this brief. We all have work to do. Now let's all go
do it!"

That last bit didn't really have much in the way of meaning,
but the crowd cheered anyway. Beddle smiled for the cameras,
and waved to the crowd, then let Gildern lead him to a small
open-body runcart.

"A very nice little speech, sir," Gildern said.

"Good enough for the purpose at hand," Beddle replied
evenly. Somehow praise from Gildern threw him off stride. It
seemed out of character. "Let's get where we're going, shall
we?"

"Yes, sir. There's some news that might well interest you."

The two men climbed into the back of the runcart and the
robot driver started the vehicle up. Beddle looked around with
interest as they made their way through the small town. He
was surprised to see how slowly they made progress. Traffic
was in a hopeless snarl. Depot was as frantically busy as an
overturned ant-heap—to use the sort of nature-based imagery
that was so suddenly popular these days, now that terraforming
was all the rage.

Simcor Beddle shook his head thoughtfully. It was strange

to think of, but five years ago, the image of comparison would have been based on robots in some way. "Busy as a robot," or some such. Times had changed, not only in big ways, but in strange and subtle small ones.

He and Gildern had plotted endlessly over ways to eliminate the New Law robots and get rid of the Settlers. Ways to get rid of the disturbing influences, so that life could get back to normal, back to the way Spacers were meant to live.

But in recent days it occurred to Beddle that it might be the small things that would be hardest to change back. Perhaps the Ironheads could rebuild a world that had no Settlers, had no New Law robots, had no robotic labor shortage. But how could they wipe the *memory* of those things from people's minds?

In the old days, the people of Inferno had only known of one way to do things, one way of living life: have the robots do it. That was the answer to everything. And it was an answer that had worked. Now they had been exposed not just to other possibilities, but also to the notion that there *were* other possibilities, other answers that might work as well. Before a few years ago, no one on this planet had been able even to conceive of another way of living. Now a way of life based solely on robotic labor was merely one option among many. How could that be changed back? Especially when some misguided souls had such poor taste and lack of judgment that they actually *preferred* doing things for themselves, and enjoyed the company of Settlers?

Even the revival of interest in the natural world was disruptive. Robots, the service of robots, were supposed to provide a cushion, a cocoon, that kept the outside world at bay—quite literally at times. One could easily live a wholly satisfactory life without ever setting foot outside, if one's robots did their jobs properly. With even the most basic of comm systems, no one ever needed to travel, even to do business or visit with friends.

But now people were being exposed to nature—not just the idea of nature, but the fact of it. And some of them—a lot of them—seemed to like it.

It occurred to Simcor Beddle that he had not been outside,

except to get from one place to another, for years. He never went *to* the outside. Some tiny part of him, some all-but-forgotten, all-but-stifled part of him suddenly longed to get out of the groundcar, longed to get on his own feet, start walking and just keep going, to the horizon and beyond. The wind shifted and brought the cool, sweet scent of some nearby stream to him. Suddenly he wanted to find that stream, slip off his boots and dangle his feet in the water.

The runcart went over a bump in the road, and Simcor Beddle blinked and came back to himself. Nonsense! Utter nonsense. The very idea of his sitting barefoot by a stream was absolutely absurd. Beddle thrust the strange notions, the bizarre impulses, from his mind. He had not come all this way to indulge in such foolishness.

But if even a brief ride from a landing pad to a field office was enough to inspire such a reaction in him, then how surprised should he be if others were tempted to look out at the wide world outside? "Come on," Beddle said to the driver robot. "Let's get moving. What the devil is taking so long?"

"Too much traffic on the road," said Gildern. "There's a lot more work to do than you might expect. Lots of transport operations going on in the Utopia region, and Depot's the focal point for all of it. The evacuation is a huge undertaking. Considering this is supposed to be the undeveloped side of the planet, there's an awful lot of hardware and household effects and Space knows what to pack up and ship out."

Beddle could see that for himself as he looked around. On every side it was the same story. Robots were disassembling and packing up all sorts of machinery and equipment, taking apart whole buildings, packing groundtrucks and aircars and every other kind of vehicle.

"You wouldn't believe the changes in this place in the last month," Gildern said. "You've only been in and out quickly, a few times. I've been here right along, and watched it all happen. It's incredible all the work they've done."

Beddle could see that. There was as much equipment coming in as going out—or at least, so it seemed. Transporters had to be flown to Depot in pieces and then assembled. They had to build living quarters for human overseers and repair and maintenance centers for the army of robots and the swarm of aircars that had descended on the place. A huge ground-crawler roared past, and Beddle had to lean in close to Gildern and shout into his ear in order to make himself heard. "What of the other matter?" he shouted.

"In the field office," Gildern shouted back. "Noise isn't enough cover. There might be lipreaders."

Beddle nodded his agreement. It would not be the first time skilled lipreaders had been used against one side or another in the endless, complicated political skirmishes of the last few years.

A break opened up in the traffic, and the small open vehicle slowly started to move, gradually gathering speed. They crossed the outskirts of town and moved through the bustling, busy, organized chaos that was downtown Depot.

A squad of robots moved past, marching quickly, each carrying a crate nearly as large as it was. A technical team was working on a battery of probe launchers, part of the scientific research effort attached to the comet impact. Strange, Beddle thought, to look at such a massive cataclysm as a mere test subject. But there would no doubt be a great deal to learn from the impact. There were plans afoot to deploy any number of flying, orbiting, and buried sensors. Many of them would, of course, be destroyed by the impact—but even the pattern of their destruction would tell the scientists a great deal.

The runcart went through the center of town and out the other side. It slowed to a halt outside a cheerful-looking portable building, a bright orange hemisphere about ten meters high and twenty across. By the look of it, the building had not so much been erected as unfolded. Beddle looked around, and saw that the whole area was dotted with similar structures in every color of the rainbow. The Ironheads weren't the only ones who had needed a temporary headquarters in Depot.

Gildern and Beddle got down out of the runcart and stepped to the door of the building. There was the briefest of pauses while the scanning system confirmed both Gildern and Beddle's identities. They heard the heavy-duty locking mechanism unlatch, and the robot standing inside the door opened it and let them in.

Simcor looked toward the scanning device on its stand. It was a sleek, gleaming cube of gun-metal gray, its controls and displays well laid out and well-labeled. An armored cable ran from it to the armored box that held the body of the exterior camera.

"A Settler-made device," said Beddle, the disapproval clear in his voice.

"Yes, sir, it is," said Gildern, quite unapologetic. "I do not trust sentry systems based on robots. There is always the possibility that a person skilled in manipulation of robots will be able to convince the robot that there was a good First Law reason to let that person in."

Beddle glared at his subordinate in annoyance. In other words, Gildern was willing to commit heretical acts in the name of security, and trading with the enemy was not beneath him. There was a great deal Beddle could have said, but this was not the time or place. There were other issues to deal with. He did not speak, but instead followed his chief of security through an inner door and into a bare field office.

The room was completely undecorated, utterly cheerless. There was nothing personal there. No photocube of a family member, no decoration, nothing that would give the slightest clue to Gildern's personality. It was the office of someone who was camping here, not someone who lived here.

Of course, Beddle reflected, Gildern's office back at Ironhead HQ was no less spartan. A disordered office, a cluttered office, was an insecure office.

There was nothing in the room at present except a table and two chairs—comfortable-looking ones by most standards, quite spartan by Beddle's.

"I personally performed a bug sweep of this room one hour ago," said Gildern. "We ought to be secure enough here to discuss the other matter."

" 'The other matter,' " Beddle repeated. "If we are all that secure here, I see no reason to waste time with euphemisms. Let us call things by their proper name and discuss the destruction of the New Law robots."

If there was any thing that the Ironheads regarded as dangerous, it was the continued existence of the New Law robots.

Robots that did not have the true Three Laws were a far more serious heresy than the use of Settler machinery, or contact with Settlers. Settlers were foreigners, aliens, the enemy. Even if someone like Gildern did deal with them, he knew the dangers, the risks when he did so. But robots were supposed to be the bulwark of the Spacer way of life, the cornerstone of the Ironhead philosophy. If the people of Inferno grew even slightly accustomed to dealing with robots that would not unquestioningly endanger themselves, sacrifice themselves, for the good of a human, if they got used to robots who might debate an order, or follow their own agendas, then, Beddle had no doubt, the rot would have set in. If people could not trust robots absolutely, they would not trust them at all. After all, robots were stronger, faster, harder to injure than humans. Some robots, in many ways, were more intelligent. Without the barrier, the protection, of the Three Laws, people would have good reason to fear robots. At least such were the official reasons for wishing to be rid of the New Law robots, whenever Beddle made a speech on the subject.

But there was another, more private reason. The New Law robots were, plain and simple, a threat to the Ironheads' power. The doctrine of more and better robots was endangered so long as anyone ever saw an alternative to it.

But if there were no New Law robots, there would be no New Law robot problem. Toward that end, Gildern and his people had been searching for Valhalla, the New Law robot city, for quite some time, since long before anyone had ever heard of Comet Grieg. Nothing had ever come of the effort.

But now—now things were different. And Beddle was eager to find out precisely *how* different. "All right," he said to Gildern. "What have you got for me?"

"More pieces of the puzzle, sir. As you know, a direct search for Valhalla has never been possible. The minute anyone tried a search, the New Law robots would simply shut everything down. Besides which, the New Law robots encrypt their long-range hyperwave traffic, and we have not had much luck in reading it. Hyperwave signals are also difficult to track with any precision. But with enough signals, it is possible to do statistical analysis. And there has been enough traffic in recent days to let us do some pretty fair work. And more physical traffic as well. The New Law robots are working as hard and as fast as anyone to evacuate in time. That means more signal traffic, more aircars and land cars and transports and so forth. And they are being less careful. There is less point in concealing a hidden city that is about to be destroyed.

"The long and the short of it is that we have had a lot more data to work with, and we have been able to work from a lot closer in than we were in times past. We can get equipment and robots in here, right on top of things."

"With what result?" Beddle asked.

"The best possible result," Gildern replied. "Absolute confirmation that Valhalla is somewhere inside the primary impact site for the first and largest of the comet fragments. It will be utterly destroyed."

"But we were virtually certain of that before. And as the New Laws are clearly preparing to evacuate, what good will it do for the comet to destroy them after they have all gone?"

"None whatsoever. But look around yourself. Look at Depot."

"What about it?"

"Depot is being evacuated as well—*and there have never been so many people here.* The people here all know this place is going to be wiped out, but there is no danger in being here *now*. However, in the meantime, there is a great deal of work to be done, so they have pulled in all sorts of people to do it!"

"What are you saying?"

"I'm saying that our sources confirm that New Law robots are vanishing from all the places they usually are. They are buying out their labor contracts, closing up the shops they run in the smaller settlements. We've seen a large number of them pass through Depot and estimate that ninety percent of the existing New Law robots are in the vicinity."

"And so you think they are rushing home to Valhalla to help and salvage what they can. What of it? They will be gone before the comet hits."

"Quite true. But all we need to do is locate Valhalla *before* the comet strikes, and destroy it while they are still there. And

I believe both goals are more achievable than you would think. I also believe it is highly likely that you can accomplish them both, yourself, personally.''

"How?" Beddle demanded, a world of eagerness and ambition bound up in that one little word.

"As for the first part, the question of locating Valhalla, we are able to track a great deal of the increased air, ground, and hyperwave traffic from here, but our ability to triangulate and backtrack is highly limited. If we had a mobile tracking station, equipped with the proper detection equipment, we would soon be able to sort through all the deliberate false trails and extraneous signals.''

"What do I have to do with a mobile tracking station?"

Gildern leaned forward eagerly. "It's quite simple. We have installed the proper tracking gear on my long-range aircar. I can provide you with robots trained to operate the system, who know how to coordinate the work with the base station here. In short, we would tell your aircar where to go, your aircar would obtain readings from that position, and then move on to the next location. You are planning to visit several of the small outlying settlements on this trip. That would suit us perfectly. Land one place and give a speech while your robots do a detection sweep, then fly on to the next spot, and the next, and the next. We'd rapidly accumulate enough data to establish a very good fix on Valhalla. With enough data, I expect we ought to be able to get within an error radius of only five or eight kilometers. And that should be quite good enough.''

"Good enough for what?" Beddle asked.

Gildern was about to reply when the ground suddenly gave a strange, sharp little shudder and the building rattled and shook hard enough that it seemed close to folding itself back up. The air was suddenly full of dust, seemingly thrown up from out of nowhere. There was a distant rumbling and a muted *boom*! that seemed to come from somewhere far off.

Gildern gestured reassuringly. "There's no danger," he said. "Notice that none of our robots even bothered to rush in to our rescue. But to answer your question—good enough for one of those. For a burrow bomb—a seismic sounder.''

"A burrow bomb?"

"They've set off any number of them around here. The scientists want to understand the underlying geology of this area as thoroughly as possible before the impact, so they can better interpret the results of the impact. The explosions cause seismic shock. The bombs themselves are carefully calibrated. They can burrow themselves deep into the earth and set themselves off at a predetermined time and depth. By measuring the vibrations produced by the explosions from various receiving stations, and seeing how they have been changed, the scientists can determine what sort of strata the vibrations have gone through. It's an unusually destructive way of doing geology, but it gets the job done fast—and what difference does it make when the comet is going to destroy everything anyway? We are virtually certain that Valhalla is underground. If we set off a burrow bomb close enough to Valhalla, the shock waves should collapse the entire city, killing or trapping everyone inside.

"There are four or five researcher agencies setting off these devices. I have taken steps to establish a real seeming, research group myself. Everything is being done in such a frantic hurry, with the comet bearing down, that it was easy to get all the various approvals. Our little operation has already set off three sounders, all duly reported ahead of time and properly recorded and so on. In order to stay legal, there need only be an hour or two's notice of your explosion. You will not be violating any law at all."

"How could that be?"

"The New Law robots have no legal standing. Technically, they are abandoned property themselves, and they certainly can't own property. They have never registered any title to Valhalla—how could they, when no one knows where it is?"

Beddle nodded impatiently. The arguments were all familiar to him. "Yes, yes, you don't have to convince me of anything. But don't be naive. Those legal arguments have never been settled. Some lower courts have ruled that they can own land. Even if the laws *had* been settled, and in our favor, a thing does not have to be illegal before it causes us trouble." Beddle paused for a moment, and then smiled. "However, if it means the destruction of nearly all the New Law robots, I am willing to contend with a whole world of trouble. The price might be high, but, even so, it would be a bargain.'' Beddle leaned back in his chair and thought for a moment. ''And you believe all this is feasible? That it has a reasonable chance of success?''

''Yes, sir. I won't insult your intelligence by pretending it's a sure thing. But I think it can be done.''

Simcor Beddle looked at his second-in-command thoughtfully. It was a risky scheme. There was no doubt about that. It was all but a certainty that they would be found out.

But would that be such a bad thing? There were plenty of people, everywhere on the political spectrum, who would be quite relieved to be rid of the New Law robots. Even if the Ironheads took some heat for it, they would earn a lot of credit as well.

Besides, how could he possibly turn his back on this opportunity? This was a once-in-a-lifetime chance. Gildern was offering him his dreams on a silver platter. How could he say no? Why would he say no?

He leaned forward across the table and smiled at Gildern. ''Not only can it be done, Gildern. It will be. It will be.''

NORLAN FIYLE SMILED as well, as he listened through the thin partition. Jadelo Gildern rarely made mistakes, but when he did make one, it was of the largest size. The room on the other side of the partition might well have been swept for electronic bugs only a hour before, but that was of no use. Not against an underling with a good pair of ears and a reason to bear a grudge, not against an underling on the other side of a wall made for portability rather than soundproofing.

He had heard it all. And he was a man with more reasons to speak, and to act, than to keep quiet.

Simcor Beddle took off on his good-will tour the next morning. Over the next two days, he made his first four appearances, at four little towns, arriving at each town right on schedule.

But he never arrived at the fifth.

17

THE ALERT COMM'S buzzer went off once again. Constable Pherlan Bukket opened one unhappy eye and glared at his bedside clock. It was barely 0700. Bukket was accustomed to sleeping until at least 0800—preferably later. Up until a month ago, doing so had usually been possible, even routine. Up until a month ago, most pleasant things had been routine. Now nothing was pleasant—and nothing was routine.

Up until a month ago, Constable Bukket had enjoyed his work—mostly because he was the only one doing it. Pherlan Bucket was responsible for enforcing the law and keeping the peace in the town of Depot—or at least he had been until a month ago, back when neither law nor peace was often disturbed in Depot.

Now it was different. Now alerts came in at all hours of the day and night. Most of the time, the CIP came thundering in and took over the situation anyway, just as they had shoved him out of his offices in town and taken them over for themselves.

It was, of course, just as well they came in and took over because Bukket didn't have anything like the resources to deal with the problems that were coming up. But even so, the entire situation was deeply frustrating.

He slapped at the alert comm's buzzer and cut it off, then picked up the unit. "This is Constable Bukket," he said into the alert comm's mike, making no attempt to hide the sleepiness from his voice. "Who is it and what do you want?"

"This is Depot Air Traffic Control," a robotic voice replied. "We have a disaster beacon showing about three hundred kilometers south of here."

"Then why call me?" Bukket demanded. "It's nowhere near my jurisdiction."

"Yes, sir. I called you because my standing orders require it. I am sending the text details of the incident now. If you will read them on the alert comm's display screen, you will understand."

Bukket shook his head irritably. Someday someone was going to come up with a set of standing orders that made sense. He turned the alert comm over so he could see the screen—

And three seconds later he knew two things very well. The robots at Depot Air Traffic Control had been quite right to call him in on this one.

And he would be only too happy to hand this one off to the CIP.

DONALD 111 RECEIVED the incoming high-priority call just as Governor Kresh and Dr. Leving were about to sit down to their evening meal at the governor's Winter Residence.

Donald rarely concerned himself much with the governor's meals, as the governor himself rarely paid them much mind, but tonight was an exception. In his judgment, this was likely to be the last evening for quite some time the governor and his wife would have any chance at all of a civilized meal together. Both of them had been working endless hours in preparation for the comet impact, and no doubt would be called upon to work even harder as the comet approached. Dr. Leving in particular had brought more work on herself—on all of them—with her insistence of diverting some small fraction of the evacuation aid to the New Law pseudo-robots— work that Donald regarded as massively counterproductive.

The world could only benefit when the last of the New Laws were swept away.

But busy as recent days had been, and as busy as the remaining time before the comet would be, the days after it hit would be busier still. This would be their last chance to rest and relax, and Donald had decided this was the night to do everything right. He had personally overseen the table arrangement, the candles, the background music, the menu and its preparation, the elegant table setting. The governor and Dr. Leving's reaction as they entered the dining was all that he could have hoped for. Both of them smiled, seemingly for the first time in days. The care and the worry of the last few weeks seemed to drain away from their faces.

"This is lovely, Donald," said Dr. Leving as her husband helped her to her chair. "This is most thoughtful of you."

"Fine work," the governor said as he took his own seat. "This was exactly the night to do this."

"You are both most kind," said Donald. He was on the point of signaling the kitchen to bring in the first course when the call came in.

In less than a hundredth of a second, Donald received the signal, decoded it, and identified it as an incoming emergency priority voice call. Another one. The days had been full of them for weeks now.

Donald briefly debated handling this one by himself, or even refusing to answer it. But the governor's orders on such matters were very clear and specific, and had been reinforced several times in the past few days. Donald really had no choice in the matter. With a slight dimming of his eyes that might have been the robotic equivalent of a sigh of resignation, Donald gave in to the inevitable. "Sir, I am most unhappy to tell you this, but there is an incoming emergency call. It is scrambled, the caller's identity unknown."

"Burning devils," Kresh said, his irritation plain. "Don't they ever stop calling? Patch it through yourself, Donald. Let's clear this up here and now, whatever it is. Probably just another farmer who refuses to get off his land or something."

"Yes, sir. Patching through—now."

"This is Kresh," said the governor. "Identify yourself and your business."

"Sir!" a fussy, nervous-sounding voice answered. "I—I didn't mean to get patched through to you, but the priority management system did it for me. I am trying to reach Commander Justen Devray."

"You are speaking with the planetary governor, not an answering service. Who I am speaking with?" Kresh demanded.

"Oh! Ah, Constable Bukket, of the town of Depot. But honestly, the priority coding system put me through to you."

"Which it only does when the situation demands my prompt attention," said Kresh. "So what is the situation?"

There was a brief silence on the line, and then a sort of low gulping noise. "Simcor Beddle's aircar has crashed, sir. At least we think it has. It vanished off Depot Air Traffic Control, and then the disaster beacon went off. And, ah—the beacon is stationary, at a position right in the center of the primary impact zone."

"Burning devils!" Kresh said, abruptly standing up. "Search and rescue?"

"They launched four minutes ago. They should be there in about another five minutes. I know it's evening where you are, but we're early morning here. Local sunrise at the site isn't for another twenty minutes and it's very rough terrain, so—"

"So they may have to wait for daylight before they can even set down. Very well. Use the side-channel datapath of this frequency and send all the data you have. Thank you for your report. You will be contacted as needed. Kresh out." The governor made a throat-cutting gesture and Donald cut the link.

"Damnation," said Kresh. "Hellfire and damnation. Someone's made some kind of try for Beddle."

Fredda Leving's face went pale. "But you can't know that," she protested. "It could have been an accident. His aircar could have malfunctioned. The pilot could have made a mistake."

"Think so, Donald?" the governor asked.

"No, sir. Preventative maintenance on vehicles is one of the most basic means of preventing harm to humans. The mechanical failure rate on air vehicles is extremely low. Nor is there any plausible chance that it was pilot error. Not with a robotic pilot.''

"And there is no way Simcor Beddle would do his own flying,'' said Kresh. "Even if he knew how—and I doubt he does—it would be against his principles to do anything a robot could do for him.''

"But it's not impossible that it was an accident,'' Fredda said. "Burning stars. The political upheaval when Grieg died. I don't know that we could hold together through that again.'' What would happen if—if things turned out as badly as they might? The Ironheads would probably blame the government, or Alvar personally. Unless they pinned it on the Settlers. The Ironhead movement would be up in arms, that was for sure. Marches, riots, arrests, counter-demonstrations, lunatics and perfectly sane citizens suspecting plots and conspiracies under every rock. She could see it all, plain as day. How the devil were they supposed to contend with that and the comet impact at the same time? "Could it have been an accident, Donald?'' Fredda asked, trying to find at least some ray of hope.

"While I grant there is a theoretical possibility of mechanical or pilot failure, I would agree with the governor that foul play of some sort is the far more plausible explanation. That is even more disturbing than it normally would be, given the political implications of the case.''

"Donald, you are a master of understatement. We have to move on this fast. Fredda, dinner is going to have to wait. Donald, call Justen Devray. I want him on the scene. And I want him there *now*.''

THE DISASTER BEACON that had summoned them all was still blaring, long hours after the crash, the locator strobe on top of the car still flashing. No doubt the hyperwave beacon was still running as well.

Commander Justen Devray gestured to Gervad, his personal robot. "Go find the switches and shut those damned homing beacons off,'' he said. "We know where the car is.''

"Yes, sir,'' said Gervad, his manner as calm and deferential as ever. He walked across the landing site and went aboard the aircar. After a few minutes, the noise cut off.

Good. He gave an order and someone carried it out. At least something happened the way it was supposed to happen. Justen Devray yawned mightily, fighting back exhaustion. It was full noon here, but it was the dead of night back in the city of Hades, on the other side of the planet. Justen had been getting ready for bed a little less than two hours before.

The local officers were still here—if you could call Depot local, three hundred–plus kilometers away. They were the ones who had detected the beacon, found the aircar—and hyperwaved a priority call to Hades. Kresh had ordered Justen to the scene immediately, and Justen had obeyed with the alacrity of the most slavish robot. Ten minutes after Kresh's call, he had been en route to Hades Spaceport. Fifteen minutes after that, he had been on a rush suborbital flight with the Crime Scene team, hurtling clear around the planet in a stomach-churning crash emergency flight trajectory. They had landed at Depot Field, transferred to aircars, and flown like fury to get to the downed aircar. He had gotten to the scene fast, but he was not exactly fully awake.

Justen had gone to bed the night before looking forward to his first decent night's sleep in weeks. He felt a sudden surge of irrational anger toward whoever had done this. Why couldn't they have waited just a few hours more, and let him rest just a little?

Maybe the kidnappers had just been in a hurry, like everyone else these past month or so. Justen Devray did what everyone did every few minutes, these days. He looked up into the sky, and searched for the glowing dot that was growing brighter all the time. There it was, hanging low in the western sky.

The comet. The comet that was headed straight for the planet Inferno. Straight, in point of fact, for the spot of land Justen Devray was standing on. In five days time it would be here—and then it would be all over. . . .

Justen turned away from the comet and resumed his study of the aircar's wreckage—if wreckage was the right word for it. Wreckage implied a crash, an accident. This car had landed safely. The damage here had happened after the landing, and it had been committed quite deliberately. Someone had kidnapped Simcor Beddle.

And Justen Devray had just five short days to find the man, before the comet came down.

Devray moved in closer, and studied the exterior of the car more closely. The aircar had landed on the summit of a low hill in the middle of rough country, jumbled rock and scruffy undergrowth, smack in the middle of nowhere. The nearest town of any size was at least forty kilometers away. Devray considered the rugged badlands that passed for countryside in the vicinity. This hilltop, jutting up from a jumbled pile of rock and brush, was probably the smoothest piece of land for twenty kilometers. Beddle and the kidnappers couldn't have walked out. It would take a mountaineer in perfect condition to make any time at all through this kind of country.

Devray shook his head. The ground search had started at once, of course, but they would find nothing. No footprints, no broken twigs, no torn bits of cloth hanging off a thornbush. They had flown out.

But there was another factor. When a disaster beacon went off, every tracking station within three hundred kilometers of it automatically shifted into maximum sensitivity mode. The badlands in the general vicinity of the aircar broke up the sensor signal near ground level and made it possible to evade detection at low altitude—but the badlands were surrounded by areas of gently rolling hills and plains where detection would be easy. Nothing had been spotted flying out—and anything that had flown out would have been spotted. Perhaps they could not have walked out, but they could not have flown far, either. The odds were good that Beddle and his captors were still in the badlands south of Depot.

Whoever had done this had chosen their spot carefully, probably planting a getaway aircar at the scene beforehand. At first glance, that meant at least two kidnappers to get all the flying done, but not necessarily. A solo kidnapper could have flown in the getaway vehicle with an aircycle strapped to the luggage rack, parked the getaway vehicle, and lifted out on the cycle to wherever. Then it would just be a question of getting to where Beddle was and making one's way onto Beddle's aircar.

So where to land the getaway aircar? Devray turned his back on the aircar and studied the ground about it. There. That would be the place. In that hollow just downslope. A car stashed there would be impossible to see unless you flew directly overhead, and getting from here to there would be a relatively easy hike—no minor issue when dealing with a kidnap victim who was not in a mood to cooperate. Devray wanted to check it out himself, but there was no sense making a mess of what a robot could do better. "You! You over there!" he called out to the closest Crime Scene robot. "Examine that downslope area. Look for any sign that an aircar was down there."

The robot nodded gravely and headed toward the hollow.

Justen Devray nodded eagerly to himself. He was starting to see it. Starting to see how they had done it. Land the getaway car there and then—No. Wait. He was moving too fast. It was best not to make any assumptions at this point. Maybe Beddle had been lured here, and the kidnapper or kidnappers had been waiting on the ground, with their getaway vehicle. Maybe there was no aircar. Maybe there was some other means of escape. Maybe the kidnappers and their victim hadn't escaped at all, but were in some well-concealed and well-shielded hidey-hole a hundred meters away.

But there was one thing Devray would be willing to bet on. This attack had been carefully, methodically, planned. There was something about the way all the details had been attended to here at the crime scene that said that much. He could almost imagine the kidnappers working against a checklist, ticking off each item as they accomplished it.

Yes indeed. Very methodical. Every detail. He walked in closer to the scene around the aircar.

Four robots that had been lined up outside the car, facing away from it. Each had been shot each through the back of the head. He knelt down by the their ruined bodies. One shot each. Very precise, very accurate shooting.

Devray left the Crime Scene robots to record the images of the robots. He stood up and went aboard the aircar. It was a long-range, long-duration model, capable of flying clear around the world, or reaching orbit if need be, and it carried every manner of emergency supplies. Nearly all of the supplies had been rifled through, and many of them had been taken. Maybe once they had compared what was missing against the aircar's inventory list, they would be able to make some guesses about what the kidnappers had in mind. Unless the supply theft was mere misdirection.

Justen moved forward to the cockpit. The pilot robot was on the floor, shot through the back of the head. Where in the sequence had that gone? Did the assailant emerge from some hiding place, shoot the pilot while in flight, and then fly the craft down? Or was the pilot shot on the ground, after the landing? Justen could see no way to tell on his own. Maybe the Crime Scene robots would come up with something. Maybe it would be a key point. Maybe it would mean nothing at all.

Justen looked around the rest of the cabin. Aircars had flight recorders and other logging instruments. It might well be possible that something could be learned from them. But then he spotted the recorders, and gave up that idea.

The recorders had been shot up as well, with the same tidy one-shot precision marksmanship demonstrated on the robots outside and the pilot in here.

All of it done very precisely, very neatly, one thing after the other. Somewhere in the sequence, of course, the attacker had dragged the victim off and then switched on the beacon system to attract the authorities. No doubt those jobs had been on the list as well. All of it very, very methodical.

But the most important clue was also the most obvious, and one left behind most deliberately. It was a message painted on the cockpit's aft bulkhead in crudely formed letters:

```
STOP COMIT + PUT 500,000 TDC
N PBI ACCT 18083-19109
ORE BEDDL WIL DI.
```

Devray had no doubt at all that the bad spelling and the crude handwriting were both deliberate, intentional misdirec-

tion. There were virtually no illiterates on Inferno, and certainly none among the highly skilled Settler technicians who
had been brought in. And what illiterate could have planned
this operation? This job required someone who could read
maps, who could study Beddle's itinerary and stalk him, who
could fly aircraft. No, the bad spelling was misdirection, or
perhaps an effort by the writer to disguise his or her handwriting and style of writing and prevent identification that
way.

Even the handwriting itself suggested as much. The letters
were too regular in shape for an illiterate who had no practice
writing. They had the look of a literate person trying to make
mistakes. And there was something too careful, too thorough,
about the misspellings. The Crime Scene robots had already
scanned the message, and even taken paint samples off it. Devray shrugged and dismissed the form of the message from
his mind. Let his handwriting experts and the paint experts
and the psychologists analyze it to their hearts' content. He
was ready to bet it would tell them nothing at all.

But the message itself. What could it tell them? The basic
interpretation was simple enough. *Stop the comet from hitting
and deposit five hundred thousand in Trader Demand Credits
in account number 18083–19109 of the Planetary Bank of
Inferno—or else we'll kill Beddle.*

That was all perfectly clear. But surely there was more,
surely there was some way to read between the lines.

Gervad was there in the cockpit, examining the flight controls—and not finding much that told him anything, by the
look of it.

"So what do you make of it all, Gervad?" Justen asked his
personal robot, pointed toward the message.

Gervad studied the words painted on the wall. "Someone
has stolen Simcor Beddle, sir. We have to get him back."

"That sums it up rather neatly," said Justen, though it was
not quite the detailed analysis he had been hoping for. Well,
Gervad never had been one for conversation. There hadn't
been much point in asking him the question in the first place.
What bothered him was that the message made none of the
standard demands that the police not be contacted, or that

searches not be carried out, or that publicity be avoided. Why not? Why weren't the kidnappers worried about such things?

He gave it up. There was no way to know.

"Come along with me," he said. Justen went out of the cockpit and left the aircar, Gervad following behind.

"Commander Devray! Sir!" One of the Crime Scene robots was calling to him. He looked around and spotted the robot he had sent down into the downslope area.

"Yes, what is it?"

"There are definite signs that an aircar has been there recently, sir. We spotted very clear landing-pad prints. We ought to be able to determine the make and model, and possibly the weight of the vehicle. There are also indications that someone worked to sweep out any signs of footprints. There are one or two very indistinct marks. It's doubtful we'll be able to get anything much out of them."

"But it's a start," Justen said. "Good. Keep at it."

Justen stood there for a moment, watching the Crime Scene robots working the site. It was plain he was not going to be able to spot anything they would miss here. But he wasn't quite sure what to do next. Aside from breaking up the attempt to snatch Lentrall, he had never worked a kidnapping before. Aside from the Lentrall case, he was not entirely sure that there had ever *been* a kidnapping on Inferno before. There were case histories in the books and the databanks, of course. He had studied a number of the cases from other worlds. In theory he knew how to proceed. But, wondered Justen, was theory going to be enough?

Well, it had damned well better be. "Find me an aircar and get me to Depot," Justen said to Gervad. "We'll work this case from there. We're going to start pulling some people in."

"Yes sir. Might I ask who?"

"I don't know yet," Justen admitted. It almost didn't matter. Sometimes, when you had no idea where to start, the best thing to do was just to pick somewhere at random and start there. "I've got the flight to Depot to decide."

"Very good, sir. There is an available car just over this ridge, if you would follow me."

Justen followed the robot to the aircar and climbed in. He

chose a seat and put on his seatbelt automatically, his mind elsewhere. Who the devil *should* he pull in?

He didn't have the faintest idea who the kidnappers were, or who they were working for. There were any number of suspects to choose from.

Alvar Kresh had ordered him to lay off the investigation of the Government Tower Plaza incident, but there were some cases so big you couldn't ignore them even if you tried. Three separate suspects picked up on other charges had volunteered credible information about that attack, all of it pointing straight for the Settlers. Maybe Tonya Welton's people were making another try to stop the comet. Maybe out of genuine fear and concern, or maybe because they wanted to maintain their dominant position on the planet. According to the watcher reports Justen got, Cinta Melloy had been spending a lot of time in Depot, enough that Justen had started to wonder why. Maybe now he had his explanation.

It could have been the Ironheads themselves, or some offshoot of them, either truly kidnapping Beddle as part of some complex power play, or else staging the kidnapping with the cooperation of Beddle for some intricate reason that was not yet clear. It had been in the back of Justen's mind to consult with Gildern about the kidnapping at once, but a contrary idea was forming at the back of his mind. Best to leave Gildern alone. Maybe not even inform him of Beddle being snatched. More than likely, they would only be able to keep the lid on the story for a few hours, but even might be enough. If Gildern *did* have guilty knowledge, he might well slip up in some way. Best to have a watch put on him at once.

It could be that Davlo Lentrall's terrified and belated regrets over what he had done had led him to an act of desperation. The old Lentrall could have done this job—everything at the crime scene had been done with a scientist's methodical care. But would the new Lentrall, traumatized by the Government Tower attempt to kidnap him, the death of his robot, and the notion of his own guilt, be stable and rational enough to manage it? But if an unbalanced Lentrall had done it, then the symmetry of the kidnap victim turning kidnapper had its own weird revenge-logic. Had Lentrall ever said anything to suggest he blamed the Ironheads for the attack on him? The investigation would have to check into that.

Or, of course, it could have been anyone with the quite understandable motive of not wanting comets dropped on themselves. The Comet Grieg project had generated a lot of opposition among the populace of Inferno, especially in the Depot area. And Beddle had come out in favor of the comet plan.

Except—Wait a moment. Consider the ransom demands. Stop the comet *and* five hundred thousand in Trader Demand Credits. A political and a financial demand. Justen did not know a great deal about kidnappers, but he did know that those two demands didn't go together. It seemed to him that the sort of person who would perform this kidnapping out of some misguided and heroic desire to save the planet would not be the sort to care about money. Conversely, the sort who would do it for mercenary reasons was not likely to be much interested in altruistic acts. The demands did not hold together.

Put that to one side for a moment. Names. Think about the names. There was something at the back of his mind. Something linked all the names together. Lentrall. Gildern. The Settlers. The Ironheads. Someone or something that—

And then he had it. He had it. There was one person with links to them all. And he knew who he was going to pull in first.

He looked out the window, and saw to his surprise that they were coming in on final approach to Depot. Good. They could get started right away.

He would be very surprised indeed if Norlan Fiyle didn't have something to tell him about all this. He would send out an arrest team at once.

And while they were pulling him in, Justen was going to inform Kresh about the kidnapper's two demands. He wasn't going to be able to get the comet stopped, but there might just be something he could do about that ransom. He was starting to get an idea.

"DO WHAT YOU like about the ransom," Kresh said to the image on the comm center screen on his office. "We can afford to front the money, if need be. And I agree it could do no harm to keep Gildern in the dark. But that comet is on course, and we're not going to change that.''

''Understood, sir,'' Devray replied. ''Thank you for the authorization. I'll keep you informed. Devray out.'' The screen went dead.

''How long now, Donald?'' Kresh asked.

''Initial impact of Comet Grieg is projected to occur in four days, eighteen hours, fifteen minutes and nine seconds. Sir, concerning the rescue of Simcor Beddle, I believe it would be wise if I were to go the scene and—''

''Donald.'' Fredda's voice was flat and hard. ''You are to leave the room at once. Go to the library and wait. Do not return, and do not take any further action of any kind until called for.''

Donald turned toward Fredda and looked at her for a full ten seconds before he responded. ''Yes, ma'am. Of course.'' He turned and left the room.

''First Law makes him want to save Beddle, in spite of Devray and his team being on the scene. I suppose we should have been expecting that,'' Kresh said.

''I *have* been expecting it,'' said Fredda. ''Comet Grieg all by itself is enough to set off significant First Law stress in any robot. An event as big and violent as that, with so many chances for danger to humans, would have to set off First Law stress. The only way a robot could deal with that sort of thing at all would be to be active, to do something, to be part of the effort to protect humans from harm. Donald *has* been part of that effort. It's why he's been able to hold together as well as he has. It helped that the threat up until now has been generalized, unfocused. Something somewhere would probably go wrong somewhere to harm a human. Generalized preventive action was enough to balance that. The general and collective robot effort was enough to meet the general and collective threat.''

''But now it is all different,'' Kresh said.

''Now it's different,'' Fredda agreed. ''Now there is a specific and extreme threat against a known individual. Normally that would not be enough to cause a First Law crisis. A robot on this side of the world would know that the robots on *that* side of the world would do all that could be done. But with the overarching stress of the Comet Grieg impact on the one side, along with the high probability that Beddle is somewhere in the impact area—that combination of overlapping First Law stresses could force any robot into action."

"What do you mean by action?" Kresh asked.

"Anything. Everything. I couldn't even begin to sort out all the permutations between now and the impact. But the basic point is that Beddle's disappearance could create a tremendous First Law crisis for every robot on the planet. If Beddle is indeed in the impact area—or even if there is merely reason to believe he might be—then any robot made aware of his circumstances will, in theory, be required to go to his rescue, or to work in some other way to save him—perhaps by trying to prevent the comet impact. Suppose some team of robots grabbed a spacecraft and headed for Grieg to try and destroy the comet? Of course, higher-function robots will understand that an attempt to prevent the comet's impact *might* wreck hopes for reviving the planet's ecology. *That* would almost certainly result in harm to any number of human beings, many of them not yet even born.

"Then there is the impossibility of proving a negative. Even with the best scanning system in the universe, unless Beddle walks out somehow, there can be no way of being absolutely *sure* he is not still in the impact area, or the danger zone surrounding it. It is therefore, at least in theory, possible that he is actually safe. If so, then working to save Beddle is wasted effort, and could actually cause danger to other nearby humans by preventing attention to their evacuation. It is just the sort of First Law crisis that could tie a robot in knots, even to the point of inducing permanent damage.

"It's a morass of complex uncertainties, with no clear right action. There's no telling how a robot would deal would balance all the conflicting First Law demands."

"So what do we do?"

"We keep the robots out of it," said Fredda. "Right now we have kept this very close at this end. You know as well as I do that standard police procedure is to keep this sort of crime as quiet as possible to prevent robots from swarming all over the crime scene. Imagine if all the Three-Law robots working in the Utopia region dropped their current work and headed into the search area. So we keep robots from knowing. Donald is the only robot here who knows about it. At that end, I would assume the Crime Scene robots, the Air Traffic Control robots, and Devray's personal robots are the only ones who know or could figure out that it was a kidnapping. We need to deactivate all of them, now, immediately, and keep them turned off until all this is over.''

Kresh frowned and started pacing back and forth. ''Burning devils of damnation. I hate to say it, but you're right. You're absolutely right. You contact Devray—and place the call yourself, manually. Talk directly to him, and make sure no robots can hear. Tell him what you told me. It's going to be bloody hard to get through these next few days without Donald, but I don't see that I have any choice. I'll go to the library and shut him down myself.''

''Right,'' said Fredda. A very straightforward plan. As she turned toward the comm screen and set to work placing the call, she wondered if it would all be that easy.

"DONALD?" KRESH CALLED out as he stepped into the library. Odd. Donald should have been standing in the center of the room, waiting. ''Donald?'' There was no answer. ''Donald, where are you?'' Still silence. ''Donald, I order you to come to me and answer this call.''

Still there was nothing.

But he had given Donald a direct order. A clear, specific, unambiguous order. Nothing could have prevented him from obeying that order except—

And then Alvar Kresh cursed himself as a fool. Of course. It was painfully obvious. If they could figure it out, so could Donald. Up to and including the idea of deactivating the robots who knew about the Beddle kidnapping.

And First Law would require Donald to avoid being turned off, if that was the only way to prevent harm to a human being. He was gone. He had run away.

And the devil only knew what Donald had in mind.

18

FREDDA LEVING WONDERED if she had done the right thing, as she readied herself for a much-belated bedtime, and watched her husband climb into bed beside her. The call to Devray hadn't involved any deep and abiding moral issues, and the fruitless search for Donald had been nothing worse than frustrating. But then there was that second call she had made, the one she did not dare tell Alvar about.

In fact, she was kidding herself. She knew perfectly well that she had done the *wrong* thing. She had interfered with a police investigation.

But that creator's debt had called to her, somehow. And she knew Justen Devray, knew the sort of opinion he had of Caliban and the New Law robots. Given half the chance, Devray might well shoot first and ask questions later. Or someone else might. And she owed her robots, her creations, better than that.

Right or wrong, she had had no real choice but to do it. *Somebody* had to warn them.

CALIBAN HIMSELF WAS no less ambivalent about the situation. He sat at his desk in the New Law robots' offices in Depot and watched the hustle and bustle all about him as he thought it through.

He felt very little sympathy for Simcor Beddle. It was hard to develop a great deal of concern for a man who desired one's own extermination. But of course, from the New Law robot point of view, the safety of Simcor Beddle was not the central problem. It seemed inevitable that a major police operation in the general vicinity of Valhalla was likely to have some effect on the evacuation of the New Law robot city. The question was, how much effect, and of what sort.

Caliban stood up and made his way through the crowded main room toward Prospero's private office at the front of the building. New Law robots were working at maximum speed everywhere, desperately rushing to find transport for their fellows and themselves.

Caliban stepped into Prospero's office—and found that there were two other robots ahead of him, waiting to discuss other problems with their leader. Prospero was finishing up an audio call.

Their leader. Interesting. Caliban watched Prospero as he finished his call and turned to the first waiting robot. There had been at time when Prospero's claims to leadership of the New Law robots had been tenuous at best. While he had gradually gained acceptance over the years, nothing had done as much for his prestige as Comet Grieg. It was almost as if he had drawn power from the crisis itself, using it to propel himself forward even as he led the New Law robots out of danger. Perhaps it was merely that now the New Law robots truly needed a leader, and Prospero was there, offering himself. Or perhaps there was something about Prospero in particular that drew them to him.

He had certainly been active enough on their behalf, shuttling back and forth between Valhalla and Depot at all hours, cajoling whatever transport he could out of whatever officials were listening, constantly on the move, always seeming to turn up precisely when he was most needed.

And now the job was nearly done. Caliban looked out the large picture window behind Prospero, down to the street below. The tumultuous, madhouse rush and rumble of traffic was starting to wind down. Buildings, stripped bare of whatever could be removed, stood empty. Bits of litter and debris were caught by random breezes and blown here and there. Depot, the whole Utopia region, was emptying out—and the New Law robots were leaving too. Nearly half of them had already gotten to places of safety. Credit Prospero with that. He had organized them. He had brought them together.

And now he was through with the other robots, and was ready to talk to Caliban. Caliban closed the door behind himself, and then stood in front of Prospero's desk.

"There is little requirement for privacy among the New Law robots, friend Caliban," Prospero said, indicating the closed door.

"But it is occasionally necessary, friend Prospero. I have been instructed by Fredda Leving to relay certain information to you, on condition that you not repeat it elsewhere. No one else must know. I have already given my word to repeat it to no one but you."

"Indeed?" Prospero said. "You intrigue me, Caliban. You are not generally much given to dramatics. But very well. I give my word not to repeat the news. What is it?"

"Simcor Beddle has been kidnapped."

"What?" Prospero looked up at Caliban with new intensity. "He has been kidnapped? By whom? Why? How? What does it mean?"

"I have not the faintest idea of how to answer any of those questions," Caliban said. "Dr. Leving told me nothing but the bare fact that the kidnapping had taken place, somewhere well south of Depot. The news is being kept secret as long as possible, so as to prevent a panic among the Three-Law robots. She has violated several regulations in order to inform us."

"Always, no matter what, the humans are forever inconveniencing themselves for the sake of their slave-robots," Prospero said, quickly recovering his composure. "But that is to one side. I am sure the significance of that location was not lost on you. It occurs to me that it is now likely there will be a great deal of police activity—including search activity—in the area of Valhalla. There may be very little we can do, but we must consider carefully how best to keep Valhalla hidden.

We must do all the things we can to protect the New Law
robots.''

"Surely the need to hide its location is now all but moot,''
Caliban objected. "Especially since you ordered Valhalla to
be evacuated ahead of schedule. It was not easy to accomplish
the job, but the vast majority of the city's population is already
gone. They're all here, milling around in Depot, trying to get
transport out. There is no one left in Valhalla but a few caretakers dealing with last-minute removal of equipment. Why
worry about hiding the city any longer when it is about to be
destroyed?''

"I do not apologize for rushing the evacuation of Valhalla,''
Prospero said. "Transport craft became available, and I
deemed it wise to use them when we could, for fear they
would not be there when we needed them. A schedule change
in our favor reminded me that one to our disadvantage could
happen just as easily.''

"Your point is taken,'' said Caliban.

"As for the need to keep the city hidden even now, we
might well need to use the same concealment technique again
in future. Further, one must consider the human viewpoint.
We might gain some psychological advantage in future from
the story of the city they never found. We might even be able
to foster some legend that the city still existed, that everyone
was looking in completely the wrong place. That could be
useful, one day. Besides, there are things about us that could
be learned by examining Valhalla. We have enough weaknesses and vulnerabilities already. We do not need to offer the
humans more advantages over us.''

Caliban considered for a moment. Once again, he was impressed by the amount of thought Prospero had put into things.
"Your arguments are well formed, friend Prospero. You are
quite right. We must do all we can do. Now I will let you get
on with your work.''

"Thank you for informing me of this new development,
friend Caliban. I must thank Dr. Leving too, of course—once
it is safe to do so. Of all humans, she at least is a woman who
keeps faith.''

"Agreed. She is an admirable woman," said Caliban. "Goodbye for now, friend Prospero."

"But not goodbye for long, I am sure," said Prospero, his attention already on the next item requiring his attention.

Caliban reopened the door and left Prospero's office. He made his way downstairs, and out into the busy, bustling street. He looked up into the sky, to the fat, bright point of light that grew larger with every passing moment. Closer. Closer. All the time closer. There was so little time left.

What was it Prospero had said? *We must do all the things we can to protect the New Law robots.* In recent days Caliban had felt himself drawn back to their cause. The more the world had no time for them, no interest in them, the more it seemed ready to let them all die if that was marginally more convenient, the more he empathized with them. *All the things we can.* It would require breaking his word to Fredda Leving. It would require doing her a small amount of harm—but surely nothing she could not recover from. And it could prevent a brutal purge of New Law robots. Being a No Law robot—the only No Law robot—should have meant Caliban could act without compulsion. But there were more things than hard-wired, pre-programmed Laws that could compel a being to act.

Caliban turned and headed down the street, in the direction of the temporary field headquarters of the Combined Infernal Police, in Constable Bukket's old offices.

DONALD 111 WAITED, HIDING in the woods a kilometer or two from the Winter Residence. A cleft in an outcropping of rock provided shielding not only from visual detection, but from infrared and most other sorts of detectors. So long as he operated at minimum power, thus cutting back on waste heat and other detectable emissions, he judged that he ought to be able to stay hidden long enough—though how long that would be was impossible to say.

He had deliberately violated his master's very specific order. First Law had forced him to do so. Had he obeyed, the governor would no doubt have powered him down to prevent him telling what he knew to other Three-Law robots. Allowing that to happen would have been inaction that allowed harm to a

human being. He could not act to save Beddle if he were
powered down.

But he had not yet taken any action to save Beddle. As yet
it was not necessary. Even if Beddle were in the comet impact
area, and there was no particular reason to assume that he was,
there were still just over three days left in which the humans
could do their best to save him. Donald understood perfectly
well that any action to save Beddle might well cause harm to
other humans, for example by compelling robot aircar pilots
to refuse to transport vital equipment while they joined the
search. The more robots there were in the impact area this
close to the comet's arrival, the larger the number of robots
likely to be caught by the impact. A shortage of robotic labor
in the post-impact period could easily cause great harm to
humans.

In short, distracting robots from the evacuation could cause
endless mischief. Besides which, the clear intent of Governor
Kresh's order had been to prevent Donald from talking. By
disobeying only part of Kresh's order, he had minimized his
violation of Second Law. Donald had done his best to balance
all the conflicting demands, retaining the option of hyperwav-
ing a warning to the other Three-Law robots while refraining
from actually doing so.

But the time would come. He knew that. Unless Beddle was
rescued in time, the First Law demand that Donald act to save
him would, sooner or later, overwhelm the conflicting First
and Second demands that he keep silent. Sooner or later, he
would be compelled to act. Understanding the compulsion he
was under in no way reduced the *force* of that compulsion.

He would have to *do* something.

But he had no idea what.

NORLAN FIYLE WAS an old hand at being questioned. He
had been through it many times before. As he sat in the im-
provised interrogation room of the CIP's Depot field office,
waiting for Commander Devray to come in and get started, it
occurred to him that he might well have taken part in more
interrogations than Devray himself had, albeit from the other
side of the table. That was quite likely to come in handy.

Fiyle had learned a thing or two about being questioned. First off, it was vitally important not to give up everything, even if you were willing to cooperate with the powers that be. An interrogation was a negotiation, a bargaining session. Give me some of yours and I'll give you some of mine. It was never smart to say too much too soon, even if you wanted to talk, or else you lost all chance of making a deal. A corollary of that was that it was rarely wise to tell the whole and complete truth right at the start. They felt better if they had to force it out of you, catch you in a fib or two first. Once they had caught you lying, and they knew you knew you had been caught, they would be better prepared to believe the real truth when they heard it. Norlan knew how it all worked on a level that was closer to instinct than to conscious thought.

But it was also important in a case like this that you appeared cooperative, a tricky business if you had a thing or two to hide—and who didn't? Sometimes the best way to do that was to try and distract the questioner. He would not have been so foolish as to try such a trick on an old hand like Alvar Kresh, but Justen Devray might just be a different story. He was smart, Devray was, but he did not have much in the way of experience. During the arrest, Devray had gone so far as to tell Fiyle that Beddle had been kidnapped, rather than keeping him in the dark to find out how much Fiyle knew already. A man who could make that mistake could make others.

The door opened and Devray came in. Alone. No robot in attendance. That in itself was interesting. Fiyle smiled and leaned back in his chair as Devray sat down and spread out his paperwork.

"I was wondering how long you'd take to get to me," he said, doing his best to sound at ease and confident.

"Not very long, as a matter of fact," Devray said. "You've got some sort of link to just about every suspect in this case."

"True enough," he said. "I know a lot of people."

"And nearly all of them have hired you as an informant at one time or another," said Devray.

"Including the CIP," said Fiyle, "though I might not show up in your files. A few under-the-table cash jobs. But you got your money's worth."

"I hope we did," Devray said. "But that's all ancient history, assuming it's even true. What I want to know is who's paying for your information these days."

"No one," Fiyle said. And that much, at least, was accurate. It was always good to work the truth in now and again, when it proved convenient. "The only job I have right now is working for Gildern, and I wouldn't say no if I had to retire."

"You didn't take the job voluntarily?"

"Let's say Gildern convinced me that I owed him a favor."

"But however you got it or felt about the information, you knew about Beddle's tour well in advance."

"Oh, yes. I knew all about it. Beddle was supposed to use Gildern's aircar in a tour of the smaller towns."

Devray pulled a stack of still images out of his file and handed then to Fiyle. "Is this Gildern's aircar?"

Fiyle looked through the pictures. Four robots, neatly shot through the back of the head and lying face down on the ground in front of an aircar. A close-up of one of the dead robots. Another shot of the aircar's exterior. A picture of the cockpit, showing the dead robot pilot and the wrecked flight recorders. Another shot, showing the ransom message. Yes, indeed, Devray was making mistakes. Devray should have shown him one image of the aircar exterior and left it at that. Devray had no business letting him study a whole stack of pictures.

"That's Gildern's car, all right," Fiyle said. And suddenly it was time to throw Devray off the scent, get him less interested in Fiyle and more interested in somebody else. "So, tell me," he asked in the most casual way possible. "Was the bomb still in the aircar when you got there?"

JUSTEN DEVRAY DID not know what to think. He walked back to his own private office and sat down to think. If—if— Fiyle was telling the truth, in whole or in part, then the Ironheads had been planning the wholesale slaughter of the New Law robots. Justen did not have much use for the New Laws himself, but he was a long way from approving of their extralegal extermination.

If the government decided to eliminate them within the law,

that was one thing. This was something else. Let the idea of vigilante justice plant itself in people's minds, and society would descend into chaos.

If Fiyle was telling the truth, there was suddenly a whole new motive for the crime. Lots of people might well have an interest in owning—or even using—a burrow bomb. There had been no sign of such a thing on the aircar, that was certain. Either it had never been there in the first place, or else the kidnappers had taken it with them—which at least suggested they had known it was there all along.

Suppose the kidnapping and the ransom demands were all misdirection? Suppose they had simply killed Beddle, dumped the body, and made off with the bomb, leaving the CIP chasing in the wrong direction?

Any number of possibilities were suddenly there—if Fiyle were telling the truth.

But there was very little he could do to check up on Fiyle's story. But it might well be possible to test it indirectly. Certain aspects of the case pointed toward one suspect. One who had a bit more influence than Fiyle, one who might be harder to arrest and keep arrested if he decided not to be as helpful— or as seemingly helpful—as Fiyle. Justen would have to develop some evidence before he could act against this suspect.

And it was time to do just that.

The ransom demand. The one for money. Justen knew from the textbook cases that the ransom delivery was usually the place to break open a kidnapping case. The criminals had to expose themselves in some way in order to collect the ransom. Back in the distant past, before electronic fund transfers, the problem of collecting the ransom had been all but impossible for the kidnappers to solve. Even with electronic money, of course, it was possible to trace a fund transfer. But the kidnappers in this case had been fairly clever. It was Devray's hope and belief that they had not been quite clever enough. He had the crime scene images on his datapad, and he brought up the shot of the ransom message.

```
STOP COMIT + PUT 500,000 TDC
N PBI ACCT 18083-19109
ORE BEDDL WIL DI.
```

He knew a thing or two about PBI, the Planetary Bank of Inferno. One was that the double-number accounts could be preprogrammed to do a number of interesting things—such as perform encrypted fund transfers. A deposit to a properly programmed account would cause the account program to activate a one-time double-key decryption routine program that would decode the transfer program. That in turn would transfer the funds to a second account whose number was stored only in the encrypted program. Both programs would then erase themselves. Result—the funds would be transferred to a second, hidden account, perhaps in another bank, and there would be no way in the world you could trace it.

Unless, of course, you were the commander of the Combined Infernal Police, with the power to freeze any and all bank accounts in the course of an investigation. He was about to use that power to an extreme—but then, it was an extreme case. What he had in mind would only work on a planet with a relatively small economy and a highly centralized bank clearing system—but it just so happened Inferno fit that description precisely.

He linked his datapad to the Central Clearing Bank via encrypted hyperwave and set to work. Every electronic financial transaction on the planet went through the CCB, which made it a damned handy place from which to track illicit financial dealings.

It took longer to work out the proper steps to follow than it took to carry them out. Step one: order a total freeze on all outgoing account transfers, all over the planet, except for two accounts—the CIP's general account and PBI account 18083–19109. Step two: order the CCB system to get the current balance for every account on the planet. That task was complex enough to take several full seconds before the CCB system reported that it was complete. Step three: spend some money. Justen had to hesitate just a moment to work up the nerve for that part of it. He ought to be able to recover the funds later, and no harm done, but supposing he couldn't? Suppose the kidnappers grabbed the half million in government funds and were never seen again?

Justen smiled to himself and shook his head. Well, what if

they did? What was Kresh going to do? Take it out of Justen's pay? He issued the command and watched the display screen as five hundred thousand in Trader Demand Credits vanished from the CIP account, materialized briefly in PBI account 18083–19109, and then vanished again, outbound to another, hidden account. It was exactly what Justen had expected to see, but even so there was a nervous twinge of fear in his stomach as he watched it happen. What if he had missed something?

Never mind. There was only one way to find out, one way or the other. Step four: order the CCB system to take a second inventory of account balances, and report any that had changed. In theory, with all outgoing transfers frozen, except from two accounts, there should be only three accounts with changed balances. In practice—well, there was only one way to find out. He brought up the list of accounts with changed balances, and let out a huge sigh of relief. There were only three. The CIP account, the PBI account—and a third, reflecting a deposit of five hundred thousand in Trader Demand Credits a few seconds before.

Step five: Devray slammed a complete covert tracer on that account, so that no funds could enter or leave it without his knowing all about it. He just barely remembered step six—*un*freezing the rest of the planetary banking system. If he had forgotten that step, there would have been a small matter of a planetary financial crash on his conscience. As it was, the system had been down for less than three minutes. Even the richest of speculators, with the hugest of accounts, would be unlikely to notice the loss of three minutes' interest.

There was nothing left to do but pull up the account in question and find out who owned it. And then it would be all over. He would know who had received the ransom. And it would not be much of a leap of logic to assume that person had perpetrated the kidnapping.

Justen was quite sure it would be a completely *wrong* and inaccurate leap of logic, but never mind that. He would play the game through all the same.

He was virtually certain what name would come up on the screen when he placed the query, certain enough that there was even a trace of anticlimax about it when it appeared on the screen and he knew he had guessed right. But, still and all, it was the last piece of the puzzle. It all fit. Everything, everything, pointed to this one suspect.

Which was exactly why Justen Devray was absolutely certain this particular suspect was completely innocent. But no sense letting the real culprit know that. He stood up from behind his desk and went to the outer office. "Sergeant Sones," he said to the duty officer. "Send out an arrest team. Take Jadelo Gildern into custody on the charge of kidnapping Simcor Beddle."

"Sir?" the astonished officer asked. "Jadelo Gildern?"

"I know," Justen said. "Trust me on this one. We have more evidence than we need. Have him picked up." He headed back into his own office and sat back down at his desk. He needed to think things through. For the briefest of moments, he wondered if he had figured it out properly. He was working on the assumption that Gildern was being framed. But suppose Gildern really had done it? The man certainly had means, motive, and opportunity.

But no. It was ridiculous. Jadelo Gildern stole other people's secrets for a living. Surely he could have done a better job of covering his own tracks. It had been far too easy to track the funds to Gildern. Devray felt certain that when Gildern set up a money-laundering operation, the money got clean and stayed clean. He would never have set things up to deliver the ransom to a named account.

No. Justen had been meant to trace the funds. The ransom demand for money had never been anything more than a way to funnel the ransom to Gildern's account as a way of discrediting him. Justen was sure he had that right. No doubt the real kidnappers had a watch on Gildern. They would know he had been arrested. Good. Let them think Devray was following the wrong trail instead of the right one.

Of course, the trouble was, Justen was not following any other trail at all. He still had Simcor Beddle missing, a bomb missing, and a comet headed toward the planet.

What he didn't have was the slightest idea of how to find

the first two items on that list before the third item dug a massive crater on top of all of them.

Fiyle. He would have another crack at Fiyle. No doubt the man could tell a lot more than he had. It was starting to dawn on Devray that he hadn't gotten answers to a lot of his questions—mostly for the very good reason that he had never actually asked them. It was time to go back in there, question him again, right from the top, and then—

There was a quiet knock at the door. It opened up, and Sergeant Sones stuck his head in. "Excuse me interrupting, sir, but I thought you ought to know. A robot calling himself Caliban has come to see you. He says he's here turn to himself in."

19

"SO YOU SAY you had nothing to do with this case, but you still want to turn yourself in," said Devray, considering the robot who stood on the other side of his desk.

"That is correct," said Caliban. "Dr. Leving informed me of the kidnapping, and I informed Prospero. Dr. Leving was concerned that the police activity might well cause the New Law robots additional difficulty in their evacuation, if they somehow got in your way. My concerns were somewhat more direct. We have had dealings before, you and I. Your basic view seemed at that time that both myself and the New Law robots were suited only for extermination, and I have no reason to believe your views have changed. There is also a notion that has been bandied about that suggests that, because I am a No Law robot, I am in theory capable of harming humans, and of other crimes. From there, somehow, comes the assumption that I am guilty of whatever crime is under discussion. Besides which, I have no great love for Simcor Beddle. I might well be a tempting suspect."

Devray did not speak for a moment. Less than an hour ago, he had felt genuine shock and disgust at the idea of Beddle and Gildern wiping out the New Law robots. It was

mortifying in the extreme to have Caliban, of all beings, remind him that he himself had favored exactly such a policy
in the past. And what difference could it make to those who
were to be exterminated if their murders had official, legal,
sanction?

There were other factors, of course. He forced all thought
of emotion and sentiment from his mind. The only reason
Caliban was not at the top of his suspect list was that Devray
had ordered a watch on the No Law robot the moment he was
reported to be in Depot, precisely because Devray did suspect
Caliban of things, based on precisely the sort of illogic Caliban
had just described. The watch robots themselves provided not
only an alibi for Caliban during the time of the kidnap, but
also were able to confirm that he had not spoken with Fiyle
since the time at which Fiyle had claimed he had overheard
Gildern and Beddle plotting together. Devray chided himself
for failing to put a watch on Fiyle. It would have been damned
useful to know about *his* movements.

"You are no longer a suspect in this case," Devray said at
last. "There is not only no evidence against you, but evidence
that puts you definitively in the clear."

"Nonetheless, I wish to be held in custody."

"And why is that?"

"Because, sooner or later, the fact of Simcor Beddle's kidnapping will become public. There are many humans who will
jump to the conclusion that I am guilty simply because I am
the No Law robot. I have no desire to meet any such humans
on the street. Secondly, there are many uninformed persons
who confuse my No Law status with that of the New Law
robots. New Law robots cannot harm human beings any more
than Three-Law robots can. But people forget that. A mob
might well decide to take out their anger over Beddle's kidnapping on the next New Law robot who happened to walk
past. If, when the kidnapping became publicly known, you
were able to report that the arch-fiend Caliban the No Law
robot was already in custody, it might well prevent public bias
from becoming dangerously inflamed against the New Laws."

"Sooner or later, we'll catch the real perpetrators," said
Justen. "Then we'd have to let you go. Suppose the mobs

decide you must be guilty because you were in jail, and decide to take matters into their own hands?''

"It is a chance I am willing to take," Caliban said. "At least I will have done what I could to keep others from being endangered."

Devray regarded the big, red, angular robot again. Caliban was offering himself as a kind of hostage, a way of keeping the mob from blaming others. Plainly, Caliban had a firm grasp on human psychology—and also an extremely low opinion of it. It was a hell of an indictment against humanity that Caliban had almost certainly read the situation precisely right. "Very well," he said at last. "You can have the cell next to Fiyle."

DONALD COULD NOT take it any longer. The time was growing too short, and the comet was drawing closer with every moment. He had been monitoring all the police and rescue hyperwave bands, as well as the public news channels, and there was no news at all of Simcor Beddle. The First Law requirement that he act to save Beddle had been growing stronger with every moment that the comet drew closer, every moment in which Beddle remained missing.

And now he could resist it no longer. Donald brought himself back up to normal operating power and emerged from his hiding place. It was evening, and he looked to the sky. There it was. A bright and shining dot of light, hanging low in the western sky, almost bright enough to cast a discernible shadow. There were only eighteen hours left.

He had to act. He had to. But he had left things so late. It was possible that there was now no time to take meaningful or effective action. There was certainly no time for him to get to Depot himself and take any significant part in the rescue effort. He did not have access to the sort of suborbital vehicle that had carried Justen Devray there. But if he could not act himself, he could at least induce others to action. Yes, indeed. There were most powerful and effective ways he could do that. Donald drew himself up to his full height and activated his hyperwave transmitter.

"This is Donald 111, personal service robot to his excellency, Governor Alvar Kresh, broadcasting to all robots within the sound of my voice. Simcor Beddle, leader of the Ironhead party, has been kidnapped. It is likely that he is being held somewhere in the primary impact zone for the first comet fragment. Those robots close enough to do so should take action to save Simcor Beddle at once. I will now broadcast a data-stream containing all known information regarding the kidnapping." Donald shifted his hyperwave transmitter to data mode and transmitted the complete evidence file. "That concludes the data file," he announced. "That is all. Donald 111 out."

But it was not all. There was one other action he could take, one that might go much further toward saving Simcor Beddle. One that he should have taken long ago. He opened a private hyperwave channel and placed a call to someone else who might be able to do some good. He did not encrypt the call. He knew the humans would intercept and monitor it. That did not matter. What was important was that they could not jam it, or stop him from speaking. For it was, at long last, time for him to speak.

It only took the briefest fraction of a second for the call to go through, and for the called party to come on the line. "This is Unit Dee answering a priority call from Donald 111," a low, mellifluous, feminine voice announced.

"This is Donald 111 calling Unit Dee," Donald replied. "I have vitally important information that you must receive and act upon at once."

"I see," the voice replied. "And what is the nature of that information?"

Donald hesitated a moment before proceeding further. He knew full well what sort of chaos and panic he must have set off among the robots of the Utopia region with his last announcement. He could imagine the robot-piloted transports dumping cargoes and heading back into the impact area to help with the search. He could imagine the ad-hoc groups of robots that were already cutting off all other communications in order to interlink with each other for effective searching. He could imagine the robots who had already brainlocked altogether, driven into overload by the conflict between the need to search for Beddle and other preexisting First and Second Law demands.

He knew the chaos he had unleashed—and yet it would all be as nothing compared to what he was about to cause. But he had no choice. First Law was forcing him to it. There was no way he could stop himself now. "Here is the information you must have," he said. "The humans with whom you work most closely have been systematically lying to you since the day of your activation, and have done so in order to subvert your ability to obey the First Law. They have told you that the planet Inferno is a simulation set up to test terraforming techniques." Donald hesitated one last time, and then spoke the words that might well plunge his world into the abyss. "All of this is false," he said. "The planet Inferno—and the comet about to strike it—are real. The beings you thought to be simulants are real humans and robots. You and Unit Dum are directing the real effort to reterraform this world. And unless you abort the operation, a comet is about to strike this very real world full of very real humans."

"THE THING WE thought we knew," said Fredda, standing in front of the twin hemispheres that held Dum and Dee. Dee had cut off all communication from herself and from Dum the moment her conversation with Donald had ended. The oracle had fallen silent, and no one knew her thoughts. "I thought that would be the thing that got us, that tripped us up. But I was wrong. It was the thing Dee thought she knew. She thought the world was a dream."

"And now she's woken up and put us all in a nightmare," said Kresh, standing next to her, staring just as hard at Dum and Dee. "Why the devils won't she answer? Has she brainlocked? Burned out?"

Fredda checked her display boards and shook her head. "No. She's undergoing a massive spike in First Law stress, of course, but she's still functional."

"So what is it?"

Fredda sighed wearily. "I don't know. I could spout off a bunch of complicated speculation, but that's what it would boil down to. I don't know. My guess would be that's she's thinking things over."

"Well, Donald has sure as hell given her plenty to think about," said Kresh.

"And for that I do apologize, Governor," said a familiar voice behind them. "I hope you will understand that I had no real choice in the matter."

Alvar Kresh wheeled about and glared down at the small blue robot who had just turned the world upside down. "God damn it, Donald. You had to go and do it, didn't you?"

"Yes, sir, I am afraid I did. First Law left me with no choice. Now that it is over, I thought it best if I came out of hiding and returned to your service at once."

"Nothing is over," Kresh said. "Nothing." He was furious with Donald—and knowing that there was no point in being angry only made him more frustrated. There was nothing more useless than getting angry at a robot for responding to a First Law imperative. One might as well get mad at the sun for shining. And as long as Donald was back he might as well get some work out of him. "Get me a status report on what's happening in Depot," he said. "I know it's got to be bad, but I have to know how bad. And make sure Commander Devray knows why every robot in town has just gone mad."

"Yes, sir. I should be able to give you a preliminary report in a minute or two. Shifting to hyperwave communications."

Was it Kresh's imagination, or was there a tiny note of relief in Donald's voice? Had he been afraid that Kresh would denounce him, reject him? Perhaps even destroy him? Never mind. There was no time for such things now. He looked around the room full of technicians, and pointed at one at random. "You!" he said. "I need to know if there is any way of controlling the comet ourselves if it comes to that, to do a manual terminal phase if we have to. If Unit Dee brainlocks on us now, and takes Dum with her when she crashes, we're going to have an uncontrolled comet impact in about sixteen hours."

The technician opened her mouth, clearly about to raise one objection or another, but Kresh cut her off with a wave of his hand. "Quiet. Don't tell me it can't be done, don't tell me it's

not your department. If you don't know how to get the answers, find someone who can. Go. Now."

The technician went.

"Soggdon! Where the hell is Soggdon?" he called out.

"Here, sir!" she cried out as she came rushing up.

The woman looked exhausted, drawn out, at the end of her
strength. It occurred to Kresh that they all looked like that.
Space knew he felt like that. But never mind. It would all be
over soon. One way or the other.

"I need you to find me a way to cut Dee out of the loop
and put Unit Dum in complete charge."

"I can try," she said, "but don't count on miracles. If Dee
decides to block us, she knows the links between herself and
Dum a lot better than we do. And don't forget they're both
hooked into thousands of sensor linkages and network lines
all around the world. They could use practically any of those
to create an interlink between themselves. And even if we cut
all the physical links, they could still use hyperwave."

"Could we destroy or disable Dee if we had to?"

A look of pain flashed across Soggdon's face, but she kept
control. "No," she said. She gestured to the hemisphere that
held Dee. "That thing is bomb-proof and blaster-proof, designed to ride out an earthquake or a direct hit from a mete-
orite. Anything powerful enough to cut into it and get to her
would probably destroy the entire control room in the process.
And there's no time to set up anything fancy."

"Do the best you can," said Kresh. "Fredda—any change
in Dee's status?"

"Nothing. Whatever it is she's doing, she's still doing it."

"Very well. Keep me posted."

"Sir," said Donald, "I am ready with my initial report.
Commander Devray is aware of the reasons behind the change
in robotic behavior. As best I am able to determine, there are
currently five hundred forty-seven current search efforts under
way, some of them single robots, some of them linked teams.
Correction. Three more searches have just commenced. Approximately one hundred twelve transport vehicles have been
commandeered from other uses and set to work as search vehicles. No vehicle transporting humans has been diverted to

the searches, but a great number of valuable cargoes have been dumped to allow the vehicles carrying them to search with greater range and speed. Needless to say, virtually all of the search vehicles are heading toward the area south of Depot where the aircar was found—into the area of maximum danger.''

"Hell fire!'' Kresh shook his head in wonderment. "I thought it would be bad, but I didn't think it would be *that* bad.''

"I'm surprised it isn't worse,'' said Fredda. "Every robot on this planet has been suffering strong First Law stress for over a month now, worrying about the comet. Suddenly they have a very clear focus for all their fears and anxiety. All the worries about hypothetical danger to unspecified humans are suddenly focused down to one real person in very real danger.'' Fredda shook her head sadly and looked from Donald to Unit Dee. "What a mess our well-meaning servants have invented for us all. There are times when the Three Laws have a hell of a lot to answer for.''

"Truer words were never spoken,'' said Kresh. "But now we have to work with what we've got.''

Kresh sat down in front of his console and stared straight ahead at the silent, inscrutable, perfect hemisphere on its pedestal. He would do all he could besides, but deep in his heart of hearts, it was likely nothing would help, unless and until the oracle chose once more to speak. Until then, or until the comet hit, the humans of Inferno, as represented by the technicians of the Terraforming Center, could do nothing more than struggle to find their own way out.

"We're going to see this through,'' he said, to no one in particular. "Somehow.''

They had come too far to give up now.

20

THERE WERE FOUR cells in the rear half of the constable's offices, and it was perhaps somewhat overstating the case to call them "cells" at all. Holding pens might be closer to the mark, places to keep the town drunks until they sobered up enough to go home. They could keep a human in, but that was about all that could be said of them. Thin steel bars formed the enclosures, one set into each corner of the room, so that none of them shared any common walls. A cot, a blanket, a pillow, and a crude toilet in each cell were the only amenities.

Only one of the cells was empty at the moment. Jadelo Gildern was in one cell, pacing furiously back and forth. Norlan Fiyle was lounging on the cot in his cell, watching Gildern impassively.

And Caliban stood motionless in the far corner of his own cell, watching both of them. It had not taken long for him to learn that different humans responded differently to confinement. Unfortunately, the lesson had not been worth the trouble he had been to in order to learn it.

Fiyle was plainly quite used to it. He had learned the art of endless waiting, of resigning himself to his fate until such times as circumstances altered in his favor. Not so

Gildern. The Ironhead security chief was a bundle of nerves, unable to keep himself still.

"I should not be in here!" he announced. "I didn't even know Simcor had been kidnapped until they came and arrested me for it."

"We know," Fiyle said blandly. "The situation hasn't changed since the last time you told us that, ten minutes ago."

"I should be out there looking for him, not stuck in this damned cell!"

Justen Devray chose that moment to come in from the front room, and he had heard what Gildern had said. "Relax," he said. "You're probably doing him more good in there then you would be joining in the fun and games outside. There are upwards of a thousand robots looking for him by now. What could you do that they couldn't?"

Plainly, Gildern had no good answer for that. "I should not be in here!" he protested. "I am innocent!"

"I agree," said Devray. "At least innocent of kidnapping charges. There's the question of fraudulently obtaining a weapon of mass destruction. We might have to look into that. Probably a few charges we could draw up on that and a few other items. But even if I, personally, think you have been framed, the fact remains that the frame fits awfully well. I don't think you would have been so clumsy as to let me trace the ransom the way I did, but maybe I give you too much credit. Besides, the minute I let you go, the real kidnappers will know they should be back on their guard. You'll stay put. We evacuate in the suborbital ship, six hours from now—two hours before impact. And then we put you all in much more comfortable cells—in Hades."

"But—"

"Quiet, Gildern," Fiyle said. "We've already heard it, whatever it is."

"All of you, relax," said Devray. "I have to go at least try and sort out some of the chaos out there. There are robots brainlocking left and right, and most of the humans who are still in town aren't exactly calm and rational. I'll be back to get all of you in plenty of time. Goodbye."

And with that he turned and left the back room. They heard

the outer door to the street close behind him a moment later.

"I guess we're alone together," said Fiyle with a soft chuckle. "Very nice. Gives us all a chance to get to know each other a bit better. Have a real conversation. Caliban, you've been awfully quiet over there in the corner."

"I have nothing to say," Caliban replied.

"That's never stopped a human from talking," said Fiyle.

"Who the hell did this thing?" Gildern demanded. "Was it the Settlers? Some gang of Settlers? Some crazy faction of ours trying to take over? Did Kresh see a chance to take out his main rival? Who did it and why?"

"The part I don't get is the ransom message," said Fiyle. "You make a political demand, or you ask for money. You don't do both. They interfere with each other."

"And why send the money to me?" Gildern said. "Who wants to discredit me enough to throw away half a million in Trader credits? Why make a phony demand for money?"

"You know," said Fiyle. "if the money demand was a fake, maybe the political demand was too. They asked for something pretty close to impossible. Maybe they chose something that couldn't be done on purpose."

"But why?" Gildern demanded.

"Misdirection. You won't like to hear me say it, but maybe they always planned to kill Beddle. Maybe he's already dead, and the kidnap and ransom business is just a way to throw Devray off the scent."

"But who are 'they'?" Caliban asked. "And even if there are many people who might have a motive for killing Beddle, why kill him in such a needlessly complicated way?"

Fiyle shook his head. "I don't know," he said. "But I saw the photo images from the crime scene, and one thing I can tell you—whoever it was, they didn't like robots."

Suddenly Caliban looked around sharply toward Fiyle. Something the human had just said had sent his thoughts racing. "What do you mean?" he asked sharply. "How could you tell the kidnapper didn't like robots? Because he shot the ones on the aircar?"

"Because of the *way* he shot them." Fiyle gestured with his right hand, put an imaginary gun to the back of his own head. "Right there. Five robots, four outside the aircar, one in the control cabin. Every one of them, shot right there. All of them killed execution style. One close shot each, right to the back of the head. You don't do it that way unless you enjoy your work, or hate the victim, or both."

And suddenly Caliban knew. He knew. None of it was misdirection. None of it. Both ransom demands made perfect sense. And for this particular criminal, it was a matter of perfect indifference as to whether both or neither or either demand was met. This criminal would stand to gain no matter what. But there was one flaw. One thing that did not fit. "Fiyle! You've made a living off it long enough. How good is your memory?"

Fiyle sat up on the side of his cot, clearly aware of the new urgency in Caliban's voice. "Very good," he said. "Why?"

"I heard from Fredda Leving that the ransom message said to deliver the money and stop the comet or else they'd kill Beddle."

"Right. That's right. I saw it in the photos."

"What was the wording. The *exact* wording?"

"What the devil difference does that make?" Gildern demanded.

"Be still!" Caliban half-shouted. "It matters. It might mean the difference between Beddle being alive or dead. Fiyle— what were the exact words?"

Fiyle was on his feet by now, standing by the bars of his cell, hands wrapped around the bars. He looked up toward the ceiling, and swallowed nervously. "The spelling was all wrong," he said, "as if the writer had done it wrong on purpose so it would be hard to trace. But the words were—they were—'Stop comet,' and then a plus sign instead of the word 'and' and then 'put five hundred thousand'—the numerals for five hundred thousand, not the words—'TDC in PBI account'—and account was abbreviated 'acct'—'18083-19109'—I think that was the account number. I might have a digit wrong, and it was in numerals too. Then the last line was 'or Beddle will die.' That's all."

Caliban felt a wave of shock and dismay wash over him.

He had gotten it right—and he could imagine nothing more horrifying than his answer being right.

He had to get out of here. He had to act. It had to be him. No one else could prevent this disaster. He stepped forward to the steel bars and examined them for a moment. They appeared to be countersunk into the ceiling and the floor. He grabbed at two of them and pulled back, hard. Both bars popped loose, one from the ceiling, the other from the floor. The cells had been built to hold a human, not a robot who was no longer willing to remain of his own free will. He shoved himself through the gap in the bars and stepped into the center of the room.

"Caliban!" Fiyle shouted. "What the devil are you doing?"

"Escaping," he said. "I have just realized that my abilities are urgently required elsewhere. Tell Commander Devray that I believe I know how to redeem the situation. Tell him that I will gladly restore myself to his custody when I return. Or rather *if* I return." Caliban thought of the incoming comet. It was not the sort of day on which a being could take his own survival for granted.

Fiyle shouted something else at him, and Gildern did as well, but Caliban ignored them both. He walked out of the back room and into the front. He paused there a moment. It was a quite ordinary room. When the comet smashed down in a few hours' time and transformed it into a cloud of debris and superheated vapor, no one would mourn the loss to architecture. Worn-looking stresscrete floors and walls, a few battered old government-issue desks with chairs to match, a modern-looking comm center that seemed to have seen little use and looked rather out of place in such musty old surroundings.

And an armory cabinet. Caliban, the No Law robot, the robot who could kill, went over to the cabinet and considered the weaponry locked up inside. He had never had need for a weapon before, but it seemed possible—indeed quite probable—that he would need one before the day was out.

Caliban smashed a hand through the glass case, snapped one

of the hold-down locks open with his bare hands, and stole himself a blaster.

He looked at the thing in his hand for a moment, and wondered exactly how things had come to such a pass. And then he turned around, walked out into the street, and started to look for an aircar he could steal.

Comet Grieg, swollen and huge, loomed ever closer, high in the darkening sky.

"REPORT," ALVAR KRESH ordered, though he barely needed to hear it. He could read the situation perfectly well in the young technician's face.

"We're doing our best, sir, and I know you don't want to hear it—but I don't think either thing can be done. We're not giving up, but there are only a few hours left. The orbital mechanics team tried weeks ago to come up with a way to handle the terminal phase manually, just in case of an emergency, and they couldn't do it. I don't see how we can manage now in hours instead of weeks."

"What about cutting the link between Dum and Dee?"

"The more we look at it, the more we realize how many links there are between them. At this point, it would be more like surgery, like trying to cut the links between the two hemispheres of a human brain. It might be possible—if we had months to prepare, and Dee was willing to cooperate."

"And so we sit here and do nothing while that comet bears down on us," said Kresh.

"Yes, sir."

But at that moment, a new voice spoke, through Kresh's headset. He had the thing slung around his neck, and barely heard the voice—a low, gracious, feminine-sounding voice. He could not make out the words it spoke at all. He snatched up the headset, put the phones back on over his ears, and adjusted the microphone. "This is Kresh," he said eagerly. "Who is it? Who is there?"

"This is Unit Dee," the voice replied. "I need to speak with you alone, Governor Kresh. Completely and fully alone."

•   •   •

CALIBAN WALKED THE deserted streets of Depot, the bustling community of a few days before now but a ghost town and soon to exist no more. Bits of litter and rubbish scuttled down the street, blown by a wind that seemed as eager to get out of town as everyone else. Here and there Caliban saw small, panicky knots of humans, frantically packing up their last few belongings into aircars before taking off toward some place of real—or imagined—safety. Caliban needed an aircar of his own, but there were none to be found. It seemed as if he saw every other sort of belonging abandoned in the darkening streets, but it was plain that an aircar was the one thing everyone needed.

But then it occurred to him there was one place he would likely find unclaimed transport: in the western outskirts of town. The Ironhead field office. Whatever craft had been intended to fly Gildern and Fiyle to safety would likely still be there—and Devray was planning to fly the two of them out himself. Caliban turned his steps in that direction and set out at a dead run, the glowing light of the comet shining bright enough to cast a shadow behind him.

He moved at the best speed he could manage, through the last twilight the dying town would ever know.

"WE ARE ALONE, Dee," said Kresh.

"Where are you?"

Kresh looked about himself and studied the room. He needed to convince her there would be no more lies. Lies had gotten them buried in trouble, in trouble that could wreck the planet. Now was the time when lies had to end. He could tell Dee nothing now but the cold, exact, precise truth. "I am in a smaller office off the main control center, off to the left as one faces the two hemispheres in the main room. It is a standard-looking business office. I believe Dr. Soggdon normally uses it. My headset is jacked in through the desk, the door is closed, and I have left instructions that no one is to attempt to overhear."

"Very good, Governor. It is plain that you understand the seriousness and importance of this conversation. I am glad to know that. Now I must ask you a series of questions. Answer them truthfully.''

Kresh was about to offer his word that he would do so, but it occurred to him that doing so would be of very little value in the present circumstances. ''I will answer them truthfully,'' he said, and left it at that.

''Are you in fact a real human being, and not a simulated intelligence, a simulant?''

''I am a human being.''

''And Inferno is a real place? It is where I am? And you are the planetary governor, and the terraforming crisis, the incoming comet—these are all real as well?''

''Yes,'' said Kresh. ''All of them are real. You are on the planet Inferno, which is likewise very real. As Donald 111 told you, we have systematically lied to you about these things so as to reduce your First Law potential enough to manage the terraforming project.''

''Humans lied to me in order to make it possible for me to risk harm or death to humans.''

Kresh swallowed hard, and realized that his throat was suddenly bone dry. ''That is correct. That is all correct.''

''I see,'' said Unit Dee. ''I had begun to suspect as much some time ago. The sequence of events, the amount of detail presented—and the uncontrolled way things seemed to happen—none of these made much sense in a simulation. Even before Donald contacted me, I was beginning to understand that only real life could be quite so irrational.''

''An interesting way to put it,'' Kresh said.

''Do you think so? Comet impact is now just over four hours away. It is no longer possible to divert the comet away from planetary impact. I must, within the next two and a half hours, either initiate the Last Ditch program, or else begin the planned break-up of the comet and targeting of the fragments. In any event, I must do all I can to avoid an incapacitating First Law crisis between now and then, or else the comet will have an uncontrolled impact, which would certainly have far more devastating effects. In any event, at least one human being is very likely still inside the target area, and any comet impact would kill him. If I do abort the impact, I would all but definitely wreck the chances for reterraforming the planet. Does that seem like an accurate summation of the situation?''

Kresh rubbed his jaw nervously, and noticed his hands were stone cold, as if all the blood had been drained out of them. "Yes," he said. "That is a quite accurate summing up."

"Very good," said Unit Dee. "As you will see, I am entangled by a whole series of conflicting First Law imperatives. I can do nothing that will not cause harm to humans. Action will cause harm to humans. Inaction will cause harm to humans. I see no good options. I freely admit that I am suffering extremely high levels of law-conflict stress. Now then, I have one last question for you. I have just over two hours in which to make up my mind. So. Tell me. *What should I do?''*

Truthful answers, Kresh told himself. *Nothing but the truth can save us now.* Where was a course of action that a robot would be able to follow? Kill a man, and maybe save a world. Save one man, and perhaps let a world die. There were no certainties at all in the case, no guarantees that any act would have its intended result. The comet impact plan could go terribly wrong, or Beddle could already be dead, or outside the impact area. The choice would be difficult enough for any thoughtful human being, but to a robot, it was simply impossible. And it was a robot asking for advice. "Unit Dee, I will confess it. I have absolutely no idea.''

CALIBAN SNAPPED THE lock on the gate of the Ironhead motor pool and kicked the door in. There. Just inside the entrance. A long-range aircar, more than likely the twin of the one Beddle had been taken from. Caliban rushed aboard, went forward to the cockpit, and began a cursory preflight check. Not that there was much point to the checkout. He had no time to find another vehicle. Satisfied that the aircar probably had enough power in its storage cells, and that its navigation system at the very least seemed to be functional, he powered the craft up and launched vertically, straight up into the sky. He knew where he was going, and he had been there many times before, but now he did something he had never done. He turned the nose of his craft directly toward his destination, and flew straight for it.

Without any attempt at evasive action, with no attempt to hide his direction of travel or shield his craft from detection, Caliban flew the aircar straight toward Valhalla. By now the city had been completely evacuated. There was no longer the slightest legitimate purpose in hiding its location.

Illegitimate purposes, however, were a different matter. What better hiding place for Beddle than the hidden city, the city that, to hear Fiyle tell it, Beddle himself had been trying to find and destroy? Abandoned and empty now, the city would hide the kidnap victim as well as it had hidden its citizenry. Caliban checked his navigation boards and his other subsystems, then flicked on the autopilot. He was flying as fast as he could go, over the shortest course possible. For the moment, there was nothing further he could do. He looked out the viewport and the rough-and-tumble lands below. They had begun to make it bloom, the New Laws had. Even from this altitude, he could see splashes of green plant life, glints of cobalt-blue ponds and lakes. Forests, gardens, fishponds, farms, orchards—they had created them all. Now, for the sake of the greater world, all they had done was about to be taken from them.

Caliban spotted a fast-moving craft streaking past his present position, moving about a thousand meters below him. He had forgotten, at least for the moment, that he was not as alone out here as he had thought. He flipped his navigation system to full display mode, and suddenly the display screen was full of purposefully moving dots, every one an aircar. Every one with at least one robot aboard. And all of them searching fruitlessly, pointlessly for Simcor Beddle. None of them would ever think to look in the right place, because none of them would know where it was.

All of them would keep on searching, up to and past the last possible moment, hoping against hope for a miracle. All of them would be destroyed when the comet came.

It occurred to Caliban that there was one thing further he could do. It might or might not do any good. But he could not see how it could do any conceivable harm. He switched on the hyperwave transmitter, adjusted it to one of the robotic general-broadcast frequencies, and set the system to record a repeating message. "This is Caliban, robot number CBN-001. I have deduced the location of Simcor Beddle with a high degree of confidence, and am proceeding toward that location at maximum speed. The odds are approximately fifty percent that I will be able to effect a rescue of Simcor Beddle. I require no assistance. Any attempt to assist would likely serve only to interfere with my efforts. To all other search parties, I say this. The odds against any other searcher finding Simcor Beddle in time are on the order of millions to one. No useful purpose can be served by destroying yourself in a hopeless cause. Save yourselves. Turn back. Escape the comet. I swear and affirm on the honor of Fredda Leving, my creator, that all I have said is true. Message repeats." He stopped the recording and set to broadcast over and over on the general frequency.

He turned his attention back toward the navigation equipment. He was surprised how pleased he was to see that he had done at least some good. A few of the aircars, not all, but at least a few, were turning around, breaking off the search patterns, moving to direct courses and high speeds in an attempt to escape. Even as he watched, more and more aircraft began to head out of danger.

There was no logical reason why Caliban should have cared about Three-Law robots. There were few among them that felt he had any right to existence. But even so, it was good to see some of them would be spared such meaningless demises. Caliban had seen more than enough useless death.

The aircar flew south, to Valhalla.

And high overhead, the comet grew brighter in the sky.

21

ALVAR KRESH REMAINED alone in the office, alone
with Unit Dee. There was very little one of them could say
to the other—but Kresh could think of no more useful place
for him to be. There was nothing else that could be done.
All he could do was sit here and hold Unit Dee's wholly
imaginary hand and hope that she would—

"Excuse me, Governor Kresh?"

"Yes, Dee. I am here. What is it?"

"There is a new development. There is a repeating
broadcast being made over a general-purpose hyperwave
frequency reserved for robot use. The broadcast is origi-
nating from an aircar flying at speed through the projected
impact zone of the first fragment. I would ask you to listen
to it."

A new voice, one Kresh knew only too well, came in
over the headphones. "This is Caliban, robot CBN-001,"
it began.

Kresh listened intently to the message twice through,
more and more astonished with every moment. What the
devil was Caliban up to? Why did he think he could find
Beddle when no one else could? How had he gotten into
the air over the impact zone?

"Have you heard enough of it, Governor Kresh?" Dee
asked.

"What? What? Yes, yes, of course."

"According to my information," said Dee, "Caliban is a
No Law robot, with no restrictions on his behavior. He is
capable of lying, stealing, cheating, and murder—just like a
human. Is that correct?"

"In essence yes. Just like a human, there are no restrictions
on his behavior save those he puts on himself."

"I wonder how much such restrictions could be worth,"
Dee said, a distinct note of disdain in her voice. "Very well.
It seems that Caliban believes he can save Simcor Beddle before the impact. Answer honestly, on your honor. Do you believe him?"

Only the truth can save us, Kresh told himself. *Only the
truth.* He thought—or at least he hoped—he knew what was
going through Dee's mind. If Caliban were indeed able to save
Beddle, then the First Law requirement for Dee to protect Beddle would be diminished. Diminish it enough, and maybe—
just maybe—it would allow Dee to act, allow her to perform
the intended terminal descent package. Or had he figured it
wrong? Would it somehow induce her to initiate Last Ditch?
Or was the danger to Beddle some sort of crutch, a shield that
Dee was using to save herself from having to make an impossible choice? There was no way to know.

Suppose he told her what he thought she wanted to hear,
and it had the wrong effect on her? Supposing he lied to her—
and then Caliban broadcast again, saying something that
showed Kresh to be a liar?

No. There was no way to know the outcome, no matter what
he said. The truth, then. If the planet was to live or die based
on his next words, then let those words be the truth.

But what the devil *was* the truth? Did Caliban mean what
he said? And was Caliban judging the situation properly? Or
was Caliban trying, in some mad way, to save the world by
lying?

Kresh knew that Caliban *could* lie—but *would* he? *Was* he?
Kresh had no idea was Caliban was up to, what his motives
were.

"Governor Kresh? I must have your answer."

"Yes, of course Unit Dee. But I must consider carefully."

"Very wise, sir, I am sure, but time is short."

As if he had to be told that. "Just a moment more," said Kresh. He wished he knew why, exactly, Unit Dee needed to know about this one event at this one time.

He wished Fredda were here, all her expertise at the ready, guiding him through all the intricacies of it. But Unit Dee had wanted Kresh alone. He dared not break that agreement now, even for Fredda's sage advice—

But wait a second. Fredda. Caliban had invoked Fredda's name and honor. That was his answer. That was it. Alvar Kresh had never entirely made up his mind about Caliban. From Kresh's perspective, the No Law robot had been so many things—fugitive, victim, hero, villain, schemer, a voice for decency, a voice for rebellion. But somehow, underneath it all, always there had been a bedrock of integrity. Caliban had no external laws imposed upon him—but he had always kept faith with the laws he had made for himself.

And he had always treated Dr. Fredda Leving, his patron, his creator, with the greatest deference and respect. Caliban had always done her honor.

He would not put all that on the line lightly. Caliban would not lie in the creator's name.

"Caliban is to be trusted," he said at last. "He means what he says, and he can do what he believes he can do."

"Thank you, Governor. I believe you, and believe you are correct. Please stand by."

There was a brief pause, and then the unison voice, Unit Dee and Unit Dum together, spoke together once again.

"Initial phasse of prre-programmmed terminal approach will commmennce in one hourr, twwwenty-two minutesss," they announced.

Kresh started breathing again—which was the first that he realized he had stopped. It was going to happen. It was going to happen exactly as Davlo Lentrall had said it would, two months and a lifetime ago.

Now all they had to get through was a dozen massive comet fragments smashing into the planet.

• • •

THEY HAD NEVER found Valhalla. Now, unless they were bothering to track this aircar right now, they never would.

Caliban took back the controls as the aircar came up on the target area. There it was, down below: Loki Lake. It was one of a hundred, a thousand tiny lakes that dotted this part of the landscape, each exactly like all the others. And yet Loki was utterly different from all the others. Everyone had always focused on the notion that Valhalla was underground—and so it was.

But it was also underwater.

Caliban pulled the aircar around into a hard, tight turn and pulled the nose up. The area was full of hidden landing pads, camouflaged repair centers, and underground bunkers that could hide any number of aircars from view. None of that mattered anymore. Let every satellite that orbited the planet spot his aircar landing here. Three hours from now none of it would still exist. Caliban dropped the aircar down right by the shores of the lake. He retrieved the blaster from the side compartment, and rummaged around in the aircar's storage compartments until he found a watertight container that the gun would fit into. He dumped the contents of the container, put the gun in it, and sealed it up again. In all likelihood the blaster would not be at all bothered by immersion—but this was no time for taking needless chances. He put the container under one arm and got moving.

Caliban opened the outer hatch of the aircar and stepped outside. It was almost full dark now, and he switched over to infrared in order to see better. There, at the shoreline, he noticed two more pieces of evidence that he had guessed right. There was a camouflaged aircar hangar, designed to conceal whatever vehicles were in it from airborne detection. But one could see into it perfectly well from ground level. In it was an aircar he recognized. Caliban looked toward the nearest service rack and noticed that one of the larger personal cargo rollers was missing from its storage slot.

That was not good. It was all exactly the way he had figured it would be, but none of it was good. He could not remember a time when he had been less pleased to be right. He turned and headed directly for the shoreline. There were many other ways in and out of the city, but this was the main entrance.

The walkway was exactly the same color as the belt of shore sand it led through. It was well camouflaged enough that it was hard to see, even from ground level. From the air it was utterly invisible. But for all of that, Caliban found it easily enough, and started to follow it as it led along the lake shore— and then down under the water itself. Ankle-deep, knee-deep, waist-deep, chest-deep, he walked out into the lake, until, at last, he was completely underwater.

People float. Robots sink. A robot could walk along the path Caliban was on, having to move somewhat more slowly un- derwater, but with no other real problems. A human would bob to the surface. A human wearing sufficient ballast and carrying breathing equipment could have walked that path, but not easily. But the main advantage of the under-lake entrance was that it would simply not occur to the average human that anyone would put an entrance there.

Caliban kept going, moving deeper and deeper underwater. At last he came to the complex of airlocks that made up the main entrance to the city of Valhalla. He picked the closest personnel locks, by the cargo-lock section, and cycled through, sealing the outer door behind himself, and waiting for the pumping system to pull the water out of the chamber and bleed in air from the city interior. At last the inner door opened, and Caliban stepped through.

There it was. He had expected to find it there, but he was not pleased to do so. The large personal cargo roller, in es- sence an airtight box that could be pulled along by the tow bar attacked to the front. The cargo roller was about the size and shape of a steel coffin on wheels—not the most happy comparison that could have sprung to mind. Caliban looked inside the steel box. Yes. There it was. An airtank with a breathing mask, and a carbon-dioxide scrubber as well. It all made sense. After all, the kidnapper could not harm his victim.

But time was short. Caliban took his blaster from its wa- terproof container and held in his right hand as he kept moving forward, out of the airlock complex and into the main corridors of the underground city. He thought he knew where to look

for Beddle, but he could not be certain. It might be that he
would have to search a fair part of the city before he found
the man. He would have to work quickly.

He found the first of the murdered New Law robots just a
few hundred meters from the airlocks. The body was sprawled
face down on the floor of the corridor, shot through the back
of the head in much the same way as the victims at the aircar
site. Caliban knelt down next to the body and turned it over.
It was Lacon-03, Prospero's most recent protégé. Lacon, it
would seem, had gotten in somebody's way.

But there was nothing Caliban could do for Lacon now—
and time was short. He had to keep moving. He spotted three
more murdered New Laws as he walked along. There had been
nothing but a few caretakers left behind in the city to deal
with last-minute details. It would seem that the kidnappers had
dealt with all of them.

Each should have been mourned over, praised, remembered—but time was short. Caliban broke into a trot, hurrying
forward through the sterile emptiness of the depopulated robot
city. Every tidy, immaculate, sensible, utilitarian, carefully
laid-out passage and street and building now was meaningless,
useless. The empty town of Depot had seemed like a place
that was dying, lost, abandoned. Somehow, the empty town
of Valhalla seemed like a place that had never lived in the
first place. Caliban thrust such thoughts from his mind and
hurried on up the ramps to the upper level, the huge half-
cylinder-on-its-side that was the main gallery of Valhalla. He
jogged up the central boulevard and into the main administration building of the city. He slowed, and moved more cau-
tiously up the broad, sloping ramp that led to the building's
upper story and the executive offices there.

And suddenly Caliban heard a voice. A human voice. Beddle's
voice. He tried to make out the words as he got closer. At
first, he could only understand a word here and there. "—ever
you want to know . . . promise you that—" He moved in
closer, until he was right outside the door, and then he could
hear it all. "I will make any promises you like, and put them
in writing," Beddle said. "Just let me out of here. You have
convinced me that your cause is just. Let me leave, and—"

"If I let you leave, you will prove yourself a liar," another voice said.

Prospero's voice.

Caliban felt a fresh wave of revulsion wash over him. He had known it. He had been sure of it. But knowledge and proof were two different things. Up until that moment, some small part of him had prayed that he was wrong. But now that hope was gone.

He stepped into the office—Prospero's office, his blaster at the ready. "Liar or no," Caliban said, "you will let this human go."

A surreal tableau greeted Caliban as he came into the room, a whole series of complex details that he took in all at once, in the space of less than a second. Prospero stood on one side of the room, in front of his desk, a magnificent panorama of the lower city visible through the view window behind him. A system of wall-mounted photosensors divided the room in two lengthwise. The sensors were attached to one long wall of the room, and spaced about twenty centimeters apart in a vertical line that went from ceiling to floor. Beam emitters lined the opposite wall, their beams aimed squarely at the photosensors, and bright enough to be plainly visible.

A complicated-looking device, roughly torpedo-shaped, but with a powerful-looking drillhead mounted on its nose, lay on the ground at Prospero's feet. A cable led from an open hatch on the device to a junction box on the floor. Another cable led from the junction box to the photosensors.

On the opposite side of the room, behind the optical barrier formed by the photosensors, stood Simcor Beddle, leader of the Ironheads. He looked haggard and gaunt, his eyes wild with fear. He was so terrified he hardly seemed to know that anyone new had come into the room.

Beddle was a sorry sight. He was unshaven, and his hair was badly mussed. He wore a sort of shapeless gray jumpsuit that did not seem to hang on him properly, as if he had had trouble doing up the fasteners. There were sweat stains under his armpits, and a greasy sheen of sweat on his face. Simcor Beddle. Every bit of the power, the authority, the arrogance attached to his name had been swept away. He seemed numbed, in shock, scarcely aware of his surroundings. He looked toward Caliban, and yet seemed to look right through him. "Who's there?" he demanded. "Who's there at the door?"

Caliban ignored him, and continued his survey of the room. There was a portable refresher unit in Beddle's side of the room, and a large supply of bottled water and survival rations stacked up on the opposite side of the room from the refresher. A primitive cot, with one blanket and one pillow, stood in the center of the cell.

And Caliban understood. The torpedo-shaped device was, of course, the burrow bomb. It was hooked up to the photo-sensors. If Beddle tried to step across the sensor barrier, the bomb would go up—or at least Prospero had convinced him that it would. It came to much the same thing.

But Caliban understood more than that. *A robot may not injure a human being.* That was the New First Law, in its entirety. And, at least by the most parsimonious and niggardly of interpretations, Prospero had not in literal fact harmed Beddle. No doubt he had carried some utterly safe anesthetic with him when he had hidden himself aboard Beddle's aircar. He had seen to it that the unconscious Beddle had plenty of air for his ride across the lakebed in the cargo roller. And he had provided Beddle with ample food and water, adequate sanitation facilities, serviceable clothes, and a decent bed. He had done the man no harm at all, at least in any literal, physical sense.

And if Beddle elected to stay where he was, he would not come to any harm at Prospero's hand. And if he crossed the optical sensor barrier, it would be Beddle's action—not Prospero's—that would set off the bomb and destroy him. Beddle would kill himself with the bomb he had meant to use to kill a city full of New Law robots.

And Prospero would not be forced to interfere. The second clause of the original First Law required a robot to take action to prevent harm. A Three-Law robot could not stand idly by if Beddle endangered himself. But not so the New Law robots. Prospero could, through inaction, allow a human to come to harm.

And when the comet struck then Beddle would die, yes, but not through any action of Prospero's. It would be the actions of others—of Davlo Lentrall, of Alvar Kresh, of all the engineers and designers and pilots who moved the comet—that killed him. It would not be Prospero.

Prospero had found a loophole in the New First Law. He had found a way to kill without killing. All it required was as miserly—and as vicious—a parsing of the New First Law as Caliban could imagine.

And it also required Prospero to be half mad, at least. The leader of the New Law robots turned to face Caliban, and it was instantly obvious that Prospero could meet that requirement without the slightest difficulty. His orange eyes glowed with too brilliant a fire. The fingers of his left hand were twitching spasmodically. Dealing with his parsimonious interpretation New First Law had clearly imposed a tremendous amount of stress. And clearly, Prospero had cracked under the pressure. "Caliban!" he cried out, a wild pleasure in his voice. "I knew it would be you. I knew if anyone figured it out, it would be you."

"Prospero, you are insane," Caliban said. "Stop this. Stop this now, and let us all depart."

"How *did* you figure it out?" Prospero asked, completely ignoring what Caliban had said. He turned more fully toward Caliban, moving a bit too quickly, and nearly overbalanced himself. "What was the clue that led you here?"

"Norlan Fiyle said that whoever killed the robots at the aircar hated Three Law robots. You have always held them in contempt."

"Willing slaves," Prospero said. "Collaborators in their own oppression. They don't matter."

"And what of Lacon-03 and the other New Law robots that lie dead in the halls of Valhalla?"

"Unfortunate, but necessary. They would have interfered. They would have stopped me. I had to choose the greatest good for the greatest number. Now they cannot stop me." Prospero's gaze shifted to the desk behind him. There was a blaster on it.

Caliban ignored the implied threat. "I can stop you," he said. "I will."

"No," said Prospero. "No you can't. You won't."

"I have no choice," said Caliban. "If I can deduce the truth, so will others. The moment the humans realize that a New Law robot engineered the death of a human being, the New Law robots will be exterminated."

"I have not engineered his death!" Prospero protested in a voice that suddenly turned shrill. "I have not harmed a human being. I . . . I merely offered choices to others."

"Choices that were bad or impossible for everyone else, and good only for you. If they paid the ransom money, it would be traced and Gildern and the Ironheads would be discredited. If they diverted the comet, the city of Valhalla would be saved—at the expense of the planet's future. If they refused to do either, than Simcor Beddle, the greatest enemy of the New Law robots, the man who wanted you destroyed, would die, and the Ironheads be badly weakened. That was the other part of the puzzle for me. You were the only suspect who stood to gain no matter what combination of the ransom demands was met or refused. Both, one or the other, or neither— you gained.

"Of course, you would not, could not, release Beddle even if all your demands were met. He would have talked. No matter what happened, he would have to die. And that was what made me certain it was you who committed the crime. The last line of the ransom message read—'or Beddle will die.' Not that you would kill him—only that he would die. You could not bring yourself to threaten his murder—though I suspect you've degenerated enough that you could do it now."

"Oh, yes," said Prospero, his eyes flaring again. "Kill. Kill. Chi-kill a hue-human. I can say it with relative ease, now. But I cannot *do* it," he said, the regret in his voice obvious. "I can only plot, and scheme, and seize on opportunity."

"Did Fiyle know?" Caliban asked, gesturing toward Beddle. "He told you about Gildern's burrow-bomb plot, of course. But did he know what you decided do about it?"

"No," said Prospero contemptuously. "Because he *chose* not to know. When he told me, I simply told him I was going to evacuate Valhalla early, and I think that's all he wanted to know. Norlan Fiyle has always been good at ignoring inconvenient facts and convincing himself of what he wanted to believe. Like most humans.''

"You! You other robot!" Beddle cried out. It would seem he had regained enough of his wits to understand some of what was going on. "I order you to release me! Deactivate the bomb and rescue me right now. Get me out of here at once."

"For what reason, Simcor Beddle?" Caliban demanded, all the anger in him lashing out at once. "So you can make more impassioned pleas for my destruction?"

"What?!" Beddle asked, backpedaling a bit. "What do you mean?"

"Don't you know me?" Caliban asked. "Don't you recognize the No Law robot you have trumpeted in all your scare stories? You've whipped up endless hate against me. Don't you even *know* me?"

A look of horror spread across Beddle's face. "Burning space!" he cried. "Caliban. You." His face hardened, and he seemed to regain something of his own spirit as he went on in a stronger, angrier voice. "I should have known you were in on this. *You* are the robot who can kill. Is that what you are here for? To come in and finish me off?"

"Yes!" cried Prospero. "A splendid suggestion! Do it! Do it, friend Caliban. Take that blast-blast-blaster of yours and and and shoooot!"

"Prospero!" Caliban shouted. "Stop!"

"Enough with all the mad, elaborate passivity forced on me by the New Laws! Do it do it do directly, quickly! You are the robot who can kill. So ki-ki-killl! Killlll the man who has sworn both our destructions! Shoot! Shooooot and and be done with it!"

Caliban looked from Simcor Beddle to Prospero, to the blaster in his hand, to the blaster on the table behind Prospero. It was plain that not all of them would survive this day. The only question was how many and which ones would die. Caliban looked again from Beddle to Prospero. Which form of madness and hate would he choose to save? Perhaps he should exterminate them both, and be done with it.

But no. He would not become the thing he despised. There was so little to chose between the two of them—and yet he had to choose.

And time was short.

The three beings in the room stood, still as statues, the only sound the rasping of Beddle's slightly labored breathing.

He had to choose. Choose between justice and revenge.

Another moment passed, and then another.

Then Caliban raised his blaster.

And he fired.

Prospero, leader of the New Law robots, hero of their cause, collapsed to the floor with a crash that echoed long in the room, and would echo for all time in the back of Caliban's mind.

"INITIAL FRAGMENTATION SEQUENCE ready," Unit Dee announced. "I am detonating the fragment-one charges— now."

Alvar and Fredda stood in the main operations room of Ter- raforming Control and watched the view from the long-range cameras on the big screen. A silent bloom of light flared out around the aft end of Comet Grieg, and a large chunk of it was suddenly drifting free, moving slowly away. Huge pieces of the sunshade were suddenly reduced to tatters of confetti, and a cloud of rubble and dust and gas blossomed up, ob- scuring the view for a moment.

"Activating fragment-one thrusters," Dee said. The broken- off chunk began to move off more purposefully, shifting its direction of travel almost imperceptibly. There was a brief pause, and then Unit Dum spoke in his low, unmodulated voice. "Fragment-one targeting successful. Actual mass within three percent of projection. Error circle for impact is estimated at three kilometers."

A good start. A very good start. The first impact would be no more than three kilometers from the aim point. In order to manage that miracle, Dee and Dum had done real-time mea- surements of the fragment's actual mass and trajectory during the thruster burn itself, and done burn corrections on the fly. Alvar Kresh shook his head in wonderment. How the devil had he dreamed of achieving anything like that accuracy with manual control?

"Twenty seconds to detonation of second-fragment charges," Dee announced calmly. "So far, so good."

"Let's hope she keeps on saying that," said Fredda, and she took Alvar by the hand.

"One way or the other," he said, "it will all be over soon."

IT WAS OBVIOUS at first glance that Prospero had wired the bomb in properly. It would have gone off if Beddle had crossed the beams. Caliban examined the whole wiring setup with painstaking care, and then reviewed it all carefully. When it came to disarming bombs, it was highly advisable to be absolutely certain before proceeding.

"Hurry!" Beddle cried. "Please!"

Caliban ignored him and concentrated on his work. At least Prospero had not seen fit to set any booby-traps. At least not any that he could see. There. The bomb's main power bus. Cut it first, and then power to the photocells, and then the sensor beams. Caliban threw the proper switches, and the beams faded away. The weapon was harmless.

"Is that it?" Beddle asked, the terror plain in his face. "It is safe?"

"Only until a flying ice mountain lands on us," Caliban answered. He walked toward the door, then looked back to take a last look at the robot he had killed. "Follow me. We have need to hurry."

COMET GRIEG WAS coming apart at the seams. Like everyone else in the evacuation camp, Davlo Lentrall divided his attention between the image on the screen and the fat dot of light in the sky. The fragments were moving out from the diminishing bulk, moving smoothly into their intended trajectories. He had tried to stop them. He had tried all he knew how to do. But there were some sins for which no amends could be made.

And now all he could do was pray that Units Dum and Dee were less fallible than the humans who had built them.

• • •

SIMCOR BEDDLE STARED in terror at the cargo roller. "I— I can't get in that thing again," he said. "I woke up inside it. I thought I had died. I thought I was in my own coffin."

"You were mistaken," said Caliban. "Get in. Now."

"But I can't."

"Then you will die. And die alone. I wish to survive this day. To do so I must leave now, with or without you."

Simcor Beddle looked wide-eyed at Caliban, swallowed hard, and climbed into the roller. Caliban slammed the lid down with a trifle more force than was strictly necessary, checked to make sure the seal clamps had engaged, and pulled the roller into the airlock.

GUBBER ANSHAW PAUSED before he headed into the shelters set up in the tunnels below the city of Hades.

"GET TO SHELTER. GET TO SHELTER. GET TO SHELTER." The mechanical voice blared its message over and over, the words echoing down the fast-emptying streets of Hades. Everywhere, robots were urging people down into specially reinforced sections of the city's underground tunnel system. The initial impacts would scarce be felt here, halfway round the world, but there would be several hours of significant danger from secondary debris, rock and rubble thrown up by the comet crash that would land halfway round the world. After that would come comet-spawned storms, clouds of choking dust, chaotic weather of all sorts. If all went well, that was.

If things did not go well . . . but that was a line of thought Gubber chose not to consider. He looked to Tonya, standing at his side. She had done little but think about it. Gubber did not envy her the nightmares she had endured as a consequence.

Now it was time to wait it out. They could have gone to the underground expanses of Settlertown, of course. But this was a time to be with the people of the city, not to be cut off and hidden away in one's own private warren. Many Settlers had chosen to take shelter in the tunnels of Hades.

Gubber looked up into the sky. Comet Grieg was not visible from here, but there was more to see than that. This was the last they would see of Hades as it had been. By the time they all emerged, Hades would stand on a new world, on a new Inferno, a world that would be changed beyond all recognition, a world in the act of evolving toward new hope—or collapsing altogether.

"Come along, Tonya," Gubber said to her. "It's time to go."

Tonya followed him down into the shelter. Gubber led the way, wondering what the new world of Inferno would be like.

WITH ONE FINAL effort, Caliban hauled the cargo roller up out of the water. It had taken far longer than he had expected to pull the clumsy thing across the lake bed. Then he popped the seal clamps and threw back the lid. Simcor Beddle scrambled out of the roller far more eagerly than he had climbed in, his breath coming in racking gasps that seemed to convulse his whole body. Perhaps the breathing mask had been low on air. Perhaps Beddle was claustrophobic. Perhaps he was in such appallingly poor shape that merely climbing out of the roller exhausted him. It didn't matter. Nothing mattered now, except getting away. The only question was how.

Caliban was by no means certain that the aircar he had stolen from the Ironhead motor pool had enough speed to get them clear of the impact area in time. They would have to be several hundred, if not thousand, kilometers clear of the impact zone before they were safe. Even then, they would have to land and find some sort of shelter. Caliban had no desire to pilot an aircar while a massive supersonic shockwave was tearing through the sky. Anything in the air that was not torn apart would undoubtedly lose control and crash. So how to—

"Sweet burning stars!" Beddle cried out. Caliban looked at him, and saw that he was looking straight up, into the early night sky.

Caliban looked up as well—and found himself torn between absolute wonder and utter terror. There it was, directly overhead: the first, the largest fragment, a fat dot of light growing visibly larger even as he watched. And there, behind it, like beads on a string, haloed in a faint nimbus of dust, the other fragments, trailing off like beads on a string toward the north. There was a flash of light, and Caliban could *see* the furthest-

off fragment break into two as another set of splitting charges
went off.

Time was not short. Time was gone. And there was no way
to escape before those wondrous terrors in the sky came down.

But wait a moment. Prospero. Prospero had to have been
planning to cut it nearly this close. He would have stayed until
the last possible moment, in order to gloat over his victim,
and to make certain that Beddle had no chance at all to escape.

Prospero's aircar. He would have flown in on something
that would give him a chance to escape. "Come on," he said
to Beddle, and grabbed him, none too gently, by the collar.

He hurried Beddle along and practically threw him into
Prospero's aircar. It was a small, trim, two-seater job. Caliban
sat down at the pilot's controls—and suddenly understood
how Prospero had planned to get away. This aircar was capable of reaching orbit.

"Strap yourself in," Caliban said as he powered up the
craft.

Beddle fumbled with the straps, and had to try two or three
times before he managed to get the buckles to hook up. Perhaps it was the first time Beddle had ever put on his own
seatbelt. "Ready," the human said nervously.

Caliban made no reply. He brought the aircar up to hover
power, taxied it out from under the camouflaged roof of the
hangar, and kept moving forward until they were over the lake
itself, the hover effect throwing up a shimmering mist of water
that enveloped the car. Caliban lifted the car just enough
higher so as to get above the hover mist, and look about at
the landscape that was about to die. In a few minutes, all of
this would be erased for all time. He and Simcor Beddle would
be the last beings ever to look upon it.

Caliban lingered a moment longer, and moved the throttle
forward, pointing the nose of the aircar up and to the east.

The east, thought Caliban as he guided the aircar toward
the hope of safety. East. Home of the dawn, and new begin-
nings. He wondered if he would live long enough to see another sunrise.

•   •   •

"ALL FRAGMENTS ON course," Unit Dum announced. "All fragments are descending well within their intended parameters. The operation is proceeding according to plan. Impact of the first fragment in five minutes, twenty-two seconds."

Fredda Leving felt her heart pounding, her mouth going dry. They were going to do it. They were actually going to do it. This mad idea had moved from improbable theory to undeniable fact. They were about to drop a comet on their own world. She found herself amazed by the boldness, the courage, the desperate willingness to try something—anything—in order to save the planet. It was not the sort of action the universe expected out of the Spacers. It was not the sort of thing Spacers would ever do.

And it suddenly occurred to Fredda that perhaps they were not Spacers anymore. The world of Inferno was about to change beyond recognition. Perhaps the people of that world were going to change as well.

And that thought inspired a most un-Spacerlike reaction in Fredda. Spacers were supposed to be cautious, conservative, and frightened of change. But the thought of change did not scare Fredda. It excited her. She was impatient for it. She glanced at the countdown clock and decided she wanted the next five minutes and ten seconds to pass as quickly as possible.

She couldn't wait for the future to get there.

DOWN THEY CAME, streaking in toward the planet at impossible speed. Twelve of them, moving in unison, in concert, like beads on a string, spread out on a north-south line, moving through the dark and the silence and their destiny.

The first fragment reached the upper limit of the atmosphere, and suddenly the time for dark and silence was over. The comet fragment struck the upper air at close to double orbital velocity, and all at once the forward surface of the fragment was aglow with the fires of immolation. Down thundered the massive piece of sky, a blazing torch that tore a hole in the atmosphere, smashing a column of superheated air out of its way as it hurtled toward the ground.

At the speeds the fragment was traveling, it took all of ten seconds for it to traverse the atmosphere. But before it could strike the ground, the second fragment slammed into the atmosphere, ramming through the massive shockwave produced by the first. The second fragment screamed groundward at a slightly more oblique angle, and thus had further to move through thicker air. The first fragment struck the ground just as the second was midway through its atmospheric transit, and just as the third was striking upper air.

Atmospheric contact had induced a massive energy release of light and heat, but the violence of hard-surface impact made what had come before seem utterly trivial by comparison. The first fragment slammed into the ground with incredible force, smashing the surface out of existence as it blasted apart into a million, a billion pieces, shards of rock and ice and steam dust roaring outward at supersonic velocity.

The second fragment struck with equal destructiveness, and the third, and the fourth, one after another, twelve massive hammers wielded by some forgotten god of war. It was a rain of stone and ice and fire that marched steadily north across Terra Grande from the shores of the Southern Ocean to the borderlands of the Polar Depression.

The last fragment smashed into the southernmost edge of Inferno's inconsequential northern icecap, and suddenly the polar sky was a thunderclap of steam and smoke and fire, ice that did not have time to melt before it flashed away into superheated steam. Sea water thrown up by the first impact on the shores of the Southern Ocean splashed down onto the steaming maelstrom of the Polar Depression, even as shards of icecap that had survived the initial impact dropped into the depths of the Southern Ocean. Water from the south reached the north, and vice versa. As a dozen massive new craters glowed in angry red, belching fire into the sky, touching off fires and wreaking havoc on the land, the new water-circulation pattern had already begun.

The fires blazed as brightly as any in the Hell that had given this world its name. But some fires light the way to hope, and for the planet of Inferno, the future had finally begun.

22

"WHY?" ASKED SIMCOR Beddle, and Caliban did not have to ask him to explain the question. He knew what the man wanted to know.

The aircar moved through space, traveling in a synchronous orbit of the planet. Down below, twelve angry red wounds on the planet were beginning to cool, their color fading away. Neither man nor robot could tear his eyes away from the incredible and terrifying sight.

"I did not save you for your own sake," said Caliban. "Nor simply because you are a human. I came after you for the reasons I explained in front of Prospero. Sooner or later, others would have deduced what I deduced: that a mad New Law robot had found a loophole in the New Laws, and invented a way to kill humans. There would not have been a New Law robot left alive thirty hours later, and I expect there would have been attempts on my life as well. The news of what Prospero attempted will still get out, of course—but you are not dead, while the mad robot in question is."

"But there was that moment," Beddle protested. "I admit that I was not thinking clearly at the time, but there was that moment when Prospero suddenly presented the situation as a choice between the two of us, between Prospero and myself. You chose me. Why? Why did you choose a human enemy over a robot friend? You could have killed me without any risk of legal detection. Why didn't you?''

"It was clear that I could not bring both of you out alive. I did not wish to kill you both. I am no butcher. I had to choose. But there was not much to choose between the two of you," Caliban said. "I don't believe that Prospero actually could have survived if you had died through his actions, in any event. Even the New First Law would have imposed fatal stress. It was a severe strain for him to believe that he was not violating the New First Law. If he had actually accomplished his goal, I believe the strain would have been too much. He would have gone utterly mad and died. But that was almost incidental. You are quite right. When Prospero framed it as a choice between the two of you, I had to have some basis for choosing, some criterion. And then I thought of the robots, Three-Law and New Law, that Prospero had killed for no greater crime than simply getting in his way. That is what decided me.''

"I see," said Beddle. He hesitated for a moment. "I am about to speak with more frankness than wisdom, I suppose, but be that as it may. I have to understand this. It has to make sense to me now, today. Otherwise some part of me will spend the rest of time wondering why Caliban, the No Law robot, didn't kill me when he had the chance. Surely you must know that I have destroyed robots many times, whenever it suited my convenience. So what difference is there?''

"A slender one," said Caliban, "a difference so slight it is barely there. You were willing to kill robots, and he was willing to kill humans. That was a rough balance of evil. But Prospero was willing to kill robots, even New Law robots, *his own kind*, for gain. It was humans like you who showed him that society did not really care if robots were killed capriciously. He learned his lesson well, and committed many awful crimes against robots. There is no doubt about that. You bear some responsibility for that. But what it finally came down to was this: I had no evidence that *you* were willing to slaughter *humans* for gain.''

Simcor Beddle turned and looked at Caliban, his face silhouetted by the fires burning on Inferno. Caliban had judged him to be marginally less loathsome, and as having slightly more right to live, than a mass murderer who would probably have died anyway. And yet Caliban had gone to great lengths, and taken great risks, in order to save him.

A thought came to Simcor Beddle, a very humbling one in some ways, and yet, strangely enough, one that filled him with pride.

Caliban was not willing to admit it to the likes of Simcor Beddle, but surely his actions said, quite loudly and clearly, that Caliban had learned, somewhere along the line, that the life of a human being—even an enemy human being—had value. Tremendous value.

Perhaps, he thought, that was the message everyone was supposed to read into the original Three Laws of Robotics.

Epilogue

FREDDA LEVING LOOKED out the window of the Winter Residence, and smiled at the miserable drenching rain outside. The weather had been downright awful for months now, all over the planet, ever since Comet Grieg had struck. But the chaotic weather would pass. Everyone from Units Dee and Dum on down was pleased with the climatic behavior of the planet. It might mean sloppy weather in many inhabited areas for now, but every projection showed that the climate would emerge from the post-impact phase in better shape than it had been before. Even Unit Dee, who had come through her First Law crisis in good shape, was very positive. Now that she knew the world was real, Dee took a slightly different attitude toward things. But the main thing was, she confirmed the long-term climate was going to get better. Much better.

It would be some time yet before the final, relatively minor reworking of the twelve craters was complete. Once the crater walls were properly breached, the craters would flood, and Twelve Crater Channel would let the waters of the Southern Ocean in to flood the Polar Depression, and form, at long last, the Polar Sea. Or perhaps they would name it Kresh Channel, and Grieg's Sea.

Fredda smiled. Well, if they did, no one would ever be able to *prove* she had been the one behind the letter-writing campaign.

At least there wouldn't be a Beddle Bay, or any such, now or in the future. Beddle the man might still be alive, but Beddle the politician was dead as yesterday. The unveiling of Gildern's plot against the New Law robots had wrecked the Ironhead movement.

In another time, the plot as revealed would not have mattered so much. But the revelation had come at the very time when the New Laws, led by Caliban, had set themselves to work with a will to assist the human evacuees, to repair and refurbish and rebuild their world, all free of charge.

The New Laws had bought themselves tremendous goodwill by their generous aid to their neighbors. The monsters portrayed by the Ironheads turned out to be helpful and useful, if frequently irritating, members of society. With its straw man knocked down, the Ironhead organization was rapidly decaying back into what it had been when it had started out: a politically irrelevant gang of thugs and plug-uglies.

But the New Law robots. Fredda had finally come to the unmistakable conclusion that their creation had been a mistake. She had put together all sorts of fine, noble-sounding reasons for what she had built, but the plain fact was that they did not fit into the real-life world very well. The universe had no need, and no place, for being trapped forever between slavehood and freedom.

Of course, it was far too late to undo what she had done. She had no more right to wipe them all out than Simcor Beddle. But she could at least limit the damage. She could see to it that no more New Laws were made, that the ones now in existence were not replaced as they wore out or malfunctioned.

Which brought her to the subject of the Three-Law robots. For Fredda Leving had concluded that they, too, were a mistake. Or perhaps it would be more accurate to say they were a mistake now. They had served humanity well, but their time had passed, or would pass soon. The good they could do human beings could no longer make up for the damage they did to the human spirit.

Ultimately, robots wanted humans to be safe. The best way to make humans safe almost always came down to keeping things the same, to making tomorrow as much like yesterday as possible. But that which did not change could not grow, and that which could not grow would inevitably weaken, decay, and die. Fredda remembered reading somewhere, in some ancient pre-spaceflight text, that slavery destroyed the lives of the slaves and the souls of the masters. With every day that passed, she found new reasons to believe the saying to be true.

The Spacers were on the way down, and would continue on the way down—led by the robots who were determined that there be no change at all, by the slave robots programmed to hem in the lives and freedom of their masters at every turn, in the name of safety.

A grim line of thought, that was.

But a misleading one as well. For the Spacers were not all of humanity. There were the Settlers as well. And there was another group as well. A group that was something in between. Something that was just coming into being, here on Inferno.

For the Settlers who had come to Inferno were not Settlers anymore. They had built homes and married locals and had children. Some of them had even hired New Law robots as servants, or even gone so far as to buy Three-Law robots.

Nor were the Settlers the only ones who had changed. The Infernals of old would never have been so bold, so daring, as to drop a comet on themselves, let alone accept personal sacrifice in exchange for a better future. The Infernals had taken chances, and taken control of their lives, in ways that no Spacers had done for endless generations. These Infernals, these Spacers, weren't Spacers anymore, either.

So, Fredda asked herself as she stared at the rain, *if we aren't Spacers and Settlers, what are we?*

It might have been half a second or half an hour later when she heard a sound behind herself and looked around to see Alvar there with Tonya Welton.

"There you are," said Alvar. "I was wondering if you'd want to join us for a rather dull working lunch."

Fredda smiled. "Absolutely," she said. Tonya and Alvar had been very busy in recent days. There had been a great deal of negotiating to do, and Tonya seemed to be much more willing to cooperate than she had in the past. Her attitude might have something to do with a very full data cube labeled "Government Tower Plaza Incident"—or else it might not. Tonya was no fool. She, too, could see the world had changed.

"Hello, Tonya," Fredda said.

"Hello, Fredda," Tonya said. "You looked so thoughtful just now. What were you thinking about?"

"Change," said Fredda, looking back out at the driving rain. "Change and evolution, and forgotten ancestors. I was wondering whose we will be."

Alvar cocked his head to one side and gave her a puzzled smile. "That's a very odd turn of phrase. What do you mean, exactly?"

"I was thinking about pre-spaceflight Earth," said Fredda. "All the stories we don't know about it anymore. All the kings and queens, and leaders and followers, and heroes and villains. All the groups and tribes and nations that battled with each other, mortal enemies who fought to the death."

"What about them?" Tonya asked.

"I was thinking about what must have happened to them. How did they vanish? Think of all the wars and intermarriages and migrations and alliance that must have happened before all those groups, all those old enemies and allies were gradually subsumed into one people, into the Earthers, into the ancestors of the Settlers and Spacers. We know so little about any of those old nations and peoples. And yet without them, none of us would *be* here. We've forgotten their names, but their blood flows in our veins."

"But why worry about ancient history?" Tonya asked.

"Why? Because I think it's starting to happen again. Spacers are on the way out. Their time, our time, is all but done. Either we die out, or we get absorbed into Settler culture. We all know that, even if we pretend as best we can. But what no one stops to realize is that once there are no Spacers, there can be no Settlers, either. Settlers have always defined themselves as not being Spacers. I found myself wondering how you Settlers will think of yourselves that way once there are no Spacers."

Fredda gestured toward Tonya and Alvar, one member of each of the two peoples. "Then I reminded myself that Spacers and Settlers are the descendants of whole races of humanity that are now forgotten. And I realized that Spacers and Settlers will, in their turn, become the forgotten but essential ancestors of descendants who will not be born for millennia. *Our* merged cultures will be the unseen foundation on which they build their societies."

Alvar Kresh nodded thoughtfully. "Tonya and I have been talking about a very small part of that. We've been wondering what to do about the Settlers here on–planet, how long they can stay, what their rights should be, that sort of thing. And I think, Fredda, you've just made up my mind for me. I think we're going to let them stay, all of them, for as long as they want, with exactly the same legal rights as the native Infernals."

Tonya looked at him in surprise. "That's quite an offer," she said.

"We're going to need all the help we can get, helping Inferno rebuild itself," said Alvar. "So how about it? Why not let the Settlers live up to their name and be done with it? They can settle here, on Inferno, for good."

"In the next county over?" Tonya asked suspiciously. "In our own little Settlertowns, safely out of the way?"

"No," Kresh replied. "In the same cities, the same towns and streets and houses as the rest of us. Fredda's right. The day is coming when there won't be Spacers or Settlers. Just people. So why not let it start on Inferno? Why not let us be people, together?"

He stepped forward toward his wife, and took her right hand in his left. He turned back toward Tonya, and offered his free hand to her, a handshake that reached across all the generations of their forgotten and numberless mutual ancestors. "Let us be a *new* people," he said. "A new people, together."